TRUSTING BL

Family is everythi

Hoping to build a rel … n to his family, as well as rei … ting on his brother remaining … appen. But Erin Langley is m … So much so that Zane is beginning to question whether they have a future after all.

Erin wasn't expecting to find an ally in Hazel Grimes, but as it turns out, Erin isn't the only one who can see that more than one person has an agenda.

But would anyone listen?

Zane's bloodline has already betrayed him in the worst possible ways, so it couldn't happen again.
Could it?

What readers are saying about *Trusting Blood*:

- *"I didn't see THAT end coming!"*
- *"Would make a great TV series…"*
- *"Hooked from the very beginning…"*
- *"Another blinding read!"*
- *"As usual, it's brilliant!"*
- *"Edge of your seat read!"*

Also by Edie Baylis

Scarred Series
Mirrors Never Lie (Scarred #1)
The Price of Betrayal (Scarred #2)
Trusting Blood (Scarred #3)
The Hard Truth (Scarred #4)

Allegiance Series
Takeover (Allegiance #1)
Fallout (Allegiance #2)
Vendetta (Allegiance #3)
Payback (Allegiance #4)
Judgement (Allegiance #5)

Retribution Series
An Old Score (Retribution #1)
Finders Keepers (Retribution #2)
The Final Take (Retribution #3)
The Retribution Series Box Set

Hunted Series
The Status Debt (Hunted #1)
The Family Legacy (Hunted #2)
The Target of Lies (Hunted #3)
The Hunted Series Box Set

Downfall Series
Until the End of Time (Downfall #1)
Escaping the Past (Downfall #2)
Vengeful Payback (Downfall #3)
The Downfall Series Box Set

TRUSTING BLOOD

SCARRED #3

EDIE BAYLIS

ATHAME
press
· LONDON ·

ISBN 978-1-916977-00-6
e-ISBN 978-1-7393009-3-7
Hardback 978-1-916977-01-3
Large Print 978-1-916977-02-0

Athame Press
Unit 13230 - PO Box 6945 – London – W1A 6US

April 1983

MY MUM, not to mention my father, will go berserk when they discover where I am tonight. But now it's official they'll find out soon enough. Official, in as much that I'm here at a Morelli family gathering.

They can't stop me because I love Zane. We're meant to be together, I know we are and I'm certain he feels the same way.

Stepping forward, I fluff out my hair and inspect my reflection in the mirror.

This ladies' cloakroom is right posh, but then so is the Savoy.

Imagine that: me - Shirley Wilson - invited to a do at the Savoy Hotel.

Frowning, I adjust the banana clip in my hair. I'm not certain if my hairstyle looks good. I think I'd have preferred to keep my hair loose. Petra reckons with a bit of backcombing, I look just like Kelly le Brock, but as this is such an important night, I thought I should make myself look more sophisticated and grown-up by pinning my hair up. Besides, a few tendrils of loose curls left to brush my shoulders shows off the back of this gorgeous red dress.

I giggle out loud at how Zane's eyes nearly popped out of his head when he met me off the tube. He said I looked gorgeous!

I'm sure my heart will burst with excitement. Now I'm about to meet Zane's father too! Could it get any better?

I straighten down my dress, making sure my breasts are placed so that my cleavage looks perfect and then I fish my lip gloss from my bag. I apply a thick layer over my red lips and rub them together like you're supposed to.

I hope it doesn't smear when Zane kisses me. He's such a good kisser, but I wonder if he'll kiss me in front of his family?

Don't people say the Italians are funny about certain things in public?

I shrug. I don't know, but the Morellis can't be as miserable and strait-laced as my *family.*

Well, I'm not with my family tonight, I'm with Zane's. And I plan on that becoming a permanent arrangement.

Calming my nerves, I take a deep breath and step out of the cloakroom, praying I don't trip in these high stilettos. As I round the corner to see Zane waiting for me, my heart leaps, my stomach filling with fluttering butterflies. The same thing happens every time I look at him.

I never get bored of Zane and never will. He's even more gorgeous than usual in his Savile Row suit tonight. We're the perfect couple!

'You really are the most beautiful girl I've ever seen.'

Zane trails his finger down my cheek and electricity runs into places deep inside me.

I smile, feeling like I might die from happiness. 'I hope your father likes me,' *I whisper, my nagging fear resurfacing.* 'What if he doesn't?'

'He will,' *Zane insists.*

With his arm around my tiny waist, I let him lead me towards the function room, my legs shaky with nerves.

The door opens into a vast room decorated with black and

gold balloons. The huge mirror balls suspended from the ceiling shine millions of little lights everywhere. I hope some are on me.

I try to stop my eyes from darting around, but I can't help it. There are so many people in here - men in immaculate suits and beautiful women.

I pull back, suddenly feeling inferior. 'I don't look half as good as these people and... well... I...'

'Hey!' Zane tugs me forward. 'Come on. It's not like you don't know anyone. You already know Marco, so don't be shy. Come and meet my father.'

I try to smile. God, I'm nervous. Plus, I don't exactly *know Marco. I remember Zane having a brother a couple of years below us at school, but I never spoke to him. The bloke is a bit odd. Furthermore, wasn't this setup at the Savoy a bit extravagant for a fourteen-year-old's birthday?*

I inwardly shrug. This is a Morelli do and everyone knows they have only the best. That's another reason why I don't understand why my parents have such a general problem with the family. 'Not right, that lot,' *my father says.* 'Bloody criminals!'

I swallow my snigger, imagining how they will react when they discover I've been going out with a Morelli for three whole months, let alone that I'm here now. And if they knew that I'd fully *given myself to him a month ago they'd have a complete fit!*

But I don't know why. Zane is gentle and loving and made my first time special. Isn't that what parents want for their daughter? A loving man?

My only sadness is that we've only done it twice since then. It's difficult finding anywhere with privacy, but hopefully that will change as I think Zane might propose soon. And when he does, I'm going to say yes.

I want nothing more than to be with Zane Morelli so my parents will have no choice but to get over their issues with him and his family because nothing will stop me from being with the boy I love.

'Dad, I'd like you to meet my girlfriend, Shirley.'

Zane's voice pulls me from my thoughts. Girlfriend? He officially called me his girlfriend! See! Zane loves me!

My eyes track up to the imposing man standing in front of me. I try to smile but my mouth doesn't do what I want it to.

'Shirley, this is my father, Giuseppe,' Zane continues.

'Pleased to meet you,' I say, my voice squeaky.

'Good evening, Shirley,' Giuseppe extends his hand and takes mine, raising it to brush his lips against my fingers. 'I hope you have a pleasant evening.'

'Thank you for inviting me,' I blurt as Giuseppe's cold blue eyes move to Zane, He has the same piercing blue eyes of Zane's, but Giuseppe's deliver a look which I can't quite decipher. Is it anger? Displeasure? Disappointment?

I feel sick. Am I not pretty enough? Does Giuseppe think Zane should be with someone taller or blonde or...

'Let's go and find Marco.' Zane takes my hand. 'I guess we should wish him a happy birthday.'

'Okay,' I mutter, allowing Zane to steer me away from his father.

As we leave, I glance back to shoot a quick smile in the older man's direction, but he's still watching me with those piercing eyes and unfathomable expression. I want to ask Zane if his father hates me or whether he's always like this, but I don't.

I won't let my mind run away with me. Nothing can spoil tonight because it's the best night of my life so far. And being with Zane, I'm sure there will be plenty more wonderful nights yet to come.

ONE

June 2001

ERIN LANGLEY shifted position in the armchair. Although her gunshot wound was healing, it was still uncomfortable if she sat incorrectly or forgot about it and suddenly moved. It should be difficult to forget being shot, but there were occasions - quite a few actually, when she managed just that. Especially when she was concentrating on what to say to Skye Wilson.

Readjusting her slight frame, Erin looked at Skye sitting in the opposite chair. This unexpected situation had been hard for everybody and although it was two weeks since the bombshell of Zane's unknown daughter was dropped and things weren't anywhere near as awkward as they were to start with, the situation was far from being what could be deemed as 'relaxed'.

Neither did it help that Zane felt they shouldn't bombard the girl with questions about her life.

'She'll tell us when she's ready,' he'd said.

All very well, Erin thought, but as they were also avoiding the elephant in the room in the guise of Skye's mother and the details surrounding that, then without being able to engage in smalltalk about Skye's life in general, it narrowed down what *could* be said.

'So,' Erin said,' You mentioned some friends? How about a boyfriend? Is there one on the scene?'

'Not particularly,' Skye muttered. 'Talking of boyfriends, I still can't believe you're getting married,' she continued, her bright blue eyes dissecting everything around her. 'Don't get me wrong – it's fantastic, but Zane said you haven't been together very long.'

Erin made herself smile. That was a veer away from the subject of Skye's boyfriends if ever she'd heard one. 'You're right. Me and Zane haven't been together very long,' she admitted. 'But Zane's the best thing that's ever happened to me.' Even under the strange circumstances in which they'd found themselves thrown together. And *those* she wasn't attempting to explain. Zane had given Skye a cutdown version of events and that was the way it had to stay. 'So, quick yes, but I guess when you meet someone and it's right, it's right.'

'I'm sorry,' Skye blathered. 'I didn't mean to insinuate that it was wrong or that y...'

'Don't worry.' Erin flapped her hand to dilute Skye's nerves, realising Skye must still be nervous and treading on eggshells, afraid to offend.

It hadn't been plain sailing for Erin either. Being discharged from Mr Solenzo's private practice to a house containing a complete stranger with links to Zane's past wasn't an ideal scenario, but Skye had been trying to get to know Zane and, to be fair, *her* too, so Erin had to cut the girl some slack.

Unfortunately, not only was it a difficult time for Skye to descend on a man with no prior clue as to her existence, but with the issues, courtesy of Marco, still outstanding and Zane's need to establish a strong new firm in record speed, his time was stretched. His guilt about being unable to devote 100 per cent attention to his surprise daughter plagued him constantly.

'Will Zane be out all day again?' Skye asked, a nervous tremor in her voice.

'I'm not sure. He'll be back as soon as he can.' Overriding

the stiffness in her torso, Erin leant forward to touch Skye's arm. 'Please don't think he doesn't want to spend time with you. He does. Unfortunately, there's lots going on at the moment.' She smiled tightly. 'Once that's all sorted, I'm sure you'll spend loads of time together.'

Skye smiled weakly. 'I-I didn't mean to sound like I was moaning. I'm grateful that he didn't shun me. I guess a lot of men would have.'

Erin's heart melted. 'Please stop apologising! Your father isn't the sort to shun his responsibilities.' She then grinned. 'Not that I'm saying you're an unwanted responsibility! The opposite in fact. He's pleased as punch to have a daughter.'

Skye's eyes glimmered with unshed tears. 'He is? Really?'

'Really!' Erin nodded. 'The only thing he's disappointed about is having missed out on so much of your life.' That his daughter had been kept from him all of these years made Zane furious.

Skye fidgeted uncomfortably. 'I don't know why my mother...' Her voice tailed off.

Erin swallowed the question pushing to escape: *Why had Shirley hidden Zane's child from him?*

Each time the subject of Shirley Wilson came up, Skye found a reason to sidestep it. No, Erin didn't want Zane to visit Shirley and ask that very question himself like he wanted to. He'd have already been to see her by now if Skye would tell him where Shirley was, but she wouldn't.

Why?

Base fear remained knotted deep inside Erin that seeing the woman he shared a child with after all of these years might rekindle his feelings.

She knew Zane was a teenager when he'd dated Shirley, but her being the first girl he'd introduced to his family must have meant something? Plus, it wasn't like he'd called off the relationship. It had been *Shirley* who had left with no word. And now to discover she'd had his child but not allowing him to be a part of that for seventeen years must hurt, so the question as to *why* would have to be answered at some point.

Erin frowned. She'd told herself time and time again to trust Zane. She'd promised both herself and him that was what she would do from now on, but the hang-ups nestled deep inside her skull haunted her like an unwanted guest, regardless.

'You know that you'll have to tell Zane where your mother is eventually, don't you?' Erin blurted, unable to help it. 'He's not the sort to leave stones unturned.'

'I don't want her knowing I'm here,' Skye snapped. 'If Zane goes to see her, my mother will know I'm here and I promised I'd never... never do that.'

Erin picked up her drink from the table, mainly to stop herself from asking anything else. *Why was it so bad for the girl to track her father down? Why did Shirley hate Zane so much when it had been her who had disappeared.*

'You said she thinks you're on holiday with your friend?' Erin watched Skye closely. It seemed odd a mother so adamant on keeping a leash on her grown daughter's choices would be happy with her going *anywhere.*

'It was easier to say that,' Skye explained. 'I wanted to get to know my father without the hassle.' She looked down at her hands. 'I don't usually lie, but Mum's not well which makes things difficult sometimes.'

Erin nodded. Yes, Skye had said her mother was unwell from the day she'd explained who she actually was, but always shut down when pressed as to *how* ill. *And in what way?*

'Let's hope your friend doesn't bump into your mother otherwise your alibi is up the wall!'

'Yeah,' Skye acknowledged. There was little chance of that, but if it made these questions about Shirley stop, it was easier to agree.

TWO

ZANE MORELLI admired the large, detached house he'd purchased in Dagenham, pleased the contractors had done such a good job of turning the façade from the dilapidated mess it was mere days ago into something that now looked perfect. Even the subtle signage reading 'Starbright Centre' fitted the image he wanted to project to the outside world.

When he'd first spotted the ten-bedroom house up for auction he'd almost bypassed it, presuming it would take too long and cost too much to get it into a suitable condition. Time was one thing he didn't have on his side.

But he was glad he'd run with his instinct and taken a look. Not only was the grotty exterior not an indication of the interior, but everyone else after auction properties had made the same assumption that he almost had.

Zane grinned. Living abroad and having inherited the property off a relative, the vendor had no interest in seeing the place. He'd wanted to grab the money while he could instead of being lumbered with what he perceived to be a useless dump, so being the only interested purchaser, the vendor had accepted Zane's knock-down offer, not bothering letting the auction run.

More fool him, Zane thought, stepping over the threshold.

Because internally, the house was in perfect condition.

In fact, everything had fallen into place better than he'd imagined. To top things off, the extra wedge he'd paid his father's old conveyancer ensured the sale went through in a matter of days, rather than weeks.

'Looking good, isn't it?' Hazel Grimes stepped out of a downstairs room that she'd taken as an office and met Zane in the tiled hallway.

'It certainly does!' Zane smiled as Hazel gestured for him to follow and sat down in the chair opposite Hazel's desk. The room was kitted out with the essentials: a computer, phone, desk and a cabinet. Nothing fancy, but nothing fancy was required. Hazel had everything needed to run the women's centre - just not to the lavish standard she'd been used to.

But, Zane thought with satisfaction, that no longer appeared to bother Hazel. Since she'd been free from his brother's clutches and the previous life she'd led as the country's most sought-after adult film star, her true persona had fully emerged. He'd been correct in believing there was a real person behind the mask of the woman publicly known as Lisa Tequila.

Lisa Tequila was no more. And Zane hoped it remained that way.

'How are you settling in?' he asked.

Hazel beamed, her face appearing years younger without the layers of thick foundation, false eyelashes and half a bag of eye products. 'Great! The website's due to go live today and then I expect to start getting enquiries.'

Zane smiled. The wounds Marco had inflicted on Hazel were now barely visible. With any luck, after a few more weeks, the more difficult to heal wounds would start to mend too.

But some wounds never fully healed...

Shaking away the thought of his brother, Zane jerked his head in the direction of the rooms upstairs. 'What about the current residents? How are they faring?'

'We've had a couple of instances of attempted escape, but I think they've started to realise this isn't a set up.' She flicked through her hardback diary to the current week. 'I've arranged for a therapist and an interpreter to come in to speak with them. I'm planning to make it a regular thing.'

'An interpreter?' Zane frowned. The Polish women that Marco had trafficked into the country to use as sex slaves' English wasn't brilliant, but it wasn't zero either.

'I thought it would be more comfortable for them to be spoken to in their mother tongue.' Hazel frowned. 'I can cancel it if you like?'

'No, it's a good idea.' Zane's face broke into a grin. He'd been adamant on opening this centre – both to give Hazel a chance at a life free from Marco, but also to try and make up in some small way to the trafficked women for the damage Marco had caused with his greed. But the women abused at the hands of his brother needed a woman's take on things and Hazel was dealing with that just fine. 'I knew you'd be great at this. You think in ways the likes of me never would.'

Hazel laughed, her respect for Zane at an all-time high. 'Ah, but you forget that without *you* this place wouldn't be here at all!' Plus, without Zane Morelli she would have suffered more damage from the end of Marco's fists than she already had. Or she'd be dead. That she wasn't, was something she would always be thankful for.

Her face suddenly fell. It was all very well things going nicely and although the majority of the time she successfully blocked out the nagging threat constantly perching on her shoulder like a succubus, it never went away entirely, and Zane's presence brought it back with startling clarity.

Zane frowned at Hazel's expression. 'Problems?'

'No, everything's fine.' Hazel played down her worries. She'd had this conversation a thousand times over the last two weeks and the answer was always the same: she'd be told the minute there was anything she needed to know.

But getting no news was sometimes worse than *bad* news and nothing could stop her from thinking about it. At some point Marco would be out and come for her. As would Damon

Sandler and *he* wasn't banged up, so whilst either of them still breathed they remained a constant threat.

Zane's frown deepened, not needing Hazel to voice what her face showed.

Marco.

His brother was on his mind most minutes of most days too. Like Hazel, he knew the luck afforded them so far could end at any time. 'I know what you're thinking,' he said solemnly, 'but please try not to dwell on my bastard of a brother. From what I've heard, it's looking promising things will go the right way.'

Hazel's mouth fell open. 'You mean...? Oh my God! This is brilliant!' She clapped her hands together, unable to contain her excitement. Rushing around the desk, she threw her arms around Zane and kissed him on the cheek. 'I'm so pleased! He'll be gone for years! Why on earth didn't you tell me?'

Zane's brow furrowed. 'I wanted to make sure that's definitely the case before I said anything and it's not. Not yet, but it's looking that way.'

Hazel's bubble of happiness began to deflate. 'But if two weeks on Marco's still detained and it's going to court, then surely that means the Crown have the evidence to prosecute? That's what you're saying, isn't it?'

Zane nodded. 'On the surface, yes, but nothing is set in stone.' And he out of anyone knew that. Even with the mountain of evidence stacked against Marco, he didn't trust his brother not to somehow wriggle off the hook.

After spending six long years banged up after the miscarriage of justice lumped on him, Zane knew things didn't always progress the way they should. Despite this, he remained upbeat. The last thing he wanted was Hazel losing faith. 'Don't panic. All I'm saying is things are looking better than they were, so let's just concentrate on that for now.'

Hazel returned Zane's smile. 'Okay, if that's what you think.'

Zane gestured towards Hazel's diary. 'Tell me what else you've got planned and then I'll be off to headquarters. Oh, and you'll be hearing from a solicitor regarding your divorce from my brother. He's come highly recommended.'

Hazel brightened. 'That's great. Thanks for arranging that. When will he be coming?'

'Sometime this week, but he'll confirm dates with you. He also needs some documentation from you, but he said he'll write to outline exactly what that is.'

Hopefully, that would be the last time Marco would have to be referenced for a while. From now on he'd steer Hazel off the subject of Marco until he knew for definite there was cause to breathe easily, or worst-case scenario - it came to the time when he had to bring her world crashing down.

Finding out further updates about his wanker of a brother was the first thing he'd do when he reached headquarters.

• • • •

DAMON SANDLER glanced around the door of the chippy before stepping onto the pavement in Battersea. He wasn't sure why he was looking. Marco had no one left on his payroll to put searches out.

At this precise moment, Marco Morelli had no viable business, no house, no enforcers and no clout. The man had nothing.

Nothing, apart from *him*.

Damon's eyes narrowed. He had no wish to be tied to Marco, but thanks to the deal he'd agreed and then signed that fucking piece of paper Marco's brief, Symonds, just happened to have ready when Marco had first been taken into custody, he was stuck with it. And from what he gathered, Marco was less than amused that none of the terms of that deal had yet been delivered…

Shoving a handful of chips into his mouth, Damon continued towards the Blacksmith's Arms, trying not to gag as more grease than potato went round his gob.

The terms of Marco's deal were unreasonable. Even Symonds thought so. Damon could clearly recall the expression on that withered old bastard's face when Marco listed what he'd expected to be fulfilled: 1) released from police custody within forty-eight hours; 2) his wife brought in to see him and then dispatched; 3) his brother Zane located and removed... Oh and 4) offloading Zane's chick, Erin Langley.

Damon braved another handful of chips.

At least he'd achieved *one* of the items on Marco's list. Shooting that two-faced bitch, Erin, who'd thought herself clever by moling her way into Luna Motion Films, had been done good and proper.

His face cracked into a crooked smile. Gunning that slut down in front of Zane's new headquarters was perfect. The half-derelict remains of Thames Canning Works made a fitting backdrop for the bitch's life to end.

Yep, he'd managed that, all right. Mainly because it was the most important item on *his* list. But how the hell could he have achieved the others once all the available men had jumped ship? He only possessed one pair of fucking eyes.

Once the clock had ticked past Marco's forty-eight-hour deadline, Damon had fully expected to be butchered in his bed. That had been promised in so many words should he fall short in delivering. But nothing had happened.

He'd laid low since then. Lower than low. He'd barely even glanced out of the window for fear of reprisals, only venturing out under the cover of darkness as far as the Spar on Battersea Park Road to buy a couple of cans of beans and a loaf of bread. He'd expected someone to be lying in wait for him wherever he went. But as one day passed and then another, Damon realised that he was the only one Marco had onside possessing the capacity of rational thought. And now, two weeks on without a hint of anything, he wasn't waiting any longer to rejoin society.

Besides, he hadn't *entirely* fallen off the face of the planet. He'd kept in touch with Symonds to maintain the illusion that he was still working on the proposed agenda. But that agenda was pointless. Marco had been officially charged and was awaiting trial. Without Hazel's testimony to get the case thrown out it was likely that Marco would get sent down.

On one hand, Damon felt this prospect was good because it meant he would not be murdered. On the flip side, he would lose out on being a partner in the firm.

But, he thought with a grin, it didn't stop him taking over where Marco left off, did it?

And that's why he was going in *here*.

Zane Morelli's men rarely frequented the Blacksmith's Arms and after receiving word that the place was clear of anyone suspicious, he'd take the gamble.

Damon's hand moved back into his bag of chips and then paused as his fingers touched another clump of melded potato. Scowling, he bunched up the packet and slung it in the direction of a bin. It missed and instead exploded all over the floor.

Shrugging, he continued. Someone could tread in that and get greasy shit all over their carpet. See if he cared!

Wiping his hands down his jeans, Damon yanked open the pub door and spotting Tel and Banjo at a table over the far end of the taproom, he made his way over.

THREE

'I'M SO GLAD you've come,' Shirley Wilson cried, ushering Martin Bolt into her living room. 'I didn't know what else to do.'

Martin steered his girlfriend's mother into the direction of a chair, frowning as he did so. He'd only met her a handful of times because Skye seemed reticent to invite him to her home. When they weren't out or at friends' places, they spent their time at *his* house - or should he say, his parents' house, rather than hers. It was almost like Skye was embarrassed about her mother, but Martin couldn't understand why.

She'd previously touched on the subject that her mother wasn't well. In what way, Martin was unsure and hadn't liked to pry on a topic that was clearly uncomfortable.

He and Skye had attended the same school. He was two years older than her and hadn't even noticed her until last year, so why would he have paid any attention to spotting her mother?

The answer was, he hadn't. The school they'd both attended, being one of the best private schools in the region, had arranged plentiful events for pupils and their parents alike. There were thousands of people milling around on those event days so he wouldn't have had a clue if he'd noticed Skye's mother or not. But since he and Skye had become an item, he'd met Shirley a handful of times. Okay, so the woman's dress sense might be a bit eccentric and she was hardly a model for the cover of *Vogue*, but she had always been pleasant and polite.

But something was clearly bothering Mrs Wilson at the moment and the rambling voicemails he'd received the minute he'd got back on English soil had unnerved him.

Martin took a seat in the opposite armchair and watched Shirley wring her hands, her eyes darting around the room. 'I'd have come sooner, but I've been away on our annual family holiday. Did Skye not mention it? We always go to Austria this time of year and being as Skye was going away with Alyson Read, I thought it wo…'

'Alyson called,' Shirley cut in, her hands picking at the hem of her inside-out skirt. 'No actually, that's not right. I called Alyson.' She looked up at the ceiling, her lips mouthing silent words. 'That's not right either. Did Alyson call me? No, I called her. I wouldn't normally call while they were on holiday, but I had to because Skye always phones when she's away and she didn't. I was worried something had happened.'

Martin frowned. 'But as they're away, maybe she didn't have a phone or...'

'Skye's not abroad!' Shirley snapped. 'She only went to Scotland. They have phones there, don't they?' She paused, her heavily creased brow folding further. 'Yes, they do! There's a programme I watch that's set in Scotland and they have phones. But anyway, Skye didn't call so I called Alyson.'

She laughed suddenly, the noise high pitched and forced. 'Why I called Alyson's house when the family's away in Scotland I've no idea, but I did.'

Martin frowned as Shirley's voice tailed off and her concentration reverted to the ceiling; her mouth jabbering silently, making her double chin judder along the fatty folds of her neck. This was the first time Martin had seen this strange side to Shirley Wilson. 'Okay, so you called and...?'

'Yes, yes,' Shirley cried. 'That's right - I called and Alyson answered!' She shifted her bulk forward in the seat. 'Alyson was at home and not in Scotland!' She grabbed the arm of the chair, her pudgy knuckles whitening. 'They hadn't been away at all. The girl didn't know what I was talking about.'

'What? They didn't go to Scotland?' Martin repeated as he navigated this woman's verbal diarrhoea.

'They went nowhere! So, if Skye didn't go with Alyson and if she isn't with you, then where is she?' Shirley paused, her head swivelling to stare at Martin. 'She's *not* with you, is she? It's been over two weeks since she left.'

'No, Mrs Wilson, she's not. I think I just said I've been in Austria for the last month,' Martin repeated, concern mounting.

'Call me Shirley,' Shirley said. 'That's if you don't mind? You don't mind, do you? It's just that Mrs Wilson is so formal and... Oh, where is Skye?'

Martin pursed his lips. He didn't know, but this was strange. Shirley was acting manic and slightly unhinged. It wasn't possible she could be mixed up because Skye had told him she was going away with Alyson too. He and Skye had been an item for nearly seven months and he'd never had reason to suspect she hadn't been truthful before, so why would she lie about this? It didn't make sense. 'Could you have misheard what Alyson said?'

Shirley's eyes narrowed. 'How? Alyson wouldn't have been at home to answer the phone if she was in Scotland! Do you think I'm mad?'

'No, of course not!' Martin blathered. Yet after this, he wasn't sure. But it was true that if Alyson *had been* in Scotland then she wouldn't have answered the home phone. And if Skye was supposed to be with Alyson...

Shirley hefted herself out of the chair and paced around the sitting room, the loose sole on the bottom of her right slipper slapping against her foot. 'I'm frightened!' she cried. 'I want to know where Skye's gone and why she's lied.'

Martin wanted to know those things too. 'Alyson has no

idea?' Not that Alyson Read would tell the truth if she was covering for Skye. Didn't friends do that?

Shirley shook her head, the movement making her fleshy chins quiver further.

A sliver of worry crept up Martin's spine. He liked Skye Wilson – liked her a lot. She was stunning both inside and out. Even having a mother who appeared to be teetering on the edge of normality wasn't enough to put him off. *Nothing* could put him off. But what if Skye had another boyfriend?

Perspiration beaded along the back of Martin's neck.

Skye wasn't the sort to play games, but what else could explain her need to lie to both him and her mother?

Hearing Shirley mumbling again, Martin ignored it. That was until he heard the same words for the second time...

Turning, he found her staring into an oval wall mirror, her face only partially visible due to the glaring reflection of the sunlight from the windows behind. 'What was that you just said?'

'I said that she can't go there! All these years she promised me she'd never do that. I made sure... How did she find out? I tried so hard... I...'

The part of Shirley's face that Martin could see in the reflection was twisted in pure fear. He moved closer, frowning at a clump of knots in the back of her matted dark brown hair. 'Promised you? Promised you what?'

Cold tendrils slithered along Martin's veins. What was this about? Were Shirley's ramblings true or figments of her imagination? 'Mrs Wilson? Shirley? What did Skye promise? What did she say she'd never do?'

With a jolt, Shirley turned from the mirror, surprised to find she'd been speaking out loud and that Martin was in the room at all. What was clear though was the unbridled fear etched on her face.

Martin swallowed nervously. Whether this was confusion or not, whatever Shirley believed Skye had done instilled the fear of God into her. 'Shirley? Where do you believe Skye has gone?'

Shirley lurched forward and Martin worried that she might be having a coronary, but she wasn't. Instead, she grabbed his hand so tightly that her nails dug into his skin.

'I-I think she's gone to Battersea.' Shirley's mouth began silently flapping up and down again.

No, no, Martin thought. *Don't start that weird shit again.* 'Battersea? Why Battersea? Shirley? Concentrate! You must tell me! I need to know. She's my girlfriend.'

'And she's *my* daughter!' Shirley countered, her eyes flashing. 'Mine!' The flare of anger evaporated as quickly as it had arrived. Her shoulders sagged, making the creases in her oversized cardigan even more unflattering. She slowly raised her eyes that were now glistening with tears. 'She's gone to find her father. And she can't. She *mustn't*!'

· · · ·

'ZANE!' Erin gasped as Zane brought her to heights previously unknown until meeting him, her aim of being quiet flying out of the window. Her climax continued to pound through her until, with a suppressed growl, Zane released into her.

Collapsing in a sweaty mess, Zane gave Erin a crooked smile. 'So much for being silent!'

Erin grinned. She pushed a tendril of hair stuck to her face away. 'I couldn't help it.' Rolling onto her stomach, she propped herself up with her elbows and stared at the ruggedly handsome face of the man she was so in love with.

Skye staying in their small, rented house in Dalston made it awkward to get much time together. It was almost amusing sneaking around snatching the odd moment, but it didn't help that only a couple of weeks ago their relationship had been fast heading down the toilet and they had lots to make up for.

'Have you given any more thought to taking back your penthouse?' Erin tentatively asked. 'You said Marco's bunch have disbanded since his arrest and no one is at the apartment anymore.' She mischievously raised an eyebrow. 'It *is* yours and if you took it back, then we'd have lots of space to ourselves…'

'That's what I've heard, yes, but I can't be sure and well, although it's tempting…' Zane pulled Erin back over him. 'I've got Skye to consider now. I don't want her experiencing any more upheaval. It's important she feels settled. I guess I would know how parents get around having a life as well as kids if I'd had more experience beforehand,' he said, a tinge of bitterness in his voice.

Shelving her idea of the penthouse, Erin traced her finger down Zane's chest, wanting to steer him off this deep seated resentment. 'There's no rule book. Besides, it's not like Skye's a kid. She's virtually a grown woman and probably well aware what happens in relationships, if you get my drift!'

Zane frowned. The thought hadn't crossed his mind that Skye might have a boyfriend - one with whom she'd... Unexplainable rage at the thought of a man's hands on his daughter's body ripped through him. It was an irrational thought process, but he couldn't help it. 'Do you think she's got a fella? Has she said so?'

Erin couldn't help but burst out laughing at Zane's expression. 'You should see your face! I pity the poor girl if she has! Imagine the interrogation her bloke would get from you?'

She wouldn't mention Skye's earlier vagueness about boyfriends. There was no point throwing fuel on the fire. Neither was there point repeating that skirting around the other questions they wanted answers to - *needed* answers to, had to be broached at some point. She owed it to Zane to support him on this unexpected situation, no matter if there were points which rang alarm bells.

It was difficult to decide if those alarm bells were ringing due to genuine reasons or whether they stemmed from her own hang ups. Until she could work that out, she had to keep her thoughts to herself.

'Anyway.' Erin pulled herself out of bed and slipped her clothes on. 'How did it go today? You didn't say much before we got otherwise "distracted"...'

The frown dropped from Zane's face. 'It went well.' He nodded towards the door. 'Are you sure that Skye's not around? I don't want her overhearing. The less she knows of the ins and outs of what I do, the better.'

'She went for a walk, but if she's back then she'll be downstairs.'

Zane's frown returned. 'Why did you let her go out? I don't want her wandering around outside. It's not safe.'

'You can't keep Skye a prisoner,' Erin cried. 'You said that yourself!' Suddenly she went cold. 'Nothing's changed, has it? Marco's still in nick?'

'Yes.' Zane nodded. 'Tiger's digging for more updates.' As much as he'd like to share Hazel's, Erin's and many others' enthusiasm that things were cut and dried over his brother being put away for the foreseeable, the prickling feeling remained that no one should relax just yet, but he wanted to offer at least *something* positive. 'We've also gained three more territories so far this week. Plus, Hazel's got things moving nicely at the women's centre.'

'I was thinking about that,' Erin took a seat back on the bed. 'Being as you can't spend as much time as you'd like with Skye at the moment, how do you feel about her getting involved with the centre?'

Zane stared at Erin aghast. 'No daughter of mine is spending time in a fucking women's refuge!'

'Christ, Zane!' Erin cried. 'You need to chill out! You can't treat the girl like she's ten years old! She'd probably enjoy doing something constructive. I bet Hazel could use the help too. At least think about it?'

Zane grunted and busied himself with lighting a cigarette. *Was he being irrational?* He could hardly expect Skye to sit around doing shag all, could he?

FOUR

'WE'VE ONLY JUST got back, Martin!' Peter Bolt said, his bushy eyebrows furrowing. 'You were out half of the evening yesterday and your mother had cooked your favourite for dinner.'

'I'm sorry, Dad. Something came up,' Martin explained. 'I didn't think I'd be so long, but it was important.' But if he'd known he'd have been stuck in Shirley Wilson's house for hours then he'd have eaten beforehand. But it wasn't like he could leave before hearing everything the woman had to say.

Peter folded his arms across his chest, his suit jacket bunching over the paunch of his stomach. 'What else is so important *now* to make you want to dash out again so soon? And to borrow the Range Rover too? You have your own car.'

Martin shrugged, hoping he'd learnt at least *something* during his two years in sixth form. 'A few of us thought we'd have a day or two away, that's all,' he lied. 'There's more room in the Range Rover than in my car.'

He watched his father's lips purse in the way they always did when he was less than amused. This would be more difficult than he'd thought. 'Come on, Dad, what's the big deal? I'm insured. You added me onto your policy for the Range Rover when I passed my test.'

Peter continued scrutinising his son. 'We've been away for almost a month, Martin. Just because you've finished your A-levels it doesn't mean you can swan off here there and everywhere!' His face grew sterner. 'We haven't spent thousands over the years putting you through private school and then sixth form just for you to get drunk with your mates! Rather than wasting time, you should be doing preparatory work for September when you go to St Andrews.'

'I *will*,' Martin pleaded. 'But I'd like a couple of days with my friends first and then I'll get things ready for September.' *And that was another thing...*

He now had reservations about going to university at all. St Andrews was a long way from Surrey, which equated to being a long way from Skye. And he didn't want to be away from her. Less now than ever being as the last month apart showed him that she was *The One*.

He wouldn't broach the subject of jacking off university with his parents just yet, but if he didn't get on with doing what he'd promised Shirley then he wouldn't need to broach the subject of not going to university at all because there might be nothing to stay around here for. He had to find Skye before something bad happened.

'Dad...'

'It's not a good idea, Martin.' Peter shook his head. 'Your mother will expect you to spend time with us here.'

Martin's hands balled into fists. 'I will afterwards, I promise. What difference does a couple of days make? We've just spent a month together!'

'No, Martin. I've made my mind up. I...'

'Peter, let the boy take the car.' Fiona Bolt glided into the room and brushed an imaginary piece of fluff off her husband's sleeve. 'Martin is right. A couple of days with his friends is just what he needs before settling down for a further three years of study.'

Martin's hopes surged. 'It's only a few of us going. It will be fun.'

'Will Skye be going too?' Fiona raised an eyebrow.

'No, she's still on holiday in Scotland with Alyson,' Martin gabbled, pleased he'd mastered the art of bending the truth.

Resting her hand on Peter's shoulders, Fiona smiled at her husband. 'Let Martin take the Range Rover, darling,' she purred. 'It will be good for him.'

Peter scowled, knowing when he was beat. 'You spoil that boy, Fiona!' he muttered, harrumphing loudly. 'Fine! Two days and that's it. But there had better be no scratches or mess inside my car afterwards!'

Smiling triumphantly, Fiona gave Martin a smug wink. 'Where are you planning on going, dear?'

Martin stopped the exhale of relief coming from his mouth just in time. 'Only to the coast.'

He wished he *was* going to the coast. If his parents knew he was heading to Battersea to search for his missing girlfriend, whose mother believed had gone looking for a father that she'd never met, they wouldn't be happy.

His parents would be even less happy if they were aware, like *he* now was, that this father Skye was searching for was linked to the criminal underbelly. Exactly *how* he was linked, Shirley wouldn't say, but either way, they would stop him from going. They certainly wouldn't allow him the use of the expensive Range Rover.

Martin swallowed dryly. *He needed that bloody car.* Planning to step off the beaten track into the back streets of the London underworld he required something with more protection and clout than his Vauxhall Nova. It had to be something fast enough to get away should he need to.

• • • •

'I DON'T KNOW WHY Erin keeps questioning me about boyfriends.' Skye played with her piece of toast and raised her big blue eyes to meet Zane's. 'I answered her questions, so why does she keep asking me the same thing?'

Frowning, Zane glanced towards the ceiling where he could still hear the upstairs shower running. His response to the conversation he'd had with Erin last night rolled through him with a shudder. He'd asked Erin if she knew of any boyfriends Skye might have, yet come to think of it, she hadn't answered the question. 'What do you mean, she *keeps* asking you?'

Skye rolled her eyes. 'She's asked me about twenty times.'

'Twenty times?' Although Erin was like a dog with a bone when she wanted to know something, Zane couldn't imagine her repeating a question to that extent. 'And what did you say?'

Skye's bottom lip trembled. 'I-I kept telling her I haven't got a boyfriend. Not anymore, but she kept on and on.'

Zane stiffened. So, Skye *had* had a boyfriend? He forced himself to remain in check. *She's seventeen years old remember, not seven!*

'H-He recently dumped me,' Skye snivelled. 'He said I wasn't pretty enough...'

Zane's jaw clenched. *What sort of cunt would tell Skye she wasn't pretty enough? The girl was stunning.*

'I might have snapped at Erin. I didn't mean to. I don't want to cause problems. I know she's just making conversation, but I really didn't want to talk about it. She kept on and on and on, saying there must be someone... It was like... like she thought I was lying...' Skye's eyes filled with tears. 'You don't think she thinks I'm hiding things because I'm one of those... those tarty girls, do you? I know Erin doesn't like me very much, but...'

'Erin doesn't think any such thing!' Zane cried. *She'd better not, anyway.* 'And why on earth you do think she doesn't like you? Look, I'm sure she didn't mean to upset you. I'll have a word with her.' He'd already told Erin not to pry into Skye's personal life but clearly she'd taken no notice. 'Who is this idiot boy anyway?'

Skye wrung her hands. 'I really don't want to talk about it. It still upsets me.'

Zane held his hands up. 'Fine. I won't say anything else,

apart from that he must be blind as well as stupid.' Seeing the sadness on his daughter's face his smile dropped. It was a good job Skye wouldn't tell him who this boyfriend was otherwise he'd be tempted to pay the little shit a visit and slap the taste out of his mouth.

'What did your mother think about him?' he asked, immediately regretting it when the colour drained from Skye's face. He might have promised himself not to push the issue with questions about Shirley, but he'd mentioned it now, so he'd run with it. 'What I mean is, I expect she wasn't happy about this boy's behaviour towards you either.'

Skye's gaze remained fixed on her hands. 'Mum never liked him, but then she doesn't like anyone.' She sniffed loudly. 'It's unlikely she even noticed I was upset. She certainly wouldn't remember if you asked her.' She cleared her throat and composed herself. 'Anyway, I'm used to my mother. It doesn't matter. As for the rest - it's in the past. I'm glad to be away from Surrey. It doesn't have many good memories for me.'

Zane looked up sharply. That was the first clue Skye had given to indicate where she and Shirley lived. 'Surrey? That's quite a way from here.'

A flash of something flitted over Skye's face before disappearing. 'The further, the better.'

Zane remained silent; his mind churning. It was unheard of for him not to ask needed questions, but he was on a steep learning curve when it came to his new daughter. And what was meant by Shirley didn't remember or notice? Was Skye hinting that Shirley was an alcoholic or worse? *Could it be that?*

He struggled to imagine the beautiful, vivacious sixteen-year-old he remembered Shirley to be the last time he'd seen her as a raving alcoholic or drug addict. It was difficult to comprehend, but anything could have happened in seventeen years. It had been *her* who'd disappeared, he reminded himself. No warning - *nothing*.

Guilt raged with the thought that he could have left his own flesh and blood to be brought up by a raving drunk with different men around the house every night.

If any men had touched Skye...

Had something along those lines happened in the past to make Skye automatically assume Erin thought her a tart?

His hands curled into fists underneath the table. He would make it *very* clear to Erin that she was to ask Skye no more questions about her personal life. Why she'd felt the need to harp on at the girl in the first place needled him. 'Perhaps you should give your mother a call? The mobile signal is good around here so you shouldn't have problems getting through.'

Skye looked up sadly. 'I-I don't have a mobile phone. I used to have a cheap one that I bought from the supermarket, but... but someone I knew from school who liked giving me a hard time smashed it up.'

'Smashed it up?' Zane frowned.

'I bumped into them in town after I left school and... W-We don't live in a nice area and, well, let's just say I didn't go to a good school either. It was rough with many problems...' Her eyes welled with tears. 'Anyway, Mum wouldn't let me have another phone. She said she needed the money for... for other things...'

Zane chewed his lip. What sort of teenager these days hadn't got a phone? Once a gadget only for the well off, times had changed and now mobiles were *everywhere* and fast becoming more vital than breathing to Skye's generation.

Furthermore, what sort of shit dump school had Shirley sent Skye to? That's what he wanted to know. Somewhere that she was bullied every day?

His anger prickled harder. Shirley was more bothered about keeping money for herself than getting her daughter what she needed?

This served to show how little he knew about his daughter. And he needed to know *all* of it, yet because of everything else he was barely here enough to pass much more than pleasantries. It wasn't good enough. Skye had gone to great lengths to seek him out, yet he was leaving her to her own devices most days and evenings.

From what Skye said, she'd been bypassed most of her life by the one person who should have put her first. *Shirley.* And to top it off she'd been treated like shit by this wanker of an ex-boyfriend?

Perhaps her spending time with Hazel at the new centre wasn't such a bad idea after all?

Zane reached into his pocket and pulled out his mobile. 'Use my phone to call your mother and let her know you're safe.'

'No!' Skye yelped. 'Please! I don't want to call her. I-I just want to be away from her... I-I can't bear it anymore...'

Zane frowned. What the hell was Shirley responsible for? Whatever had gone on had had a significant effect. It was like... like Skye was *traumatised*!

He'd get to the bottom of whatever had happened. And if Shirley Wilson or this wanker of an ex-boyfriend of Skye's had mistreated her, there would be hell to pay.

But there *was* something he could do right now to cheer his daughter up.

Reaching over, Zane patted Skye's hand. 'Do you know what? *I'll* buy you a new mobile. A top of the range one.'

Skye's eyes lit up. 'Really? You'd buy me a phone? You really mean it?'

Zane laughed. 'Of course! And I'll do so straight away. You'll have the best phone *ever*.' He raised one eyebrow. 'And if anyone tries smashing this one up, you just send them to me!'

FIVE

'WHY HAVE I COME all the way to your office for you to tell me this?' Damon griped, unable to hide his dislike for Brian Symonds. 'If you had something to say, why didn't you do it over the phone, like usual?'

Brian Symonds returned Damon's cool stare, then flicked nonchalantly through his Filofax.

Damon scowled. The man acted like it was no big deal to shell out over £20 for a taxi to Mayfair. Yes, he could have gone on the bus, but it would have taken ages and Symonds insisted he had to be here for 11 o'clock. His nails dug into his palm. 'Are you not going to answer? If what you've got to say is so important and time sensitive, I'd have thought you'd be eager to tell me what it's about.'

'*This* is what it's about.' With a flourish, Symonds pulled a copy of the *London Standard* from a drawer and laid it on the desk. 'It's happening an hour from now...'

Frowning, Damon turned his attention to the newspaper article. 'You summoned me all the way over here to show me *that*?' With the urgency of this meeting, he'd thought Marco was about to be unexpectedly released. Thankfully, that wasn't the case, but *this* wasn't what he'd expected to be twenty quid lighter in the pocket for either.

'I take it you *can* read?' Symonds scoffed. 'Because if you can, then I suggest you do so carefully and tell me what it means to you.'

Damon cut Symonds a death stare. *A real joker, this prick. Of course he could bloody read, the cheeky twat.*

Snatching the paper from under the man's pudgy fingers, he made a big show of reading the article:

New Refuge to Offer Hope to Countless Women

The Starbright Centre is officially opening its doors on 18th June at midday for the benefit of women in Dagenham and the surrounding areas.

The building, managed by Miss Fleeter, offers thirty-five beds to women in need of escape from domestic violence and other related crimes.

Miss Fleeter, herself having personal experience of domestic violence, set up the centre with the backing of an unnamed benefactor.

As part of many services offered at the centre, therapists as well as interpreters are available. Already housing several foreign victims of trafficking, Miss Fleeter believes all women should have somewhere safe to go should they require it.

If you know of anyone in need of support, please phone the Starbright Centre helpline on…

'Yeah, very nice and all that, but what the fuck has this got to do with me?' Damon snarled. 'Last time I looked, I wasn't a bloody woman!'

'Actually, I was going to ask why you'd failed to pick up on this yourself, considering you're supposed to be working flat out on Mr Morelli's agenda,' Symonds sneered. 'But being as you haven't and are clearly none the wiser, despite having the obvious thrust in front of you, then it's hardly surprising my client languishes in police custody because of your inability to deliver his requests.' He raised a bushy eyebrow. 'His wife's statement being the most important part - at least from the *legal* side...'

Damon pushed his chair back, the legs squeaking on the parquet flooring. He stood up. 'You've called me over here just to treat me like a cunt? First, you insinuate that I can't read and now you're saying it's my fault Hazel Grimes disappeared into thin fucking air? Jesus Christ! I don't have to listen to your shit, Symonds! I'm leaving before I punch the fuck out of your bastard head.'

As Damon turned to storm out of the office, Symonds grabbed his arm. 'You're not listening, Mr Sandler.' He tapped the newspaper. 'Hazel Grimes hasn't disappeared...'

Damon frowned, his anger growing with this cryptic rubbish. He hadn't got time for this. Hazel *had* disappeared. No one had seen her. Last night even Tel and Banjo confirmed that they'd been looking and there hadn't been a single sighting of the woman.

'Miss Fleeter...? The Starbright Centre...? What does that remind you of?' Symonds pushed, struggling to believe this man still hadn't put two and two together. 'Housing trafficked women...? An unnamed benefactor? That's someone with loads of money, by the way.'

'I know what a fucking benefactor is,' Damon barked, his last shred of patience evaporating.

'It's *her*!' Symonds exclaimed, giving up waiting for Damon to work it out. Miss Fleeter is Hazel Grimes. Don't you see? Marco's wife is the one managing this centre. And doesn't "Starbright" sound a little bit too reminiscent of Star*light* - you remember, Hazel's father's studios?'

Damon snorted in derision. 'That's impossible! There's no way that sh...'

'Who do you think stumped up the money to purchase the property?' Symonds asked, a smug grin on his face. 'Zane Morelli of course... *He's* the unnamed benefactor! As a solicitor, I searched the purchase and found it was a private sale a week and a half ago. There weren't any further details, but I'm sure it's him.'

Damon's mind whirred. *It couldn't be, could it?* 'We can't assume that! We don't know anything! It's just speculation!'

'You're right - we don't know for certain,' Symonds agreed. 'That's why you're going to Dagenham. The official opening is at midday. I doubt whether the press will be allowed pictures - the woman wouldn't be that stupid, but you might get a glimpse of this "Miss Fleeter". If she *is* Hazel Grimes, then we can "arrange" to secure that statement and hence remove another item off my client's agenda.' His face cracked into a sickly sneer. 'And if, like I suspect, the unnamed benefactor happens to be Zane Morelli, then that makes *two* items off the list...'

Damon blinked. Would Hazel Grimes really be so crazy to announce the opening of her new business when she was on the hit list of the most psychotic man in London?

He chewed the inside of his cheek. Then again, this was Hazel - AKA Lisa Tequila. That plastic bitch wouldn't be able to resist the temptation of public adoration that press coverage would bring.

It was a long shot, but it *might* be her. And although he'd prefer to drown slowly in a barrel of treacle than clap his eyes on that horrible slut again, Damon knew he must check it out.

• • • •

SMILING, HAZEL handed out small cards to the women she'd assembled the room they used as a common space, either to interact or to hold group meetings and discussions. 'These are the details of your personal appointments next week with the therapist.

Hearing appreciative murmurs, Hazel glowed with pride. She was doing okay here. More to the point, she was *enjoying* it.

The more she thought about what would be useful to the

women - *any* woman in this situation, both initially and going forward, the more the ideas formed. Further ideas came from there and to her delight, she found her vision for how the centre could progress and what it might offer, flowed naturally.

That there was something more to her than playing up for the lens of a camera was both gratifying and rewarding and her confidence in her latent ability grew each day.

The worry about Marco and his foul sidekick, Damon Sandler, never went away, but Zane's earlier words gave her hope and she would concentrate on that. Marco wasn't here for the time being and she trusted Zane to ensure things stayed that way.

Hazel glanced at the clock. 'Right, ladies – any time now the Starbright Centre will be officially open!' She clapped her hands together excitedly. 'Have a pleasant rest of the day.'

She smiled as the women left the room clutching their appointment cards. These women had been here since the second the keys for this place were in Zane's hand, but with today's launching of the website, the centre would be officially open and hopefully might not be long before she'd need extra help.

Imagine that - her very own staff.

Hazel opened her laptop to see if the web design company had sent the website live, but the loud buzz of the doorbell interrupted her. She frowned. She wasn't expecting a delivery, and she certainly didn't expect visitors.

Rising from her chair, Hazel moved into the hallway. She knew the drill: do not answer the door under any circumstances - that's what the guards were for. Marco may be locked away, but Sandler wasn't, so it was better to be safe than sorry.

Hazel craned her neck, hearing the muffled voice of a guard. It didn't sound like he was talking to the postman. The voice had a distinct tone of anger. Hearing the voice raise to shouting level, she rushed to the window. *There were people out there. Several people...*

She pulled aside two strips of thick vertical blinds hanging over the window in trepidation and jolted with surprise as a cacophony of flashbulbs went off in her face.

'Miss Fleeter? Can we have a picture of you outside for the official opening?'

'How about an interview, Miss Fleeter?'

'What's your opinion of the sex slave industry?'

'What about your personal experience in trafficking? Can you tell us about that, Miss Fleeter?'

Immediately dropping the blind, Hazel lurched backwards. *What the hell? Why were the press here? How did they know those details?*

'Miss Fleeter?' Fingers tapped on the window. 'How does it feel now the Starbright Centre is officially open?'

'How many women do you expect to house here? Have you had any opposition from the neighbourhood?'

'Who is your mystery benefactor, Miss Fleeter?'

Hazel pressed herself against the wall, her heart pounding. *They'd taken photographs?*

Panic swirling, sweat prickled. *They'd referred to her as Miss Fleeter.* Her eyes narrowed. The only people who knew that alias, aside from Zane and his men, was the web design company. Surely they wouldn't have gone to the press?

Running from the room, she darted down the corridor to office. She had to call Zane.

• • • •

ERIN MOVED INTO the lounge seeing Skye flicking through the *London Standard*. 'Anything interesting in the paper?'

Skye paused, a page half-turned in her fingers. 'I thought I'd see what jobs are going.' She fixed her eyes on Erin questioningly. 'Do you have an issue with that?'

Erin blinked in surprise. Was Skye intending to stay in this area permanently? Staying in this house - with them? She barely knew the girl. It was awkward enough her being here in the first place.

The expression on Skye's face was not one Erin had

witnessed before. The only way she could describe it was 'challenging'. *Aggressive*, even. The girl stared defiantly as if she dared her to comment or question her words.

Biting her tongue, Erin smiled instead. *Maybe she was reading this wrong? Perhaps Skye had no plans to stay around at all?* 'Why would I have an issue with it? Short of you getting to know your father, I have no idea what your future plans are.'

'As long as my plans don't involve stepping on *yours*, right?' Skye mumbled.

'Pardon?' Erin said, getting irked. 'What do you mean by that?'

'By what?' Skye's blue eyes transformed back to their usual innocence.

'You just said something about "my plans". What exactly are you trying to say?'

Skye's bottom lip trembled. 'I-I didn't say that! I-I said I didn't want to do anything that would affect yours and Zane's plans. I don't want to be in the way...'

Erin frowned. That wasn't what Skye had said at all. *Had she misheard?* 'I'm sure you said th...'

'I know you don't like me,' Skye continued, the innocence behind her eyes disappearing once again. 'You're so obvious, but I'm getting to know my father whether you like it or not!'

Erin's mouth fell open. She'd been nothing but accommodating since Skye arrived. Yes, she might have concerns, but it certainly wasn't that she *disliked* the girl. At a loss for words, she fumbled over what to say. 'I-I don't know why you'd think that... I...'

'Calling me a tart was low, Erin,' Skye spat, her eyes cold. 'You may have fooled Zane, but attempting to keep a father and daughter apart because you're jealous of my mother does you no favours.'

'What?' Erin gasped. 'Now wait a minute! The thought didn't even cross my mind, let alone say that to you!' As for being jealous about Shirley, that was partly true, but she hadn't tried to keep Zane away from Skye – it was the opposite. 'When did I call you a tart?'

'A tart?' Skye's hand flew to her mouth. 'I said, I wanted to get off to a good *start*.' A tear rolled down her cheek. 'You don't think I'm a tart, do you? Why would you say something like that?'

'No!' Erin cried. 'I didn't! Of course I don't think that!' Sweating, she sat down, her brain swirling.

Was she hearing things?

No, she wasn't. She'd heard every word Skye said plain as day.

About to question Skye's additional comments, Erin instead decided to keep quiet. Two things were possible here: either she had gone suddenly deaf and mad or Skye was playing games. Games of which Erin was unsure as to the point of.

It was confusing, but she'd wait. If Skye was playing games, then she'd do it again and then it would be obvious.

Now to turn the situation around. Let's see how Skye dealt with *this*. 'I must be imagining things.' Erin rolled her eyes in an over-the-top gesture. 'I'm sorry if I confused things. Anyway, talking of jobs, I mentioned to Zane that you might like to help out at the centre Hazel has been setting up. Do you remember the one we told you about?'

Skye beamed, all trace of the malicious glint behind her eyes hidden. 'Oh yes, I'd like that. But I didn't realise it was common knowledge about it opening.'

Erin frowned. 'It isn't. Why do you ask?'

'I thought there must have been a change of plans after I saw this.' Skye handed the paper to Erin, open at the article about the Starbright Centre. 'This is the place, isn't it?'

Erin scanned the article in horror. *Jesus Christ! What was Hazel thinking off by calling the press?*

She glanced at the date on the paper. It was yesterday's... Her eyes swung to the wall clock. That meant the listed opening time for the centre was today - half an hour ago...

The agreed alias to ensure no paper trail was laid had been used instead of Hazel's real name, but why would she go looking for trouble?

'You look like you've seen a ghost!' Skye laughed. 'It can't be that bad, can it?'

Erin placed the paper down and stood up. 'I don't know, but I need to make Zane aware of it.'

Six

'ALL I CAN DO is touch base every day with our contact in the force and wait for updates.' Tiger Shoreham shrugged. 'There's not a lot else we can do.'

Zane turned his cigarette packet around, controlling the desire to crush the cardboard in his hand out of frustration. 'So no news on Marco, apart from that he's still in nick and no word of impending court dates?'

'Look on the bright side,' Leo Holland chipped in. 'No change means nothing has occurred to our detriment.'

Zane nodded. It also meant they were no further forward with treading the fine line as to when Marco would either get off scot-free or be sent down. How he wished he had something solid to base his judgement on. Until then, things hung in the balance.

'But,' Tiger added. 'We *have* had a possible sighting of Sandler.'

Zane sat forward, his senses highly charged. 'Where?'

'On the way back from doing the finals on the Lambeth to Kennington triangle acquisition, one of our enforcers happened to spot who they thought to be Sandler in a pub in Clapham.'

'Which pub?' Zane frowned. 'We know the places Marco's

cronies used to hang out.'

'Yep, and it was one of those very pubs,' Tiger grinned. 'The Blacksmith's.'

Zane's heart thumped in anticipation. 'Right? So...?'

'Sandler was leaving,' Tiger continued. 'Our man spotted him as he left the pub. Unfortunately, he was unable to tail him because the fucker got on a bus, but at least we've had a sighting.'

Zane nodded. It was a drop in the ocean, but a sighting was a sighting. Now they had something tying the man to a place, it stood to reason Sandler would return there before long.

'I've already stationed one of our men in there,' Leo added. 'Karl Hartley will give us the nod the minute Sandler shows his face again.'

Zane chewed the inside of his lip. He'd hoped for something more concrete that this, but a sighting and a lead to work on was better than nothing.

Having manpower was crucial in order to keep on top of all the threads. With so few of an inner circle – his, Tiger and Leo's time was spread thinly enough as it was. Allowing Cav Fletcher to have time out to get himself together after his brother's murder didn't help, but it was the least Zane could do. But with the new men in the firm not having the background needed to fully deal with people like Marco and Sandler, it was difficult.

Zane should be happy that the firm was growing, but as much as he tried, his mind kept returning to other items: what Skye had said about her boyfriend - or should he say *ex*-boyfriend. That and the comments about Shirley...

Resentment towards this *boy* who had the cheek to ditch his daughter grew. That, combined with the base guilt that Skye might have been brought up in an abusive, dangerous environment and exposed to unsavoury individuals was getting to him.

His skin tingled with the thought of what could have happened. He knew nothing for definite so he mustn't speculate.

And what would Skye have been exposed to if *he'd* had custody? Brought up surrounded by violent criminals and a father in prison? Not a superb role model, was he?

Zane's teeth grated. At least if Skye had been with him, she wouldn't have been around perverts!

But he'd discover what had gone on and would do that sooner rather than later.

'Are you all right, mate?' Tiger said, the expressions on Zane's face obvious to them all.

'Yeah.' Zane shrugged. 'Just stuff playing on my mind.'

'Anything we can help with?' Leo asked.

'Maybe,' Zane said. Perhaps if Skye spent some time at Starbright, which in retrospect might be the best thing, then extra pairs of eyes wouldn't go amiss. 'I'm thinking of letting Skye work at... Oh, hang on a second.'

Pulling his ringing mobile from his pocket, Zane stared at the screen:

...Hazel calling...

'I'd better take this.' Zane stood up. 'Hello? Hazel? Everything all ri…'

Leo and Tiger exchanged glances as Zane's face twisted first with shock and then rage.

'Why the fuck did you do that?' Zane roared. 'Jesus! Yeah, Okay, okay.... I'm on my way.'

'What's happened?' Tiger cried as Zane stared at his phone like it was an alien object.

'The press are all over the Starbright,' Zane growled. 'Hazel reckons they've got photos of her.'

'What?' Leo cried, shunting forward in his chair.

'The press somehow knew the centre was officially launching today and turned up. They're aware of everything – the trafficking – the lot!' Zane scraped his fingers through his hair, scarcely able to believe what had happened. 'Hazel's adamant she didn't tell the papers, but for fuck's sake, how else did they know?' He snatched up his crash helmet. 'I'm going over there.'

'Wait!' Leo jumped to his feet. 'You stay here. I'll go.'

'No fucking way! It's...'

'It could be a trap!' Leo interrupted. 'Hazel ain't a thick bimbo, so someone else must have leaked this. If they have and then *you* turn up...'

'He's right,' Tiger agreed. 'It could be a setup - waiting for you to roll up to deal with it.'

Zane faltered. 'But if it wasn't Hazel, then who the hell was it? It's only us who know those details.'

'It's got out somehow,' Leo insisted. 'If it wasn't Hazel and someone else instead, then that someone could be linked with Marco.'

'And after being spotted leaving the Blacksmith's Arms, we all know Sandler is still alive and kicking' Tiger added.

Zane was about to argue but his men had a point. 'If the press have photographs of Hazel it exposes her whereabouts!' *This was the last thing they needed.*

'I'll deal with it,' Leo repeated as he shrugged on his jacket. 'I'll keep you posted.'

• • • •

MARTIN WOULD ENJOY driving this motor if it wasn't for the impending cloud of doom hanging over his head.

Even the prospect of a speck of dust left inside the Range Rover when he handed it back to his father had nothing on how he felt about venturing into the unknown. And this particular unknown was worse than he'd envisaged. Especially as he didn't have the first clue where to start now the only information he'd been given had drawn a blank.

He pulled his phone from his jacket and pressed the button to call Skye.

Drumming his fingers on the leather steering wheel as the call rang out only heightened his frustration. *Why wasn't she answering?*

Fear combined with paranoia raged. What if Shirley was wrong and Skye hadn't gone looking for her father at all? What if she *had* disappeared off with another bloke? What if she didn't want to be with him anymore and that was why she'd lied about going to Scotland? She'd have told him she'd been looking for this mysterious father of hers if it were true, wouldn't she?

But would she?

Martin felt sick. He knew his father was old-fashioned - more old-fashioned than his mother. Perhaps Skye was worried that his family would form a negative opinion of her if they knew her real father was a criminal or gangster. Or worse, maybe Skye believed *he* wouldn't want to be with her if she told the truth?

Martin brushed the sweat off his forehead and threw his mobile on the passenger seat. Not wanting to be with Skye couldn't be further than the truth. He'd want to be with her even if her parents turned out to be the Moors Murderers!

How he'd wished he'd bypassed that long holiday to Austria. Wasn't he a bit old to be going on family holidays now he was nineteen? It might have been a long-standing family tradition doing the month-long trip every year, but if he'd remained in London then Skye couldn't have disappeared without telling him the truth.

Martin's nausea increased. But if Shirley was right and Skye *had* come in search of her absent father, then why wasn't she answering her phone?

Whether he wanted to or not, he could only presume the worst and that filled him with cold dread.

So, now what?

As he got out of the Range Rover, Martin's gaze tracked back to the large building in front of him - the one Shirley Wilson was adamant was *those people's* headquarters.

His brow creased as he tried not to overthink what a building such as this could have been used for, aside from what was intended when the place was built at least a hundred years ago. Whatever it had once been or had *since* been - it hadn't been in use for some time. That was evident by the dilapidated state of the place; the dark expanse visible through the broken windows and the collection of rubbish strewn around the perimeter of the building.

He stood against the looming gates, secured with a rusty chain and scanned the weeds pushing their way through the concrete during the years nature had been left to its own devices.

'You won't get a job in there any longer, mate!'

Martin almost jumped out of his skin at the unexpected voice. He swung around to be confronted by a man, probably only ten years his senior, but due to the collection of missing teeth and raddled skin, looked at least thirty years older.

His eyes darted towards the Range Rover, belatedly realising he'd committed the first mistake in venturing into turf such as this. He'd left his vehicle unattended and it could be nicked right from under his nose. This... this freak could jab a hepatitis-infected needle into his arm and go through his pockets to thieve money for his next fix. *Stupid, stupid.*

For all he knew, this bloke might be dossing on the floor in that building. He looked the type.

Martin came to the conclusion that if he were to escape from this drongo with his life intact, he would possess more common sense when it came to his future behaviour. He wasn't in his usual neighbourhood and must learn fast because the way this was going, finding Skye wouldn't be quick.

'Do you speak English?' the toothless man asked. 'Are you lost?'

'What?' Martin snapped. 'Of course I can speak bloody English! And no, I'm not lost!' It suddenly struck him that he'd made a rapid assumption. This man didn't seem drug addled, so maybe he shouldn't have been so hasty in his judgement. 'Sorry, I'm a bit confused. I... erm... I was told this place was...... was still "trading".'

The man's eyebrows raised. 'Here? This gaff shut down six

years past when the eldest one got sent to nick.' He looked
Martin up and down with a tinge of amusement. 'You must be
after somewhere different. You don't look the sort to want work
at what that place did!'

Martin's senses jolted to life. *What did that mean?* 'This
was where I was sent, although the person who told me to come
hasn't been here for some time.' *Like seventeen years...* 'I'm
after the Morelli headquarters.'

Martin saw the man's face lighten by several shades. He'd
even taken a step back and the amiable expression he'd worn
was now replaced with wariness.

'The Morellis?' the man hissed, his voice low. 'You're right
about this place being theirs, but they're not here anymore.' His
eyes narrowed. 'What do you want with them? Are you... you
part of another gang?'

'Gang?' Martin spluttered. 'Of course not! Do I look like
I'm a ... Oh, it doesn't matter. Look, do you know where they
are now?'

The man took another step in the opposite direction. 'Where
I come from there's certain things that it's best not to ask
questions about.'

Martin frowned. This guy knew something and that he was
terrified to speak of it wasn't greatly reassuring but he was too
close not to push it.

Shoving his hand in his pocket, he fished out a twenty-
pound note and thrust it in the man's direction. He couldn't
quite fathom whether this guy was a jobless dosser or had just
had a hard life. 'Please, just tell me where you think the people
from here have moved to. Take this and buy yourself a couple
of pints for your trouble.'

The man looked over his shoulder before snatching the note
from Martin's hand. 'Word has it that the new place is a gaff
called Lunar Films or something. That's all I know, apart from
that a lot of their men used to drink in a place called the
Blacksmith's Arms. I don't know whether that's still the case
either.'

'Where is...?'

'I know nothing else,' the man barked. 'I keep my beak out of shit and my head down.' Turning, he walked off.

Martin itched to push for more information but knew he would get nothing further.

Suddenly the man looked over his shoulder. 'Cheers for the drink, pal. And good luck because you'll fucking need it!'

SEVEN

LEO SCREECHED INTO THE HOLLYWELL ROAD. It had taken longer than planned to get from Dalston to Dagenham and he could only hope he wasn't too late.

Even though there had been no way of preventing it he believed he'd already let Zane down once by not stopping Erin from getting shot outside the Thames Canning Works a few weeks ago. He didn't want another incident where he'd promised to deal with something only for it to go wrong.

Manoeuvring past an inconsiderately parked blue Volvo which was slightly obstructing the driveway to the Starbright Centre, Leo muttered a handful of expletives. If he wasn't in such a rush, he'd get out and punch whoever had parked there in the fucking head and then bounce their crappy car down the road.

Jesus! There were cars everywhere! His jaw clenched. No doubt these motors belonged to the press who'd descended on this gaff.

Screeching up the driveway, Leo couldn't help but laugh at the rewarding sight of reporters being manhandled into their motors by the enforcers Zane had left on duty.

His face then creased into a frown. How come the other

reporters were still sitting in their cars, waiting like obedient puppy dogs?

He then spotted the pile of cameras on the doorstep of the big house.

Clambering from the van, he winked at one of the enforcers busy shutting the last reporter into his car and slipping the keys into his pocket for safekeeping. 'I see I've arrived too late to join in the fun?'

The enforcer laughed, but in reality, this was no laughing matter. They had the cameras and therefore the photos which could incriminate Hazel, which was good, but in effect they were holding these reporters hostage.

Leo glanced towards one car, recognising the man inside to be a particularly slimy reporter - one of which, like most, would have no qualms in relaying the incident to the police and citing theft. Or worse, if he or any of the enforcers pulled rank and used the Morelli name to stop them printing the story, it would inevitably expose Zane as the unknown benefactor behind the women's refuge. Zane would then be linked to this place, as well as underlining Hazel's whereabouts to Marco.

Jeez. If Hazel was behind this balls-up, she'd done the opposite of keeping herself and the rest of them off the radar.

Leo turned back to the enforcer. 'What have you said to them?'

'Nothing yet. We were waiting for Zane. Hazel said he was on his way.'

'Well, he's not. I'm here instead,' Leo said, grim-faced. It was a good job too. Had the press clapped eyes on Zane, the cat would have been well and truly out of the bag. *He,* on the other hand, as far as the local media were concerned, was unknown which made things easier.

His gaze returned to the cameras piled up at the door. What justifiable reason could be given as to why nothing could be printed about this, as well as avoiding involving the Old Bill?

Unless...

'Have any of these pricks clapped eyes on Hazel – as in,

properly?' Leo glanced at the blinds concealing the window of Hazel's office. 'She hasn't been outside?'

'Definitely not. Any photos they got when she moved the blinds are in those cameras over there. Even then the pictures won't be clear.'

Leo nodded. *That was good.* With the haircut Marco had forced on Hazel when he'd last attacked her she no longer resembled what the world saw the woman known as Lisa Tequila to be either.

The idea he'd just thought of might work...

But first, he needed to speak to Hazel and find out for sure whether it was her who had informed the press. After all - for someone used to press adoration, it would be second nature to spill all in the pursuit of media attention. Maybe she'd done it inadvertently and was too embarrassed to admit it to Zane, but now more than ever it was vital that she levelled.

• • • •

FROM THE WAY Zane accelerated up the road, Erin knew something had happened. She could tell the sound of his Yamaha FJ1200 from some way away and from experience, when the throttle was thraped like that it meant bad news.

Whatever had occurred at headquarters and as Zane's phone had been engaged during the times she'd tried to reach him since seeing that article, she was still yet to break the news that the Starbright had found its way into the pages of the press.

She also had to broach the subject of Skye's odd behaviour.

And there it was...

Unable to help it, Erin jumped on the subject the second Zane walked through the door. 'I've been trying to reach you,' she gasped. 'Your phone's been constantly engaged! There's an article in th…'

'I'm aware of the bloody article.' Zane dumped his leather jacket and crash helmet on the sofa.

'You are?' Erin handed Zane a beer but he pushed her

away.

'What a bloody nightmare!' Zane rubbed his hand over his chin. 'I know about the article because Hazel called me in a panic. The place was crawling with the press trying to take photos of her.'

'Shit!' Erin gasped. 'Then Marco will know where Hazel is and that you're the one who... Fuck!' She paced the room. 'Why did Hazel tell the papers? I thought she'd left that side of her life behind and...'

'It wasn't her,' Zane said, lighting up a cigarette. He stared at the now empty packet before crumpling it in his big hand. 'I presumed it was her at first too, but it wasn't. Anyway, it's okay because Leo's sorted it.'

'Leo?' Erin cried. 'How the hell could he sort it if the papers have photos? It will only be a matter of time before Marco or Sandler sees the pictures. Hazel might have short hair these days, but Christ, Zane, they'll recognise her and...'

'The films have been destroyed. My enforcers made sure of that.' Zane finally reached to take the beer from Erin's hand. 'Seriously, it's fine. It was a close call, but it's sorted. And before you ask, the reporters have been warned from printing anything. Plus, it's been done without implicating the firm.'

Erin frowned 'I can't see how?'

'Leo told them that "Miss Fleeter" was involved with an international sex slave ring and exposing photos of her would reveal her whereabouts to the criminal operators and put her life, as well as that of the benefactor, at risk.'

Erin raised an eyebrow. 'That's not far from the truth...'

'Yeah, but the version of the "benefactor" that Leo gave was that the person in question is an extremely influential and well-known celebrity who won't hesitate to sue the papers to Kingdom Come if "Miss Fleeter's" photograph or anything else in relation to the Starbright Centre goes public - including anything about camera films being destroyed.'

Erin nodded, impressed. 'And they went for it?'

'No fucking hack will risk their job by getting the mother

ship sued or gaining the wrath of a celebrity mogul.'

'And you're that "mogul"?' Erin laughed.

'As long as they print nothing and don't expose Hazel, they can think what the hell they like!'

'You believe they'll stick to their word?'

'From what Leo said, yes I do. Plus, it was achieved without using the heavy hand of the Morellis.'

'But if it wasn't Hazel, then who was it?' Erin asked, wracking her brains.

'Hazel thought it was the web design company. She'd told them certain things in confidence in order for them to build a relevant site.' Zane's eyes narrowed. 'But she's already asked them and they've denied it, but if I find out it *was* them, they'll sorely regret overstepping the line. The only others who knew those details were us and my men.'

Erin swallowed uncomfortably with the thought crawling into her head. 'And Skye... You told her the details too.'

Zane folded his arms across his chest. 'What are you saying? That my own daughter ran to the press with something that she knew must be kept under wraps?'

'Let's face it, you don't know her very well and...'

'I don't believe this!' Zane barked. 'What's your problem? First of all you harass her about boyfriends and now you want me to believe that she's purposely sabotaged me and the centre? You think she'd put Hazel and the rest of us at risk?' He got to his feet. 'Maybe Skye was right and you *really* don't like her.'

'What?' Erin gasped. 'I haven't harassed her about boyfriends! I asked her once and all she said was that there was no one special.' *Why had Skye been lying to Zane and stirring the situation?* 'And what's all this about me not liking her? I...'

'You've had a hang up about her from the start,' Zane spat. 'I thought you'd at least make an effort! This is important to me. Did it ever cross your mind that this "boyfriend" treated Skye like shit and broke her heart? Because that's what happened, but you couldn't leave it, could you? No, you kept on and on. You've really upset her and now you're accusing her of something else?'

Erin's mouth fell open. Skye hadn't mentioned anything about that and she'd only asked the girl once in passing about boyfriends. She certainly hadn't hounded her. 'But...'

'You know that I feel like shit because I haven't been in Skye's life.' Zane's eyes flashed. 'It's not like I had any choice about that, was it?'

'I know, but...' Erin stopped as Zane pulled a box from his jacket. 'What's that?'

Zane glanced at the top of the range Nokia phone he'd just purchased. 'It's for Skye. She hasn't got a mobile.' His eyes narrowed with what his daughter had said earlier about what had happened to her last one.

Erin laid her chin on Zane's shoulder and peered at the box. 'Bloody hell! A Nokia 7650? These ones have a camera and everything! Surely Skye doesn't need such a fancy phone?'

Shrugging Erin off his shoulder, Zane stared at her in dismay. 'Why shouldn't I spend money on a decent phone for my daughter? For fuck's sake! It's not like I've been the best father when it comes to providing for her, is it?' *Like he needed reminding.*

'It was hardly your fault that you weren't aware of her existence. That doesn't mean you have to spoil her to make up for Shirley's decisions.'

'I *want* to,' Zane said sharply. 'The things she's told me... Do you know she had a mobile? A cheap one mind, but some bitch she went to school with smashed it up. It seems she got a lot of grief during her time at that shitty school which followed her after she left. Why the fuck didn't Shirley send her somewhere decent? Or maybe she had *better* things to do?'

Erin frowned at the venom in Zane's voice. 'I understand you're frustrated but...'

'I've got to go and see Shirley. I get the impression she's a drunk or something worse.' Zane paced around the room. 'If my daughter has been exposed to perverts who might have...' He shook the horrific concept from his head. 'And all you can do is make the girl feel like a tart?'

Erin blinked with shock. Skye had accused her of calling a tart earlier, but she hadn't. She'd never say anything like that. 'I don't understand wh...'

'Don't even *think* about saying I shouldn't see Shirley. Christ, Erin! I thought you'd stopped this jealous bitchy crap. I won't have it and I certainly won't have it at my daughter's expense!'

Erin was about to fight her corner and tell Zane about Skye's odd behaviour, but the second he held his hand up she realised it was fruitless.

'Don't say another word. You've said enough. Now I'm going to see my daughter.'

As Zane stormed from the room Erin sank into a chair and put her head in her hands, fighting her conflicting emotions. She'd planned to confide in Zane about her reservations about Skye. She knew it would be difficult and that he'd get defensive about the daughter he believed he owed plenty, but the girl was vague about too much and she wasn't being truthful to anyone - including Zane.

By the sounds of it, the way Skye had twisted things around this morning wasn't a one off. But why was she doing it?

Erin frowned, running back over that conversation in her mind. She *hadn't* hounded Skye, she really hadn't, yet the girl had made out just the opposite. And what was all that about Shirley possibly being an alcoholic, surrounded by perverts? Had Skye said this or was Zane jumping to conclusions? Was it a bit of both?

Erin was disappointed to notice the slight trembling of her fingers. This was supposed to be a fresh start for her and Zane - they were getting married. Or they were supposed to be - something else Skye had made a veiled dig about.

What was that girl's issue?

Erin didn't yet know, but what she *did* know was that whilst Zane was convinced *she* was the one with problems over his daughter and Shirley, he'd be deaf to everything.

Aside from being it being unlikely that Zane would listen to anything she said, how could she lump further worry on him? He was already furious at what he believed she'd said to his daughter and also worried sick that Skye could have been exposed to unthinkable things, not to mention the guilt for being absent her whole life.

But whatever was going on in that girl's head was worrying and all Erin could do was hope that it stemmed from Skye's struggle to come to terms with finding her father.

• • • •

'DOWN THE END of the road and turn left? Is that correct?' Martin asked. Seeing the man nod, he thanked him and then got back into the Range Rover.

Placing both hands on the steering wheel, he exhaled, loathe to start the car. Now he knew where the Blacksmith's Arms was located that had to be the next place to head, but what exactly would he do when he got there? Go from table to table asking the drinkers if they personally happened to work for the Morellis or knew who did?

He grimaced. Not a great idea unless he fancied getting his head rammed down his neck. And he didn't. But that was likely to happen by the general gist he'd picked up from people when mentioning particular places and names.

Since the reaction of that bloke at what had once been the Morelli headquarters, Martin had been careful not to bring *that* name into any further conversation. That the Morellis sparked such fear told him enough to realise that he was dancing with danger.

And Skye's father was one of this Morelli bunch?

He shuddered, the realisation of what he'd promised Shirley sinking in. This was a nightmare - more so now than he'd thought.

What had greeted him when he'd found his way to the place known as Luna Motion Films underlined that. That toothless bloke was right - it was indeed where the Morellis had moved to, but judging by what Martin had seen, they weren't there anymore either.

Just the police...

Martin hadn't known what to think when he'd arrived. He'd wondered why he'd been given a strange look, amounting to disgust from the cashier he'd asked for directions at the garage. All he'd asked was if Luna Motion Films was nearby, yet the woman looked at him like he was something on the bottom of her shoe before muttering in a cold, clipped tone that it was.

Now he understood her reaction...

The first thing Martin noticed when he'd arrived at the Luna Studios was the building completely cordoned off with police tape and a heavy presence of officers on every perceivable side of the perimeter. The second thing was the collection of people with an unhealthy obsession with the place, eager to fill him in over the situation.

Yep, not only was Luna Motion Films the new hub of the Morelli headquarters, but also boasted being the largest adult film studio in England.

A porn film studio.

Skye's father was involved in porn films?

Martin's head jerked with a newly acquired nervous twitch. Whether Skye's father was part of running the place or whether he starred in the films, he didn't know. And neither would he because the place was closed pending a criminal investigation into a sex trafficking operation.

Holy shit.

On top of that, the boss - a Morelli, was currently in police custody...

Martin swallowed dryly. *This was heavy shit.*

Was this person in custody - the one running the sex slave stuff - Skye's father?

He didn't know that either because Shirley had refused to give him the man's actual name. All he'd got was vague details.

Sweat gathered on Martin's back.

So, had Skye found her father and if so, where the bloody

hell was she? If her father *was* the one in police custody, how did she feel about the sorts of crimes he'd been accused of?

Martin shuddered again. He didn't have the answers, nor was he any closer to finding his girlfriend. But there was one remaining place left for further leads where to find this man - or more importantly, Skye.

Preferably without getting his throat cut in the process...

With trepidation, he took a deep breath and turned the Range Rover's ignition. Down the end of this road and then turn left that bloke had said.

Martin pulled away from the kerb, avoiding meeting eyes with a group of young men with hoods partly obscuring their faces. The hoods didn't cover enough to hide that they were watching both him and the Range Rover.

Jesus Christ, he thought, accelerating down the road. *This place wasn't good.*

Indicating, he turned left, dreading to think what his next port of call would unearth.

'Oh my God!' Martin muttered, spotting a group of men in the middle of the road having a scuffle. How was he supposed to get past with them blocking the road like...

Oh... He didn't need to.

With a rising sense of foreboding, Martin pulled the Range Rover into the one remaining space behind a Nissan Sunny and an old blue Volvo. He cut the engine and remained in the driver's seat, unwilling to open the door, let alone go in *there...*

Martin's gaze tracked to the broken-down building further up the road where the fight had spilled from. His heart sank further at the creaking sign hanging outside the pub, reading '*The Blacksmith's Arms*'. He'd been hoping the large lettering above the pub door of: '*B_AC_S_ _TH_ _RMS*' meant this wasn't what he was looking for.

Alas, it was. This was it. And it wasn't enticing.

Still, nothing ventured, nothing gained.

Martin picked up the steering lock to fix over the wheel before shoving it back under the passenger seat. There was little point putting that on. From what he'd seen so far, the people around here would snap it off with their teeth, so he wouldn't waste his time.

Besides, a steering lock would only impede his ability to make a swift exit, should he need to.

EIGHT

'THIS WOMEN'S REFUGE IS DEFINITELY something to do with them.' Damon jabbed his finger on the newspaper article he'd taken from the meeting with Symonds.

Tel frowned. 'But how do you know if you didn't see Marco's wife for yourself?'

A sickly grin slid onto Damon's face, further highlighting the mass of crooked teeth crammed into his mouth.

Parked up outside the place which was the new centre for battered women or whatever lies had been spawned in order to grab attention, Damon had patiently waited. He hadn't been convinced that Symonds's theory about Hazel Grimes running the joint under the alias of Miss Fleeter or Zane being the unknown benefactor to be correct, but out of morbid curiosity and to shut the fat fuck up, he'd gone to Dagenham as instructed on the very slim chance that the man was correct or the more probable likelihood, he could prove the old bastard wrong.

Even though Damon believed it was unlikely the centre was anything to do with Zane or Hazel, he still felt a twinge of disappointment to spot no one that could categorically be associated with Zane Morelli.

Like Symonds expected, the press were gathered for the

official opening. He'd also seen the blinds twitching at the window. There was someone in there who the reporters were interested in, but Damon's vantage point at the end of the driveway was too far away to glimpse who that figure was. It was frustrating but he couldn't go closer.

He'd also thought it strange this alleged manager wouldn't go outside for interviews or pictures, but no one had come out. Then it had got even weirder when a stream of gorillas poured from the house to manhandle the reporters.

When this happened, Damon had thought that he was in luck and that they were Morelli's army of thugs, but to his subsequent displeasure there was no sign of the trademark Morelli violence.

He hadn't recognised any of the men and he had to eyeball *someone* belonging to Zane's posse of imbeciles to warrant Symonds's theory feasible. After all, there were other people in London and Damon didn't want to stumble onto another firm's territory and open a can of worms. Not with his plan to take over Marco's empire. Besides, Dagenham wasn't anywhere near the usual territories either.

He'd been about to throw the whole idea out as Symonds barking up the wrong tree, turn his Volvo around and get his arse back to Battersea, when there was a change of plan...

'You can't say you know the place is definitely to do with them without a reason,' Banjo said after Damon's lengthy silence. 'Tel asked you how you know for certain, but you can't explain!'

'Ah, but I can...' Damon grinned. Enjoying the captive audience, as well as the power he'd recently assigned to himself, he took his time in supping his pint, keeping Tel and Banjo dangling just a little bit longer.

'This is stupid,' Tel muttered, getting to his feet. 'I ain't listening to...'

'Being as I'm in charge, you'll listen to whatever I want you to listen to and in whichever way I choose,' Damon hissed. 'If you still want money coming in, then shut the fuck up and quit with your tuppence worth!' *There. That told them.*

Confident he'd made his point and with a renewed sense of self-satisfaction, Damon leisurely stubbed his cigarette out in the overflowing ashtray. He looked at first at Tel and then at Banjo. 'I know they are behind this because if you remember, I was present when Zane Morelli and his trained monkeys stormed Luna during their failed takeover attempt not long ago.'

Seeing both men nod in acknowledgement, Damon continued. 'Well, being as I'd seen no one at the Starbright Centre who gave any hints to links to Hazel or Zane, I was about to bugger off, when I saw him...'

Banjo leant forward intrigued. 'Who?'

'One of Zane's men,' Damon grinned. 'That bastard, Leo Holland. He was on the ground floor of Luna the day of the shoot-out. He was also there the day I shot that Langley bitch dead outside the Thames Canning Works.'

Tel's mouth dropped open. 'You're certain it was him?'

'Of course I'm fucking certain!' Damon hissed, his eyes narrowing. 'I'd recognise that baboon of a bad advert for anabolic steroids anywhere. For a start, he almost clipped the back end of my car when he turned into the driveway and secondly, because he stood outside giving orders to the enforcers.'

'But you didn't recognise any of those enforcers?' Banjo queried.

'No, but as Zane is rebuilding his firm, I'm hardly likely to. A lot of men left when Marco took over and before I joined, so I wouldn't recognise them, but I *did* recognise Holland, so therefore Marco's brief was right!'

'On at least some of it,' Tel frowned. 'Holland's presence doesn't mean that Miss Fleeter is Marco's wife. Nor does it mean Zane Morelli is the mystery benefactor. Plus, Dagenham is not in any of his usual areas.'

'True,' Damon nodded. 'But would he really be so stupid to create something like this on his doorstep when he's trying to remain invisible? Holland being there gives us the link and therefore worth investigating, so that's what I want *you* to do.'

Banjo frowned. 'What does Marco think about it?'

'I'm keeping Marco out of this as long as possible. Preferably forever!' Damon said. 'If Zane Morelli's behind this, and with what I've seen seems likely, then we've got him!'

Tel glanced at a man sitting on another table. 'I'm sure that cunt is listening to what you're saying,' he hissed. 'That's three times now I've clocked him watching.'

'He could be a spy?' Banjo suggested.

Damon took the opportunity to take a look at the blond bloke sitting a couple of tables away. The Blacksmith's wasn't busy and there was plenty of spare tables, so why had this cock chosen to sit so close? His mind whirred. 'I suggest you earn your brass for once and find out if he was earwigging. If he was, then deal with him.'

· · · ·

'I'M PLEASED.' Erin pulled her face into a smile. It was difficult, considering after speaking to Skye, Zane had stormed back to headquarters rather than remain in the same house as *her*.

That's how it seemed, anyway. But because Skye was now being pleasant, so must she, when what Erin *really* wanted to do was grab the girl by the shoulders and shake the truth from her.

Skye Wilson was playing a game, Erin was certain of it.

She pushed the thoughts that had been mercilessly taunting her all day from her head. She wasn't paranoid. Neither was she hearing things. She had not said or even *thought* the things Skye had told Zane she'd said.

Had she?

It had been a rough two weeks, so perhaps...

No, she hadn't. She really hadn't.

Suddenly, Erin realised Skye was staring at her. 'What's up?'

'Nothing,' Skye said, the slight curl of a smirk playing at one corner of her mouth. 'I was trying to work out why you would say that you're pleased that I'm going to help Hazel out at the Starbright being as you were against it when I suggested lending a hand this morning. It doesn't make sense.' She paused, letting her words sink in before continuing. 'Why would you suddenly change your mind when you were so vehemently against it?'

Erin would laugh if she wasn't so flabbergasted. Instead, she folded her arms, determined not to rise to the bait. 'I said I was pleased because I *am*. Like I said earlier, when *I* suggested it to *you*, I think Hazel will be grateful for your help.'

Skye frowned, her plump lips forming a moue. 'Are you *sure* you didn't leave Mr Sorenzo's practice too early, Erin? I'm worried that the shooting has affected your memory.' She shook her head sadly. 'Zane was only saying earlier that you didn't want me involved with the centre. I can't be a prisoner, Erin. I'm seventeen, not a baby.'

'But I...' Erin stopped herself from arguing that it had been *her* who had fought Skye's corner; telling Zane that he must give the girl more freedom and that she'd be safe at Starbright - especially with the additional security and the threat of Hazel's whereabouts being exposed now diffused. But what was the point? This was another of Skye's games. Why couldn't Zane witness this? Maybe then he'd see how Skye behaved.

'Are you concerned that I'll get on with Hazel? Is that it? We all know you'd have preferred it if she'd been murdered by her husband!' A sly smile crept onto Skye's face. 'Or are you scared Zane will run off with her? After all, with all the experience she's had, she must be better in the sack than you!'

'How dare you!' Erin yelled. What had Zane said for Skye to be aware of the jealousy she'd had about Hazel in the past? Had he discussed their personal business with a daughter he barely knew? That *none* of them knew?

Skye's comments about Hazel weren't acceptable either, considering she would shortly be working with the woman. 'If

66

that's how you speak about people who've welcomed you with open arms, then...'

'Then *what*, Erin?' Skye snapped. 'Then I should leave?' Her laugh was high-pitched and shrill. 'Oh, you'd like that, wouldn't you? You'd love nothing more than to get rid of me. Or maybe get rid of everybody so you can have Zane to yourself! You must have had a really shitty life to be so insanely jealous. What next? Accuse me of sleeping with my own father? Will that be it?'

'Don't be disgusting!' Erin screamed, her eyes blazing. 'What is wrong with you? What on earth do you think you'll gain by any of this? I've had enough! Thankfully it's only a matter of time before everyone else clocks what you're doing!'

'And what is that, pray tell?' Jumping from the seat, Skye pushed into Erin's face, determined to tip her over the edge. And she *was* determined, because from what she'd glimpsed out of the window the timing would be perfect.

Before Erin had the chance to answer, Skye's whole countenance morphed from malicious intent to wounded devastation. 'I'm *not* devious and I'm *not* lying! What else can I do so that you believe what I say?' Her voice was filled with anguish. 'I don't know how to make you like me... I...' She covered her face with her hands and let out an almighty sob just as Zane pushed open the lounge door.

'What the hell is going on in here?' Zane roared. 'I forgot my phone and came back to get it only to hear *this*?' His eyes flashed between Erin and Skye's crumpled, sobbing figure on the chair. 'What have you done? Calling Skye a devious liar? What is the matter with you, Erin?'

Opening his arms as Skye jumped from the chair to sob against his chest, Zane stroked her hair, his eyes blazing.

'E-Erin accused me of leaking the story to the papers. S-She said she'd do everything so that I left here and that I'm not working at the Starbright under any circumstances. She said I was like my mother... A liar...'

Erin's mouth fell open. 'I said no such th...'

'What the fuck are you playing at?' Zane cut Erin off in her tracks. 'You're not to say a word about Shirley ever again!' His eyes danced with anger. 'You've already badgered my daughter about boyfriends and made her feel like a slut! Now you're calling her a devious liar? Jesus Christ, Erin! I told you this morning that there's no way Skye would leak anything to the press, yet you're still accusing her? And she *will* be working at the Starbright. In fact, I'll take her there right now. It's better than her putting up with your abuse!' Zane dragged his thumbs over Skye's cheeks to wipe away her tears.

Erin stepped forward. 'But...'

'But nothing!' Zane snarled. 'Sort yourself the fuck out and do so quickly otherwise there's no future for us! I will not let you or *anyone* come between me and my daughter!'

Lost for words, Erin watched Zane snatch up his crash helmet and phone and when Skye picked up her jacket she couldn't miss the triumphant smile on the girl's face.

NINE

IT WAS ONLY MID-AFTERNOON, but Martin felt like the day had already lasted a year. Raising his hand, he prodded the swollen and fast blackening flesh around his eye, wincing as it triggered more pain.

His face hurt in general. And his teeth. Come to think of it, so did his neck where that bloke had grabbed him. He wouldn't be surprised if a vertebra in the base of his spine wasn't smashed, or at the very least, fractured from landing on his arse after being forcibly ejected from that pub.

The Blacksmith's Arms had turned out to be just as troublesome as expected. But he hadn't figured that he'd end up getting whacked.

Martin shifted his position a little in the driver's seat to relieve the nerve pain shooting down his right leg every time he moved.

Great. He'd probably end up with a slipped disc or something after this.

But it could have been worse.

A lot worse...

His eyes tracked back to the driveway in the far distance along the surprisingly pleasant tree-lined road. But appearances could be deceptive and if the place ahead was linked with the Morellis, then from the opinion he was fast forming, it could be equally as dangerous as the Blacksmith's Arms turned out to be. Or *could* have turned out to be...

Martin dragged his hand over his brow. He'd got off lightly considering.

It had been a pure stroke of luck to pick that raddled old table next to those three blokes. He didn't know why he'd been drawn there - the pub was half empty and all the other drinkers were giving the trio a wide berth. But because that toothless bloke had mentioned the place being a watering hole for men connected with the Morellis, Martin felt obliged - no, *forced* by his own instinct to see if those three unsavoury characters in the corner could shed light on his quest.

Martin unscrewed the top of a bottle of Diet Coke and grimaced as the plastic of the bottle's neck scraped against his sore lips.

His instinct in placing himself close enough to overhear at least part of the three men's conversation had paid off.

Sure, his nosiness had earned him a kicking, but he'd gained information that he hadn't expected, so it was worth the black eye and the rest of the damage.

Sort of...

At least, he hoped so. What he'd overheard might not be worth anything and it had taken quite a while to drive from Battersea to Dagenham in the traffic, but surely to warrant one of those blokes to drag him up from the table, give him a swift clump and then chuck him through the door to the pavement for being such a 'nosy fucking cunt', signified something, didn't it?

Those men didn't want him within earshot. It was only because Martin had done such a good job of protesting his innocence and ensuring that his Surrey accent stood out compared to that of the cockney around him that he'd got off so lightly. Gibbering about being in the pub to meet a girl had achieved the desired result - he'd been believed and released.

He was getting good at making up bullshit. But he wished

what he'd said was true. True, in as much as he wished he'd arranged to meet Skye. Skye was the only one for him. That was why he was here in the first place.

His gaze moved back to the driveway.

From what he'd overheard, this place had nothing to do with Skye, but it was linked - or *possibly* linked with the Morellis. If he could locate someone who knew of the man she'd gone to find, then he'd be one step closer to finding *her*.

But it was weird. What would people like the Morellis want with a women's refuge?

Martin's brows furrowed further. Considering those people ran a porn film studio, a women's refuge didn't make any sense. Unless it was a means of collecting women to use in their films?

Martin shuddered. Men like the Morellis had no morals.

But he'd heard names - Marco and Zane. And something about a woman called Hazel.

He couldn't deduce how or why this Hazel woman was connected. He'd only caught snippets of the conversation, but she was *something* to do with it. Exactly how, he didn't know, but those blokes were convinced she was running this refuge.

Martin's lips formed a thin line. Okay, so now he knew Marco and Zane were Morellis, but how would he know who they were out of any men he came across?

Sweat prickled. Shirley hadn't said whether the Morellis were something to do with Skye or whether her father merely worked for them. Or rather, she *wouldn't*. Christ, this was like looking for a needle in a haystack.

He had to get into that refuge to speak to this Hazel woman and see if she knew anything.

But if Hazel was linked to the Morellis and they *were* involved with the refuge, then she must be party to whatever despicable things they were involved in too. He'd be throwing himself to the wolves.

But every minute Skye remained off radar, the temperature of Martin's blood dropped lower. He couldn't allow his girlfriend to put herself at risk by associating with those type of people. He could only hope she hadn't got as far as he had with locating anyone.

Picking up his mobile, Martin stared at it. Perhaps he should call her again. She had to answer eventually.

That's if she could...

Shaking away possible scenarios from his head, Martin dialled Skye's number, only to hear the phone ringing out. He was about to try again when the phone sprang to life.

His heart leapt. *Finally!*

He scrambled to answer the call, but on seeing the screen his heart sank like a brick:

...Shirley calling...

Martin sighed heavily. He had to answer it. He'd promised Shirley he'd keep her up to date but he hadn't called once yet. 'Hi Shirley,' he said, rustling up enthusiasm. 'How are you?'

Wincing as a cacophony of questions jangled down the line, Martin wondered how he could get Shirley off the phone. He didn't have much to tell her and what he *did* know, he'd keep to himself. He certainly wasn't about to freak her out by sharing what he *had* discovered, or his mounting panic over Skye. Judging from what he'd seen of the woman's mental state she'd have a meltdown. He needed to plough his energy into what reasons he could give to enter a women's refuge and he couldn't do that whilst Shirley was frying his head.

'What? Oh, not really. There haven't been many leads. The place you told me about was deserted. It's been closed for several years, apparently.' *At least that much was true.* 'No... nothing else... Me? Oh, I'm in the B&B,' Martin lied.

Stiffening at the sudden sound of a throaty motorbike, he sat forward as the bike slowed. *It was turning into the refuge...*

Shirley was still talking ten to the dozen down the other end of the line. God knows how many more questions she'd asked, but Martin wasn't listening. His concentration was on that bike with a big man riding it. The woman on the pillion seat...

Judging by her frame, she was slender with long legs and although he couldn't see her face behind the crash helmet, the long black hair flowing from underneath reminded him very much of...

'Shirley,' Martin gabbled. 'I've got to go! I've left the bath running. Yes... yes, I will.... Bye.'

Ending the call, Martin launched the mobile on the passenger seat and started the Range Rover.

That woman riding pillion looked suspiciously like Skye. He had to get closer and see for himself.

• • • •

HAZEL WAS MORE THAN HAPPY to let Zane's daughter help out at the centre. Even in the few hours since the launch of the website and despite the upheaval and panic surrounding the press, there had been a surge in calls from women from all over London, not just the nearby area. It was a fantastic response and she needed all the help she could get before she became snowed under.

She had thought it would have been Erin accompanying Skye to Starbright rather than Zane. She knew how busy he was, yet something was bubbling under the surface. He didn't look himself.

For once, she wasn't worried that Zane's countenance was down to unsavoury news about Marco. This was different. Something was bothering Zane - as in, *really* bothering him at a base level.

Yes, her original plan, after realising the man she'd married wasn't the true heir to the Morelli empire, was to shift her sights to Zane and bag him for herself, but that was *before*.

Since Marco's attack and the way Zane had moved heaven and earth to protect her and everyone around him from Marco's wrath, not to mention how he'd given her a chance at a new life as a *real* person by ploughing his money into a property with a business for her to run; where she could finally do some good, her feelings had dramatically changed.

Since the persona of Lisa Tequila had shattered, so had her mercenary plans to take Zane as her own. Now she'd become Hazel - her true self. Witnessing what Zane was really like, bagging him to further her own standing had been replaced by genuine feelings.

And not genuine feelings as in falling for him for real.

No, how she now felt about Zane was a novelty because she genuinely cared. She cared about him like she would a brother or a true friend. Not that she'd ever had either of those, but it was what she *imagined* it would be like. And to see something disturbing him at such a fundamental level pained her.

She'd admit at first there was the occasional blip when Lisa Tequila pushed to the forefront and Hazel had found herself wondering whether she could still pull off her original plans, but concepts like that had now disappeared. With each day that passed, Lisa became further buried and now she was gone for good, Hazel no longer worried the temptation for her old ways might win over and cause her to relapse into the person she'd never truly been.

She was starting to understand happiness, as well doing something worthwhile. And that was better than any paycheck or baubles money could buy.

But what was needling Zane?

Satisfied that Skye understood enough of what was explained about the system to separate the wheat from the chaff during the telephone calls, Hazel chanced leaving her to it for a short while.

Motioning to Zane, she left the room and walked down the corridor into the group room which was empty at present.

Zane followed, his face lined with concern. 'What's up? Has there been further issues with the press that I'm not aware of? I wouldn't have let you remain here or brought Skye if...'

'Relax!' Hazel flapped her hand. 'It's not that. And before you ask, I'm not about to badger you about whether you've heard anything further about Marco either!'

Zane frowned. 'Then wh…?'

'What's going on, Zane?' Hazel came straight to the point. 'Don't say "nothing" because something's happened and happened with *you*, so you may as well tell me. After all, you can't kid a kidder!'

Despite his mood, Zane couldn't help but laugh as Hazel wiggled her eyebrows. She was right. Things had gone wrong and he wasn't sure why. Or how to explain it because he didn't know himself.

He never spoke about his feelings. *Ever.* But if he didn't unload his building frustration on the subject it would cloud his judgement and it was vital that remained on track.

'Well?' Hazel tapped her foot on the floor in mock impatience. 'You are allowed to vent occasionally, Zane Morelli, even if you're not used to doing so! Instead of taking on the world's problems, tell me *yours*. As a woman, I will chance that whatever's needling you is something to do with Erin. Is my guess warm or completely off kilter?'

Zane sighed. *Hazel was spot on.* 'Yeah, I... I just don't know what's happened. I don't know where to start...'

'Starting somewhere would be good.' Hazel laid her hand on Zane's shoulder. 'I may be little more than a hooker in a lot of people's minds, but I do have a brain. And I do care...'

'Don't say things like that about yourself,' Zane said. 'You're a lot more than you give yourself credit for and if people don't realise that then it's their loss!'

Hazel burnt with both pleasure at the compliment and annoyance for putting herself down. 'Thank you,' she said softly. 'But I want to hear about what's troubling *you*.'

She listened intently as Zane began to speak. He was hesitant at first, like he was unsure how to articulate his thoughts. Men like Zane seldomly spoke about subjects close to the heart. Give them violence and grief any day – they excelled at that with their eyes closed, but when discussing personal topics they were like infants learning to walk.

Once Zane got over his first few faltering sentences the floodgates opened and Hazel listened patiently. She remained silent, her mind racing to make sense of his words. What he told her was strange and sounded out of character for Erin, but at the same time, Zane was too astute to mishear or be uncertain.

When Zane paused, Hazel knew she had to speak. She didn't want to voice this, but it was a question that needed asking. 'Erm, is there any chance that Erin *isn't* acting out of turn? *Could* it be Skye manipulating things?'

'I know what I heard!' Zane snapped defensively. 'Skye was really upset and Erin has a track record of being jealous.' He laughed hollowly. 'Which included about you at one point...'

Hazel glowed a deep red, knowing from her initial intent that Erin had been spot on. 'But you mentioned Shirley – Skye's mother? Has Erin got reason to think that... that you could...'

'Could I revert to how I felt about Shirley nearly twenty years ago?' Zane shrugged. 'It's not likely. She left me, remember? And... and what I felt for Shirley wasn't a patch on how I felt... how I *feel* about Erin, but whichever way you look at it, there's no excuse for Erin giving my daughter a hard time. The things Skye told me was said, plus what I've heard myself is unacceptable! I won't have my daughter's life wrecked further by adding to what's happened in the past.'

Hazel nodded. She got that. If Erin *was* doing these things, then that was inexcusable. But although she didn't know Erin very well, from what she *did* know this was the opposite of what Erin had said to *her* in the past. It was out of character.

Although some people could be manipulative as well as believable.

She should know...

Hazel understood that Erin had doubts about both Zane's feelings for her, as well as this unknown daughter. After appearing out of the blue, making everyone believe she was a threat, was Skye on the level? And of course, there was the variable about Zane's aim of getting back in touch with the woman he shared a child with - the woman who had kept his daughter a secret for seventeen years...

Hazel frowned. Erin had spoken about this during the long night they were recovering from their injuries under the care of Mr Solenzo, but she'd also clearly said that she *wanted* Zane to get to know his daughter. What had changed to make the girl out to be a liar? What would that achieve?

From what Hazel had seen of Skye, the girl was sweet with a kind nature. She was eager to help and enthusiastic, finding it easy to get to grips with stuff at the centre. Perhaps a bit nervous, but under the circumstances that was understandable. None of this made sense.

Unless…

'What?' Zane asked. 'You're thinking something. Tell me.'

Hazel sighed. 'I'll admit I'm surprised about what you've told me. The only explanation I can think of is that if Erin *is* doing these things, then perhaps she should see Mr Solenzo again?'

'You think she's ill?' Zane asked, a deep frown forming.

'No, not necessarily, but stress and trauma can do strange things to people's minds.' Hazel shrugged. 'Just a stab in the dark.'

Zane smiled for the first time in what felt like days. Skye had mentioned something similar to him as well, so Hazel could be onto something here. If she was right, then it meant there was a genuine reason for Erin's awful behaviour. It didn't make it acceptable, but it *did* mean that if he got her help then perhaps things could be saved after all.

He'd wanted a future with Erin. Still did. She was the first woman to make him want that, so he was reluctant to throw that away.

More than reluctant.

He would and could never put anyone over his daughter, however, if Erin was having some form of breakdown, then surely he owed her the chance to get fixed, considering half – no, *most* of the strain in her life had been caused directly or indirectly by him or his people?

But if Erin had gone back on her word and reverted to

jealousy and manipulation like she had in the past, then she didn't deserve to be in his *or* his daughter's life.

He had to know for sure and now there might be a way that he could.

'Thank you,' Zane said, feeling a thousand times lighter. Pulling Hazel into his arms, he kissed the top of her head. 'I appreciate what you've said and for listening. I'll get in touch with Mr Solenzo.'

Hazel hugged Zane tightly, glad to have been of help to this troubled man with the weight of the world, plus other galaxies on his shoulders.

'Oh! Sorry!' Skye blurted as she burst into the room. 'I wanted to ask a question... I didn't mean to interrupt...' Her face flushed a deep shade of crimson. 'I... I didn't realise... I...'

'Don't be daft!' Zane laughed. 'You haven't interrupted a thing! We've finished our conversation, so ask away.'

Hazel kept her smile fixed but remained focused on Skye. She'd just seen a glimpse of something on the girl's face that had been quickly masked, but it had been there for a split second. And she hadn't liked it.

TEN

WAKING UP WITH rays of sunlight streaming through the curtains, Erin felt a rush of happiness with the advent of a sunny day. That was until her memory caught up with her and she remembered that everything was far from rosy.

She didn't recall going to bed. Her final memory was exhaustion from the prolonged period of crying; her frustrated tears only serving to make her more furious over the situation she found herself in, watching the relationship she'd hoped had turned a corner crumbling into dust.

The last time she'd looked at the clock on her bedside table before succumbing to tiredness had been 3 a.m., but Zane wasn't beside her. From what he'd said, if things didn't change, he wouldn't ever be beside her again.

Impotence washed over Erin, the injustice of how Skye was making out she was behaving threatening to squeeze every last drop of semblance from her skull.

How could she protect herself against an invisible onslaught from a girl with a life mission of portraying her as a Grade A bitch?

Erin stood no chance of winning against Zane's protective urge to make up lost time with his unknown daughter and Skye was hellbent on getting her out of the picture. But why? Was the girl having a petulant tantrum because she wanted her father to herself? Or was it more than that?

Her skin prickled. Skye's behaviour was odd; even sinister in its malicious intent. If Skye behaved that way to *her* and if she had ulterior motives, what did that mean for Zane?

No one took on board that Skye was seen as a possible enemy before declaring herself to be Zane's blood.

Did in not cross anyone's mind that, blood or not, she could *still* be an enemy?

Erin felt bad for even thinking down that road, but…

'Ah, you're awake!'

Startled, Erin jumped, knocking her head on the headboard in surprise. 'Oh! I didn't realise that you...'

'You were asleep when I got back last night, so I didn't wake you,' Zane's anger towards Erin had dissipated since speaking to Hazel, but what happened now depended on Erin. 'How are you feeling this morning?'

Erin frowned, unsure how to answer. *Confused? Angry? Depressed? Worried?* 'I-I'm not sure. After yesterday... I thought... thought that...' Relief poured over her as Zane pulled her into his arms. 'You now believe that I didn't say any of those things that Skye said I...'

'Don't start that again,' Zane said, tensing. 'I want to help you, but you've got to help yourself too.'

'Help *me*?' Erin squawked. She didn't want Zane's help, she wanted his *love*. She wanted his belief in her words. 'So, you still think th…'

'I've made an appointment for you with Mr Solenzo later on today,' Zane said, fighting to keep his patience. 'I think you should have a check-up. You can tell Mr Solenzo how you're feeling and... you know... what you've been thinking and well, if necessary, he can refer you to someone who cou…'

'Wait a second!' Erin pulled away from Zane, her face twisting in rage. 'You want him to send me to a fucking shrink? Is that what you're saying?'

'No, that's not what I'm saying,' Zane said, his voice calm. 'I'm merely saying th…'

'You are! Because I'm telling you that I didn't say those things that Skye told you, you assume I can't remember what I've said or that I don't know what I'm doing. Oh my God, Zane! I don't believe this!'

'It's not just that,' Zane barked, his calmness evaporating. 'Think about it - you've tried to kill me twice in the not-too-distant past. You've killed your ex-boyfriend. Your father got murdered and for years you pretended to be someone else out of vengeance. You've been paranoid and jealous on many occasions - long before Skye came on the scene.'

He paced the room. 'You've been through an awful amount of trauma and to be honest, it's screwed you up. You getting shot seems to be the catalyst making things worse. You need help.'

Erin's mouth flapped up and down, too shocked to speak. Yes, Zane was correct on many points, but there were reasons for what she'd done – reasons that he knew about and many which they'd jointly agreed on.

Yes, she *had* done many things and experienced many more, but she'd dealt with them better than most people would. None of that meant she was crazy.

'Look.' Zane placed his hands on Erin's shoulders, only for her to angrily shrug them off. Sighing, he shook his head, forcing himself not to roar at her with frustration. 'I meant what I said. I love you and I asked you to marry me. I still want that, but that can only happen if you accept my daughter and accept th…'

'I *do* accept Skye. I have done from the start!' Erin screeched, finding her voice. 'How could y…'

'You also need to accept that for us to have a future, I have to make sure you're well,' Zane interrupted. 'If I'm wrong, then I'm wrong.' He held his hands up. 'Surely if there's an issue it's best to nip it in the bud sooner rather than later?' Hazel was due a check-up with Mr Solenzo today anyway, so I asked if he could see you too. That way you can go together.' *Okay, so Hazel didn't have a check-up. Neither did she know she'd be accompanying Erin yet, but if it softened the blow...*

Erin plonked onto the bed, deflated. She wanted to argue and refuse point blank to have her mental capacity analysed. But what if Zane was right? What if she *had* dreamt up what she believed Skye was doing? It wouldn't be the first time she'd questioned herself. Didn't mental illness start by refusing to believe that you were doing what others could see?

Fear prickled. Whether she believed it possible or not, she could be wrong. The trauma of the past *may* have finally crossed the threshold and if she refused to see Mr Solenzo and there *was* something wrong with her mind, then she was throwing away her relationship and the future she so desperately wanted.

She didn't want to be crazy.

Struggling not to let angry, scared tears brim from her eyes, Erin knew she had to do what Zane asked. If Mr Solenzo said she was fine, then Zane would have to take on board that Skye had an agenda. But if Mr Solenzo *didn't* agree that she was compos mentis...

Erin's heart thumped dangerously.

'Shall I tell Hazel that you'll go with her?' Zane asked. He watched Erin carefully, relieved to see her slight nod.

He'd get this fixed. Erin could get better and then they would all have a future.

• • • •

AS HE STARED AT the door in front of him, Damon's nerves were ragged to fuck. He wanted to punch Symonds in the throat for putting him in this shitty position. He had things to do and people to see - Marco not being one of them.

Yet here he was.

Thanks to Symonds, he'd been unable to get out of it.

Damon didn't want to see Marco. Not now. Not *ever*.

Waiting to be granted entry to where Marco waited, Damon glared at the side of Symonds's fat head. Why hadn't the muppet kept his gob shut? It was like he relished causing situations that brought the most stress, the stupid prick.

The sudden buzzing of the door release made Damon's teeth clamp together with an uncomfortable jolt. The door slowly opened with a loud squeak and it was like he'd stepped into a scene from a Hammer Horror film - the bit where a witless character glibly stepped over the threshold of an old castle or corpse-ridden decrepit house, only to be accosted by the gnashing teeth of a cape-wearing vampire with blood-red eyes.

But Damon wasn't in a haunted house - it was a police station. And Christopher Lee wasn't waiting inside dressed up as Dracula, but Marco.

Marco was nowhere near as refined or classy as Christopher Lee, neither was Marco an actor. And the expression on Marco's face made Damon wish more than ever that he'd killed Symonds during the night rather than give him an opportunity to set him up for this shit.

Because 'shit' didn't begin to encapsulate how bad being here was.

Shoving his resentment and a large smattering of fear into the base of his feet, Damon strode confidently into the small room, brushing away his screaming instinct shouting for him to leave immediately.

He extended his hand in Marco's direction, hoping it wasn't trembling. 'Hey, Marco. How are you keeping?' *Oh God.* That wasn't the best thing to say to someone being held over counts of murder and sex trafficking charges. Or that part of the reason Marco was here in the first place was because *he'd* fucked up.

Ignoring Damon's hand, Marco stared in a way which had the capacity of melting men from the inside out. His ice blue eyes narrowed into slits. 'Are you taking the piss?'

'No!' Damon gabbled. 'Of course not. I...'

'I bought Damon in like you requested, Mr Morelli,' Symonds interjected, his voice sickeningly smooth. 'He'll bring you up to speed with the details of what we've discovered regarding your wife.'

Marco folded his arms across his muscular chest; the weeks stuck in a cell having had no detrimental effect on his physique. But the enforced spell of being unable to get his hands on the immense amount of cocaine and alcohol he put away on a daily basis had made him look lined and haggard.

Damon was all too aware of Marco's legendary excesses and the prospect of having no one to sneak in his required substances was taking its toll - both on his physical appearance and undoubtedly on his already short temper. It was an unknown quantity for Marco not to have minions swarming around ready to wipe his arse at the click of his fingers and he must be seething as to why no one was queuing up to do his bidding.

Thanks to Symonds, those reasons were something else Damon had to break to his boss, who was tensed like a caged tiger ready to pounce.

'Well, Sandler?' Marco growled, his voice low and raw. It sounded like the back of his throat had been through a mincer.

Damon fidgeted on the plastic chair, his backside already going to sleep. 'Erm, well, an article was spotted in the *London Standard* and...'

'Yeah, I know about the article,' Marco snapped. 'Stop fucking procrastinating! Is this Fleeter woman Hazel or not? And is my brother the person behind this Starbright place?'

Damon internally scowled. He and Symonds had agreed that the article wouldn't be mentioned to Marco until they had cast iron evidence. Or rather he'd *told* Symonds that was what would happen, but had the bastard taken any notice? Within one bloody day the toerag had spilled the lot.

'Why am I am still waiting for a response, Sandler?' Marco's loud voice broke the silence. Despite being in police custody and not having a man or business to his name at this moment in time, he still possessed the power to render everyone terrified. 'Is it them in that place or not?'

'I... erm... I'm still waiting for confirmation about that,'

Damon spluttered. And he presumed he'd have had that by now. Not to tell Marco or Symonds – there was no intention of doing that. He'd been planning to act on the information himself and move forward with his plans of domination. But now he was back to square one. Firstly because Symonds had run to Marco, telling him about that fucking article and that he would report back today and secondly - because after Tel had chucked that earwigging bastard out of the pub last night, Damon had the foresight to instruct Tel to follow.

It was a good job he had because from the short call he'd later received from Tel, the skinny stranger had run straight to Starbright. He knew that slimy fucker was a spy!

Damon had been all set to get the full lowdown this morning, except he'd been called *here* so he still didn't know what the hell was going on.

As Marco's piercing eyes narrowed further directing laser beams of doom into the centre of his head, Damon felt a thick film of sweat form traitorously across his brow, threatening to drip over his eyebrows onto his eyelids. Against his own strict instructions not, under any circumstances, to allow Marco to unnerve him, it wasn't working.

'Did you say you were *still* waiting for confirmation?' Marco's voice held a hint of incredulity. 'For God's sake! How exactly are you running my firm in my absence?' He raked his fingers through his thick black hair. 'I knew you were a pointless bastard, but by Christ, this is something else!' His meaty fist slammed onto the table between them. 'Get some men out to do the work, Sandler, otherwise I'll pick someone else to take over the share of the business I stupidly handed to you!'

He threw his hands up in the air. 'What was I thinking by offering you a piece of my empire in return for sorting this crap out? I'd get more use out of a dead fucking cat!' He then swung towards Symonds. 'Rip up that fucking agreement! This cunt can't prove anything was signed. He can't prove shag all!'

'I'm afraid it's not quite that simple,' Symonds said,

glancing at Damon. 'I think it's time you told Mr Morelli.'

Damon's hatred towards Symonds reached a record high. He'd been just about to get out of the agreement he'd never wanted in the first place, but now this fat old turd had dropped him back in it again. Symonds had 100 per cent agreed that it was vital Marco wasn't aware of certain subjects, yet he'd put him in a position where he had no choice but to speak of them?

'Told me what?' Marco's voice held an edge which told Damon that if he hid anything it would be immediately uncovered. He took a deep breath. 'Erm, we have a lack of men…'

'Yeah, I knew a lot of them karked it during the Luna shootout, but you replenished them, right? That's what you said you were doing.' Marco cracked his knuckles, the sound echoing off the walls of the small room.

Damon slipped a finger in his collar to relieve the building heat, only to remember that he wasn't wearing a shirt and succeeded only in stretching the neck of his T-shirt. 'Erm, well, it turns out that no one wants to work for the firm,' he mumbled.

'What?' Marco barked. 'Speak up! I can't hear you.'

'I said, no one wants to work for the firm,' Damon shouted. 'They've abandoned ship!'

Marco lurched across the table and grabbed Damon around the throat. 'You're a useless fucking ba…'

'Mr Morelli!' Symonds cried. 'Please calm down. Whether you like it or not, you need Mr Sandler's help.'

As Marco grudgingly dropped his grip, Damon rubbed his throat. There was no point in Symonds coming to his aid now. Because of *him*, his plans were screwed. He'd have been better off letting Marco strangle him. But now Marco was aware of the subject, he may as well level on it. 'I have two men on the case,' he continued, determined to keep his voice free from tremor. 'They have further information, of which I would have had by now had I not been forced to attend this meeting.'

Marco studied Damon for what felt like two years. 'Why are you still here then? Get your information and report back to me immediately! While you're at it, grab some of our linked men from the Woolwich and Plumstead territories and get them on it too. They're closer to the area and will get info quicker than the two idiots *you've* put on the job.' He rolled his eyes theatrically. 'Fucking joke, this! Putting only *two* men on a case like this? Use your loaf, man! Pull on the links to my territories.'

Damon thought it preferable to have recently chosen to have his tongue chopped out rather than voicing *this*, but there was no getting out of it now. What Banjo said last night, before they'd moved onto other subjects, wasn't something he'd wanted to dwell on because in addition to losing the Woolwich and Plumstead territories things were a *lot* worse.

'Did you not hear me, Sandler?' Marco screeched. 'Get more men on it. Offer them double the brass than what they're being paid. Treble, if needs be! I don't care what it takes. There will be no reprisals from their two-bit firms. They wouldn't dare!' He clenched his fist, the knuckles glowing white with the force. 'Christ! Where's your initiative? What the fuck's wrong with you?'

'Mr Sandler felt it wise not to inform you that these territories were recently lost.' The hint of a smirk pulled at Symonds's mouth. 'I personally thought you'd prefer to know but...'

'WHAT?' Marco roared, his face reddening. 'Is this true?'

As Marco's psychotic eyes blazed, Damon hated Symonds further. That lying old cunt had told him to say fuck all about the lost areas so not to stress Marco out. 'It's true, but regardless of what Symonds just said, I was acting on *his* advice.' He nodded at Symonds, gratified to see the man flinch. 'You should also be aware that it's not just Woolwich and Plumstead that are lost.' He measured his words carefully. 'A further three were taken last night... By your brother... Lambeth, Kennington and Vauxhall have gone. All the territories have been taken by Zane.'

Marco looked like he might implode. The veins in his temples bulged grotesquely and his eyes smarted. 'What th...'

'I was busy discussing a plan of how to reclaim them, as well as getting clarification about Hazel, when Symonds insisted I come here instead. He said telling you I was awaiting information was *far* more important than territories...' *That would piss on the old bastard's toupee.*

Marco swung towards Symonds. 'You stupid fucker! Let Sandler get on with his fucking job and keep your big hooter out!' He shovelled up a sheaf of paperwork Symonds had placed on the table, scrunched it into a ball and slammed it into the man's face. 'Listen to me, you piece of shit! You have twenty-four hours to put together enough to start the process of getting these charges against me dropped. And this time do it properly otherwise you're fucking fired. And I don't just mean fired from your job - I mean your house and your bloody family will go up the fucking chimney!'

· · · ·

MARTIN OPENED ONE EYE and peered out from underneath the duvet. He searched his brain in the hope of deciphering where he'd been and how much he'd put away last night to earn such a stonker of a headache. It wasn't long before he remembered that he hadn't been drinking at all. The incessant pounding in his temples was down to the kicking he'd received, courtesy of the quest to find Skye.

Reaching up, he prodded the area around his eye. It hurt even more this morning and he dreaded to think what he looked like.

Still, that was the least of his worries.

The sudden ringing of his mobile pulled his scrambled brain fully back to reality.

Skye?

Lurching out from underneath the duvet, Martin overrode the throbbing of his head, along with his back feeling like a plank of wood and scrabbled around for his phone.

Come on, come on! He couldn't miss this call!

Locating his mobile, he snatched it up, grateful that in his haste he'd missed pressing the 'answer call' button.

...Mum calling...

Martin stared at the screen, guilt swirling. He'd never avoided a call from his mum. He had a better relationship with her than he did his father, and his mother would worry if he didn't answer, but what could he do?

Gritting his teeth, Martin waited until the call rang off. No doubt she'd continue calling until he answered. He'd call her back. But not now.

Sighing, Martin reached for the glass of water he'd placed on the bedside table last night.

At least it wasn't Shirley. But it wasn't Skye either...

Raising the glass to his lips, Martin stopped just before swallowing a dead moth floating with outstretched wings on the water's surface.

Grimacing, he replaced the glass on the side.

That summed up how he felt: floating lifelessly for eternity. And exactly what he'd be doing if he didn't tread carefully.

Wondering what to do next, he leant back against the headboard, the creaking wood not comforting his frayed nerves.

He'd been so close last night, yet still so far, but if anything, his position was more precarious now than ever.

Martin stared at his phone, waiting for it to ring again, but it remained silent. He only hoped his mother didn't panic and call the police, citing him missing.

She wouldn't, would she? He'd only been gone less than forty-eight hours.

But she would if she knew what he was up to. Especially if she'd seen what occurred yesterday.

Martin couldn't say he was enamoured about it either. It meant there was no choice but to return to the Starbright Centre. More importantly, he had to get inside there. But this time his plans had changed. It was no longer vital to speak to that Hazel woman. It *had* been Skye on the back of that bike.

89

It had taken all of his power not to rush over screaming her name. Instead, he'd been momentarily paralysed watching the rider of the bike remove Skye's helmet, cup her chin with his big hands and kiss her on the top of the head.

Had she run off to be with *that* man?

What Martin had seen didn't seem the kind of behaviour between lovers, but even so, his first instinct had been to charge over, demand to know what was going on, bundle Skye into the Range Rover and drive off. But that was before logic took the reins, reminding the sane part of Martin's brain not consumed by raging jealousy that he stood about as much chance of taking on a man built like a brick outhouse as a politician winning Miss World.

It was when the man turned in his direction that Martin found himself in a quandary.

He wasn't in direct view. He'd held back from rushing up the driveway until he knew for definite it was Skye. But he had got as far as the drive's pillared entrance. Although he'd been virtually out of sight it was obvious the man sensed his presence because he'd turned to face the *exact* direction of the pillar he'd been lurking behind, sniffing the air like a wild animal detecting a scent.

With that man's piercing eyes, a wild animal wasn't too far from the truth.

Who the bloody hell was he? A Morelli? One of their men? A random stranger?

Martin didn't know. Neither did he know what his next move should have been, but the decision had been made simple when the big man's lips moved. He couldn't hear the words but it was clear a swift exit was required when three equally large men spilled out of the doors of the Starbright and glared in his direction.

As Skye was shepherded inside, the three men moved rapidly up the drive.

Towards him...

Not needing further encouragement, Martin scrambled

away from the driveway and raced to his motor, praying he didn't drop the car keys down the drain below the driver's door that must have been placed there to taunt him.

Thankfully, he didn't. Ripping open the door, he'd jumped behind the wheel, fired the engine and turned the car around.

He'd been lucky. He'd swung the Range Rover into a tight donut, smashing up the kerb in his haste to get as far away as quickly as possible. His father wouldn't be happy with the manoeuvre, but Martin would worry about that if he'd naused up the tracking or dented the wheel rim. The only important thing was getting out of there.

He hadn't wanted to look either but forced himself to regardless. Sure enough, the view in his rearview mirror had showed the three men standing in the road, watching him disappear.

At least they hadn't followed.

Martin swallowed dryly. It wasn't like he'd left because he was *scared*. Nah - it wasn't that. Hadn't he already proved he'd risk his neck by the black eye and sore mouth he'd received?

The only reason he'd left so rapidly was because he hadn't wanted to put her at more risk. If any of those men were the Morellis or connected with the Morellis, it could mean big trouble for her.

Martin frowned. Besides, she hadn't seemed unhappy. She'd looked fine. She'd been *smiling* at that biker man and could have sworn he'd seen her laugh too.

But who was that man and why was Skye there?

Martin knew he had to return there as soon as possible. It would be all right. No one had got a clear look at him and it was unlikely they'd clocked details of his car. *At least that was what he kept telling himself.*

But then, perhaps these people were nothing to do with the Morellis? It was a women's refuge, after all, so maybe that man on the bike had rescued Skye and taken her to a place of safety?

He frowned. *Who was he trying to kid?* If that was the case, then why had those three other blokes started to chase him?

Swinging himself out of bed, Martin stretched as much as he could in a bid to limber up his aching back.

Providing that weird bloke down the corridor wasn't in the shared bathroom, he'd have a shower. Once he'd done that, he'd attempt the Starbright again. He'd only risk an approach if there was no one around, then he'd find Skye and take her home with him where she belonged.

But first he'd call her again. If she was still at that place, maybe she'd be able to answer her phone this time?

Eleven

KNOWING ZANE had left the house, Erin deemed it safe to go downstairs. There was no other movement, so Zane must have also taken Skye to drop her off at Starbright for the second day in a row. No doubt she was doing everything *perfectly* to impress everyone with her ability and eagerness to help.

Gnawing tugged inside Erin's stomach, wondering just how much Zane had discussed of her supposed 'mental ailments' with Skye, Hazel and his men. The thought of that being the topic of conversation left her with a sickening feeling that she couldn't shake. That everyone might think her to be, or *did* think her unhinged, festered uncomfortably. Yet the more she denied it, the more it appeared like it was true.

This bothered her and the longer she dwelt on it, the more she questioned whether there *was* any validity in the theory.

It was a horrifying to consider that if she *was* the only one who didn't believe there was an issue it leant more towards that there *was* one.

She'd wracked her brains half the night over another question too. How had Skye known that she and Zane had discussed the possibility of *her* being behind the press leak about the Starbright?

This had been in Erin's mind since Skye had used it as part of her argument in turning Zane in her favour. If Zane hadn't told Skye about Erin insinuating her being behind the leak, then that left only scant options: Skye had heard her voicing the topic *herself*, which meant she'd been eavesdropping on a private conversation, or she'd leaked the story and was covering her tracks, hazarding a guess that Erin doubted her.

The only other reason was that she, herself, was imagining the whole thing...

Erin trudged down the stairs to wait for Hazel, her legs reluctantly propelling her forward. She was dreading seeing Mr Solenzo. What if he agreed with Zane? What if Skye was proved right?

Her mouth tightened. No matter what anyone said, she believed - *had* to believe, that her brain worked just fine. She was *not* hearing things, neither was she getting mixed up. She might have been paranoid in the past, but this was not one of those occasions. Skye had engineered things to look a certain way and Erin was determined to prove that. But how did she go about it?

Because right now, that manipulative young woman was succeeding.

Erin's fingers tightened around the banister as she continued down the stairs. She had no choice but to go along with this both for Zane's and her own sake. She had to swallow the injustice and pray that an idea came to her or something happened to expose Skye. Fighting everyone wouldn't help.

Reaching the bottom of the stairs, she moved towards the sitting room, grateful Skye was out. Her eyes were still red and puffy from crying and the last thing she wanted was to give the girl satisfaction over the upset she'd caused.

With her hand on the doorknob, Erin froze at the ring of a mobile. *It wasn't hers, so whose was it?*

Pushing open the sitting room door slightly, she peered in, surprised to see Skye standing at the window. Her back was turned, but not so much for Erin to miss the mobile in her hand.

From this angle, she could also make out the expression of utter contempt on Skye's face as she glared at the still ringing phone.

Her mind churned. That wasn't the phone Zane had purchased for Skye. This one was completely different.

Skye had lied about having a phone of her own? Why? And who was ringing her on it?

Erin silently watched as Skye cut the call and shoved the phone behind the sofa cushions. Taking this as an apt moment to enter, she walked into the room. 'Oh! I thought you'd left!'

Skye flinched at the unexpected intrusion, quickly masking it with casual indifference. 'Zane said he needed to make a few calls and that he'd be back shortly, so don't worry, I'll be off soon. Ah, is that why you've ventured downstairs? You presumed I'd already left so you wouldn't have to face me?' She raised an eyebrow defiantly. 'Or were you sneaking around hoping to catch me doing something I shouldn't be? If that's the case, you'll have a long wait.'

Erin feigned a laugh. 'Why would I do that?' *Come on! Turn this to your advantage.* She slid a genuine-looking smile onto her mouth. 'Why would I think you had something to hide?' *Except you have, because I've just seen it… And now you're trying to work out if I clocked the phone you denied you had.*

She forced on a sympathetic expression. It took so much effort that it hurt. 'I know you're struggling being here, Skye. Finding your father after all these years must be hard, so I understand why you're lashing out, but I'm not your enemy.' *Oh, but after what you've been doing, I am now*, Erin thought acidly. But she had to keep it together. Losing her temper again would play straight into Skye's hands.

Her unbridled rage had held her in good stead in the past. The surge of hatred she'd last felt when fully entrenched in the vendetta against Anthony during the relationship she'd endured with him in order to get to Zane when she believed him to be her father's murderer, had long since been extinguished. Yet now she felt a similar but new one igniting.

She dislodged the claws scrabbling to take hold within her. She had no desire to return to that level of hatred towards anyone - especially Zane's daughter. But it was difficult keeping it at bay with the poisoned words Skye uttered out of everyone else's earshot.

'Why would you think I was lashing out at you?' Skye widened her eyes in mock surprise. 'It's the other way around, isn't it?' She paused thoughtfully. 'I was very upset last night. All I want is to be part of the family.'

It was a good job that Zane took this moment to appear because Erin was precariously close to throwing her resolution of keeping her temper to the wind.

Smiling brightly, Zane walked into the room with Hazel in tow. 'Ah, good - you're ready. We'll catch up later and you can let me know how it went.' He then jerked his head in Skye's direction. 'Come on, you. You've got the responsibility of looking after the centre whilst Hazel is out.'

'Wow!' Skye gushed. 'I'm honoured. Thanks, Hazel.'

Erin saw the smile Hazel gave to Skye's gratitude but couldn't help notice it seemed strained. Could she dare hope that Hazel had seen through Skye's pristine act?

'Will you be long, Hazel?' Skye asked, putting on the look of innocence that Erin found infuriating. 'I hope I remember everything you've showed me. I don't want to get anything wrong.'

'You'll be fine!' Zane laughed. 'Any daughter of mine will be good at her job. But no, Hazel won't be long. I'll pop in shortly too and see how you're getting on so you won't be on your own very long.'

Skye beamed ingratiatingly. 'Fantastic! I know you love being at the centre. It's nice to see how well you and Hazel get on...' Her eyes rested pointedly on Erin as she spoke, the glint unmissable.

Erin smiled tightly. 'I guess that you two had best make tracks.'

There was another reason why she wanted Skye out of the

house - before she got a chance to remember the one thing she might wish not to leave behind.

Keeping her smile in place until Zane's bike roared off up the road with Skye on the back, Erin stood to one side as Hazel opened the door ready for them to get into the waiting taxi. 'Oh, hang on. I forgot my handbag! You carry on. I won't be a second.'

Rushing back into the sitting room, Erin grabbed the handbag she'd purposely left on the arm of the chair.

An opportunity had presented itself and she was taking it.

Moving to the sofa, she slipped her hand behind the cushions where Skye had shoved her phone and thanked her lucky stars that Zane had been in such a hurry to rush Skye out of the house that she hadn't had time to retrieve it. Either that or the girl was too busy thinking of further digs that it had slipped her mind.

Sneaking through someone's personal things wasn't a trait Erin would usually resort to, nor was it one that she relished doing, but in this instance, she'd make an exception. Skye was making or receiving calls to or from someone that she had no wish to speak to. And she was doing it on a phone that she'd lied about owning.

As Erin's fingers wrapped around the plastic casing of the mobile, the outlook on her current situation brightened.

One on you, Skye Wilson, Erin thought, transferring the phone into her own handbag.

On that phone there would be contacts. If they hadn't been deleted, there would be numbers for Shirley; for this boyfriend Skye allegedly had or perhaps a friend? There must be *someone* on there. Messages, even? Finding anything to shed light on the mysterious stranger who was determined to make it look like she was losing her mind, would afford an advantage.

And by God, Erin needed an advantage right now before that troubled little cow succeeded in driving everyone she cared about away or before she got dumped under the care of a psychiatrist.

Neither of those things could happen.

Feeling happier, Erin pulled the sitting room door closed and rushed to join Hazel in the taxi. Even seeing Mr Solenzo no longer seemed so dreadful.

She wasn't losing her marbles and hopefully, very soon she would be able to prove in more ways than one, that Skye Wilson was lying.

• • • •

ZANE PICKED AT HIS FINGERS. He was only half-listening to Leo and knew he should be concentrating on the latest updates and thinking of ways to come up with ways to capitalise on the acquisition of further territories. But there were too many other things plaguing him.

There was a deep-seated worry about what Solenzo would deduce about Erin's state of mind and what that would mean for the future of both him and subsequently, his daughter. He wanted Erin in his life. *Needed* Erin in his life, but he also wanted to be able to offer Skye a secure and happy family environment. To do that, he needed his new firm to be fully functional and profitable in order to offer his daughter financial security, as well as make up for all the years he'd provided nothing. He also wanted to give her something she could call *family*. That was something Shirley had abysmally failed at doing. And if Erin continued the way she was going, the concept of family would fail again.

What Skye had said - or rather, what she'd *hinted* that had happened in the past hadn't been far from his thoughts and rang every single alarm bell he possessed.

He needed to know what had gone on and there was only one person who could give him that information. He didn't mean just words - anyone could lie. He had to clap eyes on Shirley Wilson and see what this woman - the girl who he'd once considered being in his future, was all about.

One look should be enough to deduce how low she'd stoop to allow their daughter's life to be trashed in the way he believed Skye meant. And it made Zane's blood run cold and move like sluggish, congealed gloop through his veins.

Whatever Shirley had chosen to do with her life, in addition to hiding away his daughter, she would be sorry if she'd become a drunk whore, allowing her punters to accost her own daughter.

His daughter.

A vision of the fresh-faced sixteen-year-old old beauty Shirley had once been, transfigured into a haggard, alcohol-ravaged crone with track-marked skin and cheap clothes hanging from an emaciated frame, filled his mind.

On top of this, Zane wanted to know who the fuck had been hanging around the Starbright yesterday when he'd arrived.

He cracked his knuckles and reached for another cigarette, failing to notice that he'd still got one burning in the ashtray.

'What territories do you want to concentrate on next?' Leo asked. 'We're steaming ahead and we've got plenty of men now - many more than I thought we'd have amassed so quickly and...' Stopping, he frowned. 'Is everything okay?'

'Yeah,' Zane muttered. 'It's good about the territories. Really good. I'll call a meeting with some of the new men and get them scouting other areas.' He glanced at the map of London spread out in front of him. 'Perhaps here and here.' He jabbed his finger in the general direction of Camberwell and Walworth.'

'Yes, those patches are related to Marco's connections,' Tiger acknowledged. 'Although possibly no longer - a bit like the rest of London...'

Zane chuckled. Although the other outstanding issues took a percentage of the shine off his progress, he was pleased at how things were going. And being as there were still no updates on Marco, perhaps there was time to deflect a little... Folding his arms, he looked from Leo to Tiger. 'I need you two to do something for me.'

'Whatever you need, mate,' Leo said.

'Firstly, I need one of you to dig around on that bloke I saw watching the Starbright yesterday. Can you deal with that,

Tiger?'

Tiger frowned. 'The one you mentioned was there when you rocked up with Skye? I thought you said he was just a nosy dweeb who legged it the second the guys came out?'

'That's about the extent of it.' Zane steepled his fingers under his chin. 'But I don't like being watched, no matter how innocuous it may or may not be.' With his track record, everything was a danger and he was ignoring nothing whilst a) Marco still drew breath, b) it involved his daughter and c) Erin being a target if it was discovered that shot hadn't killed her.

Plus, whether it was his responsibility or not, Hazel was also on his protection list. Although the press had kept their word and hadn't printed anything further about the centre or Hazel, the information was still out there. And that falling into the wrong hands would prove dangerous.

Even fatal...

'Nothing can be left to chance, no matter how irrelevant,' Zane continued. 'Anyone who has an interest in watching me or my daughter is of importance.' He fished a piece of paper from his leather jacket pocket. 'This is the bloke's description. I saw him myself at a distance. He looked young. And this...' Slapping the paper on the table, he prodded at three letters and a number. 'Is the reg of his car noted as he sped away.'

Leo peered at the writing. 'A private plate?'

'What young bloke do you know that has a private plate? Furthermore, a private plate on a brand new Range Rover?' Zane folded his arms. 'Answers on a postcard, please!'

Leo raised his eyebrows. 'You're thinking this is someone linked with Marco?'

'I don't know, but I can't think of who else it could be, that's why I want him checked out,' Zane muttered. 'If he's innocent and was just passing and happened to stop and watch me arriving at the Starbright, then he won't hang around. He'll have taken that motor back to whoever he borrowed it off, rather than lurking.'

'But if he *is* lurking...' Leo nodded, seeing the point.

'Exactly.' Zane sparked up yet another cigarette. 'If he *is* still around Dagenham, there's a reason for it. One, I suspect, that Marco is funding.'

'I'll get onto it,' Tiger said. 'A young bloke with a fancy car shouldn't be difficult to spot around Dagenham!'

Zane chuckled, then turning to Leo, became serious. 'And you, mate. I need you to locate someone else for me.' He'd tried to put off doing this, but it was no good. 'Skye's not giving me the info and I'm too impatient to wait until she does.'

'But things are going well between you and Skye, aren't they?' Leo frowned. 'I thought she was settling in well.'

'There's a bit of unrest between her and Erin but nothing I can't handle,' Zane said, hoping that would prove true. 'But there's missing pieces in the jigsaw concerning what might have befallen Skye during the years I've been unaware of her existence.' *And those were clawing away at a rate that he could no longer overlook.*

His eyes then brightened. 'My daughter is like a breath of fresh air,' he said proudly. 'She's so much like me with her eagerness to learn, as well as being just as stubborn.'

'Must be a Morelli trait!' Leo laughed, then his smile fell. 'But this person you want me to locate? Are we talking about Sandler?'

Zane shook his head. 'No. Karl Hartley is still in situ at the Blacksmith's waiting for that prick to show up. In fact, I'm catching up with Karl later for updates. The person I want you to find is Shirley.'

'Shirley?'

'Skye's mother,' Zane muttered. 'I need her whereabouts and I need them fast.' He stubbed his cigarette out, grinding it into the ashtray harder than necessary. Using this force resembled what he wanted to do to the skanky bitch who had screwed his daughter's life up. 'It may be easy or difficult - I don't know. All I know is that her name was Shirley Wilson and as far as I'm aware, still is. She used to be slim with dark brown hair. The first place to try is Surrey. Look in the local boozers – the shitty back street ones. I reckon that dumps full of wankers are places you'll stand more chance of finding her.'

Leo exchanged a quick glance with Tiger at the venom in Zane's voice. It wasn't like him to speak down on or insinuate anything about a woman - let alone one who had borne his child, but gauging from the rage behind Zane's cold eyes there must be just reason for this and one which he wouldn't press on. 'There's no further info?'

Zane shook his head. 'That's all I know and I'm not even certain about half of that. But I need her located.'

Because until he'd seen Shirley and got the answers he needed he'd be unable to concentrate properly on anything. And if she gave him a hint of the news he was dreading, he would kill her stone dead.

TWELVE

SITTING IN THE waiting room at Mr Solenzo's prestigious Harley Street practice, Hazel was stuck between a rock and a hard place.

She trailed her fingers along the soft leather of the oversized chair, the luxurious feel of the upholstery sparking a reminder of how much she'd loved the sumptuous leather armchairs and sofas in the penthouse. *Marco's penthouse...*

Or should she say, Zane's.

It was *his* penthouse - something else Marco had helped himself to.

She shook away the thought of how much she missed the luxury of her previous life. That life was no longer hers. Neither did she want it. She may now have next to nothing of opulence, designer goods or luxury living, but she *did* have self-respect. And that was worth more than anything.

Hazel masked the worries bouncing around her head and glanced at Erin fiddling with the strap of her handbag beside her.

She couldn't blame Erin for being apprehensive - she would be too should the boot be on the other foot, but Hazel couldn't shake the burden hovering over her. *She* was responsible for this

- at least the part about for Erin being here. Not that she disliked Mr Solenzo. Hazel held a huge amount of respect and gratitude towards the man who had so diligently patched up the horrific injuries Marco had inflicted. Soon it would be almost impossible to see the damage she'd suffered at the hands of her husband. People might notice the slight dip in her cheekbone and the hint of a tiny kink in her jaw if they looked closely enough, but it was impossible to tell the difference between these replacement teeth and her real ones. *She* knew they were there - it was something she'd never be able to fully erase, but she was getting there, thanks to Mr Solenzo, Zane, Erin and her newly found mission in life. But for Erin to have her mental state analysed and judged was something altogether different.

And it was the suggestion *she'd* made to Zane which had seeded the idea.

'I hope Mr Solenzo isn't running over too much,' Erin said, shuffling awkwardly. 'I just want to get this over and done with.'

Hazel reached out to squeeze Erin's hand. 'I'm sure it will be fine.' *But would it?* It was hard to justify her newfound self-respect right now.

She wasn't comfortable about lying to Erin over this visit or pleased to have to keep it to herself that she hadn't a checkup booked with the doctor at all. Neither was she happy with Skye running the centre in her absence. The girl had only one day's experience so far - certainly not enough to cope with running the place alone. But Hazel didn't want to let Zane down by going against his express wishes of accompanying Erin.

She'd thought suggesting this route would help. She really had. She'd thought it would help both Zane and Erin if the aftereffect of the shooting was causing Erin's erratic behaviour.

But that was *then*.

Since suggesting this route, Hazel had glimpsed other things which made her feel that she may have made a mistake.

'I'm not sure I can do this.' Erin turned to Hazel, her eyes brimming with tears. 'I didn't say any of those things to Skye but Zane doesn't believe that. She acts differently around him, but the minute his back is turned...' Her voice trailed off.

Hazel saw the fear radiating through Erin and her stomach plunged further. She'd put this woman in such a bad position.

'What if Solenzo thinks I've lost it?' Erin blurted. 'That's what Zane is expecting. Probably what everyone else expects too. I know Zane has talked to you about me. He must have.' And the horrible prospect that Zane had paid Solenzo off to agree with him had also pushed its way into her mind.

Stop! she told herself, gritting her teeth. *Now she really was being ridiculous.*

'Look, I...' Hazel faltered. She shouldn't say anything. She'd promised. But it was no good. This wasn't right. 'Zane didn't go to make calls this morning. He came to the Starbright to ask me to accompany you. He wanted me to pretend I had a checkup booked.'

Erin frowned. 'I don't understand. Why would he make that up? Why would he lie?' She snatched her hand from Hazel's. 'Why would *you* lie?'

'Because it's my fault,' Hazel said, her voice small. 'I suggested this to Zane.'

'You?' Erin cried. '*You* told him to get me carted off to see a shrink?'

'No! I-I thought after what Zane said that it would help. But not a shrink. Christ, no. I just didn't believe that you'd act the way he said you were acting without good reason or that the shooting had...'

'Had what? Confused me? Made me lose my fucking mind? Made me dream stuff up?' Erin hissed. 'I know what I've said, and I also know what's being said to me! For God's sake, Hazel. It's got to the point where I'm even convincing myself that everyone else is right, but they're not! I swear down this is nothing to do with the shooting, nor anything else. It's just Skye. She's doing it!'

'I know...' Hazel said, her voice barely more than a whisper.

'What?' Erin blinked with surprise. 'You know? If she's doing this to you as well, then why did you...'

'I suggested seeing Solenzo after Zane confided in me about how bad things were between you and how your behaviour was threatening your future. I...' Hazel sighed dejectedly. *She'd made things so much worse.* 'But no, Skye's not doing anything to me...' Her eyes narrowed. 'If anything, she's being over-the-top nice. But I saw a look on her face... There are veiled comments too... Oh, I don't know.' She wrung her hands. 'Nothing concrete, but that girl has an agenda. Something's not right, but I don't know what that "something" is. Yet...'

Erin's heart skipped a beat. 'So, you believe me?'

Hazel nodded. 'What Zane said - that you were jealous and hated Skye didn't add up with what you'd told me, but because of your fears about Shirley, then I... But now... yes, I believe you, but I've no idea how to voice my concerns to Zane. He's very defensive over the girl.'

Erin nodded. *Wasn't he just!* She opened her mouth to reply but Mr Solenzo emerged from his consultation room.

'I'm so sorry to have kept you waiting, Erin. Please come in.' He then turned to Hazel. 'I'll see you for your checkup directly after.'

Erin clocked the knowing look Mr Solenzo shot in Hazel's direction and humiliation burnt. But Hazel admitting seeing a hint of what Skye was up to put a different slant on things. There was hope to be had.

Smiling, she rose from the chair and moved to follow Mr Solenzo. She heard Hazel whisper 'good luck'. She needed it, but she'd do what Zane wanted. He thought he was doing the right thing. He thought he was helping her, protecting his daughter and making everything better. But whatever Mr Solenzo deduced from this appointment was no longer such a debilitating threat.

After they got out of here, she'd show Hazel the mobile phone safely lodged in her handbag. They could go through it, see what Skye had been lying about and then work out what the hell to do about it.

If someone had told her several weeks ago that she'd have Hazel Grimes as an ally, she'd have laughed until she dropped to the floor.

But that was then and this was *now*.

• • • •

DAMON HAD CHUCKLED most of the way back from the police station. Actually, he'd laughed out loud on so many occasions the taxi driver had started eyeing him oddly in his rearview mirror.

Oh yes, he'd got one over on Symonds. Watching the man squirm when he'd made it clear that porkies had been told over the instructions was wonderfully pleasurable. Marco might be a psychotic madman, but he wasn't absent of a brain. It was clear Symonds had twisted the truth to make himself out to be the hero. But that wasn't a patch on the man's expression when Marco shoved that paperwork in his mush.

Damon chuckled again. Bloody priceless, that was.

With the clear threat ringing in Symonds's ears that if he didn't get Marco on the way out of custody in a day then his whole family would be pork scratchings, the man hadn't even made sarky comments as they'd left the interview room. In his haste Symonds had instead scuttled off down the road to his car in his haste, leaving Damon to hail a cab.

There was little chance of Symonds getting the ball rolling for Marco's release in such a short time. Especially as a sworn statement from Hazel for Marco was required. Only *he* and his men had the ability to get that and even if Damon had it to give, he wouldn't. He'd rather spend eternity in a chicken farm than give Symonds anything to help his cause.

But he *didn't* have any further information. Not yet. But that's why he was *here*.

Yanking open the door of the Blacksmith's Arms, Damon strutted into the pub. He'd sent a text to Tel and Banjo whilst in the taxi, telling them to get their arses here for the overdue update. Sorting out the bloody territories could wait.

As he reached the bar and glanced around, Damon's jaw clenched. No sign of Tel or Banjo. They'd best hurry the fuck up. He wanted the lowdown on that nosy creep from last night almost more than he wanted a drink. *But only almost...*

'Pint of Stella,' Damon mumbled to the tired looking barman. 'Anyone been in here for me?'

'How would I know? What am I? Your fucking secretary?' the barman snapped.

Damon raised his eyebrows. Old Bob was a miserable fucker at the best of times, but the guy was lucky he was in such a good mood, otherwise he'd have earned a slap for his rudeness.

Snatching the pint off the soggy beermat, Damon chucked the money onto the bar rather than handing it over like he usually would. He was just about to pick the old cunt up over his attitude when the familiar figures of Tel and Banjo overtook as priority.

'You're late,' Damon muttered, waiting resentfully as the two men ordered their drinks. Leading the way to a corner table, he took a long slug of his pint, leaving Tel to take the seat half-behind a pillar. *He* wanted a good view of the surroundings. Everyone knew it was best to see an enemy coming.

'What happened at the meeting with Marco?' Tel asked.

'Not much.' Damon scowled. 'I had to break it to him about the lost territories amongst other things, but apart from that…'

'Shit! How did he take it?'

'Not well, but it's all under control,' Damon said. 'I made out to Marco that I'd act immediately to regain those territories, but in reality, as you know, I've no intention of doing that. Tell me what else happened last night.'

Tel sat forward, a conspiring glint on his face. 'The twat who was in here isn't anything to do with Morelli.'

Damon frowned. 'What do you mean? He went straight from here to the Starbright Centre. You told me that much last night, so where the hell does, "nothing to do with Zane Morelli" come into it? That prick was here to spy on us and then ran straight off the moment he was *stupidly* released, free to go to Zane-bastard-Morelli and tell him of my whereabouts.'

As it stood, everyone had forgotten of his existence and Damon wanted it to remain that way.

He glared at Banjo pointedly. The man should never have let that kid go. If Banjo's lack of judgement brought Zane Morelli on his case, then he'd kick Banjo's arse from here to Clapham Junction.

'That bloke is shag all to do with Zane Morelli,' Banjo snapped, affronted at Damon's comment. 'Why would Morelli recruit posh Surrey-bred school leavers to do his scouting? The skinny twat was meeting a bird, like he said.'

'A posh kid meeting a bird in *here*?' Damon snarled, his arm sweeping around the nicotine-stained, peeling wallpaper of the Blacksmith's Arms. 'Have a day off! That act was to throw us off the scent and you're fucking dead if your thick actions remind Zane that I'm still here, alive and well.'

'I agree with Banjo,' Tel interrupted. 'Aside from the posh Surrey thing, I followed the bloke, remember? He was driving a top of the range motor.' He pointed to the scrawled handwriting on the back of his fag packet. 'That's the reg and…'

Damon snatched Tel's cigarette packet and screwed it up. 'I couldn't give a toss if he was on a unicycle! That kid is part of them!'

'I don't think so.' Tel glared at his crumpled cigarette packet Damon had casually tossed to the floor. 'He didn't go in the Starbright. He lurked at the bottom of the driveway watching.'

Damon sighed in frustration. 'Okay, so I presume it was then that you brought him in?'

'I was just about to when Morelli rocked up.'

'Zane?' Damon sat forward, his heart thumping. 'Zane was there? Last night? You're sure it was him?'

'Of course I'm bloody sure! Wouldn't you recognise him?' Tel snapped.

Damon grinned. Zane *was* connected with the Starbright. A categoric, bona fide sighting meant that 'Miss Fleeter' had to be Hazel Grimes.

Oh, happy days!

But he'd not rush to tell Marco.

Damon clapped his hands together. 'So, not a dead loss after all? I *knew* that prick was worth following. Where are you holding him? We'll continue with what Banjo *should* have done last night and get the truth out of him this time, rather than bullshit about meeting a girl.'

'You're not listening,' Tel said, getting annoyed. 'I've just told you I was about to lift him when Zane showed up. The skinny guy legged it.'

Damon froze, his hands paused mid-clap.

'Like I said, he's nothing to do with Zane Morelli. The next thing I knew, three men stormed out of the Starbright after the skinny kid,' Tel continued. 'At this point I made a sharp exit before they clocked me and the last thing I saw was Zane shepherding that bird he'd brought on the back of his bike into the Starbright.'

Damon looked up sharply. 'What bird?'

Tel shrugged. 'Fuck knows. A dark-haired thing. Young, with a cracking figure. I'd do her, that's for sure!'

Damon grimaced. For a horrible moment he'd thought that slut, Erin Langley, had returned from the dead, but it didn't sound like her description. But if that nosy, skinny twat wasn't scouting for Zane Morelli, then who was he? 'We have to find that Surrey kid,' he cried, lurching off his seat to retrieve the crunched-up cigarette packet.

'What for?' Tel cried in exasperation. 'I keep telling you he's nothing to do with Zane. He's not a spy!'

'Maybe not.' Damon painstakingly straightened out the crushed cardboard to read the writing. 'But what you don't seem to understand is that he must be watching the Starbright for a reason. Why else would Zane's men want him too?' His eyes glinted. 'And that's what I want to know...'

Finally succeeding in flattening out the cigarette packet, Damon jabbed it with his finger. 'PRB 1. Very posh!' He looked at Tel and Banjo. 'Get on this straight away. It shouldn't be difficult. I want that skinny bastard located and brought to me by close of play tomorrow, if not before.'

Damon shooed away a reluctant Tel and Banjo, insisting there wasn't time for another pint. They needed to get on the road and locate Posh Boy before Morelli did. The Surrey kid must know or have something of use otherwise Zane wouldn't send his men after him, therefore time was of the essence.

Meanwhile, he'd treat himself to another pint. *He* had time and deserved it too because things were looking up.

Damon had just reached the bar, his lips curling as the vision of Symonds's horrified face seeped back into his mind, when his evening was ruined by ear-splitting shrieks.

He swung in the direction of a hyperventilating woman clinging to the doorway, her terrified voice yelling about two men who had just left the pub. One had just been shot dead in the street and the other, bundled into a car and driven away.

With a sinking heart, Damon realised exactly who those two men must be.

Fuck.

THIRTEEN

MARTIN HADN'T MEANT to answer the call, he really hadn't. Unfortunately, negotiating the traffic from Battersea to Dagenham had taken up most of his concentration and when his mobile rang, being as the remaining parts of his mind were focused on Skye, Skye, Skye, he'd convinced himself that the caller must be her. *Wanted* it to be her.

'Hang on a minute, Shirley,' he gibbered, spotting a side road ahead. 'I need to pull over.'

Shirley continued talking, or rather, offloading questions down his ear. 'Please! Just give me a second.' Throwing the phone onto the passenger seat, Martin cut across the road and took a sharp left turn.

He scanned the road for a space to pull over. Just one would do. *Come on.*

Taking a second left and then a right, Martin gritted his teeth. If he didn't keep note of the route he was taking, he'd get lost. He was less than half a mile from the Starbright and didn't want to go off course and waste time when he could be moments away from bringing Skye home.

Even though his phone was on the other seat, he could still hear Shirley's voice. It hadn't stopped yet. She probably hadn't even realised he wasn't listening, but now he'd answered the call, he couldn't just cut her off. *Damn it.*

With relief, Martin spotted a space further up ahead. Gritting his teeth, he slammed his foot to the floor and roared up the road, his eyes fixed on cars coming the other way. He was getting that space before anyone else.

The car up his arse wouldn't make this easy, but he was parking whatever happened. He had to speak to Shirley so he could get on his way.

Slamming on his brakes and ignoring the blast of the horn behind, he veered into the space. Yanking on the handbrake, he snatched up his mobile. 'Sorry about that. Have y… What? Yes, that's what I'm doing now.'

Martin clenched his jaw. *Of course he was bloody looking for Skye! What the hell did Shirley think he was doing?* 'Yes, I know... Yes... No, I spoke to you yesterday... You phoned me! I can assure you that you did... I... No, but I think I may have found a lead.' *Shit! What did he say that for?* 'No, nothing definite yet.'

He didn't know what had gone on since Skye had left. Shirley said she'd been gone several weeks so what happened if she didn't want to come back? He didn't want to get Shirley's hopes up.

Martin went cold. He hadn't thought of Skye not wanting to return being an option before. What would he do if that happened?

'No, no, I'm still here.' Shirley's screeching was driving Martin to distraction. He glanced at the dashboard clock. Time was ticking but there was one question he wanted to ask that Shirley should have answered from the start. 'I need to interrupt you... No... I... Look, please listen! This is important! I need you to tell me who Skye's father is... No, I know you said... Yes, I know...'

Martin rolled his eyes. *Christ! Didn't Shirley realise how difficult this was with the vague information she'd given him?* 'Yes, but if you could ju...'

Martin stopped talking as loud sobbing down the line assaulted his eardrums. *Jesus!* 'Okay, Okay... Forget I asked. Just give me a description. Yes... I realise it's been a long time, but anything will help to narrow down... No, I haven't seen him. I haven't seen anyone.'

His grip on the phone tightened. *Even if he had seen Skye's father, how would he know? It could be anyone!* 'It's so I have a better idea of...'

Martin listened carefully to Shirley's ramblings. Well, that narrowed it down. *Not.*

'Thanks, that's helpful,' he lied, forcing away the urge to scream. 'I've got to go, but I'll call tonight, I promise.' With that, he hung up and chucked the phone to one side.

Martin pulled back onto the road, not wanting to waste another second. He ignored the ringing as it began again. It would be Shirley calling back and he couldn't, just *couldn't* speak to her again just now.

Straining to recall the haphazard route he'd taken after leaving the main road, Martin had a horrible feeling he'd gone the wrong way. He'd also left his map in the B&B and would never find the Starbright if he'd strayed off course.

Shit!

He appreciated Shirley was worried. So was he. Plus, he was getting more concerned by the second, but the description Shirley had given applied to half the world's population: *'A tall man with dark hair...'*

That could mean bloody anyone!

But if he didn't get to this place and...

Wait a minute!

Martin peered up the road. This was the same road he'd parked on yesterday. The Starbright was somewhere along here.

Realising with his wrong turn that he'd approached from the opposite direction, Martin's heart clamoured.

There it is!

Driving as slowly as possible without attracting unwanted attention, Martin crawled past the pillared opening of the

Starbright's driveway and relief soared. The place looked deserted - there were no cars out front and no sign of a bike.

This was good.

Continuing past, Martin knew being out of the car made him a target, but he couldn't park too close. Not this time.

He pulled up in front of a truck and hopped out of the Range Rover, happy the lorry obscured his motor from anyone glancing up the road. Although he doubted anyone had been quick enough to spot what he was driving and certainly wouldn't have got any details yesterday, there was no point tempting fate.

Martin walked at a normal pace, even though he wanted to run towards where he'd last spotted Skye.

Glancing around, his heart pounded. The street was deserted. He just hoped the same could be said where he was heading. Empty of those men, anyway. Still, it looked promising so far.

Approaching the house, Martin faltered. He couldn't blatantly stroll up the driveway as he'd be spotted immediately, so how could he get near the place without…

A-ha!

Ducking under an overhanging tree on the drive belonging to the house next door, Martin waded through the shrubbery, keeping close to the fence. Cringing at the rustling and cracking noises his shoes made, he ignored the twigs scraping against his legs.

He wasn't dressed for this and wouldn't usually contemplate scaling a fence from within a random stranger's garden, but it wasn't like he had experience of surreptitiously approaching a women's refuge whilst avoiding a collection of mammoth sized men who worked for one of the most feared criminal gangs in London…

Martin shook his head at the absurdity of what he was doing but decided it best not to ponder the situation. Nor worry about if anyone else, other than the man-mountains he'd seen spilling from the Starbright yesterday saw him. If a neighbour spotted him, he might be mistaken as someone attempting to break in. That wouldn't be good. The police might even think him a boyfriend of one of the women inside the refuge.

Great. His parents would be overjoyed if he got arrested on suspicion of being a perpetrator of battering women or something equally unsavoury, but if he could save Skye from these people and bring her home, it was a risk he was willing to take.

Steeling himself, Martin took one last look over his shoulder before hoisting himself over the tall fence.

• • • •

ERIN KNEW Hazel was confused as to why they'd rushed around the corner into a side road rather than waiting for the taxi outside Mr Solenzo's practice. She also knew it was dangerous being out in public and running the risk of being spotted by any of Marco's men when they presumed her already dead. But weighing up the chances of someone such as Damon Sandler being around expensive private surgeons against going through Skye's mobile phone with someone who actually believed her outweighed all other eventualities.

'Zane will go mad if he discovers you haven't got straight back in the taxi,' Hazel gasped, struggling to keep up with Erin's brisk pace. 'You haven't even told me how you got on with Mr Solenzo.'

'I told him the truth about how Skye is acting,' Erin said. 'He then asked me a bunch of questions designed to test if I knew what day of the week it was, he wrote a few things down and that was it.'

'So, you don't know the upshot?' Hazel cried, aghast.

'Nope. He said he'd be in touch and so I'll just have to wait.' Erin pulled Hazel towards a low wall fronting a townhouse. 'Come on! Here will do. We can't be long.'

Hazel allowed herself to be plonked down on the wall and watched Erin pull a mobile phone from her bag. 'Who are you calling?'

Erin's eyes glinted as she pressed at the buttons. 'No one. It's not my phone. I just hope Skye hasn't put a lock on it.'

'That's *Skye's*?' Hazel's eyes widened. 'Why ha…'

'Skye lied about not having a phone,' Erin answered. 'Shit! There *is* a code on it.' She wracked her brain for what the code could be. 'Skye told Zane she didn't have a mobile so he bought her one, but then I saw her with this. It was ringing. Who it was, I don't know, but her face showed that it was not someone she wanted to talk to.'

What would that little cow have set as a code? Come on, think! 'She didn't realise I saw her and stashed it down the back of the sofa, forgetting it in her rush to leave.'

'Zane won't like you snooping around in his daughter's stuff. He'll...'

'Yeah, I know, but she *lied*!' Erin cried. 'Why would she lie if she's not hiding something? There has to be people listed in here who'll know what games the girl is playing and why.'

Hazel paled. She understood Erin's urge to discover what was behind Skye's behaviour which was threatening her relationship and very existence but... 'Won't this look like you're as paranoid as she's made out you are?'

Erin pursed her lips. 'Maybe. But if there's something on here which proves she's up to no good, then it's a chance I'll take. Like you said, she's not on the level, so I have to do this for Zane as well as myself.'

Hazel bit her bottom lip. Whether Zane would see it that way was disputable, but being as Erin was determined... 'Come on then, but don't attempt too many codes. It will lock out.'

Pausing, Erin stared at the phone, her heart sinking. Hazel was right. If the phone became locked it would be obvious she'd been snooping. She'd also have no evidence to justify what she'd been doing. 'For God's sake! I can't think of what her code could be.'

'Let's think,' Hazel pondered. 'How about her lucky numbers? Or half of her post code? Oh shit, I forgot you wouldn't know that. Hang on! I know! What about her birthday?'

'I don't know that either,' Erin sighed. 'Wait! I do! Skye mentioned her birthday.' She grinned with renewed hope. 'Zane asked her how old she was and when she was born.' She turned to Hazel. 'It was when he brought her to Solenzo's, remember? You were there too. Can you recall what she said?'

Hazel frowned. The memory of that night was hazy to say the least. She didn't recall much of the day she'd received the worst beating of her life and when the bottom had fallen out of her world. 'I-I can't remember.'

Erin's eyes suddenly lit up. '1984! She said 1984.' She quickly tapped in the digits and pressed enter:

INCORRECT CODE
2 tries remaining

'Fuck!' Erin hissed. 'I'm sure she said 1984.'

'She did!' A vague memory returned to Hazel. 'Skye said she was born in 1984. I remember now. *February* 1984.'

Erin beamed. 'That's it! February 1984.' She began typing in the code.

'Hold on!' Hazel yelped. 'How many digits does it need? You've only got two tries left. We have to get this right.'

Erin held the screen at an angle out of the sun's glare. 'Four stars – so four letters or numbers.'

'Well, we know it's not 1984 and 021984 is too many,' Hazel reasoned. 'Try 0284.'

With bated breath, Erin entered the four digits and gingerly pressed enter. The screen blinked and then sprang to life. 'Bingo!' she cried, scrabbling to scroll through the menu. 'There's loads of things on there. Look at this! Loads of missed calls from the past couple of days alone and tons of text messages. She hasn't replied to anyone!'

'Who are they from?' Hazel itched to take the phone from Erin. Once reticent, now she was fully involved in wanting to know exactly what and who Skye was hiding from.

Erin opened some text messages and flicked through them:

> Mum: Where are you love? Please get in
> contact. xx

Erin tensed. *Mum? As in, Shirley?* She quickly moved to the next text:

> Mum: I spoke to Alyson. She says you're not
> in Scotland. Please call. I'm worried sick
> about you. Love Mum x

Erin frowned. Skye had admitted she'd lied to her mother about going away with a friend. She then spotted a text Skye had sent to herself:

> The Gables
> Caldecotte Street
> West Horsley

Was that Skye's address? Surely she wouldn't need to make a note of it? And from Zane's references to Shirley being a down and out drunk and sending Skye to shitty schools, then 'The Gables', wherever that was, didn't sound like the sort of place where someone with no money would live.

Shrugging, she continued scrolling. There were several more from 'mum'. They spanned several weeks and were all along the same vein – all begging Skye to get in contact. There wasn't one reply. Skye had ignored every message even though her mother was clearly distraught.

This was weird. From the content of these texts, Shirley didn't come across as the sort who didn't give a toss about her daughter and off her head on booze or drugs like Skye had insinuated.

Pulling her own phone from her handbag, Erin tapped in Shirley's number.

'What are you doing?' Hazel gasped. 'You're not calling that woman, are you?'

'I don't know yet.' Erin saved the number. 'But now I've got her number, I have the choice. Firstly, I want to know who *this* is.' She prodded the name 'Martin' on the missed call list, then scrolled down them. There were hundreds of calls from 'Martin' interspersed with missed calls from 'Mum'. But the missed calls from Martin far outweighed all the others put together. 'This bloke has called several times a day. Four times today alone!'

'Who the hell is he?' Hazel gasped. 'A boyfriend?'

'Well, that's the thing! Skye told Zane she'd been recently dumped.' Erin frowned. 'That was one of the subjects she said I was hounding her about.'

'Give me that!' Hazel snatched the phone from Erin's hands and returned to the text messages. 'There's lots of texts from him too. Look at this one.'

```
Martin: missing u babe xx Hope ur having a
fab time with Alyson. I'll be back tom. Can't
             wait to c u. Love u xx
```

'That was sent only a few days ago!' Erin gasped, glued to the screen as Hazel flicked through the next few messages.

```
Martin: Where r u beautiful? Ur mum says ur
       not in Scotland? Call me. Love u xx


Martin: Please let me no ur ok? Whatever's
            happened just call xx


     Martin: Skye? Babe? Where are u? X


Martin: Please text or call. I'm going crazy
             worrying about u xx
                  I love u xx
```

'It doesn't sound much like she's been dumped?' Hazel exclaimed.

'No, it doesn't! If this is the boyfriend who broke her heart by telling her she wasn't pretty enough, then it doesn't sound like that's what he thinks, let alone that they've split up.'

'So, why...' Hazel stopped as a taxi drew up in front of them and the driver wound down the window.

'I'm so sorry!' the driver gasped. 'I've been waiting around the corner. I was sure I was told to wait outside that Harley Street place.'

Erin saw the driver's panicked eyes - no doubt dreading what would happen when it got back to Zane Morelli that he'd left these women waiting. She quickly took Skye's phone from Hazel and shoved it back in her bag. 'Don't worry. We got confused about where we were supposed to meet you. There's no harm done.'

Stealing a quick glance at Hazel, both women got into the taxi, knowing that browsing through Skye's phone was at an end. But Erin now had Shirley Wilson's number, so hopefully she'd get chance to copy down Martin's too. Maybe she could listen to some of the voicemails?

Being as Skye was single-handedly looking after the Starbright in Hazel's absence, hopefully she wouldn't have had chance to return and collect the phone. But by now she would have realised that she'd forgotten it, so retrieving it and then hiding it again would be the first priority on her return. But as long as Erin got it back in the same place before that happened Skye wouldn't have a clue that it had ever disappeared.

Erin's mouth twitched with a hint of a smile. She may not have concrete evidence of what Skye was up to, but these messages showed that the version of life Zane had received from his daughter wasn't quite as it seemed. Plus, she had two contact numbers which might prove vital. It was just a question of if and *when* to ring them.

FOURTEEN

SIGNALLING TO TWO of his men to be ready to open the east warehouse door the minute he gave them the nod, Zane steeled himself to take receipt of the delivery. He hadn't expected this, but it wasn't unwanted.

He glanced at his phone. Another ten minutes before Tiger was due back. The second he'd learned *this* was inbound he'd pulled Tiger off the job of locating the skinny young man spotted yesterday.

Zane hadn't particularly wanted to pull men off the tasks he'd set them, but this must take precedence. Not knowing any of the new recruits enough to entrust them with what would shortly follow, he needed to pull back one of his closest men and being as Tiger was closer to the Thames Canning Factory than Leo, it was Tiger on route back to base.

Clenching his fists at the telltale sound of a van reversing up to the warehouse doors, Zane stood poised. The eyes he'd placed in the Blacksmith's Arms had pulled a blinder by getting results so quickly. He just hoped Sandler had something of use to say.

Hearing the rap of specific knocks on the metal doors - the code given only to members of the firm, Zane jerked his head at the waiting men, who moved in unison to slide the heavy shutters open.

Karl Hartley panted as he clambered into the Transit's gaping rear. 'I need help unloading.'

As three men followed Karl into the belly of the van, Zane tensed, waiting to pounce on Damon Sandler when he hit the deck of the warehouse. He only hoped the man was in a fit state to talk.

Sweating profusely, Karl dragged a man out of the back of the van by his feet, the corpse's head hitting the rear step on exit. 'One's brown bread unfortunately.'

Zane flinched. *Dead? Who was dead? Not Sandler?* He needed him alive and only then would the man be granted the escape of death.

His stomach lurched as the body rolled into view. It was okay - the blood spattered face of the Afro-Caribbean man with a visible gunshot in what remained of his neck, was not Sandler. 'Who the fuck is this? Where's Sandler?'

Karl nodded to the van. 'There was two of them in the pub – one of them Sandler,' Karl said, wiping sweat from his brow with the back of his sleeve. 'They went to leave so I darted outside to wait. This geezer spotted me and jumped me, pulling a gun.' His eyes narrowed. 'I had no choice but to finish him. He nodded to the second body being dragged from the van. 'I quickly battered Sandler senseless, but he's still with us.'

Zane signalled for Sandler to be dragged further into the building, his temper spiking. Here was the wanker who had tried to kill Erin, who had shot her and left her for dead. Now it was *his* turn...

He scoured the bloody, battered face of the man being dragged across the rough concrete. His hair was clumped together, wet with blood - his own or the dead guy's, Zane didn't know nor care, but Sandler was a mess that was for sure. Unrecognisable, actually.

He took a deep breath, knowing he'd have to refrain until Tiger arrived before commencing the interrogation. He didn't trust himself not to kill this cunt before he got the required information. But there was something which could be done in the interim...

'Get some buckets of water to bring this tosser around,' he growled to a couple of men. 'Sluice this shit off him. I want to see the bastard's face.'

He also wanted to witness the panic in Sandler's eyes when he registered Zane would subsequently drain his life.

The squeaking of the tap as two fire buckets were filled with water set Zane's teeth on edge, but he didn't care. Now he was set to get the latest on his brother, retribution for the attempt on Erin's life, plus take Sandler's. It was a good day.

Zane's face was plastered with a smug grin as the first bucket of water was launched over the man on the floor. This smile spread further as a low groan emanated from Sandler's smashed mouth.

The second pail of water descended on the figure now writhing in pain and Zane's pleasure intensified as blood and dirt trickled into the man's eyes.

And then his smile fell. Taking a step forward, he frowned. 'This isn't Sandler!'

Karl blinked. 'What do you mean? It's got to be! I saw him and there were only two of them in the pub and...'

'Are you *sure* there were only two of them? Is it possible one was out of sight and only two *left* the place? Because this is *not* Sandler!' Zane roared.

Karl frowned. 'It happened so quickly. After killing the first one I didn't get to properly check out who the other one was before battering him.' He ran his hand through his blond hair in frustration. 'Shit, I had to get them into the van and out of there pronto. There was this bird screaming blue murder. She'd seen the lot!'

'Okay, okay.' Zane willed himself calm. 'You did the right thing by not leaving the body on the street.' He jerked his head in the direction of the Transit still visible through the warehouse doors. 'The van needs ditching. I doubt whether there'll be anyone sniffing around, but I need to cover our backs. Take it to the crushers. They'll sort it. Meanwhile, I'll deal with this.'

Karl nodded and scrambled out of the warehouse back into the Transit.

Sighing, Zane tugged the heavy doors shut behind him. It wasn't Karl's fault. Things like this invariably didn't go to plan half the time, but at least there was no worry that anyone in the Blacksmith's Arms wouldn't keep schtum when the police turned up.

Apart from Sandler. He was the only wildcard. But knowing that prick, he'd have exited stage left the second the shit hit the fan and do his usual trick of laying low.

But that didn't help *now*.

Zane's forehead creased. Not having Sandler here to interrogate and then kill as planned was disappointing. Now they were back to square one in knowing where the bastard was, but they at least had *this* bloke, which was a good starting point...

His eyes tracked back to the groaning stranger on the floor. It was down to *him* to get as much dirt out of this joker as possible now without the guy prematurely dropping off the twig.

Zane took the crumpled cigarette packet from one of his men who had retrieved it from the groaning man's pocket:

PRB1.

So, it wasn't all bad news. That was the reg owned by the skinny kid he'd sent Tiger to find. The dead guy and whoever this alive but mangled one was, were definitely something to do with Sandler and therefore *Marco*. Them being in possession of that skinny twat's details meant the young lad was either one of Marco's brigade or Marco's bunch were onto him too for reasons unknown.

Another question to add to the list that this muppet on the floor could answer.

'Get this dickhead secured in the back room,' Zane spat. 'I'll be in shortly.'

Turning his back, he pulled his phone from his pocket. He'd planned to call Erin. She'd have seen Solenzo by now. He'd also arranged to call Solenzo to get the lowdown on his thoughts. On top of that, he'd promised Skye he'd drop in to the Starbright, but all of that had to wait. There was no choice but to deal with this situation first.

He quickly dialled Tiger's number. He needed to know how much longer it would be before they could crack on.

· · · ·

REMAINING MOTIONLESS was difficult, but it was the only option Martin had. After drawing several blanks, this new vantage point was ideal. Plus, he'd pulled it off undetected.

Half an hour he'd been watching; his senses finely tuned for noises signifying someone was creeping up behind him, but there had been nothing. Neither were there police sirens heading this way, showing the neighbours had seen nothing. That was a relief and Martin only wished his heart would take on board that for now, he was safe. The constant clattering and thumping from within his rib cage only exacerbated the pounding in his head still going for gold.

Remaining perfectly still was playing havoc with his legs too. The cramp in the back of his calves and across the middle of his thighs was all consuming. His neck wasn't having a good time either, but standing at this angle was the only way to stay out of sight *and* get a clear view of what he'd come for.

Skye.

Martin's stomach fluttered with the thought. But he didn't have to rely on just thinking of Skye's name anymore to experience the effect she always had on him because he had a clear view of her.

Ever since he'd approached this window after the other three proved a dead loss, he'd been rewarded with the sight of his girlfriend in glorious technicolour. She looked the same as usual - beautiful. Not a hair out of place - stunning. But the most important fact was that she was *unharmed*.

The weird thing was, and what Martin couldn't work out, was what she was doing. Sitting at a desk, occasionally speaking into the phone and writing in a notebook? It was like she was *working* at this place.

But why would Skye have a job here? What were the reasons behind that unless she had no plans to return home? Had she started a new life that he wasn't part of?

Martin shoved away the thoughts that terrified him down to the marrow of his bones.

It wouldn't be that. *Couldn't* be that.

Skye loved him as much as he loved her. They were meant to be together and had it all planned. She was besotted with him. Even his friends remarked on them being so in love it was sickening.

Martin's lips turned up with pleasure and decided to think rationally about the situation.

That was it! Skye must have been forced to work here. Or perhaps she was doing it for extra money whilst she continued looking for her father? As Shirley was so against Skye seeking the man out it wasn't like she'd give her money to tide her over, so a job made sense, didn't it?

But how could he get Skye's attention?

Oh, it would have been all too easy to bang on the window so that she'd rush into his arms and then they could leave.

There was just one problem preventing this. And it wasn't a small problem...

The problem came in the size of one of those men he'd seen yesterday who was standing in the corner of the same room as Skye.

Martin swallowed nervously as the man's eyes scanned the room - the same as he did roughly every thirty seconds. He held his breath as the man's gaze fleetingly passed across the window before reverting back to the stony statue-like stance he held until it was time to repeat the check again.

Martin frowned. How could he get Skye's attention when that *thing* was stationed there guarding her?

He bristled. *Guarding her or preventing her from leaving?*

Martin had to get Skye to notice him. Once she was aware of his presence, he could think of what to do next. Or at least he hoped so, because he hadn't yet thought of a single thing as to how to bypass that man.

This guy being there wasn't part of the plan - not that Martin had one, but he'd find a way. He *had* to.

Slowly pulling his phone from his pocket, Martin brought up Skye's number, careful to keep his movements slow and controlled. He couldn't afford to catch that thug in the corner's eye.

Remaining out here, watching like a ghoul was almost impossible when every nerve ending in his body was primed to rush in and take the girl he loved away from this place and the people associated with it, but he had to tread carefully.

Martin's eyes moved to the phone on the desk next to Skye. At least she had it with her so would receive this text. He could only pray she'd got a clear signal.

His fingers fumbled over the buttons as he hurriedly tapped out a message:

```
Don't make a show of looking, but I'm outside
the window of the room you're in right now.
Distract that man and then rush out of any
door. I've got you babe XX
```

Pressing send, Martin waited with bated breath for the telltale lighting up of Skye's mobile screen to show the text as received. But there was nothing...

Come on!

Keeping still, he moved only his eyes to check his phone's signal. The text had sent, so why hadn't she got it?

With perspiration forming, he resent the message and waited, only to get no response again from the phone on the desk inside.

He frowned. *What was going on? If he had a clear signal,*

then so must she.

Suddenly, his phone burst into life - the shrill ringing sending his heart down to his feet.

...Shirley calling...

Martin scrabbled to kill the call, but it kept ringing. And ringing loud enough to wake the dead.

Fuck, fuck, fuck!

He must have mistakenly turned the bloody volume up, rather than down.

Seeing Skye's head whip up in his direction at the sound, her mouth falling open in shock, Martin even managed a smile. He'd get her out even if he had to fight that bloke. Getting beaten to a pulp would at least give her the chance to escape.

But her expression on seeing him wasn't one of joy. It was what Martin could only describe as annoyance or contempt. *Hatred*, even...

He must be seeing things. She was pleased to see him, surely? Martin mouthed Skye's name through the window, hoping she could read the message behind his eyes: *Get out now. I'll get you away from here.*

And then as quickly as it had arrived, the look of pure hatred on Skye's face morphed into terror. It happened at exactly the same time the man-mountain clocked Martin's presence.

As the large man surged forward, an unfamiliar surge of anger coursed through Martin's body to see the girl of his dreams wracked with fear.

That bastard terrified her. It was proof Skye was being kept here under duress.

Hold on a second...

Martin blinked in confusion as Skye's terror became panic, then turned into tears; her arm moving frantically in his direction. *What was she doing? Why was she giving his position away?*

Now she was screaming. He could hear it through the glass

of the old sash window as she jumped from her chair to cling to the man.

Why would she go to *that* creature for protection?

Protection from whom?

This was not something Martin understood, but as the man gently moved Skye to one side before lurching from the room, he also saw a glimmer of satisfaction flit over Skye's face, along with what looked to be a *smirk*.

And hearing the distinct crashing of twigs and gravel under foot coming closer, he knew he had to act.

Martin didn't know what to make of Skye's reaction, but what he *did* know was that he had seconds to abandon his plans and get out of there.

Realising it pointless to go back the way he'd approached now this man knew of his presence, he raced up the driveway and narrowly missed slamming into a short-haired blonde woman coming the opposite way. Not stopping to excuse himself, he ran faster than he'd ever managed in his life towards the Range Rover.

FIFTEEN

ERIN PACED the small area of her sitting room a thousand times, her anxiety over why Zane hadn't called, mounting. He'd promised he'd ring or returned to find out how it went with Mr Solenzo, but there had been nothing. Zane was super busy, she knew that, but considering his insistence that she see Solenzo she'd thought he'd at least make an effort. *Unless he already knew the outcome...*

Not for the first time fear washed over her. Perhaps Mr Solenzo had made his judgement and right now Zane was putting plans into motion to have her taken to a 'facility'. Hazel had returned to the Starbright some time ago, so was she in on it too? Was Hazel telling Zane how Erin had stolen Skye's phone and gone through it with the absurd notion of proving the girl's lies?

And even though Hazel must be back at the centre, Skye hadn't returned either, so...

Oh, stop it, Erin reprimanded herself. Hazel had seen the contents of that phone as clearly as she had. The girl was up to no good. Skye would stay at the centre as she could to further ingratiate herself.

But there was one thing…

From the extra time she'd been granted whilst waiting, Erin took the chance to listen to several frantic voicemails from 'Martin'; read a text from someone called 'Alyson' asking where Skye was and then two texts had arrived whilst she'd been holding the phone.

The latest texts were identical and from 'Martin', but they hadn't made sense. *Something about a window?*

The sudden ringing of her own phone made Erin jump, her nerves in tatters. 'Hazel! Is everything all right? What? When was this?' She glanced at the clock. 'They'll be back any minute? Shit!'

Listening carefully as Hazel continued, Erin's eyebrows raised. 'No, I think it's the boyfriend... Yeah, that Martin bloke. Skye's phone received a text from him not long ago and from what you've just said, it now makes sense. Hmm... I thought she might... Yes, I understand...'

Suddenly hearing the unmistakable roar of Zane's bike, Erin tensed. 'They're here. I have to go. Thanks for giving me the heads up. And no, of course I won't mention you called.'

Ending the call, Erin positioned herself in an armchair and snatched up a magazine. She had a strong suspicion of what was likely to happen but she'd wait to see exactly how it played out.

· · · ·

'COME AND SIT YOURSELF DOWN.' Zane steered a sobbing and pale faced Skye into the sitting room, his arm placed protectively around her shoulders.

Jumping up, Erin pushed concern onto her face. 'What on earth has happened?' She moved towards Skye, reaching to touch her shoulder, but the girl flinched away from the contact.

'Give her space!' Zane barked. 'She's had a big shock.'

Burning with humiliation at being snapped out like a naughty child, Erin retracted her hand. She must wait to see if this panned out like she believed it would. 'Did something happen at the centre?'

'You could say that.' Zane's hand remained on Skye's

trembling shoulders as she sat hunched in the chair. He dabbed his daughter's tear-stained face with a tissue, his eyes blazing with fury. 'It was that fucking prick!

'What prick?' Erin frowned. 'I don't underst…'

'Skye won't admit it because she knows what I'll do,' Zane seethed. 'Some fucker was peering at her through the window in the Starbright. Terrified the life out of her it has. She reckons she's no idea who it was, but my guard believes she does because the wanker knew her name!'

Erin concealed her knowing smile. Yep. It was the boyfriend, but she'd play dumb. Now was not the time to throw what she'd learned into the mix. She'd let Skye continue digging the hole of her own demise before pulling the plug. 'Okay, perhaps if you calm down she'll find it easier to tell you what's going on.'

'I am here, you know!' Skye hissed, then realising her lapse, turned her aggressive retort into a cascade of fresh sobbing. 'It was awful him staring at me like that.'

Yeah, course it was, Erin thought. The boyfriend who clearly loved Skye and believed her to be in danger was unaware his very existence was being denied. That was bound to scare her - only in as much if this came to light it would blow her plans out of the water.

'I reckon it's this boyfriend,' Zane snarled, oblivious of Skye's spiky reaction and centring solely on that his daughter was in tears. He gently laid his hands back on her shoulders. 'Why are you protecting him, sweetheart?' he asked, his voice softening. 'After the way he treated you, why will you not tell me?'

Sniffling, Skye sobbed a little harder for effect.

Zane turned to Erin. 'From the guard's description I'm sure it's the same person I saw watching the centre when I took Skye there the other day. He must have followed us and how he knew where to find her again.'

Erin saw Skye's eyes widen with shock. *She hadn't expected that had she!* 'Maybe we should call the police?' she suggested, knowing damn well Zane wouldn't. He'd want to mete out his own justice on the man he believed had treated his daughter so badly.

In truth, had Erin not seen those texts or witnessed how Skye twisted things then she might also think along the same lines as Zane - that this man was a creep who'd progressed to stalk Skye. But she didn't believe that was the case. This was part of Skye's plan that made no sense.

'I don't want to involve the police!' Skye screeched. 'Th-that will make everything worse!'

'You *do* admit this is your boyfriend?' Erin pressed, ignoring Zane's clear look that read *'back off'*. She watched the pulse in his neck twitch faster. Zane may warn her off but she had to keep going. 'Why would the police make things worse? If this *was* your boyfriend and he's following you, then that's stalking! It's a criminal offence!'

'Okay,' Skye sniffed, her voice tiny. 'He is. He *was* my boyfriend, yes, but I don't want him to kn…'

'What I don't understand is if he dumped you, then why is he following you?' Erin raised her eyebrows.

'Erin…' Zane hissed, his eyes speaking a thousand words.

'But it doesn't make sense,' Erin pushed. She'd got Skye cornered. She'd have to admit that none of what she'd said was true and that this *Martin*, as far as he was aware, was still very much her boyfriend. Yes, there was a slim chance that he could be a deluded ex, but it was doubtful. Folding her arms she turned back to Skye. 'You must report this man to the police.'

'No!' Skye wailed. 'He terrifies me!' A fresh round of tears spilt from her eyes. 'He said if I ever caused trouble, he'd kill me. He already took my phone, that's why I didn't have one.'

Erin gaped in disbelief. This girl had no shame. Zane had said only yesterday that a girl Skye used to go to school with had smashed it, yet now it was the boyfriend? *Didn't he remember that?* 'Zane… About the phone. Didn't you say th…'

'Not now!' Zane barked. 'I need to think.'

Erin's eyes tracked back to the sofa. The boyfriend had not

taken Skye's phone. If he had, he wouldn't be constantly ringing and texting, pleading with her to let him know she was safe. Neither would that very phone be stashed down the back of the sofa.

Her eyes roamed over the cushions where the phone was stashed behind. She had to tell Zane. She had to tell him everything she knew. *NOW.*

'Zane...' Erin reached for Zane's arm as he snatched up his crash helmet, but she was too slow. Leaving Skye amid another show of convincing sobbing, she darted after him into the hallway. 'Where are you going?'

'You couldn't leave it, could you?' Zane's eyes shone bright with anger. 'You keep on and on until you break people down.' He shrugged off Erin's hand. 'I've already set Tiger on the lookout for that little cunt. I even thought him watching the Starbright meant he was something to do with Marco, but he's not. This wanker is the bastard who has been tormenting my daughter.' His eyes danced with rage as he shrugged his jacket on. 'I got a call telling me Skye was in a terrible state, so I had to go to get her and leave what I was dealing with at headquarters. Now you see fit to wind everything up and make things worse?'

'But you can't go after this boyfriend.' Erin looked over her shoulder to the sitting room. She should have got that phone and brought it with her before leaving the sitting room. She had to show Zane the messages. 'Skye's lying. She's…'

'Enough!' Zane screamed. 'Fuck me! Is there no end to your hang ups? Whatever decision Solenzo reaches, I think I've made mine! I've got to go. I have unfinished business.'

Erin almost lost her fingers as she grasped the front door at the same time Zane slammed it.

Hearing his bike start, she pressed her forehead against the cold wood of the door in despair.

There was little point chasing after him. He wouldn't listen. She could only hope Zane didn't locate that boyfriend before she'd had chance to make him listen. Skye had done enough damage. There was only one thing to do: retrieve that phone and hold onto it as evidence.

Rushing back into the sitting room, Erin stopped seeing the deserted chair where Skye had been sobbing uncontrollably only minutes ago. Hearing water running in the kitchen, she darted over to the sofa and shoved her hand down the cushion.

Fuck! The phone was gone!

She rushed into the kitchen, her heart pounding to see Skye standing with her back to her at the sink. There was no longer the sound of sobbing.

Turning around, the smirk which had returned to Skye's mouth was stronger than ever and her eyes were dry. 'Not as quick as me, are you, bitch!' she hissed.

Erin's gaze moved to the sink and as the phone bubbled and gurgled, filling with soapy water, she realised her piece of evidence was long gone.

Sixteen

STORMING BACK INTO the Thames Canning Works, Zane didn't acknowledge any of the men. They didn't register. His mind was fixed on one thing and one thing only.

He slammed through the door of one of the small storerooms located at the rear of the east warehouse, the reverberations echoing around the vast space behind him. He kicked the door closed and removed his leather jacket.

The call he'd received telling him of the intruder and Skye's distress meant there was no choice but to prematurely leave earlier, leaving instructions for Tiger to watch the prisoner until he returned.

The whereabouts of this boyfriend of Skye's was unknown at present, but being as *this* wanker was somehow involved with him, then forcing out information on that topic overshadowed anything Zane wanted to uncover about his brother.

His jaw ached from clenching his teeth. So, that prick of an ex-boyfriend had not only broken his daughter's heart, but felt it acceptable to stalk her? He'd taken her phone, smashed it up and threatened her?

Something sounding like a gravelly chuckle rumbled at the back of Zane's throat. That skinny bastard had picked the wrong girl to piss about and abuse. It was a mistake the prick would regret for the remainder of his life - which wasn't long...

Raw fury seeped from Zane's pores as the image of Skye's distress prodded him to the point of internal combustion. Oh, that little turd would pay big time for his actions. The bastard wasn't here to kick to death, but *this* one was and now he was back, the fucker held here would be the lucky recipient of his anger.

Flexing his hands, Zane snatched up a wrench, his eyes tracking back to the man secured to a chair with duct tape and cable ties.

'What's going on?'

Zane swung around to find Tiger, unable to voice what had called him away. If he spoke of it then the subsequent rage would worsen to white. White rage took away his sense and that was required to get to the bottom of this.

Stepping forward, Tiger lowered his voice. 'What's happened?'

'Nothing.' Zane didn't take his eyes off the man on the chair busy watching the interaction through his battered face. The state of his mug wasn't as bad as it would shortly be, but the cunt was listening. 'Nothing that needs to be discussed here. All I want is to concentrate on...' Stepping forward, he snatched a handful of the man's hair. '...is *this*.'

As a loud yelp escaped the man's mouth, Zane tightened his grip and pressed the head of the wrench against the man's cheekbone. 'What you need to do is start talking. And I mean, *talking*. No bullshit, no half-truth bollocks. I presume you know who I am?'

The man nodded but remained silent.

Zane dug the wrench further into the man's already bruised skin. 'I said that I wanted you to speak. That normally comprises of your mouth making both audible and understandable coherent noises, commonly regarded as "words". So, let's try again. You nodded in response to my question, so who am I?'

'M-Morelli. Zane Morelli,' the man hissed, his scalp and face burning with pain.

'Correct. Well done!' Zane glanced at Tiger. 'Should we give the guy a round of applause?' He looked thoughtful. 'Nah, sod it!' Releasing his grip, he raised his foot and booted the man squarely in the chest, causing him to fly backwards on the chair to hit the deck.

Zane stooped down to reclaim his grip of the man's hair and pulled both him and the chair back to an upright position. He stared uninterestedly at the clump of hair in his hand which had detached from the man's head and let it flutter from his fingers to the floor. Ignoring the gasping of the winded man, he pushed on. 'I need no introduction, but I feel that you do. It's only polite, so who the fuck are you and how long have you worked for my brother?'

'T-Tel,' Tel spluttered, unwilling to look into the manic eyes staring at him.

'Yeah, that's the point!' Zane quipped, winking at Tiger. 'That's what I want you to do - *tell* me why you're working for my brother.'

Tiger swallowed his chuckle. *Whatever was eating Zane, he was on top form.*

'N-No,' Tel spluttered. 'My name is Tel. Terry.'

'Okay then, Tel,' Zane continued. 'How long have you worked for Marco?'

'A while, but...'

'But he's not around?' Zane snarled. 'Shame that. But you know who's standing in for him, don't you?' Because *he* did and wanted this cunt to back up his theory.

Tel blinked. He didn't like Damon Sandler much. Didn't like him at all. But he wasn't a grass and never had been.

'Forgotten the rules already?' Snatching bolt cutters from the side, Zane lined up one of Tel's fingers between the razor-sharp jaws. 'You're supposed to be talking.'

Tel's eyes widened. In retrospect, he didn't owe Sandler shag all. The man lorded it up around the place, speaking to everyone like crap, so fuck it. Banjo was already dead and he was buggered if he was losing his fingers for Sandler. 'It's Sandler. Damon Sandler. He's running what's left of Marco's firm, but he's a cunt.'

'That's something we agree on,' Zane muttered. He listened whilst Tel spewed what Sandler's plans were and swallowed down a chuckle. Sandler had instilled no loyalty in the men he'd got onside. And to find there were only two – one, now that other geezer was lying stone dead with a bullet lodged in his neck - spoke volumes. It also underlined that the word going around about Marco being sunk wasn't just a rumour. No men. No territories. No *nothing*.

Zane moved the bolt cutters from Tel's hand. This bloke hadn't needed further prompting to spill his guts. This guy had almost *enjoyed* offloading Damon Sandler's failings to his enemy. But discovering that Sandler had his own agenda to take over the firm for himself whilst Marco was otherwise 'engaged' and avoiding retrieving what was needed for the charges to be dropped was news to him. It wasn't altogether surprising. Sandler was a Grade-A cunt on every level.

Zane would have laughed out loud at the utter shit show Marco had running the scraps of his so-called empire if there weren't more pressing things to deal with. 'Thanks for the info, Tel,' he sneered. 'Very interesting, but I want to concentrate on someone else. I want to know where *this* bloke comes into it...'

He sensed Tiger's eyebrows raise without seeing them as he shoved the cigarette packet with the Range Rover's registration scrawled on it into Tel's face. 'Who is he and what does he do for you?'

Tel peered through the swollen slits of his eyes at the cigarette packet. 'I don't know. I don't know who he is.'

Zane's temper returned with full force. Snatching the bolt cutters back up, this time he didn't threaten to use them, he went straight in and snipped off Tel's index finger at the first knuckle.

'AAARGH!' Tel screamed, the chair juddering around as he jerked back and forth.

Zane watched blood spurting from what was left of Tel's finger with dry amusement. 'Try the correct answer, dickhead or the remains of your finger comes off, as does your cock!'

'B-But it's true! I don't know who he is!' Tel wailed, his watering eyes soaking his pale face. 'We were going to track the skinny kid down when your man stepped in.'

Zane paused, the bolt cutters hovering precariously close to the base of Tel's next finger. 'Go on...'

Sweat cascaded down Tel's face to drip onto his blood-soaked T-shirt. 'He was eavesdropping on us at the Blacksmith's Arms the other night. Banjo let him go, but Sandler went batshit, convinced he was one of your spies. He sent me to follow and the bloke went to that place of yours that Marco's bird runs.'

Zane tensed. So, Sandler and therefore, Marco, *did* know of Hazel's whereabouts, as well as his involvement with the Starbright. This was not good, but being as Sandler wasn't interested in upping Marco's chances of being released, Hazel was safe for now. 'The twat is nothing to do with me!' he growled. Except that was no longer quite true. Now Skye had admitted the man who he'd thought connected with Marco, was instead her wanker of an ex, then the piece of shit was very *much* to do with him. 'Continue...'

Fixated on the bolt cutter jaws, Tel's eyes bulged. 'Sandler sent us to bring the kid in. That's his reg number on the fag packet that was in my pocket.'

'What's his name?'

'I don't know that either,' Tel gibbered. 'We were planning to bring him in and find out everything when y...'

'Yeah, yeah.' Zane cut Tel off. *So, they'd both thought this bloke was connected with the other? What a waste of time.*

'He speaks posh. He's from Surrey, Banjo reckoned. He said he was up here to meet a bird,' Tel blathered, hoping the more info he gave, the quicker he would get out of here.

'Surrey?' Zane frowned. *Interesting.* Further proof that the skinny kid was indeed the bloke who had treated Skye like a whore. Not that he needed further evidence.

'After this, I'm finished with Sandler,' Tel continued. 'That tosser can do one. I won't put up with his shitty demands any longer.' He'd swap sides. Zane Morelli wasn't unhinged like Marco. He'd told him everything he knew. He'd got the truth - the fucking lot and Zane was a reasonable man - everyone knew that.

Tel finally met Zane's piercing eyes. 'I can work for you. I'll pretend I'm still in with Sandler and get you whatever info you n…'

'That won't be necessary,' Zane said, pulling his pistol from his waistband.

'Oh, but I thought...' Tel was cut off as Zane unloaded a single bullet into his chest.

It was over quickly really. Tel was lucky.

• • • •

LEO RETURNED THE stare of the strange looking man. It had only taken about an hour to reach Guildford from Battersea, but the journey hadn't placed him in the best of moods. Neither had the selection of shitty boozers he'd been round since getting here, so if this fucked up bloke didn't quit looking at him, then he'd slam his eyes even further back into his bloody head. He wasn't in the mood for fuckers playing silly devils thinking themselves hard enough to take him on.

He'd gladly take his frustration out on the gormless bastard, but at the end of the day, that didn't get him any closer to dealing with the task in hand. Finding Shirley Wilson was a direct order from Zane and Leo always followed given orders, but he couldn't help but feel this wild goose chase after a girl from ages past wasn't something that too much time should be spent on.

Sure, he understood Zane's urge to find out the truth surrounding his daughter, but with nothing to go on, short of a name from nigh on twenty years ago, wasn't a great place to start.

Leo didn't doubt that eventually, after a thousand years of trailing around every pub in London and the Home Counties, he'd locate the mother of Zane's child, but why wouldn't Skye just tell Zane where Shirley was? Why couldn't she be straight, rather than dishing out vague crap?

Leo slugged down the remains of his pint. He hadn't liked to pry too deeply into exactly what had been said or what had been going on in Zane's life these past weeks, but he knew the man from old and respected him greatly. Zane was more than a colleague like he'd been at the start. Zane was certainly more than the boss of the Morellis, which he was now. He was a friend - almost a *brother* and Leo knew him well enough not to need to be told that things were far from good in Zane's corner.

Even things with Erin seemed to be going awry and that was depressing, considering the woman had unearthed a part of Zane that everyone believed forever extinguished.

Yet all of this had only happened since Skye appeared on the scene…

Stubbing out his cigarette, Leo sighed. This was insane. He was getting nowhere by randomly scouring pubs in Guildford for slim woman with brown hair. This was the sixth boozer he'd been in and although he had to be careful how he worded it, no one had heard of a Shirley Wilson.

Shirley Wilson, if that's who she was now known as, may not even be in Surrey at all.

Zane had suggested Surrey because Skye had mentioned it. Leo - not that he'd voice it, wasn't sure he would give credence to anything the girl said, but as he was drawing blanks left right and centre perhaps he should start going through something as obvious as the telephone directory?

Deciding to have one last pint, Leo moved back to the bar.

'All right?'

Leo stared at the man who'd sloped up out of nowhere to stand next to him. Irritation flickered. It was the same weirdo who'd been gawping at him. 'What the fuck is your problem?' he hissed, not moving his eyes from the bar. His sights were firmly set on shouting up another pint and if the barman didn't get his arse into gear, he'd jump beyond the ramp and pour one himself. 'You've been staring at me since I came in, so if you don't fuck the hell off out of my face immediately, I'll...'

'No dramas, mate!' The gangly man took a step to the side. 'It's just that I overheard you asking about a bird called Shirley Wilson.'

Leo stared at the man. 'And?'

'I don't know whether it's connected or the same girl, but my brother worked for a removal firm years back an...'

'Is this going anywhere?' Leo snapped, itching to punch this twat in the throat.

'He did an interesting house move this once for a family called Wilson.'

Leo raised an eyebrow and as the man continued babbling, he couldn't pull his eyes from the man's filthy fingernails. It looked like he'd been digging for potatoes. This bastard might pretend he knew something, when really it was a case of distracting him with the aim of rifling through his pockets.

This was stupid and a waste of fucking time.

With clenched teeth, Leo's hand formed a fist, but before he could use it, he paused. 'What was that you just said?'

The man looked nervously over his shoulder. 'I was just saying that word had it that the move was something to do with a London gang.' His face then became panic stricken, seemingly for the first time taking on board Leo's menacing appearance. 'Erm... you... you're not anything to do with any of that, are you? What I mean is, I don't wan...'

'No, mate! Not me! Shirley's just someone I used to know, that's all.' Leo adopted a clumsy version of friendliness. *He needed to hear this.*

Leaning over the bar, he grabbed the passing barman by the wrist. 'Oih! I've been waiting for fucking ages. Another pint and whatever *he's* having.' He jerked his head in the direction of the man next to him.

'Wow! Thanks, I...'

'No worries.' Leo nodded abruptly as the barman hastened to deposit two pints of Stella on the beer towel, then pushed one of the pints in the gangly man's direction. 'When did your brother do this particular move and what made it odd?'

Taking the pint, the man grinned, exposing several gaps where teeth should be. 'It was about 83 or 84. I can't remember exactly.'

Leo jerked his head in the direction of his table. 'Come and sit back down and tell me else what you remember.' Whatever this freak said might be bullshit but he'd soon work out if it was. Either way it was worth a punt before resorting to wading through the telephone directory.

Surrey was a big county after all and if Shirley Wilson was here somewhere, then any hint narrowing down her whereabouts helped.

SEVENTEEN

SHIRLEY WILSON THOUGHT at first she'd dropped off and was dreaming. Then she thought it was the TV. Sometimes the drone of other people talking on the box helped muffle the noises in her head.

But it wasn't either of those things.

Recognising the noise coming from the hallway was the slow and strange rendition of 'Greensleeves', Shirley scrabbled out of the armchair, the skewed tune reminding her yet again to replace the doorbell batteries.

Amidst the additional thoughts of whether she had any spare AAs left, the realisation that her daughter might be on the other side of the front door crashed into her brain.

Hastening along the hallway carpet, Shirley's heart pounded. *Please let it be Skye.*

But Skye had a key, so why would she ring the doorbell?

'She could have lost her key!' Shirley mumbled to herself, momentarily closing her eyes as the off-tune doorbell sounded once again. 'I'm coming, I'm coming!' she yelled, not wanting whoever was the other side of the door to give up and leave.

How she wished she'd got one of those doors with the opaque glass panels. If she had one of those, she'd be able to immediately tell if her daughter was on the other side. But then, wasn't having glass in a door a security risk? She hadn't spent all this time being invisible, only to be viewed through a thin pane of glass should the worst happen.

Finally reaching the front door, convinced the hallway grew longer every day, Shirley fumbled with the many chains and bolts. Eventually yanking the door open, the eager smile on her face fell seeing Alyson Read on the doorstep. 'Oh!'

'Hi Mrs Wilson! After your calls I thought I should come round.'

Shirley remained fixed in position and stared at Alyson, her nerves jangling. Did Skye's best friend being here signify something awful had happened? And why did everyone insist on calling her 'Mrs Wilson'? She always introduced herself as Shirley, so why was everyone so formal? She hated it. It only served to remind her that she was a phony. She'd never married, but when someone at Skye's nursery school years ago made presumptions and referred to her as 'Mrs Wilson', she hadn't argued. It was easier that way. *Much* easier.

'Erm, could I come in?' Alyson asked, continuing to hover awkwardly.

Shirley hastily stepped aside. 'Yes, yes of course. Come in, but please call me Shirley.'

Shutting the door behind Skye's friend, she gestured to the sitting room, her heart jangling. 'Have you heard something from Skye?'

Alyson paused in the sitting room doorway and turned around. 'No? I haven't heard anything. That's why I'm here. Your calls... They... they worried me so I thought I'd better come to find out what's going on.'

Motioning for Alyson to take a seat, Shirley frowned. 'What calls?'

'*Your* calls,' Alyson said patiently. 'You keep ringing to ask about Skye. You sounded really worried and...'

'I've been calling *you*?' Shirley rubbed the side of her cheek over and over with her fingers. 'Have I?' She remembered calling Martin several times. He'd promised to call back last night and hadn't. Why not? *Oh God, had something happened to him too?*

'You've called me over twenty-five times. Four times yesterday. You keep asking the same things, but I haven't seen Skye.' If Alyson admitted it, she was also a little worried. When she'd agreed to cover for Skye, her friend had promised to keep her posted, but Skye hadn't phoned once. Neither had Skye answered any of her texts or calls. 'What's going on, Shirley?'

Shirley's hands began to tremble. She hadn't been too bad today. Probably because her mind had been so mixed up, but the realisation of how long her daughter had actually been gone returned with vengeance. 'I don't know what's going on. Skye lied to me about going to Scotland, but I haven't heard from her... I'm worried she's in danger.'

Alyson bit down on her bottom lip. The only reason Shirley knew Skye hadn't accompanied her on the family holiday to Scotland was because *she'd* told her. Skye would kill her for blowing her cover, but she'd only agreed to the alibi providing no one asked.

But then, it wasn't like she could cover for Skye forever. She hadn't mentioned she was disappearing for weeks!

'She shouldn't have gone,' Shirley wailed. 'She promised me she'd never do this!' Her hands wrung furiously in her lap, the polyester of her green skirt snagging underneath her fingers. Her hand then shot up to clutch the sleeve of Alyson's jacket. 'I think she's gone to find her father,' she blurted. 'She can't. It's...'

'Her *father*?' Alyson pretended to be surprised. Despite Skye not keeping to her side of the agreement, Alyson didn't want to let her down. She had to keep up the act as best as she could. That's what friends did, wasn't it?

'Yes, her father!' Shirley's eyes darted around the sitting room like she was following the progress of a fast laser beam. 'I don't know for certain that's where she's gone, but here...' She slammed the palm of one hand against her chest. 'Tells me that's what she's done.'

Alyson frowned. She didn't have the first clue what had gone on between Skye's mother and father. Neither did Skye. It must have been a bad break-up for her friend never to have met the man or even know who he was, but then wasn't that the case with a lot of one-parent families?

But Skye had the right to know who her father was. *Everyone* deserved to know who they were, so what right did Shirley have to play God just because she'd fallen out with the bloke? 'Let's just say that you're right and Skye's gone to find him, then what's the big deal?'

'The big deal?' Shirley screeched, her face turning an odd mauve colour. 'I'll tell you what the big deal is! Skye's father is an evil, hateful man. I despise him and I don't want her having anything to do with him. With *any* of them!' Her fingers dug tighter into Alyson's arm. 'They're criminals. Bad people...'

'Shirley! You're hurting me!' Alyson yelped, attempting to prise the fingers from her arm.

'I brought Skye up well. I don't want her associating with them. I don't want her anywhere *near* them. Even a ten-mile bloody radius is too close!'

An unexpected glimmer of unease rumbled over Alyson. *Criminals? Bad people? Whatever did Shirley mean?* Skye hadn't mentioned anything about this. She stared at Shirley, watching her manic eyes darting around, her lips moving in silence to something unseen and Alyson relaxed.

Shirley wasn't quite the ticket, so it was easy to see what had happened here. For a minute then she'd taken this seriously, but it was yet another one of those times when Shirley blew something up out of all proportion.

She patted the older woman's trembling hand reassuringly, mainly in the hope that she'd release her grip. 'Look, I'm sure Skye will be back soon and there will be a completely explainable reason as to why she hasn't been in contact. I mean, are you sure she didn't tell you where she was heading and you... erm... it... it might have slipped your mind?'

'Contrary to popular opinion, I'm not crazy!' Shirley snapped. 'I know what I know and I'm telling you that Skye had gone to find her father. She's lied to me. And she's lied to Martin!' Her eyes widened once more. 'I haven't heard from him either.'

Finally dropping her hold of Alyson's arm, she returned to wringing her hands. 'Oh god. It's my fault. Martin said only the other day that he might have a lead as to where she is. He promised to call but didn't.' She stared at Alyson in horror. 'What if something's happened to him? What if...?'

'What?' Alyson cried. 'Happened to who? Who are you talking about now? Martin?'

Shirley nodded, her chins wobbling in unison. 'Yes. Martin. I told you – he's gone looking for Skye. I asked him to, but he wanted to go anyway. Yes, he did, I'm sure he did, but oh no, oh no! What if...?'

'Shirley!' Alyson cried, unease pushing forward again. 'I'm sure nothing's happened to Martin or...'

'But *you* don't know what they're like! I do and... No, no, no!' Shirley started rocking back and forth in the chair. 'What will Martin's parents think of me if something's happened to him? I'll never forgive myself. I don't even know his parents and...'

'Why don't you just ask them?' Alyson suggested. *This was crazy.* 'Just call Martin's parents. They'll put your mind at rest.'

Shirley froze - her hand paused mid-tremble. 'I don't have their telephone number. I only have Martin's mobile that he gave me when he...'

'I don't have Martin's landline either,' Alyson cut in, 'but I *do* know where he lives. I went round there once with Skye.'

She'd miss out the part about going to a party at Martin's not too long ago when his parents were away for a bridge tournament.

Alyson smiled, sure Skye was fine. Everyone deserved to know who their parents were and it was wrong of Shirley to keep that knowledge from her daughter.

• • • •

STARING ONCE AGAIN at the scrap of paper in her hand, Erin folded it and stuffed it in her pocket. This time she wasn't giving Skye the opportunity to destroy evidence.

Pulling her fingers from her pocket, convinced they were seared with the brand of the wrongness she'd committed by sneaking into Skye's bedroom Skye, Erin's pulse raced. Yet again she'd resorted to snooping through someone else's personal belongings, but after losing the proof of Skye's hidden phone and unable to show Zane that Skye was lying about everything she said, Erin was desperate to find something else.

Although she hadn't liked going down that underhand road, it had paid off.

This piece of paper contained a number which would prove to Zane that his daughter *had* been the one leaking the details to the press about the Starbright and Hazel, thereby exposing them all to Marco and putting them in grave danger. That number on the piece of paper stashed in Skye's dressing table drawer was the newsdesk at the *London Standard*.

Although Skye's plan hadn't paid off, thanks to Leo's quick thinking in deflecting the press, it *could* have worked. It could have been fatal for them all.

Why had Skye jeopardised them all like that?

Erin felt sick. She'd wanted to tell Zane of her latest discovery last night. The minute he'd come to bed she'd planned to tell him.

But Zane *hadn't* come to bed. He hadn't even come upstairs. Instead, Erin had heard the muted sounds of his familiar voice, along with Skye's from the room below. She'd considered sneaking down to listen but decided against it. She had to think of how to go about what she knew.

Her head throbbed. After the phone incident, Skye knew for *definite* she was on to her so things would only get worse, but Zane was angry, yet so besotted with his daughter, he wouldn't want to hear a word Erin said. But would this new evidence be enough to back her story up?

Padding to the bedroom door in her bare feet, Erin pushed herself up against the frame to listen. She could still make out Zane and Skye's voices downstairs. *They'd been talking all night?*

She stared at her phone. Last night she'd toyed with calling one of the contacts she'd copied from Skye's mobile before the devious little cow got rid of it, but figured she'd best sleep on it.

Well, she *had* slept on it. She'd slept on a lot of ideas - not that an hour or so of broken sleep could be called 'sleeping', but regardless of that, she still hadn't reached a conclusion. All she knew was that she had to do *something*.

She'd even thought about handing Shirley's number to Zane. Wouldn't that prove the girl had been lying? Or she could have mentioned that address she'd seen? And getting the number for the paper found in Skye's room surely counted for something?

But she hadn't done any of that. Something told her not to. Was it because she couldn't face being disbelieved again or was it her reluctance not to push Zane into contact with Shirley? If it was, then it didn't say much about her as a person, did it? But during the long hours of the night, Erin had come to realise that in truth, if Zane rekindling his relationship with Shirley was on the cards, then it would happen at some point whatever she did, so that wasn't what was behind her reluctance.

But what *was*, Erin wasn't sure. And still wasn't.

How about Martin? What if she called him and it turned out that he actually *was* a beast who had been abusing and stalking Skye? If that was the case, and there was a remote possibility it was, then giving the man information on Skye's whereabouts or *anything* about her was a hideously irresponsible thing to do.

Erin's mind swam faster. What about the friend? Alyson?

Oh God, she didn't know. She didn't know who could or couldn't be trusted.

Time was ticking and Mr Solenzo's decision regarding her mental state weighed heavily too. If that didn't work in her favour, then she could find herself in a position where no one would ever believe her.

Zane had to see sense in the end, didn't he?

But Erin wasn't sure about that any longer either. The way he'd looked at her this last couple of days frightened her and if he believed her to be hurting or damaging his daughter, then who knew what lengths he'd go to in order to protect Skye.

Erin moved away from the door and sank back down on the bed. What about Hazel?

She pulled up Hazel's number and then stopped. Hazel had already told her all she knew about what happened at the Starbright, as well as her thoughts on Skye.

Oh God, God, God! What to do?

Erin scrolled through the rest of the minimal contents on her phone and coming to a name, stopped.

This was a gamble. Possibly a stupid one, but it might be worth it. If she was wrong, then it would backfire horribly.

The fleeting glance she'd witnessed on Leo Holland's face on a couple of occasions led Erin into thinking that Zane's friend of old might have his own thoughts on this subject and the surprising understanding they'd shared in that studio in Luna Motion Films the day of the shootout had created an unspoken respect between them.

Leo had seen Erin handling getting the trafficked women to safety: he'd watched her stand up to one of Marco's cronies who'd shot at the lot of them. She'd seen the respect in Leo's eyes. They'd also shared the moment when he'd protected her with his body after Sandler shot her outside the Thames Canning Works and clocked the worry on his face as he'd raced her to Solenzo's for emergency help.

She herself had a great deal of respect for both Tiger and Leo and felt it mutual - from Leo, especially.

Making a decision, Erin pressed the call button. The way things stood she had little to lose.

EIGHTEEN

PRESSED AS FLAT as possible against the wall, Martin's gaze remained trained on the street below. What he could see of it, that was. Aside from only having a small part of the curtains open and only one eye getting a decent view around the edge of the jutting window frame, his room offered a vista consisting mainly of the Victorian B&B opposite. But if he forced his eyes at an angle, he also got a slight glimpse of the main road.

Martin wasn't sure what he expected. It was unlikely that a black van with 'Psycho Criminals' emblazoned on the side in white writing would pull up, spilling out dozens of thugs armed with baseball bats or worse, guns, to storm the building. Criminals like the Morellis tended to be more subtle - not that he knew much about that side of life.

Martin's heart thundered away in his chest. He'd parked his father's Range Rover a couple of streets away. He wasn't stupid. He'd seen enough films to know leading people like the Morellis to his door was a death wish. But this wasn't a film - it was his *life* and he didn't know what the hell to do about the crap he found himself in.

The buzzing of his phone made Martin jump. He wouldn't move from the window. It couldn't be Skye. She never answered the phone, let alone called him anymore, plus he still didn't know what to make of the look on her face when she'd spotted him yesterday.

Adrenaline pounded. How he'd escaped that guard or whoever it was at the Starbright place yesterday he didn't know. But he *did* know that so far he'd used two lives up, so wasn't in any rush to waste the remaining seven.

Successfully blocking out the continuing buzzing, Martin remained against the wall. It would be his mother or Shirley ringing. Twelve missed calls from his mum and nine from Shirley so far this morning.

What was he going to do?

He had to think. And do so *quickly*.

Martin's jaw clenched. Skye was being held against her will. Why else would she have reacted the way she had? It was obvious she'd had no choice but to pretend not to be pleased to see him and make out she was terrified. How else would she get the chance to escape otherwise?

The contemptuous sneer she'd worn when they'd locked eyes was for the benefit of that man. It made sense now.

Martin's hands balled into fists. He'd let Skye down. He'd let her down and left her there. She'd only given away his location as a deflection tactic, he realised that now. That huge man was meant to chase him and then Martin could have doubled back on himself to return for Skye.

And what had he done?

He'd legged it like a spineless bastard, that's what.

Sweat beaded on Martin's forehead. Now he was trapped like a prisoner, leaving the girl he wanted to marry at the mercy of psychos.

His phone buzzed again.

Should he answer it? What if it was Skye after all?

Martin's mind span over and over, round and round as logic argued with his heart.

If it was Skye, what would he say? *'Oh, hi babe. Sorry I ran away like a girl. It won't happen again...'*

But would it?

He stared at the phone, the screen's glow illuminating the gloomy room behind the half-pulled curtain.

Martin swallowed drily. Now he had *two* sets of lunatics after him: the thugs holding Skye who were connected with the Morellis and the other lot, who from what he gathered, were the Morelli's *enemies*. He'd already had a narrow escape from both. This meant they'd *all* be looking for him.

But no one had come yet…

Fuck it. He'd answer the phone.

Lurching away from the window, Martin had almost reached his mobile when the hammering of his bedroom door rendered him paralysed.

Shit! They'd found him! But which lot?

His tongue caught in his throat as he held his breath. *Perhaps they'd go away?*

The door's pounding continued and the phone continued buzzing. Martin wanted to lie on the floor and vanish into the floorboards where no one could find him.

'Mr Bolt?'

Martin stopped descending into full blown hysteria. Pulling himself together, he moved to the door, his legs jerky and stiff. Opening it, he tried to make his face appear less frozen in abject fear. 'Good morning, Mrs Billard,' he croaked.

The landlady of the B&B ran her eyes over Martin, her brows knitting with concern. 'Oh my goodness! Are you all right, Mr Bolt? You look like you've had a nasty shock!'

'I'm fine.' Martin followed this statement with a strange gurgle that was supposed to be a laugh but had gone horribly wrong. 'You made me jump, that's all. I was… erm… reading a book.' He dropped his grip from the door and tucked his hands behind his back so the landlady wouldn't see them shaking.

'I was just checking to see if you wished to keep this room any longer? It's just that... erm… you were due to check out this morning and...'

'Oh! I meant to come and see you yesterday about that,'

Martin lied. *Fuck!* He hadn't bargained on staying here more than a couple of days, but there was no way he could leave now. 'Could I stay for another few days? Perhaps three?'

Mrs Billard tutted loudly. 'Hmm… I'd have to re-arrange the rooms. Someone is arriving today who specifically requested this particular one.'

Martin raised his eyebrows, not believing that anyone would go out of their way for *that* view. 'I would be ever so grateful, Mrs Billard,' he blathered. 'I'd pay extra of course...'

'Okay then, dear,' Mrs Billard said, now all smiles. 'I'll put you down for another three days. Let me know if you need anything.'

Yeah, like a gun and a map of the live location of where all of the people after me are right now would be good, he thought, shutting the door.

Martin sat back on the bed and pulled his shoes from underneath. Enough mincing around. What was he? A man or a mouse? He'd go back to the place where he should have stood his ground yesterday.

And this time he wouldn't leave unless Skye was with him.

• • • •

LEO WIPED AWAY A dribble of brown sauce escaping from the corner of his mouth and dabbed his fingers on the paper napkin accompanying his bacon sarnie. The sandwich was dripping in grease but he didn't care. It was what he needed right now.

His heavy eyebrows furrowed. So, starting to look for Shirley Wilson in Guildford was a top guess. What that gangly bloke in the pub had said – if he were to be believed, proved that Shirley *had* gone to Guildford.

With the help of a few more pints, Gangly had said that his brother had been paid a very tidy sum to move the Wilson family from Battersea to Guildford. Sworn to secrecy, his brother landed a tidy wedge never to speak of it. Enough wedge to buy a house for cash the very next month.

But *why*?

Leo frowned. Apart from the glaring reason that the Wilson family had wanted no one to know of them leaving nor of their new whereabouts.

Not wanting to drop his brother in the shit, Gangly had kept his trap shut, but now this brother had died the secrecy was unimportant.

But was it the same Wilsons?

That remained to be seen, but it was plausible. It made sense with the reference to the connection with London criminals – the link to the Morellis – Zane. And Guildford was in Surrey. It added up.

But Gangly couldn't say *where* in Guildford the address was and with the brother no long being on this mortal coil, there was no one to extract further details from. Like it or not, there was no other option but to take Gangly's information on face value. It wasn't like Leo had a host of other options.

If Gangly was to be believed, Shirley Wilson moved here in 1983 or 1984. But was she still here? And if so, where?

Back to the telephone directory and asking around the boozers again? At least he was looking in the correct area.

But where to start?

Leo stared through his windscreen at the row of shops in front of him. Having parked up just outside the town centre was as good a place as any to start, but *where* exactly?

Shrugging and not averse to continuing searching for Shirley anywhere containing bars, Leo grinned. He may as well start in *that* one. It looked ropey enough.

He squinted further along the road to where a 1960s built pub stood. That would do.

Tugging his keys from the ignition, Leo was getting out of his car when his mobile rang. Hoping it wasn't Zane wanting news, he glanced at the screen:

...Erin calling...

Frowning, Leo put the phone to his ear, hoping nothing had kicked off. 'Hey, Erin. Everything okay?' His brows knitted hearing her question. If Erin wanted to know whether Zane had sent him to look for Shirley that wasn't for him to discuss. 'Maybe you should have this conversation with Zane... What? Say that again.'

He sat forward, suddenly aware this might be helpful. *Very* helpful. 'And where exactly is that?'

· · · ·

ERIN PACED THE ROOM, the phone burning a hole into the side of her head. She knew she shouldn't be doing this - knew she was interfering. She also knew she should have gone to Zane with this, not Leo.

Her skin prickled. If she'd got this wrong it could blow up in her face. It was guaranteed to be the final nail in the coffin, that's if there were any left which hadn't already been driven home.

But she had to try for her, for Zane - even for this ex-boyfriend, Martin.

Refusing to allow her mind to wander, Erin pulled her concentration back to Leo, her head pounding. 'No, I don't know exactly whose address it is. No... I...' Pursing her lips, she moved the phone away from her ear and stared at it. *Leo was as stubborn as Zane!* 'Yes, I get that it's Shirley you need to find.'

So, Zane *had* sent Leo on Shirley's trail? Hardly surprising Zane hadn't mentioned it, considering he believed her to have a hang up about Skye and the mother. 'Listen, Leo. Like I said, it could be Shirley's place, but it could also be the address of the friend or the boyfriend... Yeah, the one that turned up.'

Erin continued pacing, the ear that the mobile wasn't against tuned for any sign that Skye or Zane had ventured upstairs. 'No, I got the address from a text Skye sent to herself... The phone? Don't ask! It's a long story... yeah...' *She'd tell Leo about Skye's mobile another time - if there was another time after this...* 'Then I saw a reference about a postcard. You know she'd made-up shit about going to Scotland? I reckon she planned to send a postcard from here pretending she was up north. I don't know how it... Yeah, that could be the case.'

Erin moved to the window. 'Wait! Don't you see? Whoever's address it is, it's *got* to be one of them. And if it's not Shirley, then whoever lives there must know where she *does* live.'

And once that was known, with any luck it should be possible to get to the bottom of Skye's lies and what she was trying to achieve.

NINETEEN

PETER BOLT scowled as Fiona paced the lounge. At this rate she'd wear out the carpet and being as she'd insisted on that Axminster stuff, he wasn't forking out another bloody fortune to patch up bald bits. *She worried far too much about that boy. It wasn't healthy.*

'Give it a rest, Fiona!' he muttered. Folding up his copy of *The Times*, he placed it on his lap. 'Martin's nineteen years old. You can't expect him to phone every five minutes!'

Fiona swung around, her stiff, lacquered hair quivering. 'He's been gone two days now and on the rare occasions he misses one of my calls, he always rings back,' she yelped. '*Always*! But he hasn't this time. That's why I know something is wrong.'

Peter wanted to roll his eyes. He almost did, but luckily stopped himself just in time. It should be *him* who was worried. It wasn't Fiona's Range Rover Martin had taken, was it? If that stupid boy had pranged it and was skulking around rather than facing the music, then he'd come down on him like a ton of bricks. If Fiona could drive and had her own car, then she'd realise it mattered.

Having received no response, Fiona's eyes narrowed. 'I

know what you're thinking. You're more bothered about that bloody car than your son! For God's sake, Peter, you've got three cars! Shouldn't you be wondering whether Martin's lying dead in a ditch?' The image of Martin's mangled body lying at the side of the road under a pile of crumpled metal made her hands tremble. 'I'm calling the police to report him missing.'

'Don't be ridiculous!' Peter scoffed. 'He's been away with his friends for forty-eight hours, which you said was fine for him to do! Do you really think the police will class that as "missing"? A nineteen-year-old at the coast with his mates at his parents' knowledge?' His eyes narrowed. 'Or should I say, *yours*. You were the one insisting I lend him the car and that the trip would be good for him, not me. I told you he shouldn't go.'

Fiona's mouth fell open. 'You're blaming me for this? *Me*?' Her eyes welled up and her bottom lip stuck out the way it always did during an argument.

Peter sighed. *Now he'd never hear the end of it.* 'No, I'm not saying that. But you spoil him, Fiona. You should back me up occasionally rather than joining forces with Martin so that he gets his own way.'

'I do not do that!' Fiona's cheeks turned pink. 'Has it crossed your mind that I want him to enjoy himself before he goes to university?'

'Then why are you mithering about him not returning your calls?' Peter countered, getting irritated. 'Has it not crossed *your* mind that the reason he didn't answer was because he *is* enjoying himself? He probably gets stick off his friends for always having his mother on the phone!'

Fiona stamped her foot - actually stamped it on the carpet. Not that it made any noise, the carpet was so thick. 'So, now I'm embarrassing my son?'

As Fiona's voice reached screaming pitch, Peter resisted the temptation to put his fingers in his ears. Instead, he did what he knew he would end up doing anyway.

Reluctantly pulling himself off the Laura Ashley sofa, he placed his arm around his wife's shoulders. After her usual initial resistance, Fiona permitted him to pull her against his chest for a stiff and uncomfortable hug. 'You don't embarrass him,' Peter soothed. 'I'm sure there's nothing to worry about. Martin will return your call by the time we sit down to dinner tonight and he'll be upset to realise he's worried you so much.' *But if the boy had ballsed up the Range Rover then he really would be sorry.*

'I hope you're right,' Fiona sniffed.

'I am!' Moving his head so Fiona's hair and the cloying stench of her hairspray didn't suffocate him, Peter stared out of the bay window overlooking the front garden and driveway at the space where his Range Rover should be.

He frowned at the figure approaching up the long gravel driveway. 'Who the bloody hell is that?' he grumbled. 'It's not another one of those oddballs from your Women's Institute thing, is it?'

'They are not "oddballs", Peter!' Fiona pulled away from her husband to see who he was referring to. 'Why do you always insist on making derogatory remarks about anyone from th... Oh my God!' Fiona stared at the overweight creature shambling up the driveway. 'Who on earth...?'

'If it's not one of your cronies then it must be one of those people collecting for charity again.' Peter's thin lips flattened. 'It looks like she could do with some help in a few departments!'

Fiona stared at the woman's unflattering cardigan and the chins undulating in waves as she stumbled closer to their front door. 'She... she looks a bit...'

'Mad?' Peter scoffed. 'Christ, she's probably one of those damned Jehovah people again.' He moved towards the lounge door. 'I'll go and get rid of her.'

· · · ·

WITH THE BACKGROUND NOISE of a woman rattling on about how unacceptable it was for John Prescott to have punched a bloke who'd whanged an egg at him, Damon glared at the radio balancing on the windowsill. Putting it there to trail the aerial up the side of the curtain was the only way to get a reception in this dump and even then it was crap.

He didn't like the radio - especially the shitty local stations. He certainly didn't give a fuck about why this stupid bitch found it so offensive for Prescott to retaliate. What did she expect? Personally, Damon thought it would have been better all round if the protester had launched a hand grenade rather than an egg. That *he* was stuck in this shithole of a flat whilst people like Zane Morelli were released to screw people's lives up only underlined the state of the country. And it was people like John Prescott's fucking fault!

But Damon only had this stupid programme on in the first place to drown out the noise of those chavs arguing in the flat above and to deflect his mind from everything else. But nothing worked.

Sitting at the kitchen table, he clenched his fists, his frustration rising to a level which had to be doing something unpleasant to his blood pressure.

What was he supposed to do now? He couldn't sit here forever. He must be rational. Following the shooting at the Blacksmith's no one had come knocking. He'd done the right thing by disappearing in the opposite direction whilst the rest of the pub remained in a state of chaos. It wasn't like *he'd* pulled the trigger, so didn't know why he'd felt obliged to keep his head down since.

He hadn't seen who'd done it either, but he knew who was *behind* it...

Damon's nails cut into the palms of his hand.

Zane Morelli. Zane or one of his men had been the one with the gun.

Which meant that one of *his* men was dead.

Damon dragged his fingers through his unwashed hair. *But which one? Tel or Banjo?*

The cold fear which had become a constant companion of late spread up Damon's back. That woman who'd witnessed the shooting had screamed that both men were shoved into the back of a van and driven off. Knowing the gaffer of the Blacksmiths, any blood on the pavement would have been immediately sluiced away. Nothing would remain suggesting anything untoward had taken place.

No one wanted the police hanging around to slow up trade. Or worse, completely shutting the place down for forensic investigation.

But where did that leave *him*?

Damon's frown was so ingrained it looked like his head was splitting. Whichever man was left - Tel or Banjo, would either be dead or grilled for information.

He shrugged, unsure why he was worrying. Neither Tel or Banjo would have fessed up information on the behest of Zane fucking Morelli!

But that meant something else. *Both* of his men must now be dead...

Standing up so rapidly it made him dizzy, Damon stumbled over to the window and glared at the radio again for good measure.

Now he had no one. *No fucking one.*

How could he get anything done on his own?

And if the woman still whining on the bloody radio didn't shut the fuck up then he'd...

Lurching forward, intent only on turning the radio off before he smashed it to smithereens, Damon paused, his hand frozen midway from yanking the plug out of the wall.

"...We interrupt this programme to bring you breaking news..."

Sweat broke out as Damon remained motionless, listening. Had the police found evidence at the Blacksmith's? Had they found something linking it to him?

If the police had interviewed people and someone was demented enough to blab that *he'd* been sitting with the men snatched from the street, then...

"...A report has just come in regarding the sudden death of a solicitor during a meeting with a client..."

Damon exhaled with relief. Thank God! It was nothing to do with the shooting, the Blacksmith's Arms, him or anyth...
Wait!
He edged closer to the crackling reception with the misguided notion that it might become clearer.

"...The incident happened in a Battersea police station around 11.30 today. At present it is unknown whether there are suspicious motives involved..."

Damon felt a rock the size of Gibraltar wedge in his throat. A Battersea police station? A dead solicitor? Fuck! Had Marco gone and killed Symonds?

"...The solicitor, who was pronounced dead at the scene by attending paramedics, has not yet been named..."

Damon's eyes swivelled towards the clock. The report said 11.30. It was now just past one. Symonds's twenty-four hours had expired. A bit like the man himself, by the sound of it. It *had* to be Symonds.
Jesus H Christ. *He* was linked with Symonds...
Fuck!
Yanking the plug from the socket, Damon ignored the chunk of plaster that came off the wall at the same time. He also bypassed the radio clattering from the windowsill to land on the floor with an unpleasant cracking sound.
He paced the room in agitation. 'Fuck, fuck!' he muttered and almost dropped dead from shock when his mobile rang.

TWENTY

WITH A FORCED SMILE at the guest perched on the edge of his sofa, Peter steered his wife out of earshot into the hallway. 'Why the hell did you invite her in?' he grumbled. 'I knew she was one of your cronies from that blasted women's group you insist on attending!'

He dragged his hand over his cleanly shaven jaw. 'For pity's sake, Fiona. That woman is never all there! What will the neighbours say? Why do you insist on being so bloody charitable?'

He couldn't believe this. He'd been just about to shut the door in the babbling fruitloop's face when Fiona had intervened and ushered that woman into the lounge - *their* lounge. That creature wasn't the sort of person he wanted in his house. She was talking to herself for Christ's sake!

God's Teeth, he hadn't understood a thing the woman said, she was talking so bloody fast. Escaped from somewhere, had she?

No, no, no. He'd had enough of this. First Fiona overshadowing his decision about Martin and the Range Rover and now this? He wasn't putting up with it anymore. 'I'm sick of you riding roughshod over my decisions and...'

'Peter!' Fiona hissed. 'You're not listening. You *never* listen. You didn't listen to what she said - the same way as you're not listening *now*.' Her lips pursed in disdain. 'It's a good job *I* listen!'

'What are you talking about?' Peter gasped. 'There's nothing a woman like that can say that I would be marginally interested in. Bloody hell! Do I look like I want to enter a raffle to win a knitted tea cosy or whatever she's peddling?'

'Keep your voice down!' Fiona spat out of the corner of her mouth. 'She'll hear you!'

'I don't care!' Peter shook his head. 'Tell her to go back to the WI and...'

'She's not from the Women's Institute, you idiot!' Fiona barked. 'She Skye's mother!'

Peter frowned. 'Skye? As in...'

'Yes, you know - the girl our son's been dating for the last seven months.'

Peter's mouth fell open, his bottom jaw slack. '*That* is Skye's *mother*?'

'Yes it bloody well is and if you'd bothered listening to anything, you'd already know that.'

Peter's head span in the direction of the lounge where he could still detect the faint murmurings of the woman on his sofa. 'But...'

'But nothing! Just shut up and go back in. We're being exceptionally rude. You know Martin is besotted with Skye, so make an effort.' Grabbing Peter's sports jacket sleeve, Fiona tugged her husband back towards the lounge. 'Has it not occurred to you that she may have heard from Martin?'

And Fiona would be lying if she hadn't toyed with the idea that maybe her son hadn't gone off with his mates after all. He could have eloped with Skye the minute the girl returned from her holiday in Scotland. It would explain his radio silence. Perhaps that's why Skye's mother was here?

Refusing to let this thought gain traction, Fiona straightened her skirt. Plastering on a smile, she glided into the lounge. 'I'm sorry about that, Mrs Wilson. My husband is fretting over something from work.'

'Please call me Shirley,' Shirley said, her wide eyes flicking between Peter and Fiona. 'I didn't mean to disturb you. I wouldn't normally take it upon myself to descend anywhere uninvited. I know we've never met and oh... I didn't know what else to do...' Her hands began their usual wringing. 'Alyson gave me your address. I presume you know Alyson? Alyson Read? She's a friend of Skye's. Her best friend, actually. I'm sure Martin knows her too and s...'

'So, Mrs Wilson – Shirley.' Peter's gaze fixed on the rhythmic knitting of Shirley's fingers. 'What can we do for you?' He still couldn't quite believe this was Skye's mother! That girl was such a pretty little thing, yet this woman - well, as far as Fiona's dismissal of his opinion of the WI, the mother *did* look like she'd just emerged from behind a White Elephant stand at the local fete.

'I... I don't know where to start!' Shirley yelped. 'I... erm… Have you heard from Martin?'

Peter frowned. 'We presumed you'd come to speak about Skye.' Had Martin got the girl in the family way? With university coming up that was the *last* thing the boy needed. *He* didn't need it either because then he'd be lumbered with dealing with this lunatic as part of the family. 'Martin's not here at the moment.'

'I know.' Shirley looked close to tears. 'I-I was hoping that he'd come back here instead of... He... he didn't phone me when he said he would and I'm worried... I mean, why didn't he call like he promised, unless something has happened? He said he would, but...'

'As I said, Martin's away with friends, Mrs... Shirley, so...'

'Wait a moment! Why did you expect Martin to call you?' Fiona butted in, her sense of alarm clanging. 'How do you know he's not here? Has Skye told you? Has she heard from Martin? He...'

'I don't think Shirley needs to know silly details or what

Martin had for breakfast, dear.' Peter placed his arm on Fiona's and gave her a sideways glance. He didn't want it common knowledge that his wife was freaking out because their nineteen-year-old son had *dared* to spend two days with friends without calling her.

'No, Peter!' Fiona glared at her husband. 'Mrs Wilson just said that she *knew* Martin wasn't here and that he'd failed to call her too. I need to know if Skye has heard anything.' She met Shirley's eyes in a show of female solidarity. 'What Peter said about Martin being away with his friends is true, but I couldn't get hold of him yesterday either and so...'

'You women worry too much,' Peter harrumphed. *This was ridiculous.* Shirley Wilson didn't know what day of the bloody week it was, so why was Fiona wasting her time attempting to translate what the hell the woman was talking about? There was obviously something wrong with the woman and he'd got better things to do than listen to crazy ramblings.

Hearing that Martin had failed to get in touch with his own mother shunted Shirley off the edge of the precipice she'd been balancing on and was unable to stop the wail escaping her mouth.

'Jesus!' Peter's stomach flew into his throat at the noise. He stared at Shirley whose eyes were rolling almost to the back of her head. 'Christ, Fiona! Is she having a fit?'

Fiona rushed to Shirley's side, but another screech stopped her in her tracks.

'I knew it!' Shirley screeched. 'It's proof something bad has happened. Both to Skye and Martin.' Her eyes implored Fiona. 'I'm so sorry. I really am. I should never have asked what I did of Martin. I should have *known* they would go for him too.' Her fingers clawed the chiffon of Fiona's ruffle-sleeved top. 'He said he had a lead, but they must have caught him... Oh God, oh God...'

'What?' Fiona yelped, looking to Peter in distress. 'What do you mean by you shouldn't have sent him? Sent him where? Who would "go for him"? What's this about?'

'Martin's away with his friends, Shirley,' Pete repeated for the third time. Striding across the room, he forcibly detangled the woman's fingers from Fiona's top. 'I'm sure Martin has told Skye his whereabouts. If you're worried, then why don't you ask her and then y...'

'I can't!' Shirley babbled. 'She disappeared a fortnight ago and I haven't heard from her! She said she'd never do this to me. Said that she'd never go to look. She *promised*.'

Fiona saw the slight shake of Peter's head but she ignored him. 'But Skye went to Scotland, didn't she? That's what she said the last time we saw her before we went away - that she was going to the Highlands with Alyson.'

'No, no! Skye lied! She never went,' Shirley wailed, her welling tears on the verge of cascading down her pudgy cheeks. 'I shouldn't have sent Martin to seek out criminals.'

'*Criminals*?' Fiona squeaked. 'Wh…?'

'Look, I'm sure Skye will be back soon,' Peter said quickly, his attempt sounding fake even to the most altruistic soul. Forcibly helping Shirley off the sofa, he steered her towards the lounge door.

Fiona moved to follow. 'Peter, I...'

'Why don't you leave us your number, Shirley?' On his way into the hall, Peter let go of Shirley with one hand to grab a pen and pad off the wooden bureau. 'We'll call you the minute Martin gets in touch. I must say, I'm not happy to hear that he hasn't called you like he promised.' *If Martin had promised to call this nut-nut back he'd eat his hat. His son wouldn't have spoken to the woman in the first place.*

'I...' Shirley turned to Fiona but the door to the lounge was already closed.

'Here you are.' Peter placed a pen in Shirley's fingers and held out the pad. 'Write your number there. We should be in contact anyway considering Skye and Martin are getting serious about each other. She's a lovely girl, by the way.'

Shirley scrawled her address and phone number onto the pad. 'You'll call me the minute you hear anything? Perhaps I should take your number too?'

'No need, no need.' Peter opened the door and cleverly nudged Shirley through it. 'You should come over for dinner one night. I'll call to arrange a convenient day as soon as I've spoken to Fiona.' *Like hell he would!* 'Take good care of yourself now, Shirley. All the best.'

Peter shut the door and sagged against the wood. Thank God for that. Just like he'd suspected the minute he'd clapped eyes on the woman. *Unhinged.*

• • • •

LEO CHANCED MOVING his gaze from the grand house at the end of the driveway to admire the area in general. Shoving his can of Tango to one side, he reached across the van's passenger seat, grabbed his phone and brought up the text Erin had sent following the phone call.

The Gables, Caldecotte Road, West Horsley

Yep, this was definitely the place.

Leo frowned. From what Zane had said, the picturesque village set in rolling countryside not too far from Guildford wasn't what he'd imagined to be where Shirley Wilson resided. Where was this shitty school Skye had attended? Where were the backstreet boozers full of slobs and perverts that were to be his first ports of call in tracking down the woman from Zane's youth?

It certainly wasn't here.

Leo looked down the wide road punctuated with trees, long driveways and equally large houses. This area certainly wasn't shabby. But then, like Erin said, this could be one of three people's houses. It could be Shirley's, Skye's cunt of a boyfriend, or a friend.

He stretched out his back to give his big frame some respite from the cramped space of the van's cab. If this wasn't Shirley's abode, then whoever lived here must know Skye and therefore know Shirley. If it was the boyfriend's place, then he'd have the added bonus of knowing where the bastard that Skye had been involved with was returning to. This could work out well.

The question was, how did he go about it? It wasn't like he could stroll up and knock on the door. Well, he could, but old habits die hard and that wasn't the way he worked.

Perhaps he should give Zane a bell to ask how he wanted him to proceed or...

Who was that?

Becoming rigid with a sudden movement in the direction of the house, Leo adopted his usual motionless poise and honed his vision in on the pillared entrance of the building.

He squinted against the glare at the figure shambling down the gravel driveway. From the rough description he'd been given that certainly wasn't Shirley Wilson. Was it a cleaner, perhaps?

Leo's eyes moved back to the now closed front door of the house. *Who was that man letting the cleaner out?*

If this *was* Shirley's house, had Skye ever mentioned a stepfather? Leo frowned. He didn't know; it wasn't his business, but it *was* his business to get the required info.

As the woman who'd left the target house reached the end of the driveway and moved towards the van, Leo toyed with getting out to speak to her. He stood more chance getting info from a cleaner than whoever was behind those fancy doors.

As the woman shuffled closer, his brows knitted at her strange gait and the way her many chins wobbled. What was even more disconcerting was that her lips were working ten to the dozen.

Was she talking to herself?

She had to be. There was no one else around. Plus, her eyes were darting around like a startled rabbit and that was the fourth time she'd glanced over her shoulder in a matter of seconds.

As she shuffled past, her eyes swivelled towards Leo's and locked on his. After less than two seconds, he experienced the urge to look away.

Turning his head to stare out of the windscreen at the empty road ahead, he shuddered, confused. He'd never been the one to break eye contact first. *Ever.* It was one of his most unnerving traits.

What the hell was going on?

He shuddered for the second time. There was something about that woman. Looking behind her eyes was like seeing into pits of despair and desperation; of longing and all-encompassing fear. They screamed of heart-wrenching misery and he didn't think he'd ever experienced anything so profound before. Or disturbing.

Shaking his head, he glanced in his wing mirror at the woman continuing up the road.

He could follow. He could find out where she was going and pick her brains about the residents of The Gables before steaming in.

But that option was not viable. Cleaner or not, she was a sandwich short of a picnic and he couldn't comfortably rely on *anything* that someone like her said, the poor cow.

Leo gritted his teeth. This left him back at Plan A.

It was fine. He'd go to the house and let himself in through a window or by whatever means. Rich folk made the mistake of believing no one had the audacity to be so blatant. And that was good because when necessary, Leo was more blatant than most. He'd been trained well.

And there was no time like the present.

TWENTY ONE

NODDING A CURT THANKS at the door being opened for him, Damon followed the police officer down the corridor. Outwardly he presented a nonplussed demeanour, but inside he was gradually unravelling.

In contrast to his assumptions, Marco had more clout in here than Damon had thought. How else could the man get access to the telephone? Had Symonds played more cards than he'd realised to put Marco in a better position than he'd been led to believe?

Damon's eyes narrowed. He wouldn't have put it past the old bastard, Symonds, to have kept him completely out of the loop.

How the bloody hell any of it had been achieved, he didn't know, but Marco had managed it and that worried him. It also meant there was no choice but to acquiesce to the demands to attend the station for an immediate meeting.

At least Marco was still here though. *For now.* But something was going on and now it looked like Symonds was dead. Dead, Damon suspected, courtesy of Marco.

'In here.' The officer pushed open the door to a room.

Seeing Marco casually sitting behind a standard police

issue interview desk, Damon's concern rose further as the door slammed behind him. *Weren't any officers going to remain? He wasn't a solicitor for God's sake, so how...*

His eyes swivelled in Marco's direction. Not fully - he didn't like locking eyes with this man unless he had to, but he forced his eyeballs in the general direction which was near enough to spot the snarl on Marco's face - his standard relaxed expression.

Damon double checked the room was definitely clear of police. 'Was it you?' he hissed.

The corner of Marco's mouth twitched and his eyebrow raised in mock amusement. 'Was *what* me?'

'You know damn well what I'm talking about,' Damon whispered. 'Symonds. Is he dead? Was it your doing?'

'You heard about that quickly.' Marco smiled benevolently. 'Hmm... a tragic incident...'

'It came on the fucking radio as breaking news!' Damon remained as far from the table as possible. If Marco had killed Symonds and being as there was no one else in this room, the same could happen to *him*.

'Forget Symonds.' Marco flicked his hand dismissively. 'I want to know about *this*.'

Damon stared at the newspaper Marco slapped on the table. Now he had no choice but to move closer. *Damn.* 'What is it?'

Marco steepled his fingers underneath his chin. 'You tell me...'

With a sinking feeling, Damon pushed through the invisible forcefield of doom and reluctantly sat down opposite Marco, He stared at the article the paper was open at.

Mystery Shooting Reported

Seeing this headline, Damon suspected his skin was turning a funny greenish colour.

'Read it!' Marco barked, jabbing his finger on the article.

Damon hurriedly obeyed orders and scanned the text:

"Authorities are baffled by a distraught call received from a woman reporting a shooting outside the Blacksmith's Arms public house yesterday.

Armed police rushed to the scene but found nothing to suggest any such incident had occurred. The pub and its customers were operating normally. Interviewing several patrons present at the time of the alleged incident confirmed nothing amiss was seen or heard. The same response was gathered from residents on the road in Battersea where the pub is located.

However, when The London Standard *spoke to the woman who placed the emergency call, Miss Levett was adamant the shooting did occur.*
Dorothy Levett, 78, said, "I've lived here all my life. I looked out of the window because I heard a van. Two men were leaving the pub - it's a horrible place - always trouble. Then another man jumped from nowhere. He shot one man, bashed the other and put both in the back of the van before screeching away. It's a disgrace!"

When The London Standard *asked the police for a response to Miss Levett's statement it was said, "...there was no evidence found to corroborate a shooting. Miss Levett is well known to us for reporting alleged crimes..."*

If anyone witnessed unusual behaviour or saw anything of relevance, please report it as soon as possible.

'Well?' Marco growled, breaking the silence. 'Why do I have the gut instinct this wasn't some old bat's dementia kicking in and that it was something to do with my brother? The Blacksmith's Arms has always been the watering hole of men working for me, so am I right?'

Damon fidgeted on the uncomfortable plastic chair. *Bollocks.* There was no choice but to level with Marco about Tel and Banjo now. Plus, he'd also have to tell him that it was definite Hazel was in charge of the Starbright Centre. And worse, he no longer had Symonds left to blame for withholding information.

· · · ·

PULLING UP OUTSIDE the Starbright, Zane jumped off his bike and loped up the entrance steps. This would only be a fleeting visit to check that Skye had arrived as planned and was getting on okay. Nothing could be left to chance at this point.

Bypassing security, he pushed himself to acknowledge the guards on the door, his mind split in far too many directions.

Why Skye was so adamant to come here today he had no idea. She'd been in such a state last night after seeing that... that *boy* who'd made her life a misery, he'd presumed, now her location was known, that she'd prefer to remain as far away as possible.

Zane ground his teeth. *When he got his hands on that bastard, he'd...*

'Ah, Zane!' Hazel rushed out of her office. 'I thought I heard your bike.' She eyed him carefully. 'Is everything okay? Erin? How is she?'

'Yeah, she's okay,' Zane muttered. Except he didn't know how Erin was and that hit hard. It bothered him that he'd roared at her last night, yet hadn't seen her today. He'd walked out of the house without so much as a backward glance. It was a hint that the relationship he'd never thought he'd have was crumbling around him, yet he also knew he was partly responsible for that.

But how could he justify allowing Erin to reside in his heart when she didn't or *wouldn't* accept Skye?

Zane managed a small smile, knowing Hazel was waiting for him to elaborate, but his mind was in knots. It was a quandary which ate away at his insides.

He'd all but told Erin their relationship was done last night. He'd seen the pain his words caused in her eyes. She'd been trying to tell him something but he wouldn't listen. He'd *refused* to listen. He knew what she'd been about to say - what she'd begun to say; that Skye was lying - lying about everything and basically, that she wasn't who he thought she was.

Well, he wasn't having it.

But regardless of her attitude towards his daughter, Erin remained firmly wedged within Zane's heart. He loved her - fucking *loved* her. The concept of her not being in his life was something he couldn't comprehend. But if that's what it took to ensure his daughter wasn't put through further turmoil then he'd live with it.

After all, he'd forced himself to switch off from so many things in the past that ripped his soul to shreds, he could do it again.

And it seemed it would have to be that way.

Hazel shifted uncomfortably from one foot to the other. After giving Erin the heads up about Zane's return last night, she'd expected things might kick off. Erin had a fire within her and it was unlikely the subject of Skye's mystery phone hadn't been brought to light. Or the suspicions - the ones Hazel now shared. From the combination of fury and disappointment on Zane's face, it seemed she was right. Unless he'd received news about Marco…

Nausea rose.

'I know I said I wouldn't keep asking, but erm… you don't seem very happy. Is it news concerning your brother?' Hazel asked, hardly daring to hear the answer she dreaded. 'Or is it Erin? Did you hear back from Mr Solenzo?'

'Why does everything have to be about Marco or Erin?' Zane's eyes flashed. 'Right now I'm more concerned about my daughter. I'd thought you'd have perhaps asked about her, considering you witnessed the aftermath of what she went through with that peeping fucking tom when you returned

179

yesterday!'

Seeing the shock of his outburst on Hazel's face, Zane's guilt rose. He stormed past into the office. He didn't want to make a choice between the woman he loved and his daughter. The thought crucified him.

Flopping into a chair, he scraped his fingers through his hair and rubbed his face, hoping the action would somehow remove this nightmare situation.

'I'm sorry I snapped,' he said, looking up as Hazel appeared in the doorway. 'Things are... well, not as I would like right now.' Refraining from getting up to smash a hole through the stud wall like he wanted to, his fingers curled to form a fist; anything to deflect from the turmoil in his mind.

'It's not that I don't care about Skye. She was fine when Tiger brought her this morning. In fact, yesterday's incident hasn't dampened her enthusiasm,' Hazel said quietly, her mind ticking over. *Skye seemed more than fine.* She was positively buzzing, like something had gone better than expected. And that grated.

'I expect that she's putting on a brave face,' Zane said. 'But this ex-boyfriend of hers will realise the mistake he's made soon enough.'

'But don't you th...'

'In answer to your other questions – no I haven't had an update regarding Marco,' Zane interrupted. That was primarily because he hadn't touched base with the people on that particular task. After pulling Tiger off his daily updates with their force contact to concentrate on locating Skye's boyfriend, that was something else he had to deal with. 'And as for Mr Solenzo - he believes there's nothing amiss with Erin. No sign of post-traumatic stress or depression.' *That was another subject gnawing away at him since yesterday.*

Hazel breathed a loud sigh of relief. 'That's great news! At least you know now that it...'

'How is that great news?' Zane looked up his eyes full of pain. 'If Erin's behaviour isn't down to recent events, then that only leaves one explanation... She won't accept my daughter and that I won't allow.'

Hazel blinked in surprise. 'But...'

'Do you know what she did last night?' Zane's anguish morphed into anger. 'Skye was in bits about that wanker peering through the window, yet all Erin could do was try to catch her out! She even started saying my daughter was lying! Lying about what, I can't imagine! Christ! Skye's mother has done fuck all, short of screwing her life up; there's a bastard of an ex-boyfriend abusing her and now my girlfriend is calling her a liar!' He looked at Hazel in despair. 'Where the fuck does that leave me? What options do *I* have?'

Getting up he moved to the door. There was no answer Hazel could give. No one could answer that question. 'I've got to go. I'll pop my head in on Skye on my way out and then I'm getting on with the rest of the shit that's piling up around me.'

Hazel watched Zane's leather jacketed back disappear up the corridor towards the office where Skye sat and her heart sank. She'd wanted to tell Zane about the phone, but there must be a good reason why Erin hadn't already done so. She'd also wanted to tell him what the guard present yesterday confided only this morning. Why would Skye have smirked at the alleged abusive boyfriend before turning on the damsel-in-distress routine?

Of course, the man wouldn't voice his comments to Zane - no one would. *She* would. But firstly, she needed to find out why Erin hadn't said anything.

Reaching down, Hazel pulled her phone from her bag and located Erin's number.

TWENTY TWO

FIONA GLANCED AT PETER over the top of his newspaper. She could just about make out his eyes above the edge of the page.

Shirley Wilson's visit had unnerved her. Well, it hadn't at first. She'd been more shocked than anything else at Skye's mother. She'd never have guessed that a girl such as Skye - such a beautiful and pleasant young woman - bright too, would have someone like Shirley as a mother.

Her usually unlined brow folded. Very, very odd, as well as worrying.

And it was extra concerning because Martin was besotted with Skye. He tried to play down his feelings in front of his parents - of course he did, but as his mother, Fiona knew her son was madly in love.

But now she *was* worried. Didn't they say insanity ran in families? If Martin were to marry Skye, like she suspected might be creeping into her son's mind, then wouldn't that give weight to any future grandchildren being not quite right?

Whatever was wrong with Shirley could skip a generation and affect her grandchildren?

Fiona shuddered. She couldn't have that.

And Peter doing nothing but going on about Shirley's absurd behaviour since the woman had left didn't help. But it was true - Shirley did appear to be mad. The things she was coming out with she *had* to be.

But could there be any truth behind Shirley's insane ramblings? It wasn't possible, was it? Peter kept saying that Shirley was talking utter tosh. Martin was away with his friends at the coast, so how could he be in danger somewhere else with *criminals*? Whatever was that about? Like Peter said - it was utter nonsense. Shirley didn't know what she was talking about.

Except no matter what Fiona kept telling herself, there was a small part that wondered if there *was* any truth behind Shirley's words.

Peter was set in his ways - he always had been. Stricter and more opinionated than her, was he allowing his judgement to be clouded by the preconceptions he'd immediately formed about the way Shirley acted or dressed?

Fiona's lips pursed. Peter was a bit of a snob. Actually, he was a *lot* of a snob and yes, admittedly, she held her hands up to having initially judged Shirley too. But one thing was crystal clear - the unspoken thing which transcended all mothers: whatever was going on, or whatever Shirley *believed* to be going on, thoroughly terrified the woman. Shirley held genuine horror at what may have befallen her daughter as well as the guilt that Martin had been pulled into it.

And this rang Fiona's alarm bells.

'Listen to this!' Peter suddenly barked, looking up from his newspaper. 'What is this country coming to? It sounds like another drive-by shooting in Battersea. Dreadful place that is.' He tapped his finger on the article, his mouth curling into a sneer. 'Although from what it says here, it could be a figment of an old woman's imagination. I wonder if she's related to Shirley?'

Fiona listened to her husband chuckling. He hadn't taken a thing of what Shirley said seriously, but something prodded relentlessly in her brain telling her that perhaps he should. 'Do you think there could be any truth in what she said?'

'Oh, for God's sake!' Peter slapped his newspaper down. 'How many times do I have to tell you that woman is off with the fairies? It's all utter rubbish!'

'But the things she said...' Fiona's brows knitted. 'As well as being worried for Skye, she's guilt stricken for sending Martin to look for her and... and that they're both in danger.' She picked at her newly manicured nails. 'I don't even know where she's sent Martin.'

'You're talking like you believe her twaddle!' Peter snorted, amazed. 'Think about what you're saying, Fiona. Why would a nice girl like Skye be associated with criminals? Ask yourself that!'

'Shirley said Skye had gone to look for someone. She didn't say who, but...'

'Claptrap!' Peter picked his paper back up. 'Skye's not looking for criminals and neither is Martin. She's probably away with friends and you know that Martin's at the coast. What that woman rattled on about was ludicrous!'

'Then why did Skye lie about going to Scotland? She told us that too, remember? She's been gone two weeks without a word and now Martin won't answer his phone.' Fiona got out of the armchair and moved to the window in the hope of seeing her only child parking up the Range Rover and coming towards the house, but of course the driveway was empty.

That Skye hadn't been in contact with her own mother, along with Martin's radio silence caused the concept of there being truth behind Shirley's words to snowball. 'Peter?'

Buried back behind his newspaper, Peter made his irritation over Fiona's continued mithering known by a loud harrumphing snort.

Fiona stared at the top of her husband's head behind the paper. As far as he was concerned, the conversation was over. It was nothing new for him to push her worries aside. He'd always been the same, but his refusal to at least take on board Shirley's fears and delve deeper into the situation, didn't mean that *she* had to.

She glanced towards the hallway. As Peter had shepherded Shirley out of the house she'd heard him telling her to write her number down. Not that he had any intention of calling the woman. But *she* could. And she'd do so as soon as possible.

How long would it take Shirley to get home? Would she be back by now?

Frowning, Fiona moved into the hallway. Peter hadn't looked up so he wouldn't notice what she did.

Her eyes darted around for the notepad she'd watched Peter take from the bureau. Spotting the jotter on the windowsill, Fiona snatched it up and flicked through it. It was completely empty.

Frustration pooled.

What had he done with Shirley's details? Fiona knew the woman had written them down because she'd heard her say so behind the closed door of the lounge.

With a flash of inspiration, she hurried into the kitchen, straight over to the bin. Popping the lid, a screwed-up ball of paper was visible on the top of this morning's empty cereal box.

'A-ha!' Extracting the paper, she rushed to unfold it and straightened it out as much as she could, finding Shirley's spidery writing still readable.

Her address was there too. Should she phone or go there? It wasn't far and she'd get more details from Shirley without Peter barking in the background.

Making her mind up to head to Shirley's, Fiona swung around only to emit a loud scream at the sight of the huge man standing to the left of her back door. The piece of paper clutched in her hand fluttered to the floor.

• • • •

'YOU'RE TELLING ME that you've been aware my fucking wife is definitely the woman running the Starbright for *days*?' Marco snarled. 'Zane's been seen there with a hot, dark-haired chick and to finish off and you allowed some fucker an insight

185

to our plans who is now hanging around the place, yet you've said nothing?'

Damon's face was a picture of pure contrition. At least he hoped it was. 'I can't understand why Symonds didn't tell you!' He'd reap the opportunity to lay the blame at Symonds's door. The timeframe fitted but from here on in it wouldn't. This was the last opportunity to pass the buck to that old cunt.

Damon felt like screaming. His plans - every single one had disintegrated. There was no option now but to revert back to working for Marco's benefit rather than his own. It was either that or starve. 'I told Symonds to immediately let you know what I'd said. He assured me he would.'

'Well, he didn't! He said fuck all!' Marco barked, folding his huge arms over his chest. 'Symonds failed on all counts. I warned him what would happen. You heard me. Now he's paid for his incompetence.'

'So you *did* kill him!' Damon hissed. And yes, he had heard Marco warn Symonds, but he'd also heard him threaten to torch Symonds's whole family too, which meant Marco's reach of power only extended so far. At present it was limited to phone calls, rather than wiping out entire families. Oh, and not forgetting the ability to kill his solicitor whilst inside a police station... 'How did you do it?'

Marco's tongue traced slowly across his bottom lip, his eyes glinting. 'Let's just say he had a bit of help with a heart attack. Shame, isn't it?' His lips twitched into a smirk. 'Amazing what you can find in a nurse's kitbag while she's otherwise distracted. Of course, air in the bloodstream is hard to detect and heart attacks are commonplace in men Symonds's age...'

The smirk then fell from Marco's face and his eyes turned to stone. 'Symonds paid for not delivering his side of the deal, as will *you* if you don't rectify it.' His fist crashed onto the table. 'This kid you told me about - the one earwigging you at the Blacksmith's and lurking outside that place my bitch of a wife runs. I want to know who he is.'

'I'll sort it,' Damon spluttered, worrying that Symonds wouldn't be the only one having a heart attack today, except *his* would not require additional help. 'I'll pick up where Tel and Banjo left off and...'

'I want that shithead. I want him located. I want you to bring him in and question him. Find out who the fuck he is and what he's doing. And then get rid of him.' Marco's eyes formed black slits. 'After that, I expect to be informed about every single fucking part.'

Noisily scraping his chair away from the table, Damon nodded furiously. *He had to get out of here.* 'I'll get onto it immediately.'

Marco remained silent and Damon thought he was about to escape the room, when the man's snarling voice shattered his illusion.

'Oh, and Sandler? Don't forget that I still expect my wife's statement. Plus, from now on you're taking over what Symonds was doing as well as your own stuff. I want the statement that will get me out of here and I want that skinny kid. After that, I'm having my brother. Got it? 'His hand jerked in the direction of the door. 'Chop, chop then. Get a move on.'

TWENTY THREE

WITH ONE HAND firmly clamped over the woman's mouth, Leo radiated with irritation. *Why did people have to be so melodramatic?* 'You need to keep your voice down, love. I ain't here for trouble, so I suggest you answer my questions.' Wailing like a banshee would earn a visit from the Boys in Blue and this kind of neighbourhood wasn't the sort to shrug off blood curling, screeching women or gunshots. He could do without the inconvenience.

Keeping his hand in place until he was confident the woman would pipe down and remain that way, Leo spun her around to face him seeing the fear blazing in her eyes. He had no wish to scare this bird and certainly had no wish to hurt her, but he needed answers.

His eyes ran over her stiffly lacquered hair and fine clothes. The affluent home hadn't bypassed his notice either. Although people could change a fair bit in almost twenty years, this wasn't the setup or look of a pissed-up slapper who sent their kids to shit schools.

It was unlikely this woman was Shirley Wilson, so who was it? The boyfriend's mother? A friend's mother? A complete stranger?

It wasn't impossible the address Erin noted was sod all to do with anything. It could be an address for an Avon customer or something that Skye was doing for extra cash. With the amount of slap this bird had on it wouldn't surprise him.

His eyes burnt into the woman trembling under his hands. 'Okay, lady, all I want to know is your name. When I remove my hand I don't want any more screaming abdabs. I just want your name. Got it?'

Seeing the woman nod, he began to take the pressure off her mouth.

'Who the hell are you and what do you mean by breaking into my house? Take your hands off my wife!'

Leo spun around, dragging the whimpering woman with him and wanted to laugh at the sight meeting his eyes. Instead, he kept his ferocious snarl in place and locked eyes with the middle-aged, paunchy man in the doorway brandishing an engraved letter opener in his shaking hand.

Leo crossed the kitchen in one stride, ignoring the muffled shriek of the woman he pulled along with him. His free hand locked around the man's wrist and squeezed tightly.

The man's eyes bulged in terror and his hand involuntarily opened; his only means of protecting himself clattering to the floor.

Leo kicked the letter opener to skitter across the tiles of the kitchen floor before grabbing the man's throat. 'I hadn't planned on spilling anyone's blood here today, but that changed the second someone threatened me with a weapon!' His lips twitched into a smirk. 'Even if that weapon is a fucking letter opener!'

Wincing at a sharp unexpected pain, Leo's attention flicked to the woman. Her mouth was still sealed underneath his hand, but her nails were free to rake the side of his neck. His eyes narrowed. 'You vicious little...'

Seeing determination behind the fear in the woman's eyes, Leo paused. She had bottle, he'd give her that. He slowly released his hand from her mouth. 'Your husband must be proud to have a wife who attempts to protect him.'

'P-Please let my husband go.'

Leo studied the woman then turned his attention back to the man in the grip of his other hand whose face was changing to a shade of deep purple.

'*Please*! You're hurting him!' the woman begged. 'Peter? Are you all right?'

'Let's see, shall we?' Leo turned, still keeping an eye on the woman in case she got the notion to whack him with the nearest object. He rubbed his hand over his neck where her nails had gouged and casually inspected the blood on his fingers. 'Peter, is it? Now, Peter, perhaps *you'll* tell me who you are being as your wife seems reluctant to.'

'Mmmphf!' Was all Peter could manage with the hand crushing his throat.

'No! I'll tell you what you want to know!' The woman grabbed Leo's arm. 'I'm Fiona Bolt and this is my husband, Peter. What do you want? Is it money? You can have money. Just let him go. I'll get my handbag and...'

'I don't want your money, lady,' Leo growled. 'I want information. That's not too much to ask, is it?' *So this bird wasn't Shirley but how did he know that for sure?* 'Firstly, I want proof you are who you say you are.'

Fiona frowned, her lips pursing in annoyance. 'Why wouldn't I be who I say I am? What ma...' She then shrieked as Leo took a steady grip of her arm.

'I don't trust *anyone*.' Leo nodded at the handbag on the kitchen table. 'Prove who you are and I'll release your husband's throat. I can't be fairer than that.' He smiled slowly. 'Providing he doesn't pull any more stupid stunts, that is.'

Judging by the attempt to shake his head, Leo guessed that Peter, if that's who he actually was, wouldn't be reaching for the nearest object. *But just in case...*

Dropping his grip of Fiona's arm, Leo's pushed his jacket to one side exposing the butt of a pistol lodged in his waistband.

'Oh my God!' Fiona squawked. 'He's got a gun!' Her eyes

darted to Peter. 'He's got a GUN!'

'Correct. But I'll have no reason to use it unless either of you choose not to play nicely.' Leo jerked his head in the direction of the table. 'Handbag?'

Fiona stumbled across the room, her fumbling fingers searching the contents for her purse. 'Here!' she cried, holding up a credit card.

Leo stared at the Platinum Barclaycard:

Mrs Fiona M J Bolt

Nodding, he released Peter from his vice-like grip, leaving him to stagger back against the wall coughing, his hands clawing at his raw throat.

'So, Mr Bolt, being as your wife has been so kind in proving her identity, perhaps you'd like to answer *this* question?' Leo stepped forward, his huge frame all but dwarfing Peter in the doorway. 'Being as neither of you are called Shirley, do you have a son?'

'Shirley?' Peter spluttered. 'Wha…'

'My son!' Fiona screamed. 'How do you know about my son?' Her eyes widened in terror. *This brute had mentioned Shirley too. Oh my God, what Shirley Wilson said was right! Martin was involved in something dire and now this lunatic was in her home.* 'What have you done to him?'

'Wait a minute!' Peter suddenly found his voice. 'What has Shirley got to do with this?'

'Shut up, Peter! All I want to know about is Martin!' Fiona's eyes darted between her husband and the stranger. 'Where is my son?'

'That's what I want to know, Mrs Bolt…' *So, these were the boyfriend's parents?* 'If you are who I think you are, then your son has been causing problems.'

'Problems?' Peter barked. 'What sort of prob…'

'Martin's a good boy!' Fiona cried. 'He doesn't cause problems! He's going to university. He's got a girlfriend and he's...'

'Does that girlfriend happen to be Skye Wilson, by any chance?' Leo raised an eyebrow.

'Skye? Where does she come into this?' Peter croaked, his throat still half-crushed.

Fiona turned a deathly shade of white. *Everything Shirley said was true.* As her legs turned to jelly she leant against the table for support. 'Whatever's happened isn't anything to do with Martin! He was asked to go. Shirley asked him to go an...'

'So, you *do* know Shirley Wilson?' Leo's mouth twitched into a smirk. Now he had the stalker boyfriend's location, who he'd learnt was called Martin Bolt, and knowledge of the woman Zane wanted. This was a good result. *Just one more thing.* 'Where is she?'

'I'll tell you where it she is!' Peter lurched forward to snatch up the piece of paper Fiona had dropped off the floor. '*This* is Shirley's address. 'Now tell me where my son is!'

Leo chuckled. The deep rumble coming from the back of his throat. His hand shot out to form an iron grip back on Peter's already mangled wrist. He snatched the notepaper from between his fingers. *Shirley Wilson's address and phone number. Excellent.* His eyes then narrowed. 'I don't do bargains, Mr Bolt.'

It only took a slight shove of Leo's brute strength to send Peter flying across the room to crash into the kitchen wall leaving Fiona shrieking in horror.

'I need to know where Martin is!' Fiona wailed, tears now flowing a trail of makeup down her cheeks.

Shoving Shirley Wilson's details in his pocket, Leo issued a warning smile. 'When *Martin* is located, I'm sure you'll hear of it...' He glanced around, catching Peter Bolt's eye as he lay trembling on the floor. 'You understand that in the interim for our peace of mind we'll need to install someone in this location. We don't want to miss your son if he decides to come home, now do we?' His eyes twinkled with mischief. 'Nice Range Rover, by the way...'

Peter blinked in shock. 'What? I...'

'What do you mean by "we"?' Fiona yelled. 'Exactly what sort of people are you, for God's sake?'

'That, I wouldn't advise you find out, Mrs Bolt.' Leo chuckled. 'I don't think I need to underline that my visit and this conversation will remain between ourselves.'

And he had the sneaking suspicion that if Fiona Bolt wanted her darling boy to retain his cock, then she'd ensure her blustering husband also honoured that request.

Next on the list was to visit the infamous Shirley Wilson.

• • • •

'I CAN'T BE LONG.' Hazel spoke slowly, wanting to keep her voice down. There was a group meeting set for this room and the women would soon be filing in. There had been an additional two women admitted to the centre today, so things were busy. 'I tried to call you earlier but your phone was engaged.'

She frowned at Erin's hasty words. 'Leo? Why would you be calling L... What? Seriously? Zane's sent him to look for Shir... Is that a good idea? Yes... yes, I know - I get that, but why the bloody hell didn't you show him Skye's phone last night? You said that y... What?'

Her eyes narrowed. *The devious little bitch! Skye was clever. There was no doubt about that.* 'Shit, Erin. Now she's got rid of the evidence wh...'

Hazel's mouth fell open at Erin's next words. 'It was *her*? Skye leaked the story?' Adrenaline thumped through her veins. All along that little cow had been the one to put her, these women, the Starbright and her own father at risk of being located, as well as the subsequent retaliation? Her heart picked up a fast pace. Marco learning of her whereabouts was getting closer by the day, but why hadn't Erin told Zane about this?

Actually, she knew why. Zane wouldn't believe her, so Erin was hedging her bets by going to Leo instead.

Skye Wilson had done a stunning job on everyone - the

enemy within the fold. 'What's Leo doing with what you've told him? He's going there now? Okay, but listen, you need to tell...'

Hazel paused as the group room door swung open.

'Oh sorry!' Skye focused on the mobile at Hazel's ear. 'I was about to prepare the room for the meeting, but I'll come back in a moment.'

Hazel beckoned Skye in. Doing otherwise would look suspicious. She turned back to the mobile. 'I've got to dash. We've got a meeting shortly. Yes... that's correct.' *Erin knew of Skye's presence.* 'Yes, absolutely... Well, I hope you manage your trip out this afternoon. Have a good time,' she blagged, hoping the bullshit sounded convincing. 'Catch up with you soon. Bye.'

Ending the call, Hazel smiled at Skye - a difficult task. This little cow had tried to set her up? Set them *all* up? She wanted to lay into her but she couldn't. She had to wait.

'I didn't mean to interrupt,' Skye said, her voice sweet, but suspicion lingered behind her eyes.

'It's fine,' Hazel laughed. 'I didn't realise the time, but you're right - the women's therapy group starts soon.'

'She likes to talk, doesn't she?' Twiddling a strand of her jet black hair, Skye looked at Hazel inquisitively.

'Who?'

'Erin. That's who you were talking to, was it not? She likes to talk... Usually about me... She's not getting any better, you realise. She's worse, if anything. I heard you say she's going out this afternoon. I didn't think she was supposed to leave the house on her own. Where is she going?'

'Oh, erm, I can't remember exactly,' Hazel blustered. 'Somewhere with Zane, I think.' *Shit! She shouldn't have said that.*

One side of Skye's mouth pulled into a smirk. 'Oh! That's surprising. Especially with everything so up in the air. Zane told me about Mr Solenzo's conclusion about Erin. Disappointing, as well as undoubtedly wrong, wouldn't you say?' Walking across the room, she pulled chairs off the stack to lay them out in a circle for the discussion group. 'Are these okay here like this?' Without waiting for an answer, she sighed. 'I wanted to fit in. For so long I've wanted - *needed* a proper family... You know, one where I would be protected from... from...'

Hazel remained silent. She didn't trust herself not to say something accusing. The devious girl presuming the phone call was from Erin spoke volumes. The question was, how long had she been listening?

Realising she wasn't garnering the hoped for reaction, Skye ramped up her act, her bottom lip trembling. 'I-I feel that I'm ruining Zane's life,' she sniffed. 'My presence is causing problems and I never meant... I didn't want me being here to be an issue.' Sitting down on one of the chairs, she looked imploringly at Hazel. 'Maybe I should go back to my mother's, despite... despite what she's like and how awful it is. Oh, is it so wrong of me to want Erin's friendship? She'll even turn *you* against me eventually.'

It took all of Hazel's willpower not to roll her eyes at this little minx. That, or punch her in the face for trying to give Marco the ability to locate them all. 'I make my own opinions.'

Skye's face broke into a wide smile. 'Zane should have picked you. You understand how difficult this is for me. You're not jealous or paranoid or...'

'Don't be ridiculous!' Hazel would laugh if she wasn't so angry. Skye was doing her utmost to convince Zane how much better off he'd be without Erin. *Christ, this girl was a serious problem.* 'Erin's gone out of her way to make you feel comfortable. We all have.' She paused. Any minute now it would slip out that she knew about Skye's weird games, so she had to keep silent. 'Anyway, I'm not arguing about this. How's your new phone? It looks fancy.'

'It's perfect!' Skye gushed. 'It's nice to have someone who cares. I've never had nice things... My Mum... well, she doesn't bother with me...' She dabbed at her eyes which looked suspiciously dry. 'A-And I hope my ex-boyfriend doesn't come back. I'm still terrified he'll show up again.'

Why are you here then? Hazel thought. She'd had enough of the fake bleeding-heart act. 'Let's finish getting the room ready,' she said, cutting the conversation. 'The women will be here any minute.'

'Okay,' Skye smiled. 'I'll pop back to your office and grab the copies of the agenda for the meeting ready to hand out, if that's okay? I won't be a moment.'

Nodding, Hazel watched Skye leave the group room. *And you, Skye Wilson - your time to manipulate Zane and everyone else will have to come to an end.*

Because if Erin didn't succeed in getting Zane to believe what this girl was really like, *she* would.

TWENTY FOUR

CRUNCHING THE GEARSTICK into second, Damon continued down the road. This Volvo was a bag of shit but it wasn't like he could afford a better motor. Had his plans paid off, he'd have soon been in possession of a shiny new Lamborghini, but now he's been forced back to grafting for Marco that wouldn't happen.

For fuck's sake, this is a bloody nightmare, he thought, scrabbling to wind down the window.

He needed some air. He was suffocating. Not from the heat or even the exhaust fumes that frequently stunk his car out, but from the responsibility wedged on his back.

Getting a statement from Hazel Grimes; finding that skinny lad, bringing Zane Morelli to his knees and putting together a case which insured Marco's charges to be dropped was a tall order...

And on his tod?

Christ!

Fear wrapped around Damon's spine. If he didn't succeed, then he was dog meat. He'd end up the same place as Symonds. Although he wouldn't be shedding a tear over that slimy fucker's demise, he had no wish to join the bloke in the local morgue, but now Marco had more clout than he'd realised, that end result wasn't impossible. If the man could casually wipe out a solicitor under the presence of a nurse, whilst in a police station, then offloading *him* wasn't a big deal.

Furthermore, that outcome was guaranteed if a) he didn't deliver this time or b) Marco discovered he'd planned to swipe the empire out from under his nose.

Bollocks. This was going from bad to worse.

Damon was convinced his brain was melting, his thoughts lurching from how to get in the Starbright to collar Hazel to achieving any of the things expected of him...

He fanned his face with his hand and turned the radio up, scowling as Christina Aguilera's *'Lady Marmalade'* belted through the tinny speakers.

He'd be marmalade if he didn't think of something and get an idea of where the bloody hell to start with Marco's unachievable list.

Fuck, fuck, FUCK!

'How much longer will this take?' he muttered, inching along the busy road through Battersea. Time was ticking and his life was running out. He didn't know where he was heading or where to start!

Jesus wept!

'Oh, bollocks to this!' Damon yelled. Yanking the steering wheel to the left, he screeched down a side street. He'd pick his way through the back streets to get rid of the traffic. All roads led to somewhere, didn't they?

Perhaps he should go to Dagenham and case the Starbright again? He may get an unexpected flash of inspiration or...

'Fuck me!' Damon gripped the steering wheel and squinted up ahead. *He was sure he'd just clocked...*

It was!

A laugh resounded around the shabby interior of the Volvo. 'There is a God!' he cried, his mouth pulling into a twisted smile. He'd asked and now he'd received...

'Don't make it obvious, he hissed, easing off the

accelerator. Wherever that car was heading, then so would he. He didn't know what he'd do after that but he'd think of something. An opportunity would present itself and he'd grab it.

In the meantime, all he had to do was keep his eyes and his car on the tail of the registration plate reading 'PRB1'.

· · · ·

'WHAT ARE YOU DOING?' Fiona cried as Peter picked up the cordless phone from its cradle.

'What do you think I'm doing?' Peter barked, one hand brushing dirt from his trousers from his time spent on the floor. 'You can't seriously expect me not to call the police after that... that *thug* broke into our house and threatened us?' His face reddened with anger over the unexpected situation he'd found himself in. 'That man even made reference to my bloody Range Rover! What other proof do we need that he's got his sights set on taking our things? I'm surprised he didn't disappear with the television!'

Fiona stared at her husband in amazement before striding over to snatch the phone from his hands. 'You will not call the police, Peter. You heard what he said!'

'And you believed him?' Peter scoffed, shaking his head. 'Dear God, you're not falling for his false threats are you? Everything he said were lucky guesses.' A loud snort came through his nostrils. 'Look around us. We hardly live in poverty! He wants whatever he can get. Most likely to fund his drug habit.'

'He didn't seem like a drug addict to me,' Fiona spat. 'That man was fully in control of his faculties, organised and certainly not averse to utilising whatever means necessary to get what he wants. How can you gloss over that he knew about Martin, as well as that he was driving a Range Rover, for God's sake! How would an addled addict know or care about that?'

'He didn't know Martin's name! *You* told him! *You* gave him that information. He just said "son", which equates to a question with a fifty per cent success rate of being correct. As for the car, well he could have got those details from the DVLA.' He moved towards Fiona. 'Now give me the phone. I'm calling the police.'

'What about him mentioning Skye, then?' Fiona deftly moved the phone out of Peter's reach. 'How do you explain that?'

Peter's lips formed a thin line. *That point was more difficult, but he wouldn't dwell on it.* 'I'm not scared of that man. I won't be dictated to by a thug. I'm calling the police!'

'You were doing a pretty good impression of it when you were grovelling around on the floor, cowering at every word he said!'

'I was not cowering,' Peter raged, his cheeks burning red. 'I didn't want to put you in danger by arguing, that's all.'

'So instead you did nothing, apart from threatening him with a letter opener? Yet now he's gone, you're prepared to risk your son's life by involving the police?' Fiona's finger pointed in Peter's face. 'I'm surprised you haven't already called the insurance company with the suspicion that your car may be about to be stolen before thinking about Martin!'

Peter opened his mouth to retaliate and then shut it again. It had crossed his mind to call the insurance company, but he wouldn't voice that. 'It's unfair to say that I don't care about my son,' he said for want of nothing else to utter.

Fiona's anger deflated. 'What Shirley said was right. Skye has gone somewhere and Martin is involved. Oh my God, we'll never see him again!' Her fingers clutched the arm of the sofa, tears welling. 'What are we going to do?'

Peter scowled. 'I've already told you! We call the police!'

Fiona flipped back into defence mode. 'That can't happen! You're not risking our son's life by calling the police. That man took nothing from this house. That isn't the attitude of a common thief or an addict. He was too organised. Too in control. He wanted information. He said Martin was a "problem". What does that mean?' Her eyes widened. 'Didn't you hear his voice? His accent? It was a London accent.'

Suddenly the truth became clear and her hands flew to her mouth. 'Oh Christ, Peter! He's... he's part of an organised gang! Whatever gang he's part of is after our son and it's something to do with Skye.'

'He should never have got involved with that girl in the first place. If I'd met her mother beforehand, I wouldn't have allowed Martin to go anywhere *near* her,' Peter muttered, not liking the prospect of a member of a London organised crime syndicate knowing his address. 'Well, good luck to him in getting sensible answers from that crazy Shirley Wilson!'

In the shock following the stranger's visit, Fiona had been concerned only with Martin's safety, but Peter's words now reminded her of something else. 'You gave him Shirley's address! You almost fell over yourself doing that. You've probably got her killed!'

'She shouldn't be involved with people like that in the first place, then!' Peter snorted. 'No wonder she's mad!'

'Just shut the fuck up, Peter!' Fiona raged. 'This is all a bloody joke to you, isn't it?'

Peter stared at his wife in abject shock. Fiona rarely swore and *never* used the 'F' word. 'What's got into you? You're...'

'I'm finding out where Shirley's sent my son.' Fiona snatched up her handbag. 'That's if that man hasn't already killed her, thanks to you.'

'Don't be ridiculous! You can't go to Shirley's place! That's where that lunatic has gone!'

Fiona stalked towards the front door. 'I'll take my chances on that, but whatever happens, I'm finding out where Martin is. And Peter, if you so much as *think* about calling the police and putting our son in further jeopardy, then I swear down that I'll divorce you with immediate effect!'

Peter stared after his wife as the slammed door echoed reverberations around the hallway, knowing that as much as he wanted to do the opposite, he'd do exactly as Fiona said.

Divorce wouldn't go down well with his friends. They

might even shun him and then who would he play bridge with?

• • • •

MARTIN CONTINUED along the road, his phone on the passenger seat. He'd called Skye twice since setting off, but something weird happened. Now it wasn't even ringing out - the line wouldn't connect. It was like the phone was out of service.

But Skye had her phone on that desk when he'd last seen her so how could it be dead? Unless the people holding her prisoner had destroyed it? They might have retaliated as a punishment for his appearance and taken her mobile as a means to exert more control. Especially now they knew *he* was aware of what they were doing.

His brow furrowed, refusing to let this prospect unnerve him. Since making the decision to go back to the Starbright today and rescue Skye without fail, he was in a much better frame of mind. He was not being reduced to lurking around the confines of a B&B in fear of someone looking for him. No, he was not. He was doing what he should have done in the first place and nothing would stop him.

In fact, he didn't know why he'd allowed himself to entertain that pathetic state of mind in the first place.

Martin concentrated on the road ahead, finding himself humming along to the radio. *There wasn't far to go now.* He'd take that shortcut he'd taken before. It avoided the traffic heading into Dagenham.

Yes, that was the best idea.

He frowned. *Now, which road was it? This one coming up?* He wasn't sure, but it was one of these around here.

Concentrating harder, Martin took the next left, tutting on seeing in his rear view that the two cars behind also took the turn. *They must have the same idea.*

He continued along the road, keeping an eye out for any landmarks he'd seen the last time he'd come this way.

He didn't recall *that*, though.

Craning his neck as he passed underneath a large viaduct, Martin saw the car behind turn off leaving just one following him.

No, he didn't remember this area at all.

As the road opened out to a half-deserted industrial area, Martin's heart sank. Had he taken the wrong turn? He must have. Perhaps he should have gone the same way as that other car?

Damn it.

He didn't want to be slowed up in his quest.

Continuing deeper into the broken-down industrial estate, Martin hesitated. *Maybe he should turn around?*

He glanced to his left at the train tracks descending from the viaduct bridge to run parallel with the road. *Oh, come on! There was nowhere to turn around.*

He eased off the accelerator. Momently distracted by the scuppering of his short cut, Martin couldn't place the strange clanking noise from behind at first. He glanced in the mirror to see an old blue car inches from his bumper swerving from left to right.

What the fuck?

His eyes widened when the car behind veered further to the left and then to the right. He gripped the wheel to accelerate away, but he was too late.

The crunch as the blue car's metal bumper collided with the back of the Range Rover was ear-splitting and as Martin lurched forward, his hands fighting with the wheel, there was another loud crunch.

His head impacted with the dashboard as the car spun out of control.

The last thing Martin remembered before everything turned black was hitting a metal fence and the horizon turning upside down.

TWENTY FIVE

SITTING OUTSIDE the house in East Horsley, Leo had watched, weighing things up for half an hour before he made a move. He'd hoped to catch sight of Shirley Wilson to work out whether she was alone or even if it was her place at all...

His jaw clenched. From what he'd been told none of this added up and he was starting to believe that prick at the other house had cunted him off with false information.

Leo contemplated the possibility that Peter Bolt was cannier than he'd given him credit for before dismissing that concept as negligible.

That man in his posh house, with his bolshy wife and the saddo son would get his comeuppance before long, the slopy-shouldered coward. His wife was the one with the balls. Peter Bolt would sell his own grandmother to keep himself out of the shit.

How Leo hated tossers like that. The man had spawned an equally offensive piece of crap in the son he'd fathered too.

No, Peter Bolt hadn't the nous nor backbone to pull a fast one. Plus, he'd sold Shirley Wilson out quicker than he could neck a cup of Earl Grey!

Getting a second sighting of the woman hovering in the

window before disappearing, Leo flicked his cigarette butt out of the car and snatched up his phone. He had to get Zane's opinion before doing anything else.

'Hey, mate, it's me. Yeah, can you talk?' Leo frowned. 'Why are you going home to check on Erin? Has something happened? Okay... well, yes, I have got somewhere actually... I've been to an address...'

He faltered over Zane's next question. If Zane was heading back to check on Erin for some reason, then he didn't want to add to the edge he heard in Zane's voice by telling him Erin was the one to give him this address. He wasn't being responsible for driving an additional nail into the coffin of Zane and Erin's relationship.

'Getting this address is a long story... But I had some hints off over Shirley's whereabouts from a guy in a boozer too. Yeah, she originally went to Guildford from Battersea... That's right... I also know the boyfriend's parents' location... I've just come from there... No, he's not, so he must still be in London... His boyfriend is Martin Bolt.'

Leo quickly explained some men should be sent to keep watch on the place. 'I'm confident the Bolts will say fuck all. They're too worried about their baby boy, but we should send men as a safety precaution... No, not at the moment... The address I'm at now apparently belongs to Shirley...'

Leo held the phone away from his ear with Zane's thousand questions. 'The thing is, I'm not sure about this... Something's not right...'

His eyes tracked back to the big house in his sights. 'It's a nice place and looks to have cost a fair bit. What? I don't know exactly, but the geezer in the pub heard that the family came into money... But get this – it was said the cash came from a London gang... No, I haven't a clue what about...'

He squinted at the pretty window boxes and the immaculately painted fences surrounding the house. 'But it's a fact that whoever's lives here has money, mate.'

Leo winced. *Yeah, he knew that made no sense from what*

Skye said. 'No, I haven't sighted her yet. Just the cleaner... This woman cleans for the Bolts too. I saw her when I was waiting to go in to see th... No... I was planning on speaking to her but she's a bit... well, what I mean is, she looks nuts.' *Or more truthfully, that cleaner woman was the saddest, most troubled soul Leo thought he'd ever clapped eyes on.*

'The question is, mate,' he continued, 'do you want me to see if Shirley's in there as well or... Yeah, I don't want the cleaner overreacting and calling the cops.' He frowned. 'Som what should I... Okay... Yep... I'll text you the address.'

Ending the call, Leo sat back in the driver's seat. Fine. He'd stay put and wait until Zane arrived. Then he'd head back to Dagenham and see if he could get any more sightings of this Martin Bolt prick.

• • • •

'WERE YOU PLANNING to tell me you were leaving the house without any protection?' Zane's relief on finding Erin still inside the house in Dalston fast turned to frustration. Whatever he did to keep her safe; whichever way he turned, she thwarted his efforts in one way or another. 'Don't you realise the dangers? Don't you understand that I have no idea of the state of play regarding Marco's movements at the moment?'

There was too much going on to keep track of. He and his men were spread too thinly as it was and Leo throwing Shirley's whereabouts into the mix, as well as requiring additional cover made things even more threadbare. Now Erin was adding to the problems?

Christ! He didn't know how long he could keep everything together when threads were fraying everywhere. It was like he was drowning. He dropped into a chair. The way he felt right now he'd never get up again.

Finally able to get a word in edgeways now Zane's ranting since bursting through the door, shattering her initial delight at his return, had run out of steam, Erin's shock turned to fury. She knew *exactly* where this tale of her going walkabout stemmed from. 'Who said I was going out?' she asked, fighting to keep her voice under control. 'Skye, by any chance?'

Zane's face reflected his frustration. *This was like walking in treacle.* 'There you go again! Another conspiracy, right? Skye cares for you, Erin. She's worried about you. Why can't you see that?'

'*Cares* for me?' Erin sneered. 'That girl cares for no one apart from herself!'

'I won't have this!' Zane roared. 'Skye overheard Hazel talking on the phone to *you*. She had no choice but to tell me because Hazel said you were going out with *me* this afternoon.' He studied Erin suspiciously. 'Skye knows I'm not taking you anywhere today because I'm busy with...'

'Busy sorting out everything else, yet unable to see the wood for the trees?' Erin interrupted.

Jumping from the chair, Zane paced the floor - anything to stop himself ripping the sitting room door off its hinges or punching through the wall to the neighbour's house. 'Okay, I see... Because I'm making sure everybody, including *you*, are safe, fend off my brother - who could be coming at us from any direction, track down the bastard who's been stalking my daughter, as well as getting my firm in working order, I'm not paying *you* enough attention? Is this because I haven't chucked everything else to the wayside to take you to the cinema armed with a bunch of fucking flowers the reason why you're putting everyone in danger by making yourself a target? Again?'

His eyes grew wilder. 'You have a short fucking memory, Erin. The last time you went against my instructions to swan about of your own accord, you got yourself shot! You nearly died! So where were you going? And who with?'

'Nowhere and no one! How dare you accuse me!' Erin yelled, raising her head to slap Zane around the face. 'It's not me who's clamouring for attention!'

Gripping Erin's wrist, Zane pushed her against the wall with his body, his eyes blazing into hers. 'Isn't this how things first started between us? You trying to attack me? We're not going back down that road.'

Erin's breath caught in her throat. The muscled weight of Zane's body crushing her was her undoing at the start. The confusion of the raw attraction she felt for the man she believed to be her father's killer had been suffocating, as well as intoxicating. Now, it frightened her because she loved him - loved him with all at heart, but she wouldn't continue being misjudged. Neither would she watch whilst Zane was gradually destroyed by the enemy within their house whom he believed he was protecting.

Taking a deep breath, she dragged her temper under control. She'd get nowhere by screaming, but Zane had to know the truth and this time he would listen. 'I wasn't going out. Hazel said that because Skye interrupted the conversation. Your daughter obviously felt this a good opportunity to cause more trouble between us.'

Confusion flashed in Zane's blue eyes before a wash of what could only be classed as despair poured over him. He kept making allowances for this shit but as much as it pained him, the time had come to draw the line. And it *did* pain him. More than he thought possible.

He shook his head sadly. 'I love you more than I thought possible for someone like me, Erin. You're everything I ever wanted, even though it took me a while to accept that. I still feel that way. Why do you think I go crazy when I think you're in danger?'

Erin blinked. *Where did that come from?* This wasn't about Skye twisting Hazel's conversation. She opened her mouth to speak, but Zane silenced her with his finger against her lips.

'I still love you, Erin. I do. I always will, but Skye is my daughter. One I didn't expect, granted, but nevertheless, she *is* my blood and will always come first - even above *you...*' Dropping his fingers from Erin's lips, he raked them through his hair. 'I was hoping Solenzo would say you have a mental imbalance – shock or something - *anything* that meant I could continue justifying what you're doing, but he's adamant you're fine and that you know exactly where you're at.'

Erin frowned. 'Of course I'm fine! I'm completely sane! I only went along with seeing Solenzo for your benef…'

'But don't you see? I'd rather you were mad because now I have no choice but to accept that you don't and will *never* accept my daughter.'

Erin suddenly realised where this was heading. Zane had said similar before, but it was different this time. It was also different this time for her. *This time* she wasn't taking it without a fight. This time, Zane *would* listen to everything she'd got to say however much it hurt. She had little to lose and she wasn't letting Skye win. *This* time, Zane would listen and listen well.

Not telling him would cause more pain in the long run to the man she loved beyond anything.

TWENTY SIX

DAMON EYED HIS GUEST with derision. This piece of shit swanned around in a fucking brand-new Range Rover with a private bastard plate. The tosser wasn't more than twenty, yet here he was - double that with years of toil under his belt and what had he got to show for his hard bloody work? A crappy rented flat?

Damon booted the spare kitchen chair across the room. It came to land against an overflowing bin bag propped against the wall sporting a suspicious-looking trail of orange fluid seeping from the bottom. The cunts in the flat below could have a taste of his Co-Op ready meal dripping through their bloody ceiling, the bastards. Perhaps it would stop them fucking arguing day in and day out?

But this shithole he lived in had its plus points: no one batted an eyelid at a bruised and bleeding skinny young man being manhandled up the grotty stairwell. If anyone had noticed, they hadn't said anything. Neither would they. Nobody gave a rat's arse around here. Life was cheap.

But nowhere near as cheap as this fucker's life was about to become.

'Don't pretend to be half-unconscious, you little turd,'

Damon growled, digging his fingers underneath Martin's jaw, forcing his head up. 'Start talking. And make it fast.'

His first reaction once he'd run his bastard off the road and dragged him out of his suped-up motor was to kick ten bells out of him. Today had been crap so far and Damon needed a laugh, but he also needed info from the little scrote before battering the fucker senseless.

Had it not been totalled he'd planned to have that Range Rover for himself. He'd have easily put fake plates on and no one would be any the wiser, but the state it was in now it wasn't in any better nick than his bloody Volvo. How unfair was that?

'I said,' Damon snarled, applying more pressure to Martin's jaw, 'that you needed to start talking, so talk!' If this tosser remained schtum, he'd be sorry. Info would be prised from him one way or another. There was no way Damon was being the second recipient of Marco's Needle of Death. Not when Lady Luck had shone on him and handed over one of his targets on a silver platter today.

His eyes flicked towards the pathetic kitchen his flat offered. What implements did he have in here to torture this dickhead? Not a fat lot, short of a kitchen knife and a rusty can opener. He'd got his gun of course, but if he used that he'd get no information whatsoever.

Dropping to his haunches, Damon shoved his face level with Martin's, aware he could deliver a fierce look when required. He'd try that first. This plonker was barely out of nappies, so Zane Morelli must be desperate to employ jokers like this in his new firm!

Deciding to use his gun for motivational purposes only, Damon tugged it from his waistband and jammed it under Martin's chin. 'Last chance, fuckface. My colleague should have done this when he had the chance, but now your boss has killed him, this is your final opportunity to tell me what you're doing for them and what you've already spouted about me.'

Martin blinked rapidly, barely able to comprehend this was happening. The blood dripping from the cut on his forehead after faceplanting the Range Rover's dashboard steadily dripped down his face to congeal on his cheek. It felt stiff, like his face was made of plasticine. His whole body ached and his head throbbed relentlessly.

Amid the fear of the cold metal muzzle of the gun pressing painfully into his jaw he clawed around his jolted brain to string words together. This was surreal. It was like watching a disjointed home video of himself.

His mind was scrambled. Possibly concussed. But he was sure this man was one of the ones who'd been sitting in that pub two days ago, but in the fuzzy mess of his brain, nothing was clear enough to fully decipher.

'Are you taking the piss?' Damon screeched at the lack of response from this cockend even with a gun jammed in his throat. 'See this?' Yanking the gun from under Martin's chin, he waved it in front of his eyes. 'Are you aware what these things do?'

Martin attempted to nod, but with his body frozen in fear, nothing happened. His mind was now centred on what his father would say about the Range Rover being beyond help.

'Just for reference, this is another way of using one.' Damon smashed the butt of the gun into Martin's cheek. 'Next time I'll pull the fucking trigger! Now what do you do for Zane Morelli?'

The searing flash of pain exploding in Martin's face had the effect of pulling his attention to his current predicament. 'I-I don't have anything to do with him. I'm looking for my girlfriend. She...'

'Not this girlfriend bollocks again?' Damon snarled, shoving the gun back under Martin's chin. 'Don't think that spiel will work a second time. Fuck me, they must be paying you well to keep schtum to this extent!' He laughed coldly. 'Either that or you're just plain stupid!'

Panic finally set into Martin's frazzled brain. *Shit*. He had a gun shoved in his neck. If he got shot, he'd abandon Skye again to those monsters holding her. He had to make this man -

whoever he was, see that he was nothing to do with those people. 'No, truly! I'm here for my girlfriend. I...'

'Why were you seen hanging around the Starbright then? You think I don't know that Zane Morelli is involved with that place?' Damon sneered. 'Oh, wait! Of course you do because you were fucking eavesdropping on me at that pub and then ran straight over to tell them I was onto them!'

'No! No, I didn't.' Martin shook his head, stopping as the pain in his temples worsened along with the scraping of the gun against his skin making his teeth on edge. 'They're after me too.'

Damon's lips curled into a twisted smile. 'Why would they be after you?'

'Because they've kidnapped my girlfriend!' Martin cried, his stress mounting. 'I was going back there when you ran me off the road. I need to get her away from them.'

Damon hesitated in pushing his thumb into Martin's eyeball. 'Why would they kidnap your girlfriend? Who the fuck is she? Princess Anne?'

'I-I don't know why they've taken her. I came to find her. She's looking for her father. Her father's something to do with the Morellis.'

'Her father?' Damon paused, his brain ticking over. 'Who's her father?'

'I don't know that either.' Martin reached for his neck only to get his hand promptly batted away. 'He works for them. That's all I kn...'

'Bullshit!' Damon screamed. 'Who is he and who is this girlfriend of yours?' *It had better not be Hazel.* Surely even that tart wouldn't stoop quite so low to bed a skinny runt who looked about sixteen? Still, he had a new Range Rover, so maybe that was enough?

'I-I genuinely don't know who he is. Neither does my girlfriend. Or she *didn't*. I haven't seen her for weeks. I've been on hol...'

'What does your girlfriend look like?'

'She's beautiful,' Martin said proudly. The vision in his mind's eye of Skye made him smile despite the circumstances. 'She's quite tall with dark hair and...'

'Okay, that will do,' Damon muttered. It wasn't Hazel, thank fuck, but it did match the description Tel gave him of that bird arriving on the back of Zane Morelli's bike...

A warm feeling radiated through Damon as the cogs in his brain clicked into place. 'Zane Morelli!' he muttered, feeling like all his Christmases had come at once. *The bird in question must be Zane Morelli's daughter! He hadn't realised the bastard even had kids.*

His face split into a wide grin. Now he had the bonus of all bonuses. Zane Morelli had an Achilles heel and knowing the bloke as he knew him, Zane would go all out to protect the fruits of his loins. And that gave *him* an important bargaining chip.

His eyes swivelled to Martin who stared at him with confusion. This knowledge, if he was right - and he believed he was, also gave him another advantage...

'Are you saying Zane Morelli is my girlfriend's father?' Martin asked, the horrible prospect making the words difficult to voice. Zane Morelli was one of the head psychos, he knew that, but which one? The one in prison or the other one? Either way, the man was after him now. *This was getting worse by the second.*

'I don't know for certain whether he's her father or not, but I think he must be. It makes sense,' Damon answered truthfully. 'But what I *do* know is that you'll bring her to me.'

Martin's eyes widened. 'I'm not rescuing my girlfriend only to bring her to...'

'I think you find you will,' Damon growled. 'Because if you don't, then I'll kill her.' His eyes glistened. 'If you want both her and you to be safe and ever walk away from this, then you'll do exactly as I say. Of course, at the end of the day, the choice is yours...'

• • • •

FIONA CONTINUED up the road towards the address Shirley
had written down. Had she not been in such a rush to leave the
house away from the husband who had today infuriated her
beyond all limits during their twenty-year marriage, then she
might have considered calling a taxi rather than walking to East
Horsley. The next village was only just over a mile from her
home, but a half an hour walk in stilettos wasn't the best idea
she'd ever had.

Wincing at the forming blisters on her heels, she pressed
on, determined to reach her destination and get the information
about exactly where her son had been sent.

But going to Shirley's also brought additional problems.
Her rage at Peter being diluted by her uncomfortable feet
allowed her mind to consider what she might walk into at
Shirley's. The adrenaline which coursed through her veins at
the threatening stranger who had inside information about her
son's well-being had fallen away to be replaced by worry and
fear.

She was following that man to his next target.

Fiona yelped as her ankle went over on a patch of gravel.
Gritting her teeth, she patted loose strands of hair back into her
stone-effect hairstyle and continued, conscious that sweat stains
must be visible through her chiffon top by now.

By the time she got there that thug could have murdered
Shirley. She could be about to walk into a murder scene. Or
worse - walk into the middle of the act being committed...

Aside from desperately wanting to know every detail of
what had made her son lie in order to search for Skye, Fiona
also felt obliged to check Shirley's welfare. Peter offering the
woman up to that lunatic was beyond acceptable, but it didn't
change that she was walking into what could be a very
dangerous situation.

What good would she be to Martin if she was butchered by
the underworld gang she was trying to protect him from?

But what choice did she have?

Fiona eyed a bench at the side of the road longingly, the

pain of walking tempting her to sit down and give this up as a bad job. Instead, with sweaty fingers, she pulled Shirley's address from her handbag to check it again. It wasn't far now. She must push on.

As her phone began ringing from within her handbag, Fiona ignored it, presuming it to be Peter.

But then it might be Martin?

She pulled her mobile from her bag.

...Peter calling...

On the verge of shoving it back, Fiona hesitated. What if Martin had returned in her absence? She'd answer it, but if Peter started bleating about calling the police again...

'Unless you're calling to... What? Why would the police call to ask if the Range Rover's been stolen?' she cried. 'I presume you've told them our son has our permission to drive it and that he's on the insurance? You'd better not have mentioned anything about that man who... What?'

The blood emptied from Fiona's head and pooled somewhere around the bottom of her legs which only exacerbated the throbbing of her growing blisters. Stumbling to the bench, Fiona leant against it to prevent herself from crumbling to the pavement. 'When? When did this happen? It's what? Written off? Oh my God!'

Her breath came in long rasping pants as she dragged air into her shrinking lungs. Her recent visions of Martin lying in a ditch amidst a pile of mangled metal crowded her brain. She'd foreseen this. She'd felt something like this would happen. 'Tell me Martin is all right? Peter? Is he in hospital?'

She'd call a taxi to wherever Martin was. It didn't matter how far she had to travel or how much it cost. She'd be by her son's side and...

'*What*?' Fiona squeaked. 'What do you mean? How can they not know? How can they call about a dreadful accident without... What? What did you say?' Her mouth dropped open.

Surely she was hearing things? 'What do you mean the car's empty? How can it be mangled, splattered with blood and have no one in it?'

Fiona realised her voice had reached screaming pitch, but the passersby over the other side of the road could stare all they liked. Her son had been in an accident which left the car he'd been driving wrecked beyond repair, yet there was no sign of him?

Bending over the bench, she expelled the contents of her stomach over the neatly cut verge.

TWENTY SEVEN

ERIN WATCHED ZANE CAREFULLY. She could sense the internal battle inside his head, but she wasn't backing down. Not until he'd listened to everything he needed to hear. And by the look on his face, the number he'd just called had proved at least *something* to back up her words. 'Well? Was it them?'

'The newsdesk for the London Standard, yes.' Zane stared at the number Erin had found in Skye's drawer. 'But that doesn't give a cast iron guarantee Skye gave them details of the Starbright or Hazel. There could be a perfectly reasonable explanation.'

'Like what? Oh, come on! The press "somehow" gets wind of the details that only you, me, your men and *Skye* were party to? It wasn't me or you who called them. It wasn't Hazel either and I can't see it being Tiger or Leo, so doesn't that only leave Skye?'

'And the web design company...' Zane muttered. 'They knew those details.'

Erin rolled her eyes. *Would he not believe anything?* 'What about Skye's phone then? Why did she lie about that? You told me that a girl she knew destroyed her mobile, then yesterday she changed her story and said it was this boyfriend! Don't you remember?'

Zane looked pensive, his mind swirling. 'I don't. So much stuff has happened and all of this "he said, she said" stuff - it's like being back in fucking school! My brain switches off from that shit.' He looked at Erin with renewed suspicion. 'You're dumping all of this on me now just when I'm about to head to Shirley's? Leo's got an address. What you're doing is a ploy to stop me going even though you know I'm desperate to find out about my daughter's past.'

Erin bristled. 'So, you *were* going to see Shirley? Without even mentioning it? Regardless of what you think of me and whether you believe I'm jealous of Shirley or hate your daughter, you're wrong.' She folded her arms. 'I don't trust Skye. She's lying.'

'Because of *this*?' Zane held up the phone number on the scrap of paper. 'And because you allegedly remember something I said which I can't recall? Shouldn't you ask yourself why you're so paranoid to snoop around someone's private things?'

Erin gritted her teeth. 'Then explain how Leo got the address you're itching to go to! I'll tell you, shall I? I knew you'd see Shirley at some point because a) you already said you would soon as she was located and b) It was *me* who gave Leo the address. I thought she might be at the place or linked to it.'

Zane frowned. '*You*?'

'Yes, I told him rather than you because you won't listen to anything I say. You're too busy getting me labelled as crazy. You don't want to hear what I've got to say because you don't like it.' Erin pointed her finger in Zane's face. 'How did I get that address? I found it on Skye's phone - you know, the phone she said was destroyed before arriving here!'

'You did *what*? You gave information to one of my men rather than me?' Zane's eyes narrowed. 'And what phone? What are you talking about?'

'Skye hid a phone.' Erin stomped over to the sofa and yanked off the cushions. 'She shoved it down here. I caught her using it, but she wasn't sure whether I'd seen, so she stashed it. But then you then took her to the Starbright and she didn't get chance to move it, so after you both left, I took it.'

'Where is it then?'

'Well, that's just it. Skye realised I'd got it and knew I'd show you, but guess what? You were too busy stomping away from me and by the time I went to fetch it, she'd trashed it.'

Erin saw the disbelief on Zane's face. 'I know you don't buy this. I realise it sounds bizarre, but it's true. Ask Hazel. She saw it. She saw the texts from Shirley and the boyfriend, who I might add is desperately looking for Skye. If that boy dumped her and was stalking her, then you could have fooled me!'

'You went through my daughter's phone?'

'Is that all you care about? Whether I went through her phone?' Erin yelled. 'Yes, I went through her fucking phone! She lied about what I said, she's lying to you and I'm pretty certain she's lying about her mother too. The texts I saw from Shirley don't sound like they're from a pisshead who doesn't care.'

'You've had access to Shirley's number and haven't told me?' Zane muttered, barely able to believe what was unfolding. That's if he did believe it. And that, he wasn't sure.

Rushing over, Erin knelt on the floor and put her hands on Zane's thighs. 'I get no enjoyment from this, believe me. I haven't kept anything from you because I don't want you to contact Shirley.' *It was true. All of it.* 'I know I had concerns that you might rekindle your thing with her, but if you do, then you do!' Reaching up, she cupped his face. 'If that's what's going to happen, I can't change it, but what I *do* know is that I don't want Skye ripping out your soul. I know how you feel about her and that she's the most important thing to you. She *should* be - she's your daughter, but... Oh, I don't know... There's something very wrong about all of this.'

Zane remained silent, his brain working overtime. Why would Skye do this? It made no sense. He didn't *want* it to make sense. Her turning up might have been the most unexpected thing ever and yes, it had caused a great deal of hurt as well as anger over unknowingly being absent from her life, but his daughter being here gave him a feeling deep in his heart that only having a child could bring.

He'd move heaven and earth for the young woman who was his blood and the concept she was playing games or lying was like a blade to his heart.

'Zane?' Erin's voice remained quiet at the confusion on Zane's face. 'Maybe she's testing us? Despite what she said about being glad to have finally found you, perhaps she's resentful that you haven't been there? I know it's not your fault,' she added quickly, 'but people sometimes react in ways th…'

'I need to think.' Gently moving Erin's hands, he stood up and resumed his pacing. 'I have to talk to Skye. I want to hear her side.'

'She'll deny it!'

'Then what else am I supposed to do?'

'Believe me?' Erin cried. 'Or ask Hazel. She saw the phone messages. She knows what they said.'

'Give me Shirley's number,' Zane muttered. 'I have her address, but I can't go there now.' His fists clenched. 'Fuck! Leo's still there waiting for me.'

He tugged his phone from his pocket. 'Leo? Change of plan. There's something I need to sort. Yeah, just get yourself back. No… I'll explain later.'

Erin's mouth fell open. 'You're not going anymore?'

'Not right now. I have to speak to Skye first, but give me Shirley's number, Erin. Now.'

Erin reached for her phone only for Zane's to ring again.

Scowling, Zane snatched up his mobile again. 'Tiger? What is it? I've got things I need to do here at the mo… What? When?' His eyes moved to Erin. 'Fuck's sake. Okay…'

Erin hovered where she stood, reluctant to even ask what the call was about but she didn't have to.

'It's that car. The one with the private plates…'

'The boyfriend? Oh God, Zane! You sent Tiger to bring him in?' Erin gasped. 'He hasn't hurt him, has he? I don't believe that boy has been doing what Skye says. I think...'

'Tiger hasn't got him.' Zanes brows knitted. 'But it looks like someone else has. It's been on the news – a smashed up Range Rover in Dagenham bearing that reg plate, splattered with blood, but no driver. The police are appealing for witnesses.'

'What?' Erin gasped. 'You... you think it's...'

'I think it's Sandler,' Zane spat. 'And therefore, Marco's behind it...'

• • • •

'THANKS TIGER.' Zane nodded as Skye was shepherded into the house under Tiger's watchful eye.

'What on earth has happened?' With wide eyes, Skye looked around the sitting room. 'Are you all right?'

'We're fine,' Zane said, cutting Erin a look to keep the remarks he knew were itching to spill from her mouth to herself.

'By being summoned back here I thought something dreadful must have happened. I haven't finished my shift at the Starbright yet, so what's so urgent?' Skye pouted.

'I'll catch up with you tomorrow.' Zane nodded to Tiger and waited until he'd left the room. Not speaking until the man's large figure moved back down the path towards the car, he turned to Skye. 'I need to talk to you.'

Skye slumped into an armchair, cutting a narrow-eyed glare in Erin's direction. 'What has she accused me of this time?'

'*She* is my fiancée, Skye, so have some respect! There's a few things I'd like you to explain.' Zane pulled the folded-up square of paper from his pocket and slid it across the coffee table. 'Why did you have this number?'

'What is it?'

Erin gritted her teeth as Skye frowned at the piece of paper. *Pretending she'd never set eyes on it before, was she?* 'It's the number for the *London Standard* newsdesk.'

Skye stared at Erin and then Zane. 'Okay, but why do I need to know that?'

'Perhaps because it was in your room?' Erin sniped, unable to stop herself.

'You've been going through my things?' Skye gasped. She swung to Zane. 'Why do you think it's acceptable for *her* to go through my stuff?'

'I don't,' Zane admitted. 'But it's a reasonable question to ask why you've got this number, considering…'

'Oh, I understand!' Skye rolled her eyes towards the ceiling. 'This is about the Starbright, isn't it? She's accusing me of that again, is she?' Looking at Erin, her eyes glowered. 'I've already told you that leak to the press was nothing to do with me!'

'Then why do you have the newsdesk's number?' Zane pressed, noting the look he'd just seen in his daughter's eyes. It was very much like his own when he'd been wronged.

Skye folded her arms. 'I had the number because I was going to call them about a job.'

Zane frowned. 'A job?'

'Yes, a job. Erin has clearly forgotten that she came in when I was looking at job adverts in the paper.' She turned to Erin. 'Maybe you don't remember? From what I recall, you were more interested how long I was staying around here for, so perhaps the other parts slipped your mind? Anyway, there was a job going for a junior reporter at the *London Standard* which I thought might be interesting, so I wrote the number down. That's it.'

'Why didn't you apply for it?' Erin asked. *The lying little bitch…*

'There didn't seem much point.' Skye shrugged. 'I was then offered work at the Starbright, so what was I supposed to do? Work with a pile of strangers or grab the opportunity to be closer to my father?'

Zane glanced at Erin. 'Well? Do you remember any of that?'

Erin fidgeted. 'I remember her looking for jobs because I thought th...'

'But you conveniently jumped to conclusions?' Skye interrupted, then stared imploringly at Zane. 'See what I mean? See what she does? I can't do anything right.'

'Ah yes, I remember. That was the day you accused me of having "dubious plans" and I didn't want you "stepping on my toes"?' Erin laughed hollowly. 'Yeah, I certainly remember that.'

'Except what I *actually* said was that I didn't want to be in the way and affect your wedding plans.' Skye's bottom lip trembled. 'Then you called me a tart...'

'I most certainly did not!' Erin barked.

'For fuck's sake!' Zane yelled. 'This isn't an "outbitch each other" competition! I just want the questions answered so nothing gets taken out of context.'

'By her, you mean?' Skye snapped sulkily.

'Skye! I mean it! Answer the questions gracefully. And Erin, don't take every single comment the wrong way!'

Erin silently fumed. *Take things the wrong way? Was Zane still blind to this?*

'There's also an issue about a phone,' Zane continued.

Erin smiled inwardly at the flash of panic flitting over Skye's face. The girl may have concocted a feasible story to explain the newsdesk's number being in her possession - not that she believed *that* by any stretch of the imagination, but the phone was another story.

Skye had trashed the evidence so it couldn't be physically proved, but Erin didn't need that phone. How else would she have Shirley's, Skye's boyfriend and a friend's number, as well as an address which had proved relevant otherwise? There was no way she could dream up correct numbers on the off chance. It proved *everything*.

If Skye denied this one, then Erin would make Zane dial one of those numbers right *now* to prove that they were indeed correct and could only have come from Skye.

Disturbed by Skye's silence, Zane asked again. 'Erin told me you had another phone in addition to the new one I bought you. Why would you say your phone had been destroyed if it wasn't?'

'You changed your story on that too!' Erin added. 'First it was a girl you knew from school that smashed up your phone and then it was your boyfriend...'

'Erin!' Zane warned. 'You're not helping.'

'You're taking *her* word that I had another phone? I keep telling you that she hates me and doesn't want me here. I'm your daughter, so you should believe what I say!'

'It's not a case of believing one of you over the other. Erin said there were texts on your phone from your mother, your friend and your boyfriend,' Zane muttered, not enjoying this conversation. 'How is that possible if the phone didn't exist?' Something was telling him not to mention that Erin had also noted the numbers down and prayed she'd also keep that fact to herself. The concept that his daughter may have lied weighed heavily, but he had to be sure before making judgments over something so important.

'From what I saw, the boyfriend isn't aware that he's "dumped" you either,' Erin jibed, getting a certain amount of satisfaction. The girl was drowning. She'd got her now. There was no way Skye could get out of this.

'You know nothing,' Skye snapped. 'You can't prove anything. You just want to turn my father against me, like the jealous cow you are.'

'Skye! That's enough!' Zane barked, horrified.

'I'm sorry,' Skye whimpered, turning on the tears. 'I'm just upset she's gone through my personal things.'

'So, you *do* admit lying about another phone?' Zane said, his heart sinking. 'Why? Why would you do that?'

Skye rested her head on the arm of the chair and the sobbing began in earnest. *Here we go again... Don't fall for it, Zane*, Erin thought, hoping the strength of her words would transmit through the ether.

'I know it's pathetic.' Skye raised her head slightly, her hair falling over her face. 'I admit I *did* make it up about the phone...'

Erin sat forward. *Wait! What?* The girl was admitting it? No! She was supposed to continue denying it. That would be her downfall.

'Why would you make it up?' Zane gently pushed.

'Because...' Skye sniffed loudly, her voice punctuated by sobs. 'I... I wanted you to buy me something. I wanted something from my father... I've never had anything and when... Oh, when we were talking, the stuff about the phone just came out. I shouldn't have said it. It was pathetic and wrong.' She looked up beseechingly. 'I really am sorry.'

Erin watched Zane's expression soften. *Oh no - he was buying this bullshit? It was obvious Skye was lying.* 'Then what was all the stuff about the boyfriend dumping you?'

'I was embarrassed,' Skye muttered, her voice small. 'It was *me* who didn't want to be with him anymore, but he... he wouldn't leave me alone. He still won't. If you've been through my phone, then you must have seen that I didn't reply to his texts. I just want him to leave me alone, but now he's followed me here. He's obsessed!'

'And your mother?'

'What about her?' Skye stared at Erin. 'She acts like a normal person half the time but not the rest. What else can I say? She's crazy and I'm embarrassed about it. Why do you think I don't want my father to go and see her. He loved her once...'

Zane was torn. He could see Erin's disbelief, but Skye was so upset he didn't know what to think.

'Is that it or is there anything else you want to accuse me of?' Skye mumbled.

'I think we're done here.' Zane watched Skye mope across the room looking like she'd had her soul extracted. 'Skye...' He reached after her but she avoided his hand.

'I just want to be on my own for a while, if you don't mind?'

Nodding, Zane's eyes remained trained on his daughter as she left the room, guilt beating within him like a bass drum. He turned to Erin. 'Not quite how you thought it to be then?

'I still don't believe her.'

'Oh, for Christ's sake! I think I'm the latest person to trample on that girl's heart.' And that knowledge was like a poker through Zane's own heart. 'No, she shouldn't have bent the truth about the boyfriend, but the guy is a stalking bastard. That's a fact. Thankfully, it looks like he's now out of the picture. She shouldn't have lied about the phone either, but I guess I understand that she just wanted something from me. I haven't exactly been around…'

Erin pursed her lips. 'She made it sound feasible, I'll give her that, but please for your own sake, as well as mine - whatever you're thinking, please, *please* promise me you'll ask Hazel about it. Hear what she's got to say.'

'Okay, okay,' Zane agreed, exhausted. 'If it means this can be put to bed once and for all, then I'll see Hazel tomorrow.' Perhaps then a line could be drawn under this as a horrible misunderstanding and they could all start again.

But whatever happened, if the boyfriend hadn't been dispatched, he needed to be. Secondly, if Shirley was crazy, then that was something he'd have to follow up on.

TWENTY EIGHT

'HE'S NOT GOING anywhere, trust me,' Damon grinned. 'I've tied the twat up good and proper and you know I'm excellent with knots.'

'Yeah, yeah,' Marco sneered. 'Send off for your fucking Blue Peter badge if you like! What's the situation then?' *As for trusting Damon Sandler, that was something he'd never do.*

The smile dropped from Damon 's face. He'd expected praise for locating one particular bloke out of millions in London and its surrounding areas. Personally, he thought he'd done bloody good. That it had been a stroke of luck wasn't the point.

Neither did Marco appreciate that the skinny twat secured in his kitchen had spent the night sobbing like a fucking girl. The constant whining had kept Damon up the entire night and he could have done with some kip. Instead, he was knackered. Then when checking on him before leaving to discover the cockend had pissed himself over the kitchen floor hadn't helped either. Making this trek to deliver the good news to Marco was something else he could do without.

And now Marco was asking what the situation was? He'd already told him, hadn't he and would have presumed there would have been excitement over this information. 'I've said that I reckon the hot chick seen at the Starbright is Zane's daughter. She's the girlfriend of Martin Bolt - the bloke in my kitchen.'

'Yeah, interesting,' Marco sneered. 'I didn't think my brother had it in him. Surprised he's not firing blanks because his spunk must be as dead as he should be.' He laughed coldly. 'That girl isn't my main concern right now.'

Damon frowned. 'But isn't Zane's daughter the first target to use to get him running to do whatever we want?'

'No!' Marco barked. 'Not yet anyway. It's something to consider down the line, but what you're failing to grasp is the most important thing is getting *me* the hell out of here.'

Damon watched Marco wave his arm around the police station interview room. He was becoming a frequent visitor here and he didn't like that. Not being here *at all* would be the best scenario.

Marco's beady eyes tunnelled into Damon. 'So, just in case I need to spell out priorities *again*, I want my wife signing that statement which I presume you've prepared, like instructed?'

'Yes, yes I've done it.' Damon rummaged in his inside pocket and pulled out a crumpled sheet of A4. He pushed it across the table separating him from the man he wanted nothing to do with. 'See what you think.'

Marco squinted at the document, pleasantly surprised. 'This isn't bad. I expected it to be littered with mistakes.' He smiled coldly. 'Where did you get this wording from? Hold a seance and ask Symonds?'

Damon pretended to join in with Marco's laughter whilst hiding the relief that Marco found the document acceptable. 'Erm, I copied it off the internet. Is it all right?'

Marco slid the paper back across the table. 'It's suitable enough. Just my bitch of a wife's signature to get now.'

Damon's worry grew. *How was he supposed to do that?* He was so involved in formulating a suggestion as to how to achieve this impossible task, he was slow to react when Marco jumped up to materialise in front of him and pull him into a headlock.

Fear pulsed through Damon, his hands flailing pointlessly. *This was a setup? He would die just like Symonds?* Then he realised Marco wasn't going for his throat. Instead, he was playfully ruffling his hair.

'Poor Damon,' Marco chuckled. 'You weren't blessed with the ability to use initiative, were you?' He lightly slapped Damon's forehead as an afterthought.

A strangulated half-laugh escaped Damon's mouth as he choked from being pressed against the hard muscles of Marco's torso. Suddenly he found himself thrown back in the chair.

'Glad you find your inability amusing,' Marco hissed, all traces of joviality gone. 'Leading you by the hand on every single thing is getting on my fucking tits!' Sitting back down the other side of the table, his fist crashed onto the document Damon had painstakingly copied. 'Take this and get it signed. This is where your mate tied up in the dump you live becomes of use.'

Damon didn't want to ask how exactly that would happen and instead waited to be told.

Marco leant across the table. 'This is so fucking easy even *you* can manage it, Sandler,' he growled. 'I have a feeling my brother's thin on the ground with available cover. He's got a lot on his mind and spreading his men too thinly and *that* we will use to our advantage.'

'From what I've seen, Zane's built up a number of men who...'

'He's distracted.' Marco thumped his fist against his chest. 'I can feel it here.' He yanked Damon forward by the front of his T-shirt. 'Pick a time when there's least cover at the Starbright and use your skinny mate to distract any remaining monkeys' attentions. My brother is after this lad too, you say? This means they'll be on the lookout for him. Skinny Boy can be a decoy. Once you've got a clear run, go inside and force my fucking wife to sign the document. Easy! And then,' he added with a wink, 'I'll let you offload her.'

. . . .

FIONA STARED IN THE MIRROR. The bags under her eyes needed a kilo of concealer. That's what happened with no sleep along with being told that your child was missing following a car wreckage found at the side of the road in an industrial estate.

She looked different without makeup and her hair not scaffolded into place, but right now she didn't care. She'd walk around naked with a bin bag of banana skins perched on her head if doing so meant news of Martin. News that he was alive. *Safe...*

She stared at Peter reading the paper; a half-eaten piece of toast clutched in his hand. He was acting like this was a normal day. How could it be a normal day? Things would *never* be normal until Martin walked back through that door where he belonged.

'Is reading the paper all you're going to do?' she hissed, glaring at the shiny expanse of Peter's forehead. 'We should go to where the car was located.'

Sighing, Peter folded up his newspaper and placed it at the side of his plate. 'We're doing what we were advised. The police said there was nothing to do or see in Dagenham and the best thing was to remain at home where it's more likely Martin will return or get in contact.'

'He won't do that if he's dead or has been kidnapped by that *thing* who was here yesterday, will he?' Fiona screamed, what was left of her hairstyle dislodging further. Her eyes filled with fresh tears. 'You called the police, didn't you? You've caused this. It's *your* fault! You did what I expressly told you not to do and it's because of that...'

'Enough!' Peter slapped his hand on the breakfast table. 'Get a hold of your senses, woman! No matter how quickly that thug could shift, he's not that bloody fast! Think about it rationally. You hadn't even reached that crazy woman's house when I called you with the news about the car.' Despite his irritation at Fiona's accusations, he found himself reaching across the table to take her hand. 'Martin must have crashed *before* that man was even in our home, so whatever happened can't be anything to do with that lunatic.'

'Maybe not but it could be *linked* with him.' Fiona gripped Peter's hand to lessen the shaking of her own.

'Shirley mentioned Battersea was where she thought Skye had gone and where Martin followed, yes?' Peter waited for Fiona to acknowledge his words before continuing. 'And you pointed out that thug's accent was London. Cockney, right?'

'Yes, but...'

'The police said the Range Rover was found in Dagenham,' Peter explained slowly, determined to get his wife to see reason. 'That's not Battersea. And for the record, I didn't call the police.'

Fiona had the good grace to look contrite. 'I'm sorry I said that. I know you wouldn't put Martin in danger.'

'I do think that we should now tell the police about yesterday,' Peter suggested. 'It's the sensible thing to do.'

Fiona's head snapped up. 'No! No, it's not. What if...'

'The police asked if Martin had any enemies. They also, in as many words, said the scene of the crash hinted at signs of a possible kidnapping. So, you're right that whatever Martin's involved in because of that girl could be linked to what we now know.'

Fiona's eyes widened. She put her head in her hands and openly sobbed once more. 'I-I don't know what to do,' she wailed. 'I just want my son back.'

Standing up, Peter walked over to the phone and lifted it from its cradle.

'What are you doing?' Fiona screeched. 'Don't call the police yet! I need to think about this. I...'

'I'm not calling them. I'm trying Martin rather than it always being you who phones. You never know - it's worth a try. Then I *will* call the police back and tell them the whole story. Regardless of what you think, it might just be what saves

Martin's life. That's if he's still on this earth.'

TWENTY NINE

MARTIN FELT ONLY RELIEF to be untied from that chair in the hovel he'd spent the night. What wasn't a relief was that he stank of piss and was back in the blue Volvo with his captor.

What was even more horrifying than both those combined things was what was expected of him. All night he'd been haunted by patchy dreams of torture, along with never seeing Skye or his mother again. How he wished he'd answered the phone on at least *one* of the occasions his mum had called. By now his parents must have been informed about the crashed car. It was registered to his father, so they'd be going out of their minds.

Too exhausted through lack of sleep and fear to care that it wasn't manly to allow tears to drop onto his bruised cheeks, Martin let them flow.

There had been a glimmer of hope that he might escape when this man, who he'd since learnt was called Damon, disappeared first thing this morning, but he'd failed on that too. To make things worse, from his tethered position, Martin had been unable to reach his mobile. It had been placed on top of the only cupboard the kitchen possessed to taunt him by ringing on what seemed an endless basis.

He stole a glance at the man driving the car. Damon had just informed Martin what it was that he expected him to do in order to grant Skye's safety. And Martin would do anything - *anything* to protect her. He wouldn't let her down this time. But now he knew exactly what *was* expected, it filled him with the kind of cloying desperation that only stemmed from something offering no chance of a positive outcome.

'We'll be there soon.' Damon nudged Martin non too gently. 'Are you straight on what to do when I give you the go ahead?'

Martin flinched at the sound of Damon Sandler's gravelly voice. He'd almost convinced himself that this ghastly situation wasn't real for a split second. *Sadly, it was.*

Although he was hell bent on rescuing Skye, like he'd promised himself before getting run off the road, he hadn't factored in having to blatantly walk into the place where everyone was primed to rip him limb from limb. 'I don't know how I'll get away with this,' he muttered. 'I keep telling you that they're after me in there.'

'That's your problem,' Damon sneered. 'Switch your brain into gear and think of something that will work. Only when the job is done and that girl is safely under my roof, do *either* of you get to walk away intact. Got it?' *Not that this prick would be doing that*, Damon thought, chuckling to himself. The girl - yeah, *she* was still required. But this one, once this particular job was crossed off the list, was not.

Damon stiffened at the vibration of a phone ringing in his pocket. Steadying the steering wheel with his knee, he shoved his hand into his jacket and pulled the mobile out. 'How many calls do you get on this bloody thing? It never stops!' He glanced at the screen. 'Aww look! It's mummy and daddy. How sweet.'

Martin's eyes prickled with tears. Even getting a round of abuse from his father about the Range Rover was better than this.

'Answer it!'

Martin stared at the ringing phone in horror. 'I can't! What would I say? They'll have heard about the car by now.' It wasn't like he could say, *'Oh, hi. Sorry about the car. I'm okay, apart from that I'm trapped with a lunatic and I stink of piss...'*

It was almost a relief when the call rang off. In fact, he was surprised his phone still existed. Didn't people in the habit of snatching others off the streets and keeping them prisoner usually destroy their captive's phone in case they were traced?

Damon glared at Martin. 'Phone them back.'

'What? I...'

'Phone them back and make up some shit. We don't want them calling the police - that's if they haven't already.' Plonking the phone into Martin's lap, Damon tapped the screen. 'Go on. Ring them but don't say anything fucking stupid. And do it quickly because we'll be at the Starbright in a couple of minutes.'

· · · ·

ERIN STUDIED ZANE with concern. After Skye had retreated to her room last night, he'd barely said a word. He'd gone to bed shortly afterwards himself, which gave Erin the opportunity to call Hazel to tell her what had happened.

Zane hadn't had said much this morning either; locked inside his own head with thoughts he didn't want. The responsibility of bringing this chain of events to a head sat heavily in Erin's heart. 'I know what I said last night has upset you, but you will do what you said today, won't you?'

Zane pulled his eyes away from the wall he'd been blankly staring at. 'When do I not do what I say?' he asked, a trace of resentment in his voice. 'I'll speak to Hazel later on.'

Erin frowned. 'You're not going there now? You can't brush this under the carpet, Zane. I know you don't want to hear it, but...'

'I'm not pushing anything under the bloody carpet! I have a firm to run in addition to everything else. That's why Tiger has taken Skye into the Starbright this morning, rather than me doing it. I haven't had chance to swing a cat this past couple of days and I need an update from my contact on the force. I'm meeting him this morning.' Zane lit a second cigarette off the back of the one he'd just finished. 'I need updates about Marco. I can't prioritise Skye's fibs about a few things when it looks like my wanker of a brother has somehow, via Sandler, got hold of the boy connected with my daughter. Marco may be out by now for all I know. I presume you haven't forgotten that he and whoever else he has on side remains a threat?'

Erin chewed the inside of her cheek. She was hardly likely to have forgotten Marco. Nor about the man who'd already tried to kill her once. And yes, updates on Marco were needed, but this business with Skye amounted to a bit more than a 'few fibs'.

Giving Tiger the task of ferrying Skye around again was Zane's way of delaying facing the mounting issues surrounding his daughter. That the girl had flounced off the second Tiger arrived to collect her without so much as a word to either of them underlined that she would be using the 'allegations' from last night against them – or more to the point, against *Erin* for as long as possible.

Erin sighed. She appreciated the situation with Skye was difficult for Zane. *All* of what was going on was difficult: his brother; his daughter; the firm; *everything*. It was a lot for one person to shoulder. Him playing down what Skye was doing might be the most palatable way to deal with it, but not the best.

She frowned. If only she could think of what Skye's agenda could be. Although Erin had offered it up as a feasibility, Skye's behaviour couldn't all be down to resentment over Zane's lack of presence, surely?

But even once Hazel had backed up what had been said, as well as mentioning the other incidents she'd noted within the Starbright, would that be enough for Zane to accept that his daughter wasn't on the level?

Erin didn't know, but there might be a way she could help ease the pressure...

'Would you like me to get in contact with Shirley?' she asked tentatively. 'I could speak to her about Skye - at least let her know that she's safe and...'

'You're not serious?' Zane snapped. 'You seriously think that *you'd* be the best person to speak to Shirley and grill her about Skye? About *me*?'

'That isn't what I'd do,' Erin said, refusing to bite at Zane's hurtful tone. 'I'm just trying to help.'

'No.' Zane shook his head. 'Dealing with Shirley is something that has to come from me.'

'How about I call and arrange a day and time for you to visit then?'

'Just fucking leave it!' Zane roared, his knuckles whitening as he clenched his fists. Closing his eyes, he exhaled slowly. 'I'm sorry. I know you mean well, but this is something I must do alone.' Stubbing his cigarette out, he pulled Erin onto his lap and brushed a tendril of hair from her cheek. 'I need to get my head above water with this backlog, starting with the bloke I reckon Sandler's got and an update on my brother.' His lips brushed against Erin's – the tender gesture at odds with the subject. 'Once I've done that, I'll be in a better frame of mind. I promise I'll speak to Hazel before the end of the day, okay?'

Erin smiled weakly, knowing that Zane's mind was set. 'Okay.'

• • • •

PETER'S REMARK about whether Martin was still on this earth had shaken Fiona to the core. Although she knew it was the likely truth, it wasn't something she wanted to acknowledge. If she believed her son was dead - *definitely* dead, she'd crumble into dust.

The chance, however small, that Martin was okay and that he was alive was the sole reason she was still functioning. But the horrific thought that the worst *could* be a reality had been pulled back to the forefront of her mind with Peter's comment. And that dread made Fiona feel worse.

Her heart sank even lower watching Peter hang up the phone.

'Still no answer.' Peter replaced the phone in the cradle. 'At least Martin's phone is still ringing. Surely that means something?'

Fiona wasn't sure that it made any difference. Martin was still missing under worrying circumstances. Taking a deep breath, she made the conscious effort to pull herself together. Having a breakdown wouldn't help Martin. She had to do something, however pointless that something may be.

Both Fiona and Peter suddenly froze as the cordless phone's shrill ring punctuated the silence. It took Peter a couple of seconds to bring himself to answer it.

'Hello…?' Peter's eyes widened. 'Martin? Son? Is that you?' He batted Fiona's fingers away as she went to snatch the phone out of his hands. 'Where are you? We've been worried sick! The car… it…'

'What is he saying?' Fiona yelped. 'Is he okay? Are you okay, love? It's Mum. Martin? Can you hear me? Where are you?'

Peter turned his back on Fiona, straining to hear the words from the other end of the line. 'What?' His eyebrows moved further down his nose and his mouth twisted in anger. 'You think that's acceptable? You've put us through hell and y…'

'What is it?' Fiona shrieked, her abject relief at her son being alive dissolving back into panic. 'What's happened? Peter? What is Marti…'

'Shut up, woman!' Peter roared, turning back to the phone. 'Now Martin, you listen to me. Get yourself home right this very minute and…' Stopping he pulled the phone away from his ear and stared at it in disbelief.

'What is it? Peter? Just bloody well tell me what's going on!'

'He's hung up!' Peter raged. 'Martin goddamn hung up on me, the cheeky little sh…'

'But where is he?' Fiona shrieked. 'Is he all right? Is he…'

'Oh, he's absolutely fine!' Peter snarled. 'But he won't be if he doesn't get his backside home immediately!'

'What do you mean? Wh…'

'Listen to this,' Peter snarled. 'Our son only decided to get hammered in a pub the other day and succeeded in leaving the keys to *my* Range Rover lying around for the benefit of an opportunistic thief! It wasn't our son's blood in the car. He hasn't gone missing. It was the thief's! Our son is, at present, still at the coast with his mates, nursing a massive hangover!'

Heart pounding with relief, Fiona fished her compact mirror from her handbag and dabbed at her eyes with a soggy tissue. *Martin was okay. He was okay. He was ALIVE!*

Standing up, she smoothed down her hair.

'What are you doing now?' Peter asked, still raging over his son's unbelievable behaviour.

'I'm doing what I planned yesterday. I'm going to see Shirley – that's if she's still in one piece.'

Peter's bushy eyebrows settled almost as low as his nose. 'Why would you waste time with that babbling nutcase? I've now got to call the police to say that our son is fine – merely an irresponsible little shit! The insurance company probably won't pay out now because of this. Martin can pick up the tab for that! You wait until he gets back. I'll…'

'I'm going to see Shirley,' Fiona repeated. 'You deal with talking to the police. I'm going to see her.'

And why she was doing that, she wouldn't explain. Her husband would only pooh-pooh her reasoning. But *she* knew differently. Had Peter let her speak to Martin herself, then she'd know for certain whether she was right or not.

Whatever Martin had said to Peter just now, Fiona didn't believe it. Her instinct screamed that something was very wrong. Her son was in big trouble and Shirley was the only person who could shed light on exactly what that trouble may be.

THIRTY

HAZEL TIDIED a section of paperwork and began placing it neatly into the drawers of her desk. Her gaze flicked to Skye doing the filing that she'd been tasked with this morning. Unusually, there was no excitable chatter from the girl - only a solemn moroseness emanating from her like a thick fog.

And Hazel knew exactly why Skye was not her usual whirlwind of energy.

The rushed phone call from Erin last night explained Skye's odd demeanour. Hazel was wondering whether Erin would ever broach the long list of things Skye had lied about with Zane. She'd been all set to take the bull by the horns and do it herself. She had a meeting with Zane pencilled in for their weekly catch up tomorrow, but now Erin had said what was needed, she didn't have to. Zane was coming to see her today to hear her side of things.

But from what else Erin said, last night was not all plain sailing. Zane wasn't fully convinced. Skye had done a cracking job of making out like everything had explainable reasons. Plus, she'd thrown in an admission of guilt over one of the points in order to muddy the waters and make her denial of the rest more convincing.

Hazel's brows knitted. The girl was good. So good, Skye could give Lisa Tequila a run for her money. Although Lisa Tequila was long since retired from Hazel's psyche, she could still *think* like Lisa when the need arose.

And that's what she'd do now.

Based on Skye's arrival at the Starbright sporting perfectly executed, crestfallen behaviour meriting an Oscar, Hazel knew she was playing the Victim Card for support.

Oh, it sounded like a witch-hunt – with Hazel on the instigator list, but Skye had handed her enough proof to see she was a wrong 'un and that would be relayed to Zane when he arrived.

Erin hadn't needed to remind her to tell Zane her opinion. Not that she'd asked. Hazel would gladly give her thoughts about Skye whether he wanted to hear them or not.

She frowned. From what had been said, Hazel expected Zane to be here first thing so the matter in question could be addressed straight away, but there was still no sign of him. However, one thing was sure - the way Skye moped around, shooting occasional glances in her direction to see if notice was being taken of her stellar act, Hazel was confident the girl had zero knowledge about *her* being aware of last night's events.

As far as Skye was concerned, Hazel was the perfect candidate to fight her corner against the hate campaign lumped upon her.

Securing another bundle of paperwork with a tag, Hazel rummaged through the partitions in the drawer for the correct place to store it. Organisation was paramount and being as things were going well so far and good progress had been made with the women resident here, that was the way Hazel wanted it to stay.

But she'd have to break the silence in this room soon. The atmosphere was stifling.

Frowning, her fingers rested on a partition. *That was strange.* She'd placed the documentation here for the meeting with the divorce solicitor Zane had organised.

She sighed. She must have advertently placed it elsewhere. How annoying. It showed just how busy she was to put things in the wrong place. She didn't have time to turn the contents of her desk inside out to look for it, but she'd have to at some point. *Not now though.*

Her attention moved back to Skye over the other side of the room, the heavy silence punctuated only by the occasional overdramatic sigh coming from that direction.

Hazel closed her irritation over her lost paperwork by shutting the desk drawer. 'Are you all right? You don't seem yourself today.'

Skye paused from filing and turned to Hazel, her shoulders sagging. 'Not really if I'm honest. Everyone has got it in for me.'

'Got it in for you?' Hazel exclaimed, her eyebrows raised. *And when was Skye ever honest? That was a joke in itself!* 'What do you mean?' *Like she didn't know...*

'Things aren't working.' Skye picked her fingers. 'I think it's best if I go back to my mother's.'

Hazel said nothing, waiting for the blame game to start. Noticing a twitch of irritation on Skye's face from the lack of immediate response to her words she decided to humour the girl. She didn't want Skye getting wind that she was aware of what had come to pass. 'I thought you were happy here?'

'I'm happy *here*,' Skye said, opening her eyes to maximum effect which contrasted the darkness of her thick lashes to the ice blue of her eyes. 'But... but it's the house... It's getting worse...' She brushed an invisible tear from the corner of her eye. 'It all kicked off last night. She's now got Zane on side. I can't believe he's falling for the lies.'

'By "she", I presume you mean Erin?' Hazel asked, already knowing the answer.

Skye nodded. 'I admitted that I lied about the phone, but now I've done that, it makes the other accusations more believable.'

'Phone?' Hazel frowned. 'What phone?' She could act just

as well, if not better than this seventeen-year-old expert of manipulation.

'It was silly. I pretended I hadn't got a phone when I had,' Skye whimpered. 'I wanted Zane to buy me something. I know it sounds pathetic, but I've never had a father...' The documents in her hands creased as her fingers twisted with angst. 'Erin found my original phone and went through it. She's been going through all of my things. Then she accused me of destroying the evidence. She's mental.'

At this point the tears switched on. 'I-I don't know what to do. I want to stay there but I can't bear it with Erin. I was so hoping we'd be good friends, but she hates me.'

When Skye's shoulders jerked with sobs, Hazel swallowed the urge to say what she thought and instead played the game. She gave what was expected - *sympathy*. 'There, there,' she soothed, pulling Skye into her arms to cry against her chest. 'I'm sure things will work themselves out.'

'H-How?' Skye hiccupped, her hands clutching the back of Hazel's blouse. 'I can't see how anything can be resolved while Erin remains here and is against my very existence.'

'I'm sure things will improve,' Hazel stroked Skye's silky black hair. 'It just takes time.'

'M-Maybe you could talk to Zane?' Skye's voice was like that of a terrified little girl. 'He listens to you. If you told him how badly Erin is affecting me, maybe he'll make things change.'

And there we have it, Hazel thought bitterly. If that didn't translate as *'get rid of Erin or I'm leaving'*, she didn't know what did. 'I'll speak to him.'

And she would speak to Zane - hopefully very shortly. The only problem was that she wouldn't be saying what Skye expected. She'd be telling Zane that everything Erin had said was true, plus *more*, and that sadly, his daughter was a manipulative little bitch.

• • • •

244

LISTENING TO THE scrabbling from behind the front door of the surprisingly well-presented house, Fiona pursed her lips. The addition of unintelligible muttering didn't make her any more convinced that this visit would grant the answers she so desperately wanted.

However, the weird noises from along the hallway showed that yesterday's visitor from London hadn't carted Shirley off or killed her.

Fiona continued to wait patiently as the front door opened an inch and an eye appeared in view through the crack.

'Oh!' Was all Shirley said as she finally opened the door fully. 'Mrs Bolt.' Her face then crumpled. 'You've heard something? Oh my God, they're dead, aren't they? They're both dead!' Throwing her hands in the air, she staggered down the hallway and off into a room.

'Shirley, no! It's not that. It's...' Remaining on the doorstep, Fiona glanced behind her and then took it upon herself to enter the house. Shutting the door behind her, she tentatively made her way down the long hallway, following the anguished wailing.

She couldn't help but notice the nicely decorated space as she went. She didn't know what she'd expected, but based on Shirley's odd behaviour and dress sense, it wasn't this. This was normal. *Classy*. Even the carpet was better than the Axminster in *her* house.

Edging into the lounge, Fiona was greeted with an equally nicely furnished, neat room, but with Shirley slumped in an armchair sobbing.

Approaching, she laid her hand on the woman's shoulder. 'Shirley, calm down and listen to me. No one is dead.' *At least she hoped they weren't.* 'Martin's car was found wrecked with...'

'Your son!' Shooting to an upright position, Shirley clutched Fiona's arm. 'I'm so sorry. It's my fault! I asked him to go. I...'

'Martin's not dead,' Fiona hastily interrupted. 'Peter spoke to him not long ago, but I don't believe the things my son said.' Pausing to sit in the next chair with Shirley still firmly attached to her sleeve, she continued. 'I need you to tell me the truth as to who Skye has gone to find. I need to know where Martin is. He says he's fine and at the coast, but I know he's not. I think someone's taken him.'

Shirley blinked repeatedly, her eyes registering only panic. 'And Skye? Did Martin mention Skye? I can't reach him at all and Skye's number is no longer connecting.'

'Shirley,' Fiona said calmly. 'Did you get a visitor yesterday after you returned from my house? Did anyone approach you? Knock the door? Speak to you?'

'Visitor?' Shirley shook her head, her chins wobbling. 'I never get visitors. I didn't see or speak to anyone.'

'A man from London appeared in our kitchen,' Fiona said, shuddering with the memory. Shirley's attention was now on the ceiling, her mouth working silently on its own accord. 'Shirley! Listen to me. We had a man from London break into our house and threaten us. He was looking for you!' She watched all trace of colour drain from Shirley's face. 'You know who he is, don't you? Who is it?'

'W-What did he look like?'

'A huge man with brown hair. Looked like a bulldog.' Fiona watched the cogs grinding in Shirley's mind.

Shirley expelled the breath she'd been holding. 'It's not him. It's not him.'

'Not who? Please, Shirley, if you know who he is, then...'

'It's not him. That man. But they've sent him. They must have,' Shirley babbled. 'All these years and they've sent someone. I knew it would happen eventually.'

'You're not making sense,' Fiona cried, getting agitated. '*Please*! Martin's in trouble and Skye, she...'

'Skye shouldn't have gone. She promised me she'd never...' Shirley's eyes grew wide. 'They sent that man. He's coming for me and I can't! I *won't*!'

'Who, Shirley? For Christ's sake, who?'

'The Morellis. They sent that man!' Shirley's hands flew to her mouth where she began scrubbing at her lips. 'Get the name out of my mouth. Get it out. I can't believe I uttered it. No, no!'

'Say it again. That name?' Fiona was now the one clutching Shirley's arm. *She hadn't quite caught the name. Chelly, did she say?* 'Is that the man who was here? Chelly? Shelley? Who?'

'No, no, NO!' Shirley ripped Fiona's grip away with surprising force. 'They sent someone and...'

The loud ringing of the phone stopped both Fiona and Shirley in their tracks.

'Skye!' Shirley screeched, jumping from the chair. 'Martin rang you and now Skye's phoning me. They've escaped!' Laughing hysterically, she skittered across the room and snatched up the receiver. 'Skye! Thank God! Where are y…'

If Fiona believed Shirley couldn't turn a whiter shade of pale than she had been a minute ago, she was wrong. All remaining droplets of blood in the woman's veins drained somewhere unknown, making her complexion translucent. Shirley stared at the receiver like it was made from nuclear waste and then something really strange happened.

Shirley's ghost-like complexion changed to a deep red and she appeared to grow in size, her face twisting with an expression that made Fiona want to run away.

Realising she was cowering in the chair, she forced herself to concentrate.

'Don't you dare call me after what you've done? After what your family did! You. Do. Not. Exist!' Shirley then pulled the phone cable out of the socket, slung the phone on the floor and brought down a slippered foot hard on top of it.

Fiona flinched as shards of plastic shot across the patterned rug in the centre of the lounge. 'W-Who was that? The man from yesterday?'

Shirley stood paralysed, staring at the phone on the lounge floor. The expression of rage melted away as quickly as it had materialised. 'No, NO! I cannot speak to him. I *will* not speak to him.'

Getting out of the chair, Fiona approached Shirley. 'Shirley? Was that the man from yesterday? Tell me!'

Shirley stared blankly, her eyes holding only terror. 'It's too late. They have her. *He* has her.'

Fiona was just in time to break Shirley's fall as she passed out and crashed to the floor.

THIRTY ONE

ZANE TURNED THE pint glass around on the beermat. It was a rarity for the White Saddle in Dalston to offer the indulgence. Normally glasses aquaplaned on the surface of the table, along with the remnants of the last several hours' worth of spilled drinks. Perhaps the landlord was attempting to impress him? Takings must have dropped considerably since he'd moved his meetings to the Thames Canning Works rather than renting the pub's backroom, which prior to acquiring the new headquarters was where he'd been forced to gather his men.

But procrastinating about the reasonings behind the unexpected appearance of beermats wasn't taking his mind off Shirley's reaction to his telephone call.

It was odd hearing her voice again after all these years. She sounded exactly the same as when they'd been dating. She hadn't sounded drunk or wasted and he'd heard the desperation in her first words. It wasn't 'hello', it was 'Skye?'.

The nagging prod of Erin's conversation from yesterday rushed into Zane's mind. *'The texts I saw from Shirley didn't sound like they were from a pisshead who doesn't care'.*

She was right and that Shirley was worried about Skye was clear.

Zane frowned. He'd wanted to tell Shirley that Skye was safe and well. Despite what Skye insinuated Shirley had or hadn't done, he should give the woman the peace of mind that her daughter was safe. But he hadn't been given the chance.

Yes, Shirley's voice was the same as he remembered, but the innocent wonderment which had radiated from the sixteen-year-old beauty he'd last seen at that family do and what had made him like her so much back then was now far removed.

The rage he'd sensed down the line he hadn't imagined to be possible to come from the same girl he'd once known.

But it had.

The utter hatred in Shirley's spewed words to him had achieved the rare effect of rendering Zane speechless: *'Don't you dare call me after what you've done. After what your family did...'*

Zane focused on the amber liquid in his glass as if the beer held the answers.

It didn't.

What did Shirley mean by what he'd done and what his family had done?

He, nor his family had done anything. It was *Shirley* who had vanished into thin air. It was *Shirley* who had abandoned him, knowing all along she was pregnant with his child.

He'd have stood by her. He'd have ensured their child was looked after. He wouldn't have let either of them down. *Ever.*

But the final words Shirley screamed before hanging up had shocked him to the core. He hadn't expected them.

You. Do. Not. Exist.

Yes, Shirley cared about Skye more than he'd given her credit for, but whatever else Skye may not have been honest about there was definitely something not right with Shirley and it was deeply worrying.

He'd tried to call back. Of course he had. Several times in fact, but she wouldn't pick up. So much for his plan of softening the blow of turning up on her doorstep. Now he had no choice but to do exactly that because she clearly wasn't willing to speak to him on the phone.

And that visit needed to happen as soon as physically possible.

Zane shook his head, still bemused and shocked. For all the uncertain things right now, one was crystal clear: Shirley Wilson despised him with a vengeance, yet he had no idea why.

It was all very well him wanting to let her know that Skye was safe and well, but how long would that be true? Leo was on the task of searching for Sandler and Tiger was overseeing the Starbright along with all the other guards, being extra-vigilant for intruders on or around the building's perimeter. But would it be enough?

If he was right and Sandler had Skye's boyfriend, then Sandler would get or already *had* extricated information. If Sandler and therefore, Marco, were aware Skye was his daughter, then they'd use that knowledge to get to him by doing something to Skye.

And that thought sickened him more than anything. Now his daughter, Erin and Hazel could be facing a bigger threat than ever.

Suddenly aware someone had moved into his personal space, Zane's senses snapped to red alert. His head shot up, his hand moving to the gun in his waistband in a knee-jerk reaction.

'Sorry I'm late.' Dave Richards nodded towards the empty seat beside Zane before helping himself to it. 'Bloody traffic.'

Zane gritted his teeth. Allowing himself to become so bogged down to almost forget he'd been waiting for his contact from the force was unforgivable. Blowing a hole in the head of a copper in a pub would be something that even *he* would be unable to buy his way out of. He *had* to get a grip.

Forcing himself to relax, Zane pushed the stress surrounding everything else to the back of his mind for a few minutes. He must concentrate on the long overdue update about Marco. All he could hope for was that it was good news that would tip the balance in his favour.

· · · ·

ERIN STARED OUT of the bedroom window onto the street below. She didn't expect to see anything out of the ordinary or even anything interesting. She was doing it for no other reason apart from passing the time.

Being a spectator of the world going about its normal routine sometimes took the edge off the mind-numbing sameness that she was stuck here, waiting.

Waiting for what, she no longer knew.

Everyone else was getting on with what was required, despite what risks that may or may not bring. Yet all *she* was doing was treading water whilst the grand scheme bypassed her, merely waiting to see what everyone else did in order to perhaps be of use with an opinion.

This wasn't how she normally operated and it was difficult. Since being shot down in flames over her suggestion that she call Shirley she was now waiting for Zane to tell her what had been said when he called. Being as he'd been so insistent she gave him the number she'd copied from Skye's phone, he *would* call Shirley today.

But would he disclose what was said?

Erin just hoped that whatever Shirley was like, and whatever cost it had on her and Zane's relationship, the conversation would shed light on why Skye had been kept out of Zane's life and what was going on inside the girl's head.

Shirley was the only hope Erin had. Depending what was said it could sway Zane's mind into seeing the daughter that he'd placed on a pedestal wasn't as innocent and hard done by as she'd led him to believe.

Getting fed up with staring through the rain droplets gathering on the window pane, Erin moved back across the room, picking her phone up as she went.

Bringing it to life, she flicked through her sparse contact list. Was it worth calling Leo again to see if he'd discovered anything else in his quest for the elusive Shirley?

From her conversation with Zane, she knew Leo had gone to the address she'd given him, but that was all she did know.

Plus, calling Leo again after already angering Zane by running to one of his men, rather than him in the first place, wouldn't help. Being as Zane's anger towards her had slightly abated, she wanted to keep things stable. She'd be unable to help him if he reverted to keeping her at arm's length.

What about Hazel?

Erin picked at the hem of her top. Zane wouldn't have been to the Starbright yet, so there was little point asking Hazel for an update.

Her mind diverted onto what info Zane might have received from his contact about Marco. What if that despicable man had been released?

Oh God, this was unbearable.

Erin scrolled further down her list.

Martin

Now the general consensus was that Martin was dead or that Sandler held him hostage somewhere there was no point calling him.

Alyson

Erin frowned. *What about her?* Would a friend of Skye's know anything?

Possibly.

But would this Alyson person divulge any information to a stranger? *Unlikely.*

• • • •

MARTIN THOUGHT it plausible that he might have a cardiac arrest before he'd even properly *started* this insurmountable task. Could it get any more suspicious than lurking half-in and half-out of a bush within the expanse of the front grounds of the Starbright?

In his opinion it couldn't. But that was the point.

He *wanted* to be spotted.

Crazy? Yes, indeed. But the baseline was that *he* didn't want to be spotted. He wanted to be obscure – sneak in, get Skye like he'd planned and then sneak back out with her in tow. But unfortunately, that was not the order. And no matter how much he'd protested - *begged* even - to do it his way, he'd been shot down in flames.

Damon's was the only way this was allowed to happen and there was zero room for manoeuvre. Martin must get spotted by the guards and distract them, then he had to get Skye and whilst the guards were otherwise engaged, Damon would go in and do what was needed.

Whatever *that* entailed, Martin wasn't party to. He hadn't asked and neither did he care. All he wanted was the guarantee that both he and the girl he loved got out of this nightmarish setup and back to real life.

With any luck, he might eventually forget that any of this had ever happened.

Martin felt the unwanted lump form in his throat once again. Hearing his parents on the phone just now hadn't helped his state of mind. All it achieved was to make things worse. His mother's angst-ridden voice in the background had almost finished him. But in a way, it was a blessing in disguise that it hadn't been his mum who'd answered the phone.

Knowing the ability she possessed at detecting hints that he wasn't being honest, she'd have immediately known that the story he'd dreamt up under Damon's insistence was utter bollocks. She'd know from his voice alone that he hadn't been slack with the car keys and got them stolen. Neither was he hungover. Or at the coast.

He was in the middle of a bush somewhere in Dagenham about to sacrifice himself to the lions.

Martin suddenly felt the absurd urge to laugh. His father had believed his story though. He'd believed it immediately. That alone showed that his father didn't hold him in high esteem. This wasn't too much of a surprise and he just had to hope his dad would finally understand that he hadn't had any choice but to say that load of welly and that the trashing of his beloved Range Rover wasn't down to drunken shenanigans.

That's if he ever made it out of here.

Taking a deep breath, Martin stuck his head over the top of the bush which doubled up as a parapet. Surprisingly, there were very few guards around. Damon wasn't kidding when he said the place looked thin on the ground.

And that was typical. The one time in his life that Martin *wanted* to be spotted by a thug toting a gun and they'd all buggered off.

Since he'd got here, he'd only seen one guard patrolling the perimeter. And he'd been here about a year. In reality, it was about ten minutes, but the lone guard Martin had seen hadn't been spotted since and he couldn't afford to hang around forever. There could be a mass load of guards on route and then the chance of pulling this off would be dead in the water - along with him.

It was time to change to another plan.

Never thinking he'd find himself in the position of blatantly walking into a place where people were on standby to kill him, Martin extracted himself from the bush and ran diagonally across the garden in the direction where he'd last seen the guard.

His crawling panic only intensified hearing a shout from across the lawn.

Knowing he'd achieved his wish of being spotted, Martin diverted in the opposite direction while the guard continued yelling for backup. Martin's lungs screamed, his legs powering at record speed, he bolted around the corner of the building, pulling his T-shirt off as he went.

'Do not trip over, do not trip over,' Marting chanted, taking the fire escape steps three at a time.

Crashing through the door whilst pulling on the spare top Damon had given him, he skidded down to the first floor.

Still not a soul about.

Grabbing a large box as a prop, he breathed a sigh of relief to find it empty. He clutched it close to his chest and half over his face, then slowed his run to an ambling walk, overriding his burning instinct to scarper.

Now he had a change of top and assumed the identity of a delivery man. He was sure he'd read this ploy in a Famous Five book when he was a kid. Wherever he'd read it, the idea was working all right so far.

Now, just to find Skye.

Keeping his ears open, Martin hastened along the hallway. *Where was the room he'd seen Skye in before?* He pictured the office where he'd seen her working from outside in relation to where he was now.

It was down here somewhere.

Continuing down the hallway laden with the pseudo heavy box, Martin glanced in each room as he passed. *Come on Skye - where the devil are you?*

And then he saw her.

Martin stood in the doorway transfixed, his muscles turning to sludge at the sight of the girl he loved so very much.

Look at the state of her - she was upset. She was sobbing against a short-haired blonde woman.

Unable to rationally process what he was about to do and what consequences it might bring, Martin dropped the empty box to the floor with a clatter. 'Skye! Babe!' he gasped, moving into the room towards her.

The following occurred in slow motion: Skye's eyes raised to meet Martin's and then her mouth opened. At the same time, and whilst Martin's legs kept propelling him forward, the blonde woman also turned, her eyes widening. Then there was a strange sound - one which hurt his ears.

Martin couldn't work out what it was until he realised it was his girlfriend's ear-splitting screams. And someone – Skye or the blonde, shouting at the top of their voice about an animal. A *tiger*?

Martin had reached halfway across the room when he heard the clatter of boots in the distance. He was also sure he saw the blonde mouthing words to him: 'go' and 'quickly'. She looked desperate.

He only had time to catch the same look of hatred that he'd seen before on Skye's face, before he turned on his heels and ran for the second time.

• • • •

PETER'S FACE bore the traces of the scowl that had remained embedded ever since calling the police to explain they had since heard from their errant son. 'It was downright bloody embarrassing,' he moaned. 'I'm sure the officer I spoke to was trying not to laugh! That's what we are - a laughingstock!' He glared at Fiona. 'If you weren't so against me informing them of our visitor then our embarrassment wouldn't be as scathing.'

He paused, watching his wife pick at one of her fingernails. 'Are you listening? You're sitting there doing silly things with your hands like that Shirley woman. Don't tell me you're still mithering about Martin?'

Fiona didn't answer. With her mind elsewhere, she hadn't heard a word Peter said.

'FIONA!' Peter bellowed. 'What is wrong with you? I knew I should have stopped you from seeing that nutty woman. It's done you no favours! All it's achieved is making you dream up all sorts of nonsense in your own head. I don't need to ask what she said. I can see she's made you believe her ludicrous conspiracy theories again. What is it this time?'

Fiona slowly raised her head. 'That's the point. That's the way you see things and yet you haven't even asked. After what you did yesterday, I could have arrived at her house to find her dead!'

Peter gaped incredulously. 'After what *I* did? What on earth do y…'

'You gave that man her address,' Fiona snapped. 'It would have been entirely *your* fault if he'd killed her!'

Ignoring Peter's expression, Fiona was on a roll. *She'd* been the one to see how Shirley reacted to that phone call, not Peter.

'You know *nothing* of what's going on! And why is that? Because you don't *want* to!' she spat. 'You'd rather cling to the lies our son was forced to spout by whoever's holding him against his will, but I'll find out what's going on with or without your help.'

Snorting loudly, Peter placed his coffee cup on the occasional table, not caring that it missed the coaster and the scalding liquid splashed out to stain the surface of the polished wood. 'Have you heard yourself? Why do you have to look for things that aren't there?'

'Aren't there?' Fiona cried. 'Shirley was so angry, stressed and terrified after that phone call that she collapsed! The person Skye went to find - the person who I believe has our son hostage and the person who's connected with the man who threatened us yesterday, is dangerous. These people are *dangerous*, Peter.' She pointed a long-nailed finger in her husband's direction. 'If you're so sure that Martin is fine, then why isn't he back by now?'

'Because he knows he's in big trouble, that's why!' Peter scoffed. 'He's putting off returning for as long as possible before facing the music.'

Shaking her head in frustration, Fiona got up from her seat. 'Martin's *already* in big trouble, but not from you! Don't you understand? We've got to find him.'

'If that's what you *really* believe, then we should call the police and tell them everything, like I keep saying!' Peter spoke slowly like he was speaking to a difficult child. He then frowned as Fiona stalked across the room towards the door. 'Where are you going now?'

'Away from you! That you haven't even asked why Shirley behaved the way she did to the person who called, why she collapsed afterwards or how she is now, says it all!' Slamming the lounge door behind her, Fiona hurried up the stairs before the tears threatening to escape rolled down her cheeks.

Shirley Wilson was hiding something - something so bad that merely talking of it sent her spiralling.

Fiona knew that if she wanted to get the bottom of where her son was and who this Chelly or Shelly person was that she believed had Martin, then she'd have to do it alone. Because she wouldn't get any help from her husband.

THIRTY TWO

FROM HIS HIDING PLACE, Damon watched the proceedings with interest, his veins thrumming with anticipation. The kid hadn't done badly - not badly at all. Even ear defenders wouldn't have muffled the screams he'd heard which coincided with Martin's appearance. The screaming had gone on for ages before it stopped.

Now there had been several minutes without any sign of Zane Morelli's trained orangutans, therefore this was the break he'd been waiting for.

With the guards rushing in one particular direction and not wishing to lose the window of opportunity which may not open again, Damon clattered up the fire escape. From what Martin had said he knew that if he took the back staircase once inside, it would lead him near to the room that Hazel Grimes used as an office.

Oh Zane, not training your idiot guards to share brain cells and have at least one man watching at all times is stupid, Damon thought, his face showing the hint of a sneer.

But for all his bravado there wasn't much time. After leading the goons on a merry dance, Martin would now be doubling back to grab the girl and so getting a shift on with forcing that slut, Hazel, to sign the statement Marco depended on had to be done quick. *Like now.*

Then he had to get his arse out of here and back to the Volvo, ready to intercept Martin and the most important bargaining chip of all - Zane's daughter, before they thought it a good idea to attempt an escape from *him.*

And that would be extremely stupid because they wouldn't get far.

Damon grinned. With any luck, the guards might even gun Martin down, saving him the job, meaning he would leave with both Hazel's signed statement *and* Zane's daughter in his possession. No need to bother about the lad.

He'd be fucked if he was spending time he hadn't got offloading Hazel. Bollocks to that. If Marco wanted the slag dead, the man could do it on his own time.

Besides, what did Marco deem more vital? His freedom or the death of that plastic bitch?

Making short work of the back staircase, Damon paused. One last check to make sure no grunts were lurking.

Pressed against the wall, he fine-tuned his hearing. *Nope. Not a sound. Complete silence.*

No doubt Hazel, along with Zane's sugar-titted daughter were in that room too scared to breathe from the unexplained chaos, aware something untoward was going down.

With one hand on his gun and the statement in the other, Damon charged through the open door of Hazel's office. It was better to take the women by surprise and then getting this job done wouldn't take long.

Damon's confident smile froze as he entered the room.

What the fuck?

Momentarily stuck in suspended animation, his eyes centred on Hazel on her chair behind the desk. After stopping for a several seconds his heart restarted its steady thump.

What. The. Actual. Fuck?

The document in Damon's hand fluttered to the floor as he stared at Hazel's corpse. Coming back to life, he lurched towards the woman he'd spent so long despising. He didn't *want* to go near her but his body had other ideas.

His gun slid in his hand, his palm slick with sweat.

How the hell would he get the statement signed now? And furthermore, who had done this?

Damon's eyes narrowed. *That little prick! He'd never told Martin to do this!*

His gaze locked on Hazel's over-inflated breasts exposed through her torn blouse.

Something had been carved into her chest.

Bile rose up his throat. His hand swiped away the sweat dripping down his forehead as he pulled his eyes to Hazel's mouth - forced wide open and stuffed full of money, her dead eyes locked as wide, bulging orbs.

The tart had been suffocated - choked to death with a pile of cash?

Damon edged closer. *What was it? Fifties? Twenties? He wouldn't have even wasted a fiver!*

Stopping, he took a pace back.

What the hell was he doing?

Hazel had been bumped off in her own office, but it was *him* standing here. It was *him* who was Zane Morelli's known worst enemy, short of his own brother - who Damon should add, now had a dead wife…

His heart thrashed around like it was connected to a defibrillator.

He'd kill Martin for this. The bastard was setting him up and he'd succeed if he didn't get the fuck out of here because those guards would be back any second!

Fuck, fuck and fuck.

Damon's head swung around the room in terror. They'd find him in here… with this...

He had the motive and he also had the...

Without wasting any more time analysing the situation, Damon dashed back the way he'd come, praying he could escape in time.

. . . .

'SO THAT'S ABOUT THE EXTENT OF IT', Dave Richards said, taking a long pull of his pint. 'Without proof it doesn't matter how many of us suspect it was no accident.'

Listening, Zane's jaw set in a hard line. The belief Marco had bumped his own solicitor off was shocking, but not altogether surprising. Nor was it astounding that, as usual, his brother wouldn't be held accountable.

Zane picked his pint back up, scowling to notice the small trace of gas within the beer had long since expired. 'It seems my brother gets away with everything.'

Dave shrugged. 'The powers that be can't be arsed with the extra rigmarole which would come with it, not to mention the expense of proving his guilt.' He raised his eyebrows. 'Avoiding drawing attention to a murder taking place within police custody is priority to the force.'

'That doesn't give me much hope that he'll finally get banged up. Like *I* was…' Zane grumbled, resentment brewing.

'Hmm, well, that's the thing...' Dave continued. 'Checking the latest developments this morning, it seems we've used our last available extension to hold your brother.'

Zane stiffened. 'So he's getting out? Released without charge?'

'We'll have to release him within the next forty-eight hours unless he's charged,' Dave explained.

Zane's hopes plummeted further. The CPS hadn't yet charged Marco despite all the extra time granted to hold him, so it was unlikely to happen now. *Fuck*. Would two days give enough time to wrap up the mass of loose ends so that full defence was in place? His fists clenched under the sticky tabletop.

'But I've saved the best till last,' Dave's eyes twinkled. 'Just when I thought I'd be bringing bad news, I received another update… The CPS are going for it.'

'What?' Zane sat forward. 'They're doing Marco after all?'

'Yep. As there's been no forthcoming evidence supplied in Marco's defence to counter the charges, the CPS hold the opinion that they have enough of a case to prosecute and gain a conviction.'

Zane's face broke into a grin. 'So, he's going down?'

'With any luck!' Dave winked. 'The documentation is being prepared now and if no evidence from your brother's defence suddenly comes out of the woodwork, then he'll be formally charged within forty-eight hours. And,' he laughed, 'let's face it - being as Marco topped his own brief and hasn't replaced him, any changes on that front look unlikely.'

Zane found it difficult, almost impossible not to punch the air with joy. *Marco was going down. And there he would remain for a very long time.*

Shaking Dave's hand, Zane rose from the seat. Now he could go to the Starbright to give Hazel the good news. This unexpected bonus about his brother almost diluted that he also had to speak to her about Skye.

He was in the process of connecting his crash helmet strap when his mobile rang. If that was Hazel asking when he'd be coming, then he'd keep the good news to himself until he arrived. He didn't want to spoil the surprise.

• • • •

TIGER SHIELDED SKYE from the conversation as much as possible, but it was difficult with the girl clinging to him, her uncontrollable shaking making him feel like he was on a vibrating platform.

He kept the phone pressed to his ear, his other arm holding Skye upright. 'Yeah, I'm serious… I heard screaming and ran down the corridor only to slam straight into Skye. She was the one doing the screaming.'

And it had all but bust his fucking eardrums.

'I don't know. She hasn't made much sense. She's pretty hysterical.' Tiger tightened his grasp on Zane's daughter. 'No… She said she saw no one.'

He glanced at the trembling head pressed against his chest and lowered his voice further - almost hissing into the mobile. 'Yeah, there was an alert... Someone spotted within the ground and then entering the building. He matched the description of.. yeah... And all the men, including me, were searching for him... That's right... yeah... either him or the *other* one...'

Tiger peered at what he could see of Skye's face to see if she'd cottoned on to his words. The girl would be more distressed if she realised her stalker had been seen on the premises again. But Zane knew who he meant. Zane also knew 'the other one' translated to Sandler. Both him and Zane suspected that tosser, Sandler, had hold of Skye's boyfriend, so it stood to reason he was behind this.

Plus, there was another big hint...

'Yeah,' Tiger agreed, 'that's definitely the motive if you get my drift... And she had a word carved into her chest. Yeah... above her fucking tits...' He glanced at Skye. She'd already seen enough to last her a lifetime. 'The word? Yeah... it said "MINE"... What does that tell you? Yep... Exactly!'

Tiger cleared his throat. 'There was something else too... A document on the floor... A statement. I haven't read it all, but basically it was stuff relating to Marco... Yeah, saying he had nothing to do with any of the allegations made against him with the trafficking and all of that stuff.'

He inadvertently moved his hand to trace the pocket where he'd stuffed the piece of paper. 'No, it wasn't signed.' He nodded in response to Zane's take on what had been said. He thought along the same lines: whoever had been in here wanted Hazel to sign that statement and when she'd refused, she'd paid for that loyalty with her life.

There was nothing else to say. It was clear the order to kill Hazel had come from Marco. And the person holding the knife had to be Damon Sandler. That cunt had motive in the shape of pleasing his fucking psycho of a boss and was using Skye's boyfriend to aid him with that job. Skye's boyfriend throwing their guards off kilter had given Sandler the perfect opportunity to strike.

Tiger's brows knitted into a deep frown. 'Yep... he was bloody quick!' Sandler must have been in and out within seconds. There were barely any gaps where there wasn't at least one man on guard anywhere. Hazel and Skye topping the priority list. Whatever Sandler had pulled off had been precisely executed. *A bit like Hazel...*

He turned his attention back to Zane down the other end of the line. The man was upset. Since she'd turned her life around, Zane had a lot of time for Hazel. They all did. And for that life to have now been extinguished was bad. Gutting, even.

Such a horrible, twisted way to go too. But on top of the upset of what had happened to Hazel, this incident made Skye's and Erin's safety extra precarious. Zane would feel that pressure more keenly than any of them.

'Yeah, that's done without saying, mate. I haven't left her side since. Yes, we're as far away as possible. The rest of the men are still patrolling... No... not yet...' *Sandler and the boyfriend would be long gone by now. But heading where, was the worry.* 'Yep... I'll sort that... Mate, she's with me. No harm will come to her.'

Even if he had to die protecting Skye, Tiger would honour his promise and protect Zane's daughter with his life.

Finishing the call, Tiger gently held Skye at arm's length, his usual stony heart softening at her wet cheeks as she looked up, her eyes bottomless pools of anguish. 'It will be okay, you hear me?'

'I-I can't believe someone would do that to Hazel,' Skye whimpered, her words jerky from the hiccupping sobs wracking her body. 'She's such a lovely, kind woman. *Was...* She *was* a lovely, kind woman.' Fresh tears flowed. 'Oh God! How could this happen?'

'There's some shitty people out there, sweetheart.' And it just so happened in this life of theirs these happenings were far too commonplace. They all knew what this life entailed and what it brought, but for the likes of Skye it was an anomaly - a frightening and horrifying prospect. Today she had seen something that she would have never before got hints of, let alone witnessed.

'But what about all the women housed here?' Skye asked, her eyes filled with horror. 'They can't stay here with this going on.'

'No, they can't,' Tiger agreed. Those poor cows had already escaped from a horrible, violent setup once and now they were back in one? 'Your dad wants them to be taken back to Solenzo's immediately until this shit is over.'

Skye clutched at Tiger's sleeve.' Don't go! I don't want to be here on my own.'

'I'm not going anywhere.' Tiger brought his mobile back to life. 'I'm about to instruct some guys from here to move the women now.'

THIRTY THREE

RAW FEAR COURSED THROUGH Zane - each surge stronger than the last.

His sweaty fingers slipped over the buttons on his mobile as he stabbed in Erin's number. He hadn't experienced this level of crippling terror since that day he'd heard she'd been shot. Now it was likely she was back in the firing line again. Or she *would* be if Sandler learned the bullet which had left the barrel of his gun that day had failed in killing her.

Zane didn't know whether his brother and Sandler were aware Erin was still alive or not, but he had to act as if they were.

And this meant Erin was in danger. *Big* danger. Right *now*.

With Sandler succeeding in evading capture after killing Hazel, he could be heading to Dalston. *To Erin.*

A vein pulsated rapidly in Zane's neck. *Come on, come on! Answer the fucking phone!*

He had to get through to Erin and do so fast. Back up was on its way, but that wouldn't happen as quickly as it needed to.

Zane wanted to be there with her. *He* wanted to protect her, like he'd promised himself, yet here he was - too far away to be of use; split between her and the Starbright where his daughter had just stumbled across Hazel's body.

'Come on, Erin!' he roared, booting over a trade bin at the side of the pavement, his head pounding with frustration, fear and anger.

Raging anger. Anger for Sandler; for Marco; that his brother's actions over the past few months had culminated in spreading his influence and power so thinly that he could protect no one.

Now Hazel was dead...

Gritting his teeth, Zane pushed down the burn of tears brewing at the back of his eyes. *Hazel was fucking dead!*

She's been doing so well. She was an asset to herself and to him. Now she was gone.

His fists clenched around the phone. *And all because of Marco.*

Since receiving Tiger's call, the pleasure of his brother's impending prison sentence had long since faded into oblivion. Marco could go to prison but that wouldn't bring Hazel back. Nor would it protect Erin if Sandler reached her first. Neither would it protect Skye who, if Sandler or Marco were aware of who she really was, had probably become even more of a target than Erin.

It scared Zane to the very marrow of his bones.

Sweat soaked the back of his T-shirt as the call rang off. Snarling, he redialled, his earlier theory resurfacing. If the boyfriend - that Martin-fucking-Bolt knew he was Skye's father and given Sandler the info…

His teeth bared in a furious snarl. *Sandler would die for this.*

Jolting as Erin finally answered the phone, Zane dismissed with pleasantries. 'I don't care if you were on the fucking toilet, just listen to me... Hazel's dead... Yes, dead! It was Sandler...' A low growl emitted from his throat. 'How? I know it was him and on my brother's orders because the word "MINE" was carved onto her fucking tits with a knife!'

His hands shook with uncontrollable rage. 'Go to our bedroom. Barricade yourself in there and take the spare gun from the wardrobe... No... No, Leo is coming. He's on his way to you now.'

He stared at the phone. *Was this sinking into her head?* 'Erin!' he repeated. 'Do not move from the bedroom until Leo arrives. He's got a key... Yes... Do you understand? No, I don't know if Sandler's coming for you. This is a precaution.' His eyes narrowed. 'Until I find the bastard, no one is safe. I *need* you to be safe. Yes... yes, she is... She's upset, but okay. I'm heading there now... No, Tiger's with her.'

Zane glanced at his watch. 'I've got to go... Yeah, I will... Promise me you'll do what I said... I love you.'

Ending the call, he jumped on his bike and fired the engine. He'd ride like the devil himself to the Starbright.

All he was grateful for at the moment was that a trusted colleague and friend was protecting his daughter. Skye was in good hands with Tiger and he hoped his other most trusted man would reach Erin and the house in Dalston before anyone else did.

• • • •

TIGER WAS FRAZZLED. It was difficult speaking to the troops on the mobile to give them specific orders to mobilise them into the correct place for optimal cover without rubbing Skye's face in what she'd witnessed by having to listen to Hazel's fate over and over.

It was even harder explaining the situation to the men in the new territories across London in order to send at least half of them to headquarters, plus a quarter more here to wait for Zane.

Leo would meet the men going to the Thames Canning Works and split them into sections to comb the capital and its surrounding areas for Sandler and Skye's boyfriend.

Zane, when he arrived here at the Starbright, would do the same for the men coming here. All remaining men would be left where they were to oversee the territories and ensure nothing untoward kicked off.

He glanced out of the window, watching as the remaining

women from upstairs were covered from all angles by the guards as they clambered into two vans. They'd be safe at Solenzo's for now.

Tiger sighed. This was an utter shit show. This stunt with Hazel meant the start of a war. A war coming from where and featuring exactly who Sandler had under his command, no one knew. Perhaps the news that Zane had been given by his contact in the force was wrong? Perhaps Marco wasn't dead in the water after all? This could be the start of something huge which they had to face blind.

Conversely, it could be Sandler and Sandler alone behind this. As far as they knew, that wanker was the only person Marco had to fall back on. But things could have changed...

Whatever happened, that bastard had done serious damage and successfully thrown them off balance today. Not to mention Hazel losing her life in the process.

In the office he'd chosen as a safe place, Tiger's attention fell back to Skye curled into a ball on the chair. He couldn't let her out of his sight until Zane arrived. Then what would be done with her, he didn't know. She would need guarding 24/7 tighter than before, as would all the women.

Zane should be here any minute and that couldn't come too soon. Comforting people wasn't high on Tiger's list of strengths and judging by the state of Skye, he wasn't doing a particularly wonderful job. But for fuck's sake, what was he supposed to do?

Tiger shifted his big frame and made his way to the chair Skye was curled in, her legs tucked underneath herself as if to make her body as inconspicuous as possible. He tentatively reached to touch her shoulder - his hand pausing mid-air before making contact.

Hell, he didn't know what to do. If only Erin was here. Women dealt with others' grief better than men - or at least, better than *he* did.

Skye would end up having to be sedated at this rate and Zane wouldn't be happy if his daughter ended up in hospital with trauma-induced panic attacks. Having to explain the reason behind her distress would be awkward. Plus, hospitals were less guarded than any of their locations would *ever* be.

Tiger glanced at the wall where two rooms along the body of Hazel Grimes remained. What they would do about her was something else to deal with.

'Erm...' He hesitatingly touched Skye's shoulder. 'Do you need a glass of water? I think there's some bottles down the hall which I could...'

'No!' Wide-eyed, Skye leapt from the chair and threw herself against Tiger's barrel chest. 'Don't leave me!' A single tear slid down her face and dripped off her chin to leave a wet patch on his shirt. 'I don't want to be on my own. W-What if they're still here? The people that... that... killed Hazel?'

'There's no one here,' Tiger said calmly. 'We have men everywhere. The building is clear. No one will hurt you.'

'H-Hazel said that too and look what happened. What if...'

'I won't leave you,' Tiger said gruffly, still smarting that Sandler and his sidekick had somehow got past their defence. 'Your dad will be here soon. He's on his way.'

'I can't believe Hazel's dead!' Skye wailed, the sobbing ramping up both in pitch and ferocity.

For want of not knowing what else to do, Tiger pulled a tissue from his back pocket to clumsily dab at Skye's cheeks that were running with rivulets of black mascara, only succeeding in smudging her makeup.

'I'm not making a very good job of doing this,' he muttered. 'I'm sorry you had to see... well... Hazel like that. Young girls and women shouldn't have to see this side of life.'

Skye's sobs quietened as she looked up into Tiger's stern face. 'But I'm not a young girl. Young girls are kids and I'm no kid.'

Tiger frowned, unsure why Skye would be so shirty over his comments as to what women should or shouldn't be exposed to in this bitch of a life.

'I can easily prove why you should start looking at me like

a woman, rather than a *girl.*' Arching an eyebrow, Skye began unbuttoning her top.

Tiger stepped back, unsure he was processing what he was seeing. *She wasn't taking her clothes off? Surely she wasn't?* His answer was confirmed to be the affirmative when Skye's top fell to the floor and she then unclipped her bra, leaving it to follow suit.

Tiger's mouth opened but nothing came out. He immediately averted his eyes from the pert globes of Skye's breasts and instead bent down to snatch her clothes from the floor. 'What on earth are you doing?' he gasped, shoving Skye's clothes at her.

'Don't tell me you're shy?' Skye pushed back up against Tiger's chest, her hand palming his crotch. 'I find it difficult to believe that a man like you doesn't know what to do...'

Taking Skye's wrist, Tiger yanked her hand away. 'Just put your bloody clothes back on now!'

'Hmm...' Skye pouted, her teeth coquettishly digging into her lower lip as her hand found its way back to Tiger's crotch. 'There doesn't seem to be much life here. I've never had that response before. I'll have to make an extra effort to get you going.'

Before Tiger could pull Skye's hand away for the second time, she crashed her mouth onto his, her nails digging into the side of his neck to pull him further towards her.

'Christ's sake!' Tiger snarled. Wrenching away, he grabbed Skye's shoulders to hold her at arms' length. 'What the fuck has got into you? You can't just...'

'What the fuck is this?' Zane roared, bursting into the room, his eyes widening in horror to see his daughter naked from the waist up.

'Oh, thank God!' Skye shrieked. 'He won't leave me alone!' Rushing to Zane, she clung to the sleeve of his leather jacket. 'He said if I didn't do what he wanted, then he'd...'

'You touched my daughter?' Zane screamed, his eyes burning with raw fury at Tiger. 'How fucking dare you abuse my trust! Abuse my daughter's trust and take advantage! I'll kill you! I'll...'

'Fuck off! She's crazy!' Tiger roared, his face equally fired. 'She's wrong in the fucking head! I was just standing there when...'

'His hands were everywhere,' Skye sobbed, tears appearing on cue. 'He took my top and...'

Physically lifting Skye out of the way, Zane lost the ability to think rationally before he vaulted the desk and launched at Tiger, his fist connecting with the man's jaw.

He was so primed to kick the living daylights out of the man - his trusted colleague - his *friend*, who had taken it upon himself to touch his daughter against her will, that he completely missed the smirk of amusement on Skye's face.

Thirty Four

RIGID WITH FEAR, Martin remained motionless - the same way he'd been for over an hour and wondered, not for the first time, how long it would take before he ran out of oxygen.

His fingers traced the join between the tightly fitting doors of the cupboard he'd sought refuge in. *There was no gap. Didn't that mean he'd eventually run out of air?*

Cold sweat beaded on his forehead which only fuelled his panic. He'd done biology at school and knew that sweating used up the body's water supply. If he had to remain in here for hours and hours - possibly *days*, then he'd run out of oxygen if dying of frustration didn't kill him first.

Oh God.

The back of his legs burnt from the unnatural position he held, but he couldn't move. He *dare* not move - not that there was anywhere to move to. Although it was pitch black in this cupboard, his eyes had adjusted enough to see there wasn't room to squat down. Or turn around.

His heart pounded.

He couldn't stay in here forever but if he opened the door, then they'd see him. What if he couldn't open the door at all? He'd be entombed until the air ran out or he died of thirst.

Panic spiralled. Martin screwed his eyes tightly shut in the dark claustrophobic space in an attempt to calm his burgeoning hysteria.

How could he get out of this place? And what about Skye? He'd left her again.

Martin pressed his forehead against the wooden door. He'd slam his bonce against this hard thick wood over and over to stop his brain from pounding if he wasn't so terrified of being detected.

His teeth clenched. He was doing it again. Being selfish and only thinking about himself. Pathetic! That's what he was. Goddamn pathetic!

He didn't deserve Skye. He'd let her down and failed to protect her. What sort of man was he?

The truth was, he wasn't a man. He was a joke.

Tears burned in Martin's eyes at this glaring realisation. He'd allowed that Damon man to dictate what he had to do and he'd glibly nodded like a good little boy and followed instructions.

Why?

Because he was a snivelling, pointless, useless piece of...

But what choice did he have? It was the only way to protect Skye. And now he'd failed in doing that because Damon said that if he didn't complete the instructions, then both him and Skye were finished.

Well, *he* wasn't finished yet. Mainly because he was hiding in a cupboard. But what had happened to Skye? Had Damon taken her? Raped her? Killed her?

Martin began trembling. He needed the toilet now as well.

Oh, this was hopeless!

Amid throes of unbridled panic, he felt more like a child than he could ever remember and desperately wished his mother was here to help him.

Wait! That was it!

Forcing his arm between himself and the tight constraints of the side of the cupboard, his fingers felt for his pocket.

Was it still there? Please let it still be there...

Touching the hard outline of his mobile, Martin's heart surged with hope. *How had he forgotten he'd kept hold of his phone?*

After following Damon's orders to call his parents back, the man had been too fired up about getting into the Starbright to notice Martin slipping his phone into his pocket rather than back near the gear stick where Damon had instructed to put it.

Now Martin just had to get it out. *If he could get it out...*

But there wasn't room to get his hand in his pocket...

Shit, shit!

Martin gingerly pushed two fingers into his jeans pocket to form a pincer hold of his mobile. *If he could pull it out without dropping it...*

If he dropped the phone, he'd be unable to bend to retrieve it. He had to be careful.

As the phone inched higher out of his pocket, Martin dare not breathe.

Come on, nearly there. Don't drop it, he prayed, his fumbling fingers clammy with sweat.

Got it!

Martin exhaled, his breath juddery. Then he listened.

He couldn't hear a sound. The footsteps and shouts milling around in the hallway and nearby areas had died down and disappeared some time ago. He was as certain as he could be that no one was in this room or nearby now.

Bringing his mobile to life, he smiled seeing the two bars of signal. *Not great but it would do.*

His fingers fumbled on the keypad. Would the police get here in time to save Skye? Save him? Would they even believe him?

No! He couldn't risk it. He'd phone his mum instead. She'd know what to do.

With shaking hands, Martin dialled the number, hoping his father didn't answer. If that happened, then any conversation would be pointless.

. . . .

ERIN BARELY HEARD THE front door open when Leo arrived. She'd done what Zane asked and barricaded herself in the bedroom, but her mind wasn't consumed by fear that Damon Sandler would appear to gun her down for the second time. Instead, all she could think of was that Hazel - the woman who had become an unlikely friend and ally, was dead.

The full extent of her heartbreak hadn't fully sunk in but the desperate misery, combined with hatred for the person responsible, threatened to squeeze the very life out of her.

'You okay?' Leo asked, concern clouding his face. Erin didn't look fine. She looked destroyed. *Shattered.*

'I just can't believe it,' Erin mumbled, her voice sounding like it belonged to someone else. 'Poor Hazel.' She swiped away a lone tear making its way down her cheek. 'Fucking Sandler! That bastard, he…'

'He'll get his,' Leo said, his voice cold. He couldn't get his head around the fact that there were all those guards in the Starbright and not only had the skinny kid had been sighted and not found, but the worst mistake of all was that the people most needing it had been left unguarded.

They may have the numbers and the men who had recently joined the firm were solid and trustworthy, but they didn't understand the way things worked with the backstory that played such an important role in dealing with Marco. The new men lacked the experience to deal with things occurring under Marco Morelli's command. The psycho issued orders in ways that only people aware of his way of thinking had a chance of outsmarting.

Out of all of the men in Zane's new firm, the only ones possessing enough knowledge to make the right decisions on that score was Zane, Tiger and himself.

Leo grimaced. Tiger was the one on duty at the Starbright today, but there were only so many places he could cover alone so it wouldn't be fair, nor reasonable to point the finger of blame for what happened to Hazel at his door.

Zane was spreading them all far too thinly. Everyone knew that and now a price had been paid, Leo had to ensure there were no further payouts.

'The women at the Starbright?' Erin asked, panic rising. 'They...'

'They've gone back to Solenzo's temporarily,' Leo said. 'Or they will be shortly. They'll be safe there, don't worry'.

Erin nodded, unsure whether anyone could be safe anymore. Would it *ever* be safe? 'And what about me? How long do we have to stay here?' she mumbled, guessing what that answer would be.

'Zane's pulled in as many men to scout for Sandler as possible,' Leo shrugged. 'He won't rest until the bastard is apprehended, which reminds me - I don't suppose he got the chance to tell you that Marco's going down after all?'

Erin's eyes widened. 'He is?' *That was good news. Except...* Without warning, her face crumpled. 'Hazel will never know that now.' How ironic for the woman to be cut down a matter of hours before she'd have been free from Marco for the foreseeable.

Hazel would have been able to breathe easy once again. Despite her putting on a brave face and ploughing her energies into the women in need at the Starbright, Erin knew how deeply the prospect of Marco's release played on her mind. Hazel's death also proved that the fear Sandler was just as much of a threat as Marco to be well-founded. They were *all* targets – more so now than before.

Seeing the silent tears falling from Erin's eyes, Leo placed his arm around her shoulders and pulled her into a hug. 'Sandler will be stopped, you'll see.'

'And you should be out there doing just that, rather than babysitting me!' Erin said, bitterly resenting that her existence was slowing down removing Sandler from this earth. 'Christ! He carved Marco's message into Hazel's fucking chest!' she spat, not wanting to focus on her friend having died forever branded by the words of her psycho husband.

'I'd rather be babysitting you, if that's the way you see it, than allowing that fucking wanker to chalk up another strike,' Leo smiled. 'Oh, who's this?' Pulling his ringing mobile from his pocket, he got to his feet, his whole posture changing as he readied himself for news that danger was heading this way in the form of a sighting in Dalston of Damon Sandler. Instead, his mouth fell open. 'What? When? Fucking hell! Is it still going on? Shit! Where are they now?'

Erin sat forward, aware that whatever this was, was not anything Leo expected. She didn't think she'd ever seen his swarthy complexion go pale regardless of what was going on. *Until now...*

'Yeah, okay... Keep it that way.' Leo glanced at Erin. 'I'll be there as quickly as I can.'

The second Leo ended the call, Erin jumped on the situation. 'What's happened?' she asked, her nerves buzzing.

'It's Zane,' Leo muttered, snatching his jacket from the back of the sofa.

'Zane?' Erin cried, nausea surging. 'What's happened to him? Not Sandler? He... he hasn't...'

'No, not Sandler,' Leo said sharply. 'That was a guard from the Starbright. Zane arrived to find Skye half-naked being pawed by Tiger.'

'What?' Erin stepped back in shock. 'Tiger? Tiger was doing *what*?'

'You heard correctly.' Leo's face was grave. 'The guard didn't see anything but heard a commotion from the room Tiger was in with the girl and rushed in to find Zane beating seven tons of shit out of him.'

Erin's head swam. 'But...'

'Tiger was giving as good as he got.' Leo shook his head with disbelief. 'A bunch of guards have separated them for now but the shit's hit the fan good and fucking proper.'

'I-I can't believe it!' Erin gasped.

'Nor can I, but that's what's happened! Tiger was all over

the girl. He'd ripped her clothes and everything.' Leo jerked his head at the door. 'I have to go and sort it out. Which means so have you. I can't leave you here.'

Erin scrabbled for her shoes. 'Are they *sure* that's what happened? I can't see Tiger behaving like that!'

Leo pulled his gun ready for opening the front door just in case. 'I can't either. I've known Tiger for twenty fucking years. He wouldn't pull that stunt on anyone, let alone the daughter of one of our own.'

'Hmm and what's the common denominator here?' Erin's eyes narrowed, picturing the victorious sneer on Skye's face – one similar to the many she'd personally received.

Was this the next facet in Skye's plan? Breaking up yet another association which Zane relied on to function? Because *that* was the common denominator - anything upsetting the dynamic and chipping away the glue holding the threads of Zane's firm together was fair game.

Without a doubt, *this* latest episode would achieve that.

Following Leo out of the house and into the car, Erin bristled with unknown but growing trepidation.

What else was going to happen today? First Hazel and now this?

THIRTY FIVE

'MARTIN?' Fiona cried. 'Is that you?' Relief swarmed through her body as she wiped away the tears she'd allowed to flow freely out of desperate frustration.

She kept a steady grip of the bedroom's cordless phone, praying Peter was too engrossed in the newspaper like usual, to warrant picking up the extension downstairs. What mattered was hearing her beloved son's voice and finding out what was going on without her husband interfering.

'Where are you? I don't believe what you said to your dad. You were forced to say that, weren't you? I know you were. You're not at the coast - am I right? You can tell me, just... What?'

Fiona's forehead crinkled in concentration. 'I *am* listening, but I can't hear you very well... The line... It's not very good... It's...' She frowned harder. 'Can you speak up a little? I can't... Oh! What? You're *where*?' Fiona's blood ran cold. 'You're in a what? Oh my God, Martin! I...'

Fiona paused. *She must keep a grip of herself.* If Peter heard her talking, he'd either pick up the downstairs phone or come to investigate.

But trapped and hiding in a cupboard? 'Hiding from who,

Martin? Who are you hiding fr...' Her eyes widened. 'Is it them? Those people? I spoke to Skye's mother and she told me that these people... Are they called Chelly? Or Shelly? Something like that? Shirley said they... What?'

Fiona forced her racing mind to slow. She could barely hear Martin - his voice was little more than a whisper. *People were looking and would kill him if they found him? What on earth?*

Her blood crashed in her veins, her hand flying to her mouth in case the rising bile made a sudden exit. 'Chelly, I said. Or Shelly? I couldn't quite understand Shirley and your father, he said th... Who? *Morelli*? Who is... He's Skye's father? Morelli who? What? Damon? Damon Morelli? No?' *Oh God, she was getting confused.* 'Martin! I can't hear you, I... What? Hang on!'

Fiona propelled herself off the bed and scrabbled around the dressing table for a pen. She ignored the Yves St Laurent eyeshadow palette falling off the side, her favourite sparkly nude shadow crumbling into pieces.

It didn't matter. Nothing mattered apart from making sure her son was safe.

'Say it again? Right... Okay. Got it!' Fiona scribbled the word 'Starbright' on the back of her leather-bound journal. 'I'll get help, I promise. What do you... Martin? MARTIN? Are you still there?'

Taking the phone from her ear, Fiona stared at the handset in horror. The line was dead. Martin had said something about the signal getting worse. And now he'd gone.

Okay, breathe, breathe.

Now she knew the truth.

Fiona's lips straightened. She'd been right all along. Martin was not at the coast - he'd been taken hostage by someone - one of those people to do with Skye's search or someone connected with them.

She raced from the bedroom across the landing. There was no time to waste. She'd go to this Starbright place and make those people let her son go. Martin was nothing whatsoever to do with what Skye had got herself mixed up in and she'd tell them that herself when she got there.

Her face set in determination. This time, Peter *would* listen and take her seriously because he would have to drive her there. And he'd be doing that right this very minute.

. . . .

ALTHOUGH DAMON WAS STIFF, covered in things he'd rather not know about and thoroughly pissed off, he found he still possessed the ability to gloat over his good fortune. It showed what a shit show Zane Morelli's firm was.

Okay, so Zane's grunts had surrounded the perimeter of the Starbright, closing off all routes of escape whilst getting a view of all other possibilities. That was the sole reason why he was forced to lie low *here*. But failing to spot him whilst he'd still been inside that building or since, was priceless.

What wasn't priceless was in the time he'd been lying low there had been no sign of Martin or the girl. He had as good a view of the place and the grounds as the guards who were trying to find him, which could only mean one thing: Martin, the fucking idiot, had got himself a capture. Making the stupid decision to waste time offloading that plastic bitch, he'd not receive a friendly experience inside there. Something had kicked off since Damon had been watching, so the twat was probably already stone dead.

Some time ago, Zane himself had arrived and then shortly after that, half of the guards had rushed back in too. What it was about, Damon didn't know or care. As long as it wasn't to do with *him*, he didn't give a rat's arse.

Oh, and there was one other thing...

Damon raised his body up a little, the pressure on his ankles crucifying, to bring his eyes level with the inch-wide gap he'd fashioned to keep the lid of the trade bin ajar. Using a bin full of shitty half eaten crap and God knows what else wasn't the first choice had there been others. The smell alone would take a fucking month to get off his skin and out the inside of his nose. But this hiding place was all there was on offer to avoid joining

Martin being tortured to death, so he'd taken it.

He was getting mightily hacked off having to remain in the fucking thing, yet here he must stay until the goons stepped their search down. Only then could he risk getting the hell away from here.

Damon swallowed uncomfortably. Getting out of this place unscathed would be difficult enough, but if he succeeded there was another issue to deal with...

Marco...

Marco would not be pleased to hear that not only had getting the statement signed by his beloved wife failed, but it would never happen now because she was dead.

Suddenly hearing a car, Damon lowered himself a fraction from the crack the bin lid offered.

Who was this?

If it was one of Zane's men who knew their stuff, then that wouldn't work in his favour if *they* insisted on scouring the grounds.

Heart pounding, he watched the car door open and a large figure jump out.

Shit. *Leo Holland?* That man knew his stuff, so he...

What the fuck?

Damon's throat instantly dried up at the sight of the person emerging from the passenger side.

No way! Just no!

She was dead! He'd shot her himself! He'd seen her die on the floor surrounded by a pool of her own blood!

How. The. Fuck. Had. Erin. Langley. Lived?

Sweat ran down Damon's back, his jaw clenching.

How could this happen? He'd seen her fucking die! Even then he'd put feelers out just to be doubly sure, but she hadn't been sighted anywhere since. *Ever.*

Snapping his eyes shut, he took a deep breath, wishing he hadn't as the bin's stench rushed further into his lungs. He quickly reopened his eyes.

Yep. It was her. Erin Langley was alive. For fuck's sake.

Marco would go tits!

Damon wanted to scream. He hated that bitch. He'd wanted her dead more than Marco had, the horrible whore.

He shook with frustration at being unable to jump out of the bin, rush over and stave Erin Langley's head in for daring to defy him by being alive, but he wasn't getting gunned down because of her.

Snarling, he watched Erin and Leo rush into the building.

Do you know what? Damon thought, reaching a decision. *Bollocks to it.*

He wouldn't tell Marco. What was the point? Without Hazel's statement giving Marco a defence, the man would go down. And if he remembered correctly, Marco was due to be formally charged within a day, so what could be done to get at him then?

Once he got out of here all he had to do was stay out of the way and lay horizontal until Marco was jailed and then that was that.

Sure, he'd still have Zane Morelli after his blood, but judging by the brainpower of the man's staff, Damon reckoned that perhaps he shouldn't be overly concerned.

THIRTY SIX

'ARE THEY IN HERE?' Leo crashed into the room without waiting for an answer.

Following on Leo's heels, Erin gasped at the spectacle: a set of guards surrounded both Tiger and Zane at opposite ends of the room, sweating profusely with the immense effort of controlling the raging men. She moved forward only to be held back by a large arm.

'Stay back!' Leo growled. 'I ain't having you getting hurt as well!'

Erin did as she was told for once, her shock morphing to despair as her gaze darted between the man she loved and one of his closest friends. Blood flowed from Zane's split lip; his one eye swollen almost shut. His remaining eye blazed with psychotic rage to an extent she'd not before witnessed, even during the unbridled fury he'd unleased on Anthony - the man partly responsible for Zane's wrongful incarceration and who Erin had become engaged to in order to pursue the vendetta over her father's killer.

As the men continued restraining him, growls and expletives spewed from Zane's mouth to join into one unintelligible roar.

His rage was equally matched by that of Tiger who was pressed against the opposite wall by guards also struggling to keep control.

Erin took in Tiger's split lip which mirrored Zane's but with the difference of a missing tooth. Tiger's eyes were undamaged, but severe bruising on one cheekbone showed he'd received a hefty whack.

'Oh my God,' she gasped. How the hell had things come to this? Beating on each other? Never attack your own - that was the unspoken rule - the firm was *family*. But then, this being over Zane's daughter put a different slant on those rules.

Was it possible that she was wrong and Tiger *had* taken it upon himself to force himself on the girl? She hated even thinking such a thing of Tiger, but was it possible? Had she got this and everything else wrong?

As if Erin's thoughts transmitted through the ether, Skye's voice rose above the rabid roaring of the men.

'What is *she* doing here?' Skye screeched, lurching forward in an oversized T-shirt clearly foisted on her to cover her modesty. 'She'll be loving this!' Fresh tears sprang to flow down her cheeks. 'I don't want her here. Get her out!' Her voice was high-pitched and hysterical. 'She'll say I'm lying like she does about everything.'

Despite having his hands full foiling Zane's latest attempt at breaking free, Leo stopped Skye's advance towards Erin with his other arm.

Bewildered and beyond upset, Erin stared at Skye. Despite the tears, the venomous hatred in the girl's eyes was unmissable.

'I did NOT touch her!' Tiger suddenly bellowed - to whom, Erin didn't know. But what she *did* know was that she believed him.

Oh, she believed him all right. And this wasn't because of the previous stunts Skye had pulled, the lies, nor the girl's unknown agenda. Tiger was innocent of this because Erin had clocked the smirk Skye shot in his direction before turning around, making sure the expression she now wore contained only anguish.

'Zane!' Erin risked moving forward once again. 'You must calm down.' He wore a look that both terrified and worried her. It was as if the man she knew and loved had been replaced by a monster whose sole purpose on earth was to destroy mankind. He looked crazy; animalistic. *Deranged*.

'This isn't going to fucking work,' Leo muttered to the guards who were at risk of exhaustion containing Tiger's immense strength. 'Get him out of here.' Grabbing hold of one of Tiger's arms, he helped manoeuvre the thrashing man towards the door, pulling Erin with his other arm. 'You're coming too.'

Erin had no choice but to allow herself to be dragged out of the room. Zane was too busy thrashing out of the guards' grips to notice her departure. Skye, on the other hand, sent a smug smile in her direction.

'Where are we going?' Erin shouted, her feet struggling to keep a grip of the floor.

'I'm taking Tiger to a separate room, then I'll go back to speak to Zane and try and sort this out,' Leo hissed as the group moved with difficulty up the hallway.

'I'll come with you,' Erin said. *If she could just get Zane to calm down: to listen...*

'Hang fire!' Leo pulled up the shuffling group and used his foot to boot open another door. 'You're to wait in here, Erin.'

'What? Why? I...' Before Erin knew what had happened, Leo had pushed her inside the room. She immediately darted back to the door.

'Stay there!' Leo growled, his face showing there was no room for argument. 'Your presence is aggravating the girl and I've got nowhere to put her. Skye can't be left on her own. She needs to be with her dad. Let me calm Tiger down, try and do the same with Zane and then I'll come and get you. You're safe from harm in here and I can't be everywhere at once.' Giving Erin a look that hinted at apologetic, he slammed the door in her face.

'Leo! No!' Erin banged on the door until she heard the unmistakable sound of the key turning in the lock and realised her argument was pointless.

. . . .

PETER GLARED AT FIONA, fast losing his patience. He straightened down the creases on his shirt from where her fingers had clutched at his sleeve to pull him from the chair. 'You're unhinged! You come racing in here, pulling me about and making absurd demands! Stop it now!'

'I will not stop it! It's important!' Fiona ran back and forth in the lounge unable to decide what to do first. 'Have you not listened?' Her hands flew into the air like she was chucking a pile of confetti. 'I just told you that Martin called me. He's hiding in a cupboard in a place he's been forced into by a man. He's got two lots of people trying to kill him!'

Peter sighed, his lack of patience moving towards full blown annoyance. Fiona's state of mind these past couple of days had been concerning but was now at the point of being irritating. 'This is to do with what that stupid woman said, isn't it? Whatever she's put in your head has sent you crazy! Martin in a cupboard? Don't be absurd!'

'But he is!' Fiona's delicate hands clenched into fists. 'We must drive there now. He's in a place called the Starbright. Look!' She thrust her journal at Peter. 'I wrote down what he said.'

Peter smiled sadly. 'Martin hasn't phoned at all. It's just what you *want* him to do. You need an answer why he's not home because you're worried. I understand after that hoo-ha with the car, but I told you what he said - he's still at the coast with his friends. The car was stolen, Fiona. He's fine!'

'Oh my God!' Fiona threw the journal and watched Peter duck to avoid being hit in the face. 'It's there in black and white. The "Starbright". I wrote it down and I *did* speak to Martin. He's locked in a cupboard.' Her eyes widened. 'You must drive me there now, Peter. They're going to kill him!'

Peter shook his head, partly in disgust that his wife would actually *throw* something at him and partly from exhaustion over dealing with her outbursts. 'I'm driving nowhere.'

'Then I'll phone Shirley. I'll tell her where Martin is and see if she's heard of the place or of this Damon Morelli or whatever his name is.' Fiona stomped across the room and picked up the phone.

'You're not speaking to that lunatic again!' Peter moved to snatch the phone from Fiona's hand. 'That woman has done enough damage by filling your head with this nonsense.'

'It's not nonsense! Martin said th…'

'Okay, where is this Starbright place, then?' Peter asked, holding the phone out of reach of Fiona's grasping hands.

Fiona paused. *Where was it? Had she asked Martin that?* 'Erm, I think it must be in Battersea or...'

'You don't actually know?' Peter couldn't help the chuckle escaping his mouth. 'For God's sake, this is madness! This place doesn't exist. It's all in your head.'

'It's not! I'm telling you that Martin…'

'Fine! Have it your own way!' Peter punched a number into the phone.

'Who are you calling?' Fiona screeched. 'Don't call the police! That will make things worse. They'll...'

'I'm not calling the police,' Peter spat. 'Do you not think I've had enough public humiliation as far as they're concerned for one day? It's... Hello? Directory Enquiries? Yes... Hello. Could you give me the number for the... erm... the "Starbright" please... No, just "Starbright".' He drummed his fingers on the sideboard impatiently. 'Yes, it's in London... Pardon? No… I'm not sure exactly where, just somewhere in London, I think... No, I'm afraid I don't know what type of business it is...' He raised his eyebrows at Fiona. 'Okay... No, that's it. Thank you very much.'

'See? I told you!' Fiona cried. 'Now let's go!'

'Go where?' Peter said, thoroughly exasperated. 'There's

no record of anything called the "Starbright" in London. The only place coming up was an adult film studio – but that was called "Star*light*". It recently burnt down too, so no, Fiona, I won't be driving you to the Starbright.'

'Then I'll call a taxi!' Fiona scurried around looking for her handbag.

'No. You. Won't!' Peter said slowly. 'You're not going on a crazy goose chase to somewhere that doesn't even exist!'

'I promised Martin I'd get help!' Fiona screamed, her eyes wild. 'You're happy to wait until he's murdered? I hate you for this, Peter. *Hate* you! I'll never forgive you if something happens to him because of you!' Storming over, she pummelled Peter's chest with her fists.

'Stop that immediately!' Peter shouted. 'Enough is enough!'

'I HATE YOU!' Fiona yelled, her hand swinging to slap her husband around the face.

Flashing red with rage, Peter shoved Fiona away hard enough for her to stumble into the armchair. 'ENOUGH, I said! Right – now you listen to *me*. I'll ring Martin myself right now. If he confirms what he said to you, then I'll gladly drive to London and sort this out or call the police - one or the other. If, on the other hand, Martin is too drunk to answer or tells me he's still at the coast, then this will be the last time we shall speak of this because I'm at my wits end with this rubbish!'

Snatching the phone back up, Peter dialled Martin's number.

THIRTY SEVEN

MARTIN WANTED his teeth to stop chattering but he couldn't control them. He wasn't cold - far from it. If anything, he was burning up because this cupboard was a sweatbox.

It was because there was someone in the room where he was hiding. He'd heard them come in. A man's voice at first, then a woman's, plus lots of other noise. But it wasn't Skye's voice he'd heard – he'd recognise that anywhere. It was another female's voice.

Martin remained motionless, hoping the persistent humming and buzzing in his head making his face shake wasn't as loud in reality as it sounded from within.

It was now quiet outside of the cupboard. The voices had stopped and everything was silent, apart from occasional footsteps. And they were from nearby - from *inside* the room. Someone was pacing up and down. And if he concentrated really hard, Martin was sure he could hear breathing too.

But even when the sound of pacing and breathing was absent, he could *sense* someone's presence. Were they standing the other side of this wooden door able to sense *him* just as strongly?

Furthermore, who was it?

Was it the person he'd heard earlier with the gruff voice who sounded like it belonged to a large and muscly man who would batter him senseless with one punch? Or was it the woman?

Either way, it didn't bode well. Perhaps it was the short-haired blonde he'd seen with Skye before turning on his heels?

Martin frowned. He was sure he'd heard the door being locked. That blonde woman clearly worked here, so why would she be locked in a room? It didn't make sense, so it must be someone else being kept prisoner here.

It could be Damon... If these people had cornered that man it made sense to lock him somewhere until they decided how to deal with him.

Sweat prickled. *How long would this person remain in the room? And how long should he wait before trying to escape?*

Although Martin hadn't yet attempted escaping, he hadn't tried the cupboard door to see if he could get out either. He was too afraid to in case he found it locked.

But it wasn't like he could do anything now. Not while someone was here.

Praying he wouldn't sneeze or cough, Martin concentrated on anything else to take his mind off the unbearable situation, reminding himself that his mum was getting help. The police would be on their way by now. His mum wouldn't let him down, he *knew* she wouldn't.

Then the worst thing happened. Worse than Martin could have foreseen.

The ringing of his mobile phone was louder than if it were spliced through amplifiers serving a football stadium.

'Fuck!' he hissed under his breath. Or had he shouted it? He didn't know - he couldn't hear anything other than the deafening noise of his mobile in the otherwise silent enclosure.

His fingers fumbled to pull his phone out of his pocket, but he couldn't get hold of it. *Come on, come the fuck on!*

Finally getting hold of his mobile, Martin hastened to pull it free to cut off the call, but in his rush it slipped from his fingers and fell to the floor where now it wasn't just ringing, but vibrating noisily against the cupboard's wooden base.

Shit!

Pushing the phone along with his foot, he tried to crouch down to reach it, but his arm didn't span the required distance.

God, no!

Martin glanced at the screen:

```
...Home calling...
```

What was his mum calling back for? Had she not thought that ringing might give his position away?

Sweat poured freely down Martin's face and just as he contemplated stamping on his only connection with the outside world, the door of the cupboard flew open.

• • • •

ERIN'S FIRST REACTION on seeing the stranger in the cupboard was to attack him. Either that or scream for Leo.

But something about the young man's terrified countenance as he squinted through the light rushing into his hiding place and the livid bruising of his face, stopped her in her tracks.

Now she was glad that she hadn't reacted off the cuff.

After talking to him it was obvious this young man possessed no knowledge of Hazel's murder. The shock on his face when she'd grilled him about it showed he hadn't a clue.

Furthermore, she believed what he said. His injuries backed up his story, but the question was, would anyone else agree?

It wasn't exactly the best day to expect Zane or his men to behave rationally towards the person they believed had a) stalked Skye, b) killed Hazel and, c) worked for Marco under the command of Damon Sandler.

It was unlikely Martin's presence would go down well now Zane and one of his men were at each other's throats. But Leo could return any second and he wasn't the sort to ask questions first either.

Erin chewed her bottom lip. She needed facts from Martin Bolt to prove his only involvement in this was to look for Skye on her mother's request. And it was up to *her* to get those facts, otherwise Martin would be ripped limb from limb. But now she'd upset him further and she could do without him having hysterics. He was treading a thin line as it was, but it was vital he understood the picture Skye had painted of him rather than remain in the make-believe world that the girl loved him. *Because she clearly did not.*

'Why would Skye say I'd dumped her?' Martin gibbered. 'I love her. I want to marry her.'

'I don't know but she soon changed that story, saying *she* didn't want to be with *you*, but you wouldn't accept it and were stalking her.'

'That's not true! I've never stalked anyone! I wouldn't! She...'

'But there were no texts on her phone that she'd sent to you,' Erin said, playing devil's advocate. Martin Bolt looked sincere enough, but he could be lying. Skye was proof that people put on convincing acts.

'No texts?' Martin gasped. 'Until she disappeared here two weeks ago, she texted me constantly! She was texting so much when I was away on holiday that my father threatened to throw my phone away!'

Erin frowned. 'Show me.'

Fumbling with his phone, Martin opened the messages. 'Here. Look.'

Erin scrolled down the list of texts. Some days Skye had messaged Martin seventy or eighty times! The last ones he'd received were mere days before she'd first been spotted watching Zane.

Erin opened a text:

> Babe, I so can't wait to see u.
> I miss u.
> Love u more every day

```
xxxxxxxxxxxxxxxxxx
```

Jesus, how many kisses? Erin moved on to the next:

```
Y did u have to go away 4 so long?
U no I can't live without u.
Love you soooooo much.
xxxxxxxx
```

And the next:

```
Love u love u love u
Love u love u
I LOVE U
xxxxxxxxx
```

'My God! Are they all like this?' Erin muttered, flicking to another message.

```
Marty, u r my life
2gether 4eva
xxxxxxxxxx
```

These weren't sent from a girl who wasn't interested, Erin thought and weren't in the sent box on Skye's original phone, but they'd definitely been sent from that number. They must have been deleted. *Why?* 'How long have you been together?'

'Seven months, nearly eight,' Martin said. 'I've known Skye for years. Well, not "known" her as in known her *well*. I saw her about at school. She was a couple of years younger than me and then I left to go to sixth form, so I didn't see her for a while. We got together last year.'

Erin saw the smitten expression settle on Martin's battered face as he talked of how he and Skye's relationship had blossomed and how he'd never felt about anyone the way he felt about her. He wasn't making it up. Neither was he deluded.

But Erin remembered what Zane said about Skye's school being awful. Well-spoken and polite, this lad didn't seem the sort to have gone to a rough school. Plus, he had a Range Rover with a private plate...

'What school did you go to?'

Martin seemed surprised at this question. 'There's only one decent school near where we live. People come from all over to attend, but luckily we didn't board because we're local.'

'Board?' Erin raised her eyebrows. 'Skye went to a *private* school?'

'Didn't she tell you?' Martin looked confused. 'She loves telling everyone she was Head Girl. Everyone wanted those top positions.'

'I see,' Erin muttered. Head Girl of a renowned private school? Not exactly a place that someone with no money and living in a hovel like Skye had made out would go to. 'Okay, so now I want you to tell me *everything* you know about Skye, her mother and why she's here.' She frowned. 'You can also give me your phone.'

Martin nodded and dutifully handed his mobile to Erin, who placed it in her pocket.

She'd need this to help convince the others of Martin's innocence, as well as providing her with security so if she was wrong about this bloke, he had no contact with the outside world.

THIRTY EIGHT

RED-FACED, Peter glared at Fiona, his whole body trembling with rage and humiliation. There was him saying he'd had enough public humiliation today, thanks to the embarrassment of calling the police to explain how stupid his son had been. Now *this*?

Fiona had gone one step too far. The neighbours would have seen that police car arrive. They'd have seen it coming up the drive. They'd also have witnessed the police entering their home, primed for trouble.

And not only would they have seen all of this, the reason the police were here right now was because one of these neighbours - the people who they'd lived amongst for *years*; who they'd invited to their annual garden parties and who they'd accepted invitations to countless barbecues, felt that Fiona's unearthly screeching and screaming, audible even from their well-spaced detached house, warranted placing an emergency 999 call, citing domestic disturbance.

Christ!

Peter felt his face may fold in two. This would get back to *everyone* at the bridge club. They wouldn't be invited to any upcoming tournaments ever again.

'Like I said, officer, it's a misunderstanding.' He forced his face into a more genial expression. 'My wife has been under an immense amount of pressure these past couple of days.' Peter's hands wrung in his lap. *Now he'd have to explain everything again from scratch. God, this was so humiliating.* 'Are you aware that we... erm... that we had to report our son as...'

'I know what's happened with your son and the car,' a grim-faced officer said as he perched awkwardly on the edge of a floral armchair. 'But we have to respond and act appropriately when receiving calls regarding possible domestic assaults.'

'Domestic assaults? I can assure you there was no domestic assault here!' Peter barked, his usual arrogance coming to life. 'My wife was unhappy that I was unable to reach our son on the phone.' He'd miss out the part when Fiona flew at him, clawing at his face and screaming expletives that he hadn't realised she even *knew*, let alone would voice. 'It's all sorted out now.'

The officer pointedly glanced at the cordless phone still lying on the rug where it had fallen from Peter's hands before his eyes moved to the scratches on Peter's face. 'How may I ask did you get those marks? The ones on your face?'

'Shaving,' Peter blustered. 'My razor, it's...' His voice tailed off seeing the policemen swapping glances. He glared at Fiona again. Why wasn't she saying anything? *She* should be damn well telling them why she'd lost the plot and attacked him! If she *really* believed Martin was in a wardrobe or wherever the hell she reckoned he was being held against his will by someone sounding like a cherry variety, then why wasn't she speaking up?

Because she knew it was rubbish, that's why.

Maybe he should tell the police what Fiona was convinced of? Then they would understand.

No, he couldn't. If he did *that* they might insist on Fiona's mental health being evaluated. However much she'd angered him today and no matter how much her recent behaviour frustrated him, she was still his wife and he had no wish to see her locked up in a mental hospital.

Besides, that would be even more embarrassing.

Out of the corner of his eye, Peter saw one of the officers staring intensely at Fiona, his expression that of concern at her increasingly agitated behaviour. She'd get herself carted off at this rate regardless of what was said.

'H-How much longer will this take?' Fiona asked, her eyes locked on her watch.

Peter exhaled with relief as both policemen got to their feet. *Finally!* He also got out of his chair. It didn't pay to have no manners. 'Right then, officers. If everything's been cleared up, I'll see you to the door. Sorry you've had a wasted journ... What are you doing?' He gawped in shock at the pair of handcuffs being slipped onto his wrists. 'What th…'

'A precautionary measure, sir,' one officer said. 'Now if you'd please come with us.'

'NO!' Thrown from her state of suspended animation into panic, Fiona jumped to her feet. 'He can't go anywhere! I need him to drive me to...'

'It's protocol in cases such as this, Mrs Bolt. It's to safeguard your well-being. Providing your husband does nothing to obstruct us, then he won't be arrested. Once he's arranged for somewhere else to stay for twenty-four hours as a cool-off period between you, he'll be free to go on his way.'

'*What*?' Peter roared, pulling at the cuffs. 'This is *my* house! Why should I have to go anywhere else?'

'How am I supposed to get to London now?' Fiona wailed. 'Peter! Don't let them take you! I need you to dri…'

'I'm afraid this is the way we have to do it, Mrs Bolt.' The officers manoeuvred an unwilling Peter towards the door. 'Come on, Mr Bolt. Behave yourself and things will be much easier for everyone.'

As the front door shut behind her husband and the police, Fiona wept in despair. *How was she supposed to help Martin now?*

· · · ·

LEO RAKED HIS FINGERS through his hair with exasperation and exhaustion. 'For fuck's sake,' he muttered. 'This puts me in one hell of a position.'

'I know,' Erin said, her brow lined with stress. 'I realise I'm asking you to go against Zane and I also know it's not the first time I've put you in an awkward position. I'm sorry for that, but I didn't know what else to do. Martin Bolt isn't what Skye said. He's not a stalker. Neither did he kill Hazel.'

'I can buy that Sandler was the one who killed Hazel, but being as this bloke is involved with Sandler, I can't assume he's innocent.' Leo's eyes moved to the door of the office they sat in, knowing Martin Bolt – the one they'd all been primed to bring in since learning he'd put Zane's daughter through terror and his suspected involvement with Sandler, remained locked in for his own protection.

Erin chewed her lip. Locking Martin in the room to speak to Leo was something she'd insisted on, but that in itself was a gamble. If she couldn't persuade Leo to trust her instincts, then Martin was dead. Except it would be via Leo's hands, rather than Zane's.

But even this precarious gamble had more chance of working in her favour than speaking to Zane about it at the moment. Although Leo hadn't gone into detail over how his attempt to calm Zane and Tiger down had gone, judging by the exhaustion on his face and that the sound of breaking furniture and yelling had subsided, he must have achieved something. How much, she was yet to learn, but whatever happened, she had to sort out the situation with Martin before his presence was discovered by someone other than her, and now Leo.

'In my opinion, being as Sandler ran him off the road, yet didn't kill him, Bolt is working for Sandler,' Leo said. 'This could be part of Sandler and Marco's plan.'

'Martin told me that if he didn't follow Sandler's instructions, then both he and Skye would be killed,' Erin countered. 'His job was to distract the guards and get Skye out of here.'

302

'What, so Sandler could kill her, or what I suspect he'd planned - use her against us. They must have found out - presumably through your friend in there,' Leo jerked his massive head towards the neighbouring office, 'that Skye is Zane's daughter and wanted to use her as bait.'

Erin shrugged. 'I don't know. Damon told Martin that he had things to do in here but didn't say what.'

'Yeah, and we all know what *that* was...' Leo hissed.

Erin prickled with what had befallen Hazel. In the resulting chaos, *that* felt like years ago rather than a few hours. Hazel's body was still lying within this very building like forgotten meat. She shook her head to remove the distressing image. 'Bolt genuinely doesn't know much, if anything. I can read people fairly well and I'm rarely wrong. He's a well-to-do lad from a posh school. You'll see for yourself if you speak to him.'

'I'm not sure I want to.' Leo didn't trust himself not to let rip at the bloke just to release some frustration. He couldn't deny that Skye had lied. He'd developed misgivings about her himself lately. The discrepancies between what she'd told Zane about her life at home did not tally in any way, shape or form with the house he'd parked outside of in East Horsley. Now he had the additional knowledge that she'd gone to a private school?

The list of texts Erin had just showed him from Skye to this Bolt character – proved the opposite of what she'd said too. He'd heard the lies about the phone and then what he'd seen for himself in the room with the girl and Zane just now...

It was playing on his mind something chronic. Tiger and Zane at each other's throats like that had shocked him to the core. All the years they'd worked and known each other, covering each other's backs and risking death for each other, never had any of them been *close* to laying into one another.

Until today...

Now everything had changed and as much as Leo disliked thinking it - all of this had happened only since Skye had arrived on the scene.

His brows furrowed, the weight of decision bearing down hard. He'd also witnessed something he'd seen many times before, but never from within the fold or with anyone connected with the heart of the firm - the inner circle.

Yet now he had.

And he hadn't seen it on Tiger, Zane, Erin, Hazel - *any* of them. He'd seen it when Skye recounted the 'facts' to Zane about what his trusted friend had allegedly tried to do. He'd seen it when Erin had first stepped into the room where the men were being restrained. He'd seen it flash across Skye's face before *and* after she spoke several times.

But Leo had only just clocked what that unusual expression he'd caught glimpses of meant in relation to Skye.

Manipulation.

And the second he'd labelled it in his own mind he knew his instincts were correct...

Tiger had not touched that girl.

Trying to convince Zane of that was not as straightforward. Anything Leo said which even *smelt* like his opinion was in Tiger's corner gave Skye an excuse to bleat that no one believed her.

In any other situation, taking a stance against somebody claiming to have been assaulted would be unthinkable. But this was Skye. And Skye - for whatever reason, was lying about Tiger. There was no question about it.

But mud had a habit of sticking and whenever the truth came out - because it *would* – Tiger's reputation could be in tatters. All those guards heard the allegations. The whiff of *anything* along those lines becoming public would never be exterminated. It would also ruin the firm's fledgling reputation.

Erin watched Leo closely, hope glimmering. 'You believe what I'm saying, don't you? You believe all of it. About Martin; About Tiger... About Skye.'

Leo remained unresponsive. He knew the moment he made his decision known there was no turning back. *What if he was wrong?*

He clenched his jaw.

He wasn't wrong. He could feel it.

'Leo?' Erin pushed.

Raising his eyes, Leo gave a slight nod. 'All right, yeah, I believe you. I have own reasons too. The long and short of it is that girl's a fucking problem. A big one. But not as big as the problem of what the fuck we're going do about it.'

THIRTY NINE

DAMON WASN'T SURE how long it had taken him to get this far. Nor did he know if he'd ever stop sweating.

Snatching up the can of warm lager he'd bought from the One Stop somewhere along the route, he tipped it into his mouth with trembling hands.

Fuck! Today wasn't something he wanted a repeat performance of for anything. And it wasn't quite over yet...

He scowled as a twig fluttered from his hair onto his mud-caked jeans.

After taking the chance to leg it across the grounds of the Starbright to the main road, he hadn't stopped until he'd reached the tube station. But as the chances of Zane's henchman jumping out from nowhere lessened, the prospect of being apprehended by the police for being a tramp or a druggie, grew.

And it was getting worse...

Damon willed his heartrate to slow down. He could do without having a cardiac arrest to top this day from hell off. He usually avoided going anywhere involving the Great Unwashed, but today was different. He'd thought he'd feel relief being in the proximity of 'real life' amongst masses of people on the underground, but it was the opposite. Unable to risk stopping for his Volvo, he hadn't much choice but to use public transport. Now he'd lost his car and that fucked him off big time. It wasn't like he could go back and pick it up. *Ever.*

It could be worse... He could be on the bus.

But this was still far from good.

Noticing a woman staring in his direction with suspicion and paranoia to the levels Damon hadn't believed existed suffocated him. Then she looked at him for the second time. And then a third...

After that, she did something with her phone.

Was she phoning the police?

Damon fidgeted as the man sitting next to him got up and chose to stand.

Fear pounded.

Casually pushing his hand underneath his jacket, Damon traced the outline of his gun. It was still there, thank God. He thought for a moment it might be sticking out underneath his jacket which would explain why people were staring at him. But it wasn't, so why the fuck were they looking?

Just when he thought things couldn't get any more unpleasant, his mobile rang. Ringing phones were hardly unusual, so why were more people turning to gawp at him?

Damon pulled his mobile from his pocket, the action dislodging an old piece of pie stuck to him from the bin. Getting a strong waft of his own body odour, along with the disgusting aroma that only crouching neck deep in a rubbish bin for hours could cause, he let the pie drop to the floor and stared at the phone.

```
...Marco calling...
```

Buttoning the call, Damon's teeth clenched against his aching jaw. He wasn't answering it. No, no and no again. That was five missed calls from Marco now. He'd be ringing for an update but he wasn't getting one.

He had to get home and lie low until Marco was sent down.

That. Was. All. He. Had. To. Do.

The mobile sprang to life once more.

'Go away!' Damon hissed, cutting off Marco's call for the second time.

Now even *more* people were staring. Convinced these people - especially that bloke at the far end of the carriage, must be undercover police, Damon was sure he was slathering with fear. These people knew *everything*. He had to get off this tube and back to his flat.

His dirty fingernails scraped against his jeans as he fidgeted. His stop was ages away yet. Plus, he had to change lines in a moment.

Damon's gaze darted around the train. Changing tubes would give them the perfect opportunity to pounce.

With renewed panic, he gulped in mouthfuls of air.

Perhaps he should go to the penthouse? It being half empty was an insult. It wasn't like Marco needed it. If he took up residence there in Marco's absence, what was the difference? Marco had helped himself to the place when Zane was sent down, so why couldn't *he* do the same? Having a percentage of interest in Marco's firm entitled him to perks when needed, didn't it?

And somewhere better to live *was* needed.

Damon's sweating increased as the many eyes continued boring into him and his whole body vibrated when his mobile rang again.

...Marco calling...

Jesus Christ! Marco would keep phoning until he got an update. The update required would never come, so this phone needed to stop bloody ringing.

The sinews on Damon's neck stood to attention as he clenched his jaw harder and harder. *Shut up, shut up, SHUT UP!*

He couldn't bear it.

Suddenly jumping to his feet, he threw the ringing mobile

to the floor and stamped on it with his size elevens. He then stamped on it again and again.

As the phone's broken casing ricocheted across the carriage, he kept bringing his foot down until the phone became silent.

There! Now no one could fucking ring!

He'd got Martin's phone, so he'd use that one from now on. Marco didn't have *that* number. Ha ha ha!

He glared at the people still openly staring at him, now with the hinge of concern. Let them think he was an escaped psycho. He didn't care. 'Having a good fucking look?' he yelled.

As the tube screeched into the next station, Damon took the opportunity to dart off the train, leaving the remnants of his phone in situ. He didn't need it anymore.

He didn't bother looking to see what station he'd disembarked at. *Fuck it.* He'd walk back to the flat from wherever this was even if it got him killed. He wasn't going to the penthouse. He didn't want shag all of anything Marco had touched ever again.

And that started right now, whatever the consequences.

• • • •

ZANE HAD CALMED DOWN sufficiently enough to be brought back to the house. He was no longer smashing things up, but neither was he so calm that psychotic undertones weren't alight deep behind his eyes.

Holding a fresh ice-cold compress on the purple flesh of Zane's eye, Erin continued working on reducing the swelling as much as possible.

Skye had accompanied Zane on his return, but instead of sitting here with them, she'd taken one look at Erin, huffed loudly and flounced up to her bedroom, leaving just her, Zane and Leo.

It was Leo who broke the heavy silence. 'What happens from here, mate?'

Zane winced as Erin dabbed TCP on his split lip. Leo's

question was one he needed answering himself, but that he'd broken his own cardinal rule - the rule each and every one of them stood by, bit deep.

That his trusted comrade, his friend of old, could betray him in such a way and do that to Skye, cut deep gouges that could never be filled. 'Thanks. That will do for now,' he muttered, steering Erin's hand away from his throbbing face.

Erin tidied away the dressings and bowl of water, glancing at Leo as she did so. She knew he saw the internal battle raging within Zane's head as clearly as she did. Zane hadn't taken the news well that Martin Bolt was being held in the Starbright. Unsurprisingly, he was unhappy that he hadn't been made aware of this development until now, but how could he have been told that information with the state of mind he'd been in?

Erin knew it was the right decision. Even Leo agreed that Skye must not get another opportunity to twist anything.

'So now you've heard my take on things, including the discrepancies about Skye's home life and seeing the texts Erin has on Bolt's phone, do you really think she hasn't an agenda?' Leo waited for the fallout from Zane. He'd volunteered himself instead of Erin to be the one to broach the subject, aware that she had recently been taking the flack alone, but would it make a difference?

He sat on the chair opposite Zane and rested his elbows on his thighs. 'I appreciate she's your daughter, but this is *Tiger* we're talking about. Do you really think he'd do something like that to a woman? To Skye? To *you*?'

Picking up his tumbler of whisky, Zane sipped at it, hissing as the spirit burnt the raw flesh on his lip. His all-consuming rage was ebbing - one receding tide being replaced with another that brought additional problems - ones that in many ways were worse.

How long could he find explanations for the long list of things that just didn't add up?

Turning his attention back to Martin Bolt's phone, he scrolled through the hundreds of texts sent by his daughter.

They showed that what Skye said about the lad was untrue.

If Skye had lied about that, was Erin and now Leo right that she was lying about *everything*?

Zane's need to watch his daughter's back; to protect her at all costs and to be unwaveringly loyal to his blood, clashed with the mounting evidence leaning in the direction that the only explanation was that she was lying.

Feeling a soft hand on his arm, Zane looked up.

'Leo's right,' Erin said quietly. 'Tiger hasn't done anything. I don't know why Skye said what she did and what she's hoping to gain by it, but I don't believe Tiger's guilty.'

'No do I,' Leo muttered.

Placing the phone down, Zane picked up his whisky. A stinging lip might detract from this plague of disbelief. No matter how horrific the concept, he had no choice but to take on board that Skye could be lying. There was another reason he had for that too…

He knew Tiger - *really* knew him. If the man was guilty, then he'd have accepted the beating. But Tiger hadn't. He'd fought back with equal viciousness and rage.

Zane frowned. If he hadn't walked into that room and Skye had told him this story in a different situation, would he have approached it differently?

He'd have gone for Tiger regardless and found out the truth one way or another, but walking into that room, seeing only his panicking, half-naked daughter was all he'd been able to focus on. There was only one thing he could do.

'Skye!' Zane roared.

'What are you doing?' Erin cried. 'She'll just play her usual trick of...'

'You're to say nothing, Erin,' Zane said, his eyes hard. 'I'll deal with this.' Getting up, he yanked open the door and called up the stairs. 'SKYE! Come down here. I need to talk to you.'

Erin glanced at Leo and then back to Zane. 'What will you do?'

'What I really don't want to do,' Zane muttered. 'I'm

calling Skye's bluff and see what that brings.'

FORTY

A LARGE GRIN spread over Marco's face as he placed the phone down and nodded to the policeman who had been useful these last few days by retrieving his mobile out of 'safeguarding' and back to where it needed it to be - in his pocket.

That there were still people around that he could buy only bolstered Marco's belief that this was far from over and this was only the beginning.

As the officer shut the door behind him, Marco glanced around the cell he'd been forced to occupy these past few weeks.

Would he miss it?

Would he fuck!

It wasn't quite over yet, but it would be very shortly.

'I'd like you to arrange a meeting with a duty brief tomorrow morning,' he said, smiling coldly at the policeman making his way out of the cell. 'Say about 10 o'clock?'

The officer frowned. 'I'm not sure whether that will be possible, Mr Morelli. Paperwork is already being prepared in relation to... erm... you know, the charges against you. That's all due to happen tomorrow.'

Marco sat forward, his face morphing into a snarl. 'I think you'll find it *is* possible. Need I point out that it is my right to have a solicitor present in the event of being charged with these fake allegations?'

And until the moment he was charged, he had every right to present a defence. But he wouldn't mention that. There was no point. Let this bunch of bastards carry on believing he'd accepted this load of shit. He knew differently.

Marco pulled his face back into a sickly grin. 'Just arrange it, will you?'

Nodding, the officer left the room and Marco leant back against the extra pillow on his bed.

Just a few hours and then things would be sorted.

And by fuck he was looking forward to it.

For the first time since he'd been in this dump, Marco smiled – a *genuine* smile.

Shortly he would be putting a few wrongs right. And it would be most enjoyable.

• • • •

SKYE'S FACE was getting hotter by the minute. She glared at Erin, then turned back to Zane. 'What's this? Now you don't believe me because she's filled your head with lies?' Blinking rapidly, her eyes glistened with tears. 'Have you any idea what it's like not to be believed? Had you not come in when you did I'm sure that man would have... would have gone further... He'd have...'

Zane winced at the reference to one of his trusted men being a potential rapist, nausea brewing deep in his gut. He hoped he was doing the right thing. Not believing someone - especially over something like this, only for it to turn out to be true would be catastrophic. Something *else* he'd never forgive himself for.

But he had to know. And this was the only way.

If his worst nightmares were realised and Tiger *had* masqueraded all of these years being someone he wasn't, then no one would stop him from killing the man. He'd have done that already had he not been stopped. 'I'm well aware what it's like not to be believed, Skye,' he said dully. 'Years in prison taught me that.'

'Then why do you want me to "think carefully" about what I've said?' Skye pouted, turning to glare at Erin. 'And why is *she* still here? And *him*.' She turned to Leo. 'What do *you* know? You weren't there. None of you were!' Facing back to Zane, she continued, 'I'm your daughter, your blood, yet you're taking Tiger's word and those of these two over mine?'

Zane folded his arms across his chest. 'Yes, you're my daughter and therefore I'll do everything to protect you. All I'm asking is whether you could have misread the situation?'

Skye's eyebrows raised to almost hit her hairline. 'How can I misread someone ripping my clothes off and putting their hands on me?' she shrieked.

'You can't,' Zane said. 'But the CCTV shows otherwise…' He kept his face in check but inside he was dying. There was no CCTV. None at all. He planned to install it at the Starbright but that had fallen down the list. How he wished it hadn't - for this situation, for Hazel, for *everything*.

But if he was wrong...

It was only then did Zane pick up that Skye's defensive outburst had morphed into a cloying silence. 'Skye?'

Erin watched the colour drain from Skye's face and the tears flow. *Let's see what she comes up with this time.*

'W-What with finding Hazel's body it's being such an awful day... I... I don't know... M-Maybe I did take the top off myself…' Her eyes widened, her face filling with horror. 'It was covered with Hazel's blood. I panicked... I had to get that top off… I don't even remember doing it, just that I had to remove it...'

Erin went to speak but a firm grip of Leo's hand on her arm reminded her to honour what she'd faithfully promised. *Stay quiet.*

'You took it off yourself?' Zane cried. 'You said that Tiger...'

'I-It must have been me!' Skye wailed, her hands clutching at the fluffy dressing gown she'd wrapped herself in. 'That was what the CCTV showed, didn't it? I wasn't lying... I thought...' She put her head in her hands. 'I-I wanted Hazel's blood away me... I needed reassurance... I was frightened... I...'

Zane's heart sank. 'You accused my man of touching you when he didn't?' He felt his temper rising. 'Why would you do such a thing?'

'I-I didn't mean to, I really didn't.' Tears cascaded down Skye's face. 'I thought he had, I swear... It... it must have been a flashback. I...'

Unable to keep quiet any longer, Erin stepped forward. 'A man's reputation gets ruined because of these kinds of allegations. There are people out there who have been assaulted for *real*, yet you decided to say something like that, like it doesn't matter?'

'Erin!' Zane warned. He turned to Skye. There was something else bothering him. Something which she'd alluded to before. 'What do you mean by "flashbacks"?'

Skye's hands fanned her face. 'I... erm... sometimes... sometimes things come back in my mind... No! I don't want to talk about any of that. I...'

Zane bristled. 'What do you mean? Who touched you? One of my men?'

'No!' Skye scrabbled off the chair and looked at Zane, her eyes wide. 'Please. I don't want to talk about it. Don't make me. That part of my life is over now... I...'

'I have to know what's happened to you in the past,' Zane roared, jumping to his feet. 'Tell me!'

'No! I can't! Please... I'm sorry,' Skye sobbed. 'Tell Tiger I'm sorry. It's... it's just with what happened a long time ago... I'm sorry, okay?' Sobbing hysterically, she ran out of the sitting room and thundered up the stairs.

Hearing Skye's bedroom door slam, Zane went to follow, but Erin grabbed his arm. 'Leave her,' she said softly. 'Let her calm down and get her head together, then talk to her.'

'Erin's right. You won't get straight answers out of Skye like this.' Leo shook his head in disbelief. 'Now we know that Tiger did nothing.'

'Someone has though,' Zane muttered. 'So, who did?'

Erin shrugged. 'I don't know.' *And she didn't.* It might be another one of Skye's lies, but as much as she hated to admit it, it could equally be true. Deep seated trauma caused flashbacks, she knew that well enough.

She despised herself for thinking this might be another one of Skye's games, but she thought it all the same.

And if Zane knew that she wished more than anything that Skye Wilson wasn't here and had failed to find her father in the first place, then he wouldn't like that either. But that was also true.

FORTY ONE

'IT WILL WORK OUT SOMEHOW.' Erin propped herself up in the bed and gently caressed Zane's damaged face. 'You'll put things right with Tiger.' Although at this moment in time, she wasn't quite sure how.

This wasn't something that Tiger would shrug off and forget. Despite not voicing it, she wondered whether that particular relationship had been damaged past the point of no return, regardless of what apology Zane offered. What Leo said was true - mud had a habit of sticking and accusations like this, should they get out, would tarnish both Tiger's and the firm's reputation beyond repair.

What Skye said last night, although the change of tune seemed timely and 'convenient', *was* feasible for something – a horrible experience, perhaps several, to have happened in the past now manifesting as difficult to explain flashbacks.

A glimmer of doubt crept into Erin's mind. Was it possible her long-standing theory about Skye not being on the level was wrong after all?

Hazel would say that flashbacks could explain a lot of Skye's odd behaviour and Erin understood that, but there was still something that just didn't add up.

Erin sighed. Even thinking about what Hazel's take on this would be made her well with sadness. What she would give for Hazel's opinion, but that she couldn't have. And she never would again.

'I have to go and see Tiger,' Zane muttered, wincing as he pulled himself out of bed. Even though he'd been exhausted to the point of death last night, his sleep had been sporadic - plagued with nightmares and thoughts of 'what ifs'. 'As well as sorting things out with Tiger, I've got to make arrangements for… for Hazel's body. I also need to get to the bottom of what is making Skye do the things she's doing. I need to know about her past. What occurred yesterday underlines that more than anything.'

Erin kept her opinions to herself and instead concentrated on the facts. 'She's certainly a troubled girl.' She then frowned. 'What about Martin?'

Zane sighed. He hadn't forgotten the boy who had caused so much upheaval, rightly or wrongly, was still under lock and key at the Starbright. Nor had he forgotten that Sandler was still on the loose. For that reason, leaving Skye or Erin without him present wasn't something he relished. 'I'll deal with Martin, but he's not my priority.'

Erin nodded. 'I understand, but do you think it might be an idea to bring him in to speak to Skye? See what her reaction is?' *Putting the girl on the spot might unearth further truths.*

Zane remained stony-faced. The texts Erin had shown him from Martin's phone last night showed that Skye was not an unwilling recipient, frightened or stalked. 'Tiger and Hazel first. Skye's got enough to mull over. I should go and see how she is though.'

Erin watched Zane pull a pair of jogging bottoms on and leave the room and wondered if the hours of the night had given Skye time to dream up more excuses.

Getting out of bed, she pottered over to the wardrobe and rummaged around for clean clothes. As soon as she found out whether Zane felt it best for her to remain here or go to the

Starbright, then she'd grab a shower and...

'She's gone!'

Spinning around, Erin found Zane standing in the doorway. 'Gone? What do you mean, *gone*?'

'I mean, gone! Skye's disappeared!' Zane dropped onto the bed, his head in his hands. 'I knew I was too hard on her last night. I pushed her too far. This is my fault and now she's gone. Shit!'

Erin trembled with rage. *Had the devious little cow done a flit now she'd realised her game was up?*

Then her rage subsided and instead, paranoia fluttered.

Had wishing Skye away last night somehow made it manifest?

No, that was stupid.

But what if last night's conversation had sparked a meltdown? If the girl *was* telling the truth about unsavoury incidents in the past and thought no one believed her, then she could have taken it upon herself to disappear.

If something happened to Skye it would destroy Zane completely. She knew how much Zane loved the girl and how important it was to him for her to be part of his life. Panic bubbled. 'Has she taken her clothes? Taken all of her stuff?'

'I don't know. I...' Zane's eyes filled with fresh pain. 'For fuck's sake! I've screwed everything up. What if all of this is wrong? If it is, then I've basically accused Skye of lying about *everything*. I've let her down. I've let everyone down – Tiger, Hazel, you...'

'No, you haven't,' Erin said, her resolve returning. This was just another well-executed ploy Skye was using to derail her father to take the heat off herself. Why had she even entertained that there could be truth in anything coming out of Skye's mouth?

But there was somewhere Skye could have gone... 'Could she have gone back to Shirley's?'

'Shirley's?' Zane frowned. 'She wanted to be away from there. Why would she have returned?'

'Because she threatened to go home several times. She told Hazel that things were so "bad" here with *me* that it might be best to return to her mother's.'

And wasn't that a discrepancy in itself? If things were as bad at home with Shirley as Skye made out, then wild horses wouldn't make her return there - even the embarrassment of last night's accusations and her subsequent admissions.

'Do you really think it's possible that she's gone back there?' Zane asked, hurt clear on his rugged face.

'Yes, it's possible.' Taking a deep breath, Erin suggested something she didn't think she ever would. 'You must go. Go to Shirley's and see if Skye is there.'

Zane's head snapped up. 'I can't leave you alone here. Not while we don't know where Sandler is.'

Throwing her arms around Zane's neck, Erin smiled. 'Yes, you can. I'll be fine.'

'It's too much of a risk. I won't put you in any more danger.'

'Zane, you must go and see Shirley and see if Skye's there. If me being here bothers you that much, then why don't you ask Leo to send Tiger over,' Erin suggested. 'He can bring Martin and that sorts out leaving him with the guards. You can straighten things out with Tiger once you've seen Shirley?'

Zane's brows knitted. 'That could work, but Tiger might refuse to come after last night.'

'No, he won't.' Erin brought her lips to Zane's. 'He'll come.'

'You're a good woman.' Zane pulled Erin close. 'I don't know what I'd do without you.' *And he didn't.* Erin went above and beyond. He didn't deserve her. He didn't deserve *anyone* the way he kicked off sometimes.

Making a solid decision that from now on he would curb his temper until he could think rationally, he smiled. 'Okay, I'll go. But the same applies as before. Don't move a muscle until Tiger gets here.'

• • • •

WAKING UP, Damon looked around, the usual panic sitting around his shoulders like a heavy mink stole - the same way it did every single morning.

And then remembering what had occurred, the panic lifted - just like that! The burden of being linked to Marco Morelli disintegrated and fell away, never to weigh him down again. That worry and the all-encompassing stress and dread was no longer applicable.

He glanced around his bedroom just to make sure this wasn't part of a twisted dream, cruelly hoaxing his brain to believe something that wasn't true. But it *was* true.

The chink of sunlight spilling through the tear in the thin curtains showed it was morning. This leak of light normally bothered him; the sunlight disturbing what little sleep he got and invariably making each day start unpleasantly. That mood gradually worsened as the day went on - not that he needed much assistance with that. But today it didn't apply. The light burning his eyelids brought nothing but relief.

He'd made it through the night. He hadn't been picked off the street by one of Zane Morelli's trained retards to be tortured to death during the frantic and nerve racking last few miles he'd done on foot after getting off the tube. Neither had he been carted off by the undercover police he'd been convinced were everywhere he looked on the train last night.

He'd done it.

He'd escaped from the Starbright undetected and made it back without anything untoward occurring. No one was lying in wait at his flat when he'd finally returned, utterly exhausted either.

Damon never thought he'd be so glad to see his shithole of a flat, but he was. In fact, overjoyed was an understatement.

Never again would he find the skanky dump with its piss-soaked stairwells and arguing chavvy neighbours a problem.

He'd even enjoyed the cold shower he'd taken the minute he'd got in to wash the bin juice off him. That the boiler no longer worked and hadn't for some time and was probably slowly poisoning him was a mere triviality.

Life was good.

And listen to that...

Closing his eyes once more, Damon lay back on the lumpy pillow and sighed contentedly.

Aside from the clanking and squealing of the dustcart and the neighbours shouting upstairs, there was no sound.

There was no phone ringing and there wouldn't be either.

Sitting up in bed, Damon reached to retrieve his jacket from the chair and stuck his hand into the pocket. His phone was no longer in existence, but he wasn't stupid. He'd got a spare in Martin Bolt's phone.

That prick's mobile was a much better model than the one he'd had which was now lying smashed up somewhere inside the London Underground. And best of all, Marco didn't have Bolt's number, so he couldn't call and hound him about...

Hang on! Where was the phone?

Damon frantically searched the other pocket. He even checked along the seams in case there was a hole and it had slipped through into the lining.

Bollocks. It wasn't there.

He must have left it in the Volvo. The last place he'd seen it was by the gear stick just before Bolt made that last call.

Shrugging, Damon tossed his jacket in the direction of the chair. It was a pain in the arse, but on the grand scale of things it didn't matter. He only got another twenty-four hours to keep his head down before Marco was carted off for his stint at Her Majesty's Pleasure. And it would be a long one, so a day without a phone was hardly a major bother.

Lying back down, Damon placed his hands behind his head and smiled smugly. While he waited for the time to pass he'd do what he never got chance to do.

He'd have a lazy day.

And why the hell not. Out of anyone, he bloody well deserved some well-earned rest.

FORTY TWO

GRIM-FACED, Leo watched Mr Turner zip up the body bag, hiding Hazel's once beautiful face forever.

It would be difficult remembering anything other than what she looked like *now*. Her purple-blotched and bloated face in the throes of rigor mortis would be hard to erase. The mouth that scores of men dreamt of claiming remained stretched full with the money which had succeeded in choking her, forcing her lips forever into an anguished gape.

As Hazel's body was loaded onto a gurney, Leo held the door open as Mr Turner and two of his staff wheeled it out into the corridor towards the back exit. He nodded his thanks. 'I'll be in contact once I've got a schedule.'

It was lucky Mr Turner was available. The old school firm who had worked with Zane's father were worth their weight in gold at times like this. There weren't too many undertakers who would accept and hold a corpse, no questions asked, until further notice.

Normally, deaths of their own or others in circumstances acting as red flags to the authorities warranted different methods of disposal. But Zane was adamant Hazel be dealt with *properly* and with utmost respect. Her body wasn't destined for the car crusher or a meagre under-the-counter funeral held during the hours of darkness. She'd get a proper funeral, not an unmarked grave. It was something Leo wholeheartedly agreed on. Hazel deserved that much.

But arranging that was too risky at the moment. Things had to settle down first. Thankfully, Mr Turner understood and was willing to play ball, so that was one less thing Zane had to worry about.

But agreeing with Zane's stance over Hazel was one thing. What Leo didn't understand was why Zane hadn't yet come to speak to Tiger.

After Skye's admission last night, Leo had assumed the first thing Zane would do today would be to apologise to the man who'd been so unfairly accused, but so far, there was no sign of him.

Leo returned to the room where Tiger had spent the night. 'Right, shall we...' His eyes darted to the small bag on the seat. 'What's that?'

'I'm out of here.' Tiger's voice sounded not his own thanks to his newly missing teeth and swollen face.

'But Solenzo's coming to look at your injuries in a couple of hours and...'

'Thanks, but with all due respect, I'm not waiting around for anyone,' Tiger said, his voice cold. 'I wanted to see Hazel off in my own way and now that's done, so am I.'

Leo's disappointment snowballed. 'But I told you Skye admitted last night that you'd done nothing. She passed off her accusations as flashbacks. Whether you buy that or not is up to you. I know I fucking don't! The girl's a problem.'

'Yep, she certainly is.' Tiger's monotone voice was missing the camaraderie he and Leo had always shared.

'Zane will apologise, you know he will. He's coming to do that. He...'

'The trouble is, mate, it doesn't make any difference,' Tiger said flatly. 'Look, I have no gripe with you. I don't even have a gripe with Zane. I get where he's coming from – the girl's his

325

daughter.' He picked up his bag and slung it over his shoulder. 'But what I *do* have an issue with and what won't go away with a fucking apology, is that Zane thought I was capable of it. Or *could* have been. That *any* of you thought it feasible - even for a split second, isn't something I can overlook.'

Leo turned away, ashamed. He'd be lying if he denied that. 'This sort of shit fucks with your head. I admit there was a moment when I wondered whether I'd got you wrong.'

'One moment or a thousand - it's all the same. You still gave it a second of credence,' Tiger said hollowly. 'Zane gave it a lot more than that. He believed that little bitch over everyone and everything.' He tapped at his temples. 'She's fucked up in here, so no, whatever happens I ain't staying.'

'I get that you need some space, but you're not going for good, surely?' Leo gasped. 'Oh, mate, you're part of the fabric. You *can't* go! It's always been us three. At least hear what Zane has to say and...'

'As I said, an apology can't erase this,' Tiger spat. 'I need out. Whether it's forever, I don't know, but for now it is.'

Leo's shoulders sagged. He knew the altercation between Zane and Tiger would cause issues, but Tiger walking away from the firm?

It was the last thing anyone needed.

He couldn't say he blamed the man. How would *he* react if it was *him* on the receiving end of that little cow's lies? Leo suspected he wouldn't glibly shrug off the accusations and the accompanying hurt either, but he was desperate to change Tiger's mind and say something - *anything* to make him reconsider. It probably wouldn't make a difference but he had to try. He opened his mouth to speak, only to be cut off by his ringing mobile.

Glancing at Tiger, now halfway to the door, Leo snatched his phone from his pocket. 'What is it? Oh, Zane, yeah, I am. I thought you'd be here by now. We have a problem... Tiger, he's... What? When? Okay... I'll get onto it.'

Ending the call, he turned to Tiger, hoping *this* would be

the situation to change his friend's mind. 'Skye's done a flit. Zane's gone to see if she's at Shirley's place and wants me to search Battersea. If Skye's not at Shirley's, then Sandler could have somehow got her. Zane has asked if you can take Martin Bolt and go to the house and watch Erin's back in the meantime until he...'

'And that's the upshot, isn't it? Skye takes precedence over everything. While that girl is allowed to call the shots, Zane is fucking doomed.' Tiger shook his head. 'She's either got a screw loose or is determined to bring him down. I don't know which, but I won't take the flack for her. I'm not going to Dalston.'

'But what about Erin? Zane needs you to cover her until he returns.'

'I'm not Zane's lapdog,' Tiger spat. 'After what he did yesterday I have too much self-respect to do his bidding. Anyway, Erin's a tough chick, she'll be fine.' He then smiled sadly. 'All the best, mate. Maybe see you around sometime.'

'But Tiger. If...' Leo's voiced tailed off as the door shut behind his friend of old.

He booted the wall in frustration. Tiger was right. Skye was calling the shots. She was diluting Zane's concentration and pulling him away from the firm. The worst thing was, Leo suspected that was her aim. Why, he didn't know, but now he'd got to go and look for the manipulative little cow and then get back to Dalston as quickly as possible.

The only saving grace was that Tiger was right - Erin could hold her own and he could only pray that she didn't need to do so.

• • • •

FIONA WASN'T SURE how much she'd slept. Or even if she had. Any amount of rest achieved during the night had been punctuated by pacing up and down and wringing her hands whilst sobbing with impotent frustration and panic about not knowing what to do to help her son since Peter had been taken off by the police.

She'd even tried calling Martin again several times, but there was no answer. There was no point calling the police. Without an address for the place Martin said he was, how could she? Plus, she knew from Peter's previous attempt to get an address for the 'Starbright' there was no record of it.

But judging by the stiffness of her neck, she must have fallen asleep in the chair at some point, even if it wasn't for long. Now it was morning again and there was still no sign of Peter and Martin was God knows where. That's if he was even still alive.

Fiona pushed away the burn of tears. She couldn't waste any more time panicking. She had to do *something*.

That was it! She'd call Shirley. Shirley might have heard something or might know of this Starbright place.

Fiona frowned. Why hadn't she thought of this before? Why had she let panic and Peter's absence floor her? Shirley might have a car and therefore they could *both* go to this Starbright place and demand the safe return of their children.

Getting out of the armchair, Fiona staggered over to the phone, her legs as stiff as her neck. She picked up the receiver, grateful that it still worked after yesterday's stint on the floor.

With trembling hands, she plucked Shirley's number from her pocket and dialled, her heart sinking hearing it ring out. She tried dialling again only to find the same thing happened. 'Oh no! Come on, come on,' she muttered.

'Who are you calling now?' Peter asked as he walked grey-faced into the lounge. 'I hope it's not the police!'

'Peter!' Fiona put the phone down and ran to her husband's side. 'You're back! How are you?'

Peter stared at Fiona coldly. 'Not the best. I discovered that cells aren't the most comfortable. And before you even *mention* it, no - I won't drive you to London. That conversation is over!'

• • • •

GETTING OFF HIS BIKE, Zane peered at the plaque at the end

of the driveway: '*Gatefield*'.

Pulling the scrap of paper from the inside pocket of his leather jacket, he checked the address Leo had handed him. *It was definitely the right place.*

He scanned the neat garden and large house set back at the end of the drive. Leo said the place bore little resemblance to Skye's version of her life at home and he'd been unsure whether Shirley even lived there, but thanks to Erin getting Skye's address from Martin Bolt yesterday, it added up.

Zane glanced back up at the property. So, who was inside? Shirley and Skye, the cleaner or no one?

He was aware things were all over the place at the moment, but no matter how fraught things were and the uncertainties hanging in the air, he hadn't wanted to drive his daughter away. He'd only just connected with Skye and wanted to make things work, not bin her off because of difficult issues.

But if this was where Skye lived, then why had she said those things about her dreadful, impoverished upbringing? From where he stood it didn't look feasible. But he'd find out.

Shirley might have acted weird on the phone and refused to speak to him, but she couldn't ignore him now he was here, could she?

Zane made his way up the drive feeling uncharacteristically nervous. *Would he recognise her after all this time?*

He shook away the vision of the sixteen-year-old stunner from his mind. He'd recognise Shirley if it was indeed her who lived here. Even if she despised him for reasons he was also determined to uncover, the most important thing was their *daughter*. Shirley's issues with him and the other burning questions he had for her could wait.

Approaching the door, Zane rapped the brass knocker and then stood back. The house was quiet - almost eerie in its silence. *Was anyone here?*

Knocking again but getting no response, he fidgeted with impatience. He banged on the door with his fist. 'Shirley? Skye? Are you in there?'

Sensing movement out of the corner of his eye, Zane's hand moved to the gun in his waistband, sure he'd just seen a curtain twitch.

There it was again.

Dashing over to a large bay-fronted window, Zane tapped on the glass, careful not to thump it with the same relish he'd used on the door. Although it was tempting to smash the pane and gain entry, he had to remember he wasn't in Battersea and in this house was the mother of his child.

Whatever his beef was with Shirley for keeping Skye's existence a secret, he must tread carefully. 'Skye? Are you in there? Shirley? I need to talk to you.'

Zane leaned close to the window, convinced he'd just heard talking. Was it Skye, Shirley or someone else? Although Skye hadn't mentioned anything about a man, short of the hints about copious 'visitors' over the years, before now it hadn't crossed his mind that Shirley may have a partner.

Feeling his fists clench at what his daughter may have been exposed to, Zane moved back to the front door. He wasn't having this. Fuck the neighbours and fuck Shirley. If his daughter was in there then he wanted to know about it.

His fist crashed back on the door, this time so hard the whole frame shook. 'Shirley! Open the fucking door!' Zane roared. 'If Skye's with you then at least have the decency to tell me!'

'Get away from here now!'

The voice came from behind the door. It was loud and clear and one which Zane remembered well...

'SHIRLEY!' he yelled, his fist connecting on the wood with an almighty crash. 'I need to talk to you. It's important!'

'Go away!' the voice screamed. 'You're nothing to do with me!'

Zane blinked. *Was she crazy? Nothing to do with him? She'd had his child for Christ's sake!* 'Where is Skye? I'll break this door down if I have to. I know she's in there.'

With renewed silence from the other side of the door, Zane

looked over his shoulder to see if any neighbours had come to investigate. Thankfully, the houses were widely spaced and Shirley's place was surrounded by trees that muffled his shouting.

Turning back, he banged again, his temper frayed. 'Whatever your problem is with me, put it aside, for God's sake! Is Skye with you?'

The door flew open. 'She's not here. You know she's not because you and your family have stolen her.'

The woman standing in the hallway wasn't one Zane recognised which threw him momentarily. 'I... erm...' In that moment, he realised that this bedraggled, overweight, shabbily dressed person was the very same, once beautiful, Shirley Wilson. Pulling himself together, he continued. 'Skye's disappeared. She was with me last night and now she's gone! I need to make sure she's all ri...'

'What have you done to my daughter!' Shirley screeched. 'She should have kept away from you cursed people.' Lurching forward, her hands raked at Zane's face.

As the woman clawed his already battered face and without thinking what he would do next, Zane did the only thing available. He blocked Shirley's attempt to disable his one working eye and manhandled her back into the house, kicking the door shut behind him.

FORTY THREE

LEO DIDN'T FEEL LIKE making conversation with anyone, let alone Martin Bolt. If the bloke didn't quit making small talk then he'd shove the cunt out of the van and save the hassle later if he turned out to be lying.

He hadn't wanted Bolt accompanying him to start with, but Zane didn't want him left with the guards and now Tiger was no longer present to escort him to Erin and Zane's house to wait, Leo he had little choice but to bring the twat along.

The only saving grace was that the skinny prick had been kept prisoner at Sandler's flat, so it stood to reason he knew where the place was. He said he did, so that had better be the truth.

'You don't believe me, do you?' Martin said, Leo's rabid expression making him more uncomfortable than being trapped in a van with this man in the first place.

'Did I say that?' Leo snarled, his concentration focused on battling the traffic from the Starbright to Battersea.

'I *do* know where he lives,' Martin bleated. 'Well, not the actual postal address, but once we get into Battersea, I'll be able to direct you.'

'Good!' Leo hissed. 'Because if you can't, I'll fucking kill you.'

Martin laughed nervously, unable to tell if Leo was joking. Judging by the man's demeanour, he probably wasn't. Sweat beaded at the back of his neck. 'Erm ... how is Skye? Erin said she was back at her father's.' His countenance brightened at this prospect. 'I hope she'll be glad to see me when we get back.'

'Will you shut the fuck up?' Leo snapped, his massive head swivelling to stare at Martin. The boy didn't know Skye had gone AWOL and he had no intention of telling him. If the girl was present at Sandler's gaff, then Bolt would find out soon enough. 'I don't give a toss what Skye thinks. I just want to reach Sandler's.'

Abruptly closing his mouth, Martin remained silent. He wanted to sort things out with Skye; ask her why she'd said all those weird things about wanting their relationship over and that he'd been stalking her. After that, he wanted to go home back to normal life.

That the police hadn't arrived at the Starbright following his mother's promise to get help was a blessing in disguise the way things had turned out, but the reason as to *why* they hadn't showed bothered him. His mum wouldn't let him down, so he hoped she was okay.

Then, with his thoughts returning to where this van was heading, a horrible concept descended and he decided risking Leo's wrath was slightly better than not knowing. 'Erm, you're not planning to kill Sandler, are you?'

'I haven't decided yet,' Leo muttered, but he'd happily kill Sandler if the chance arose. Actually, he didn't know how he would refrain. In addition to all the things that bastard had done - all of which warranted the death penalty, the mood he was in, venting some rage wouldn't go amiss.

Tiger walking out was a kick in the guts. He still couldn't get his head around it. After two decades of being all but brothers, the man's absence was akin to a missing limb. For the first time, Leo had a better understanding of how Zane must have felt after Marco's betrayal. Not that Tiger had betrayed him or *any* of them, but for circumstances to dictate that his trusted friend and colleague was no longer be by his side left a deep cut that wouldn't stop bleeding. *And the way he felt, it never would.*

Leo took his eyes off the road, Martin's hands constantly wringing in his lap grinding on what was left of his patience. 'What the fuck is the matter with you?' he barked. 'I don't expect *you* to kill Sandler, you pathetic turd. You're just supplying his address!'

'I know, I know,' Martin gibbered. 'I... I just... Oh God, it doesn't matter.' *Except it did matter.* He didn't want to witness a murder. He hadn't wanted to experience *any* of the things he'd been forced to endure the last four days. Along with not knowing what was going on with Skye, how would his parents cope if they knew he'd been party to a *murder*?

His life was going down the toilet...

'Pull yourself together, for fuck's sake! You're breaking my heart!' Leo sneered as a tear trickled down Martin's bruised cheek.

Martin turned away so Leo was no longer privy to his desperation and stared out of the window at the bustle of the London streets in an attempt to quell his escalating panic. It wasn't working. The panic was still there and now not being far from Battersea, it surged. They'd be at Sandler's soon and then...

'Right, we're on the A202. Where is Sandler's from here?' Leo grunted. 'I take it your conscious hasn't made your memory patchy?'

'No,' Martin sniffled. 'It's...' Pressing against the window, every nerve ending in his body fired. 'Stop! Stop the van!'

'You what?' Leo roared. 'I ain't stopping the van just because you're having a fucking meltdown! Tell me the route to Sandlers, Bolt. And do it *now*!'

'No! Just look!' Martin slapped the passenger window. 'There! It's Skye!'

Leo rolled his eyes, wondering why he was bothering even

looking in the direction Martin was frantically pointing, but then he saw what Martin saw: a girl who looked very much like Skye Wilson disappearing down the stairs into Vauxhall underground station.

'Shit!' Leo stamped on the brakes. Swerving up the kerb half on a pedestrian crossing, he slapped on his hazard lights.

Martin yanked off his seat belt as Leo pulled the keys from the ignition. 'I'll come with y…' The driver's door shutting in his face, followed by the click of the central locking showed he wasn't going anywhere. Instead, his only choice was to watch Leo's massive frame dart through the traffic and disappear from view into the underground.

. . . .

HAVING DEDUCED THAT Skye was not in the house and showed no signs of having been recently either, Zane stared in horror as Shirley's venomous diatribe continued.

'How dare you show your face here. You and your family disgust me! You're all evil!' Shirley screamed. 'And barging into my home? It's *my* house not yours, no matter what they paid. It's *mine* and so is my daughter!' She snatched up a glass decanter. 'What have you lot done with her? I said, what have you done?'

Quickly reacting to the threat of receiving heavy crystal against his skull, Zane lurched forward and grabbed Shirley's arm. 'Please put that down. I'm not here to argue. But what do you mean by "what they paid"? What are you talki…'

'DON'T TOUCH ME!' Having no choice but to relinquish the decanter, Shirley wrenched her arm from Zane's grip. 'Worst mistake I ever made having anything to do with you!' Moving away, she pressed her face against the wall. 'Why did she do this? Why has she opened this cesspit? I told her... I told her not to ever do this!'

Placing the decanter down, Zane watched in both disbelief and shock. Had he not known this to be Shirley Wilson by her eyes, he'd have never recognised her in a million years. Where had the beautiful, sweet girl that he'd once dated disappeared to?

His gaze moved over the shapeless clothes hanging on Shirley's overweight frame; the stained blouse; her unbrushed hair... It was like she'd chucked together the most ill-fitting, unflattering things she could find - honing herself to look as unkempt as possible. Plus, her constants mutterings made no sense. It was like she was arguing within her own head.

A huge wave of sadness engulfed him for what Shirley had once been, compared to what she now was. He had no idea what had happened to the girl he'd once thought so highly of, but that girl was certainly no longer part of the person now calling herself Shirley Wilson.

But he'd got one thing wrong - Shirley was no drunk, nor a drug addict. She wasn't part of reality or rather, didn't *want* to be part of reality.

'Shirley?' Zane stepped forward, his voice calm even though his mind was reeling. 'Why did you not want Skye looking for me? She has a right to know about her fa...'

Shirley froze where she stood then slowly turned to face Zane. 'That's a joke! After what you allowed... After what you believed to be acceptable? Your family... No! No, I'm not going there! How come it's you who's here, anyway? Come to gloat? Where are the rest of them?'

'Gloat?' Zane frowned. 'Gloat at what?' Despite his promise to remain calm it was difficult. 'What have I got to gloat about? Not being made aware of Skye? I don't think so! Where were *my* rights then?'

'Why should you have rights over *that*?' Shirley paced up and down, her loose slippers flapping on the carpet. 'It's *me* without rights. The same as the rest of the goddamn world, aside from the Morellis. That you stood there and allowed others to make the... Oh! What am I doing?'

She flung her hands in the air, the flabby skin at the top of her arms jiggling. 'What am I doing? What am I doing? All these years I've waited for one of you bastards to show up and try and take what's mine.' She pushed closer to Zane's face, her finger pointing perilously close to his one decent eye. 'Well, you're not having it! To think I used to think you were everything! Ha!'

Spinning around, Shirley made a strange pirouette-type dance in the centre of the room. 'Skye's my daughter and I've bought her up well. She's not like you lot.'

That's where Shirley was wrong, Zane thought. Skye was very much like him – not in her strange behaviour and manipulative techniques being unearthed by the bucketload, but by her zest for life – her *spirit*. It was like looking at a carbon copy of himself when he'd been younger before his world and view of life clouded. The fire in Skye made her a Morelli. Like Leo said – it was a family trait.

As Shirley stomped from the lounge into the kitchen, Zane followed. Pointing out the similarities between him and his daughter wouldn't have a positive effect, but regardless of this, Shirley's words didn't add up. *Nothing* she said added up.

'You're not making sense,' Zane cried, perplexed and aggravated. 'You disappeared on *me*, remember?' A strange unearthly noise assaulted his ears before he realised the noise was coming from Shirley. *Was... was that a laugh? What the hell was wrong with her?*

The memory of Skye's remarks about Shirley 'not being well' and 'crazy' flooded Zane's mind. With renewed vigour he concentrated on the other burning question he needed the answer to. It was clear he wouldn't get a reason why she'd left all those years ago or why he hadn't been informed he had a daughter, but he had to know the answer to one *other* thing. 'Put your strange and undeserved hatred towards me to one side and...'

'Undeserved? UNDESERVED? You knew *everything*! You made the choice. You...'

'I keep telling you that Skye's gone missing. She's been acting strangely and I need to know the truth. Has she ever been abused?'

Shirley's mouth fell open. '*What*? Abused? Skye?'

'She hinted that someone you knew or someone you were friendly with had...'

'Get out!'

'What?' Zane frowned. 'I'm trying to get to the bottom of why Sk...'

'Get. Out. Of. My. Fucking. House.' Snatching up a knife from the worksurface, Shirley held it out in front of her.

It was Zane's turn to be astounded; not just from Shirley's language – she never swore - or never used to, but for *this*. 'Okay, okay, put the knife down, Shirley.' He held his hands up submissively. He could tackle her to the ground and disarm her but he didn't want to do that. But neither did he particularly want to get cut.

'You lot!' Shirley snarled, her teeth bared. 'You're all the same. You allowed what your father arranged. You thought it was okay. You knew everything and as for your brother... Oh, I can't bear to... What does it matter? You got what you wanted. You all did! I hope you're pleased. I'm surprised your father hasn't come here himself and...'

'My father's dead, Shirley, so whatever is in your head, don't speak badly of him,' Zane said. *And God knows what was in her head!*

'Dead? Good. I'm glad!' Shirley spat. 'I wish the same on all of you. Now, I'm warning you, Zane Morelli. Get out of my house. You think I'd *ever* allow anyone to touch my daughter? I don't want her around anybody and certainly none of *you*! There is not one drop of Morelli in Skye, do you hear me? I've made damn sure of that. Now get the hell out of my house!'

Swallowing his anger, Zane shook his head. He was wasting his time. Skye wasn't here, but what she'd said about her mother was true. Shirley was ill - crazy.

What a cruel world this was.

He pulled a piece of paper from his leather jacket pocket. 'Here's my number. Please call me if Skye gets in touch.' Holding it out, Shirley stared it like it was radioactive and made no move to take it, so he placed the piece of paper on the table instead. 'I'll leave it there.'

Zane let himself out of the house before he grabbed the crazy bitch around the throat and got the answers out of her that way. He suspected even if he did that, he'd be wasting his time. She was well gone and talking rubbish.

Shutting the door behind him he darted down the side of the house. Through the sash window of the room he'd left her in he watched the woman he'd once thought might become his wife sitting in a kitchen chair rocking backwards and forwards. Tears poured down her pudgy cheeks and her mouth flapped up and down in conversation with someone in her head who didn't exist.

Sighing with raw disappointment, Zane made his way down the drive back to his bike.

Forty Four

LOOKING WILDLY from left to right, Leo craned his neck above the throngs of people pushing their way around Vauxhall underground station. *Which way had she gone?*

He'd only glimpsed a fleeting view of the woman from the back, but from what he'd seen it had resembled Zane's daughter as much as anyone could.

If it *was* Skye, then why was she in Vauxhall? It was close to Battersea, so had Damon taken her but she'd somehow escaped?

Lurching down the escalator, taking the moving stairs three at the time and pushing people to one side as he did so, Leo made it to the bottom in record time. Feeling the telltale rush of wind from the tube line he darted towards the platform.

Overriding the flickering overhead lights causing a strobe effect on the tiled walls around him, he peered through the mass of people moving in front and behind the map on the wall, his concentration was pushed to the limit deduced which platform Skye might have taken.

He must hurry.

Receiving another blast of hot air and the screech of an incoming tube, Leo pushed his way down one of the forks, not caring who happened to be the recipient of his elbows.

Vauxhall was on the Victoria line, so if Skye was heading back to Dalston she'd change at Highbury and Islington to take the overground to Dalston Junction.

But if she was heading to Shirley's instead...

Then again, if she was doing that, then why would she be in Vauxhall in the first place?

He'd have to take a guess. *Any* guess...

Leo raced onto the platform, his eyes darting through the crowd.

There she was. Up the other end, boarding the tube.

'Skye! he roared. 'SKYE!' Shoving more people out of the way, Leo raced along the platform, realising that he could get on any carriage and find Skye once on the tube. Now he'd seen it was definitely her, he had to get on this train.

Frantically pushing forward, the beeping of the door closing sounded. 'Don't you fucking dare!' he screamed. Sweating, he reached the door just as the tube pulled away.

Banging the side of the train, he ran alongside to no avail as the tube, along with Skye, disappeared into the tunnel's mouth.

Leo bent over, leaning on his knees to get his breath back then turned on his heels.

Clattering his way back up the steps to the main road, he jumped back in the van. Ignoring Martin's questions, he instead tried unsuccessfully to call Zane and tell him Skye had been sighted.

'Surely she's heading back to the house?' Martin said.

'Not if she's going to Shirley's.' Leo continued along the road as fast as the traffic would allow. 'Answer the phone, Zane!' he barked. *Should he continue to Sandler's?* He didn't know. *For fuck's sake! This was a bloody nightmare.*

Sparking up a cigarette, he gritted his teeth as he drove into Battersea, the fourth set of lights turning to red. Drumming his fingers on the steering wheel as he waited, he willed Zane to hurry the fuck up and call him back. He had to know what to do for the best.

'It was definitely Skye?' Martin repeated for the thousandth time. 'I knew it was. It's the way her hair flicks to one side when she walks and...'

Leo suddenly went rigid, his knuckles whitening on the steering wheel. 'What the...?'

Martin stared at Leo's rapidly paling face. 'Surely it's not that unusual to recognise the woman you love purely from a fleeting glimpse, is it? I mean, there must be times when you've...'

'Shut up!' Leo screamed. The lights had now turned to green but he made no move to pull away; his eyes fixed only on something ahead. 'I don't believe this! How? How the fuck?'

'You need to turn left down here for Sandler's flat,' Martin continued, oblivious. 'I'm pretty sure it's that one. If not, it's definitely the next.'

Martin's voice continued droning, but Leo zoned out. The only thing he heard was the buzzing in his own head as the door of the black cab further along the road closed and the car pulled away. Jolted back to reality by horns blaring behind him, he scraped the gearbox into first. He could just about see the black cab in the distance. *Keep on its tail.*

He hadn't been sure about Skye until he'd got a closer look on the platform, but he was sure about this. *Jesus Christ! How could this happen?*

Marco Morelli was being charged! He was going to prison. Zane's contact from the force confirmed that only yesterday, so how the bloody hell could the man himself be sauntering down the road and getting into a taxi?

Because that's what he'd just seen.

With the back of his hand, Leo swiped away the sweat threatening to drip into his eyes off his forehead. Now there really was no choice where to head next.

Marco was out. Fucking *out*! Not only was Skye somewhere on a tube not far away, but Erin was alone in the house in Dalston.

And now the black cab had disappeared from Leo sights. *Fuck!*

Marco could be heading to Dalston or he could be tailing Skye. He could be going *anywhere*.

Shit, shit, SHIT!

Leo slammed his foot on the accelerator, ignoring Martin's yelp when his head bashed into the headrest. Whatever happened, he had to drive like the clappers and get back to Dalston. *Fast*.

Wherever Marco was going, he didn't know, but what he *did* know was that he had to get there first. Catching up with Sandler would have to wait.

* * * *

'IS SHE BACK?' Zane crashed through the door of his house and rushed into the sitting room.

Erin thundered down the stairs from with the noise of Zane's unexpected entrance. 'No, she's not. I haven't be…'

'Where's Tiger?' Zane darted into the kitchen and then back again. 'Where is he? I told Leo to send him over here and bring Bolt, so where are they?'

'No one's here yet.' Seeing Zane's stress, Erin placed a hand on his arm. 'It's fine, but how did you get on with Shirley?'

'What do you mean no one's been here yet?' Zane raged. 'Are you telling me you've been alone the whole time I've been gone?' His anger grew. 'I made it clear to Leo that Tiger needed to get his arse here and that we'd sort out the shit from yesterday when I returned, so where the fuck is he? Is this his way of punishing me?'

'But I'm fine!' Erin insisted. 'I did what you said. I stayed out of sight. There's been no problems.'

'Oh, but there is!' Zane seethed. 'I'll kill him! How dare Tiger nor Leo ignore instructions! How am I supposed to trust anyone if no one does what I say?'

'Calm down,' Erin said sternly. 'Something must have

happened. There's no harm done.'

Zane sank into the chair, realisation dawning. 'But there could have been harm done. This is my fault. I'm being deluded! Why the fuck would Tiger honour my orders after what happened yesterday?'

The fact was that he wouldn't. There were some things which could be glossed over and shrugged off, but accusing someone of rape was hardcore. 'Christ, Erin. What's happening to me? I've alienated one of my best men, I've lost my daughter and I've exposed you to Sandler because I failed to remove him. He could have come here and...' He jumped from the seat and paced the room, the veins bulging in his temples.

'Everything will work out.' Erin hoped that would be the case. 'But Shirley? Did you see Shirley?'

Zane stopped pacing, his ice blue eyes pained. 'I did. It was fucking awful!'

Erin's heart pounded. Zane didn't usually get in states like this, but he was manic – overloading on nervous energy. Her prior fears about him setting eyes on his first love resurfaced. Had seeing Shirley brought his feelings flooding back? Had Shirley fallen into his arms over the joint anguish of the daughter they shared going missing? 'W-Why was it awful?' she whispered, her nails digging into the soft flesh of her palms.

Snatching up a bottle of whisky, Zane unscrewed it and then thinking better of it, replaced the cap. Putting the bottle down, he flopped into the chair and put his head in his hands.

Erin inched closer, her fingers shaking within her clenched fists. *He was about to say he was leaving, wasn't he?* 'Zane? What's going on?'

'I-I barely recognised Shirley,' Zane muttered. 'She looked like she'd been sleeping in a hedge. She went mental at me. First, she tried to clump me with a decanter and then she pulled a knife.'

'What?' Erin pushed away the relief and the glimmer of satisfaction to hear that Shirley looked dreadful. Out of everything Zane had just said, surely she shouldn't be pleased?

Probably not, but there was a tiny part of her that was. 'What else did she say?'

'Not a lot,' Zane sighed. 'Skye wasn't there and hadn't been for some time, but what *was* clear is that she's been lying.' His eyes narrowed. 'She hasn't been brought up in a hovel and went to a *good* school. Lastly, Shirley is certainly not a raving drunk.'

'Then why...'

'When I broached the possibility of someone having abused Skye, Shirley went berserk. She's extremely protective - overprotective, if anything,' Zane continued, his mind reeling with what it meant. 'She's frantic about Skye - anyone can see that.'

Once again, Erin pushed away her satisfaction that she'd been proved right about Skye being a lying little bitch. It wasn't right to gloat, but neither did it explain why the girl was doing it. 'Why didn't Shirley tell you that you had a daughter? Did you ask?'

'I tried, but fuck, she hates me!' Zane glanced up, his eyes holding a mixture of pain and confusion. 'I still don't know why. She was ranting and saying all kinds of stuff.'

'Like what?'

'Stuff that made no sense. But one thing Skye hasn't lied about is that Shirley's crazy!' Zane rubbed his hand across his face like the action would erase his exhaustion. 'I don't know whether she's had a breakdown, whether it's insanity or what, but it was dreadful. She's barking mad and it's just so bloody sad.' He held Erin's eyes. 'I'm so very sorry that I didn't believe what you said about Skye. It seems I'm making a habit of doing that with everybody...'

'What's important now is that we find Skye. We have to make sure she's okay,' Erin said. 'Call Leo. He might have some news.'

'You're right.' Zane pulled his phone from his pocket just as it rang. 'This might be him now. Leo? Oh! Yes, what's up?'

Erin's blood froze as the colour drained from Zane's face, the paleness accentuating the purple of his blackened eye.

'*How*?' Zane's eyes darted to Erin's. 'It couldn't have been! Hazel wouldn't... Right... I see...' He didn't say anything else - just ended the call and stared vacantly at the dark screen of his mobile.

'What is it?' Erin prayed this wasn't news that Skye's body had been found. However much she didn't like the girl's behaviour, she wouldn't wish *that* on her; or on Zane. *How much more could he take?* 'Zane? Who was that?'

Leo suddenly crashed through the front door, dragging a confused looking Martin Bolt with him. Clapping eyes on Erin, he exhaled with relief. 'Thank fuck!' He then turned to Zane. 'Look, I don't know how to tell you this, but...'

Zane silenced Leo with a raised hand. 'I already know... Marco's been released. I've just had a call from my contact in the force.'

'*What*?' Erin shrieked. 'Released? He can't have been! You said...'

'It's true.' Leo turned to Zane. 'I've just seen him getting into a taxi in Battersea. I tried to call, then came straight here. I didn't bother with Sandler. He's not important compared with this. And there's something el...'

'I don't understand. How could Marco be released?' Erin spoke more to herself than anyone else. Nausea engulfed her. 'Marco had no defence. He...'

'He had a signed statement from Hazel absolving Marco's involvement in everything,' Zane said.

'But Tiger told you about that statement being on the floor. It was unsigned!' Erin cried.

'I know that,' Zane acknowledged, reluctant to entertain the possibility that Hazel had betrayed him either, but he had to weigh up all odds. 'The one found – it may have been a copy because my contact confirmed that document they received was definitely signed.'

'Hazel wouldn't sign something like that!' Erin gasped. 'She...'

'We'll talk about this later.' Zane snatched his jacket from the chair. 'I need to find my daughter.'

'That's the other thing.' Leo quickly added. 'I saw Skye boarding a tube in Vauxhall. I wasn't fast enough to get on it.'

'What?' Zane spun around, his face flushed with relief. 'That means she's okay!'

'She was, but Marco could be gunning for her. We need to find her,' Leo pressed.

'So, she *is* going to Shirley's?' Erin yelled.

'I'm certainly not going back to my mother's,' Skye said, casually walking into the room. 'What's all the commotion about anyway? I can hear you lot from outsi... Martin!' she squeaked. 'What are you doing here?'

HAVING SPENT THE DAY lying in bed, sleeping on and off and eating crisps, Damon received no warning of a visitor until he was ripped from his dream as well as his bed.

Suddenly finding himself on the floorboards, Damon looked up in confusion. The boot to his jaw which followed sent him sprawling onto his back. 'What in fuck's name?' he yelped, pain exploding in his face.

'Lying around doing fuck all as usual, Sandler?' Marco drawled. 'How unsurprising...'

Hearing that voice, Damon forced his head to stop spinning to check whether this was actually happening or if it was a horrible nightmare. Because if it *was* a nightmare, he needed to wake up immediately.

Blinking as the figure standing above came into focus, bile rushed up Damon's throat. *Fuck! How could Marco be out? It was impossible! Completely impossible.*

'Hmm, you seem surprised to see me.' Marco rubbed his chin. 'Isn't that strange...'

'Well, I...'

As Marco dropped to his haunches, Damon scrabbled to sit upright, but instead of getting traction on the bare floorboards, he collected only splinters. His elbows scuffed against the wood as he levered himself back against the wall, but any distance away from Marco was better than none.

Marco's reach was long enough to lean over and grab Damon around the throat. 'It appears you were in no rush to give me an update. I called you but you didn't fucking answer.'

'M-My phone bust,' Damon garbled. 'I couldn't get the statement you wanted either. I...'

'Really?' Marco raised an eyebrow. 'Could that be because you didn't *try*?' His eyes changed to fiery pits of hate. 'Because you wanted me to go to jail?'

'No! No, of course not!' Damon's fingers clawed pointlessly against Marco's hand as it tightened around his throat. 'I did what you said... I went to the Starbright with Bolt, but Hazel was dead. Bolt killed her! I don't know why... I never asked him to... I...'

Marco dragged Damon away from the wall and slammed his head into the floorboards. 'So, you ran away like the cowardly cunt you are and lay here fucking sleeping until I got sent down?'

'No! It wasn't like that... I...' Damon dragged whatever air he could into his lungs. 'I can't breathe! You're hurting me!'

'Yeah, brilliant analysis,' Marco snarled. 'So my wife is dead? Did you not think I might wish to know about that?'

'Well, yes, but you...'

'Hazel's absence hasn't stopped me from being here, has it?' Marco released Damon from his grip. Brushing his trousers down, he stood to his full height and stared down at the man quivering on the floor beneath. 'I'm surprised you're still living in this shithole, Sandler.'

Damon watched Marco casually walk around the bedroom staring scornfully at the peeling wallpaper and damp patches. His eyes darted around for something - *anything* he could use to defend himself. *Where did he put his gun? Was it under all that stuff on the chair?*

'Yeah, I'd have thought you'd have taken the opportunity

to move from this dump into my penthouse, being as you presumed I wouldn't need it again.' Marco ran his finger along the windowsill and glared with revulsion at the dust collected.

'I didn't... I...'

'The truth is that you didn't want me to be released, is it not? You've done everything possible to ensure I remained where I was.' Bending down, Marco wiped the dust down Damon's cheek before pushing the end of his finger, along with a dead spider, into Damon's mouth. 'You could do with a fucking shave as well. Have you no self-respect?'

Spluttering, Damon spat out the mouthful of dust and hopefully the dead spider and raised his hand to wipe the rest of the dust off his cheek, but he didn't quite manage that before Marco's shoe came down on his hand.

'AAARGH!' Damon screamed, the sound of breaking bones almost as dreadful as the pain.

This couldn't be happening. How had Marco been released? He had no solicitor; no statement from Hazel; no one on the outside to pull in favours. It just wasn't feasible, yet he was here. *In this bedroom.*

Unable to stop the tears of both panic and pain from escaping, Damon clutched his shattered hand.

'Stop. Fucking. Whining!' Removing his foot, Marco continued pacing. 'Do you really think I haven't been onto you all along?' His eyes sparkled with malice. 'Do you really think that for some time now I didn't know your aim wasn't about me, what I needed or the instructions I gave you? Instead, you wanted what was *mine.*'

'That's not true! I...' Damon flinched as Marco laughed heartily. The manic laughter - a trademark of the man was something Damon had never liked and now, given the situation, it sounded even more sinister. *He was dead. Marco had come to kill him. It was over.*

He'd almost been there - literally a few more hours were all he'd needed. Marco would have been sent down and then he'd have been free. He'd have triumphed. He'd hav...

'You lying cunt!' Marco growled, spinning around to boot Damon in the face for the second time - this time removing teeth. 'You wanted my business, my empire - the *lot*! You hid all sorts of shit from me thinking I wouldn't know - like that you couldn't even manage killing my brother's whore!' He laughed once more. 'You think I didn't know that your shooting didn't finish Erin Langley? Well, I do. But did you tell me? Of course you didn't!'

Damon spat out a mouthful of blood along with the remains of a few teeth, leaving further blood to drip down his bare chest onto his underpants. *How the fuck did Marco know Erin was still alive? Where was he getting his information from?* 'I-I only found out about her myself the other day,' he mumbled.

'Then that makes you even more pointless,' Marco snarled, watching Damon intently.

Damon remained motionless, scared to breathe. If he lurched towards the chair, could he grab his gun and shoot Marco before the man had time to react? It was possible if he timed it right. The gun was just underneath his jeans - he could see the edge of the butt poking out just where his belt lay over the…

'Oh dear… Your eyes always give you away, Sandler,' Marco chuckled. Striding over to the chair, he used his finger and thumb to gingerly pincer up Damon's jeans. 'If you hadn't made it so fucking obvious, I might not have found this so easily. Cheers!'

Damon's heart crashed to basement level as Marco swung the gun straight at him.

And here it was… Time to die.

Marco cocked the gun. 'Nothing to say, Sandler? No, "Sorry Mr Morelli for being an abject cunt and letting you down on a regular basis?" No? Nothing?'

'Fuck off,' Damon mumbled, having nothing to lose anymore.

From the loud crack, followed by a second one, Damon only heard Marco's maniacal laughter as the gun discharged.

Then the pain started…

'AAAAAARGH!' Damon screeched, the two bullets having ripped both his kneecaps apart with expert precision. Sweating copiously, he could only hope that Marco finished the job quickly.

'The thing is…' Marco moved his aim to Damon's chest, 'I could kill you…' He chuckled quietly. 'Don't get me wrong - I'd enjoy that. I'd enjoy it *immensely*, but…' He emptied the gun's chamber of the remaining bullets and shoved them in his pocket. 'It's just that I hate you too much to do that. I'd much rather you suffered.'

Stepping over Damon writhing around on the floor, avoiding the blood seeping into the wooden boards, Marco placed the gun back underneath the clothes. 'Being crippled and living in fear as to exactly when I'll come to finish the job is a more satisfying outcome,' Marco grinned, his teeth shining bright in the sunlight spilling into the room. 'Because you know that particular ending is guaranteed, so it's just a case of when… Now be a good chap and tell me where you keep the keys to my penthouse and I'll leave you to enjoy the rest of your day off.'

• • • •

SKYE LOOKED TO ZANE AND ERIN, then onto Leo and finally to Martin before turning back to Zane, her face a picture of angry resentment. 'You've been to see my *mother*?' she exclaimed, incredulous. 'Even after I made it clear that I didn't want you to? Well, now you know for yourself that she's crazy!'

She swung towards Erin, her blue eyes flashing. 'I suppose you're loving this now you can have a good laugh at my embarrassment?'

'We thought something had happened to you when you disappeared this morning,' Zane said, determined not to lose his cool.

'Why do you think that was?' Skye snapped. 'After accusing me of all sorts last night did you really think I'd be here this morning pretending like nothing happened? But if you must know, I went for a walk.'

'A long walk, I take it?' Leo added. 'One which involved getting on the tube at Vauxhall?'

The flash of panic on Skye's face before she masked it was clear.

'Well?' Zane hissed. 'Not just a walk, was it? Seeing your mother today showed that you've lied about many things. You weren't brought up in a hovel, you didn't go to a shitty school, your mother isn't a drunk surrounded by lecherous men and...'

'What?' Martin piped up. 'Shirley's not...' He silenced himself as Zane glared at him, raising his hand for quiet.

'Neither was this bloke here, stalking you. Judging by the texts you sent *him* that I've seen, it was *you* acting obsessed,' Zane continued. *He'd get to the bottom of this without fail.*

'If that's what you want to believe,' Skye sniffed haughtily. 'You see things whichever way you wish. You will do anyway and the reason I was in Vauxhall,' she glared at Leo accusingly, 'is because I *was* going home - I admit it, but I changed my mind. I was so upset I got on the wrong train. It was then that I decided it was more important putting things right with *you* - my father than running away. Now I wish I hadn't bothered!' Getting to her feet, Skye went to stalk from the room.

'You stay here and explain yourself!' Zane barked. 'Why all the lies? Why make out that Erin has been unkind to you when it was the other way around?'

Stopping in her tracks, Skye stared at the many pairs of eyes around the room focused on her and she blinked like a rabbit caught in the headlights.

She glared at Martin. 'Why is he still here anyway? Why are *any* of them here? This is nothing to do with anyone else. I'm *your* daughter, not theirs!'

'Your behaviour has affected everyone in this room, as well as one that isn't here.' Zane gestured for Skye to sit back down and waited until she reluctantly obeyed. 'Because of your lies one of my most trusted men walked away from me today after years! And no, I won't ask Martin to leave either. As much as

I've spent the last week wanting to kill him, again based on what *you* said, he has as much right to hear your explanation as we do.'

Suddenly, almost in slow motion, the well-maintained wall surrounding Skye Wilson crumbled. At first, one pebble dislodged and then a few seconds later the entire structure fell away like it had been whacked with a demolition ball, leaving Skye to dissolve into body-wracking sobs.

'There's no point crying,' Zane spat. 'I want an explanation. We *all* want an explanation.'

'I was jealous, all right?' Skye yelled. 'I don't know why, but I was. Doing and saying all of that stuff wasn't my plan. I'm not like that. It… it just happened.'

She caught Erin rolling her eyes. 'I know what you think of me and I don't blame you. I've been a bitch and I'm sorry. As for Martin, he scares me because he loves me. I'm scared I'll end up hurt and it makes me panic. Everybody leaves me in the end.'

Skye stared at her feet but continued to talk. 'My mum said you were awful, Zane, but I wanted to know where I came from. I-I found you and then instead of being grateful you'd accepted me and weren't awful at all, I... I resented you.'

She then turned to Erin. 'And you. I resented you most of all. Actually, I resented *all* of you. You have a life and act like family, even though no one is blood. Family is everything. Everything I never had. And I... I hated you all for being part of one when all of these years, I wasn't. All I can say is that I'm sorry and hope you can forgive me.'

With that, Skye dissolved into a fresh but exhausted round of sobbing leaving everyone sitting in stunned silence.

Erin especially. She'd expected more bullshit, more lies, even angry outbursts of denial.

She hadn't expected *this*.

FORTY SIX

HAVING SUCCESSFULLY TALKED Fiona out of calling Shirley again, possibly out of her guilt over his night's stay at Guildford police station, Peter did a double take seeing the woman herself hurrying up his drive.

There was absolutely no way Shirley Wilson was putting one foot, or even a single hair in his house after the hassle she'd caused.

He opened his mouth to make the position clear to Fiona, when to his horror, she also spotted Shirley and rushed towards the door. 'Don't even think about it!' Peter cried, jumping from the chair.

Seeing his wife continuing down the hallway oblivious to his instructions, he followed. 'Fiona!' he bellowed. 'Do not let that woman in!' His panic mounted further as she reached the door, her hand on the knob. 'I expressly forbid you to talk to that woman! Do not let her into this house! I…'

Ignoring Peter, Fiona opened the door. 'Shirley! I've been trying to call you. I… Oh my God! What's happened?'

'H-He turned up! He turned up at my house!' Shirley gibbered, her eyes darting around. 'I didn't know what to do or where to go. I'm sorry… I shouldn't have come.'

'Nonsense,' Fiona said, batting away Peter and steered Shirley into the lounge.

Peter stared at Shirley. The woman looked even more deranged than the last time he'd been stupid enough to allow her anywhere near his family. 'Fiona, Shirley shouldn't be h...'

'Thank you, Peter,' Fiona snapped. 'Can you not see Shirley's upset? Go and put the kettle on.'

Clutching at his hair in desperation, Peter glared at the back of Fiona's head - not that it made one iota of difference. He stomped towards the kitchen, making sure he could still hear what was being said. He wasn't allowing his wife's head to be filled with any more rubbish.

Fiona glanced over her shoulder, making sure Peter had left the room. 'Tell me exactly what happened. You said "he" turned up? Who? Shelly? Chelly? Whatever his name is who phoned you?'

'Morelli,' Shirley spat like the name rotted her mouth. 'One of them, anyway.'

'Damon Morelli?' *That was the name Martin mentioned on the phone yesterday.* 'Is that Skye's father?'

'No!' Shirley cried. 'And I don't know a Damon Morelli, although God knows how many Morellis there are now. I only knew...' She stopped, not wishing to discuss that family. 'They had Skye. He admitted it.'

'Then why did this... this person come? Was it blackmail? Money?' Fiona frowned. 'What did he want?'

'Money? They don't need money! They have more than anyone, the evil twisted...' Shirley swiped at her face to delete the sight of Zane from seeping under her skin after all these years. 'He said Skye disappeared this morning. I threatened him.' Her eyes were wide; glazed. 'I scratched his face and pulled a knife on him. I would have stabbed him. I hate him. I...'

'Skye's escaped?' Fiona gasped, barely able to breathe. It was bad enough Shirley had been wielding knives but if Skye had escaped, then so might have Martin. 'Where is she now?'

'I don't know.' Shirley grabbed Fiona's hand. 'I don't know what to do.'

'Do you know a place called the Starbright? Martin said that's where he was. Where *both* of them were, but on record it doesn't exist. I want to go and look, but I don't know where to start and then Peter, well, he...'

'I don't know anywhere called Starbright,' Shirley admitted. 'The only place I knew is abandoned - so Martin said when he got there.' She had distinct memories of *that* place too. Ones that could never be erased.

'Where did you send Martin?' Fiona's nausea heightened with the thought that her son had been trailing these animals for days without her knowledge and now... now he might be dead. But then, he might have escaped... 'Oh! The phone!' she yelped as a sudden shrill ring cut through the air. *She must reach it before Peter. It might be Martin again.*

Lurching towards the handset, she snatched it up. 'Martin? Thank God! Are you all right? Tell me where you are. I tried to call the police, but the Starbright doesn't exist... What? You're not?' Fiona's eyes darted to Shirley. 'But... No, just tell me... Well, when will you... What? Okay, yes… I promise. Oh, and Martin? I...'

Fiona stared at the phone, the line dead. 'He's hung up.'

'That was Martin?' Shirley gasped. He's okay? And Skye? Is Skye with him? Where are they? When are they coming back?'

'That's the strange thing,' Fiona frowned. 'Martin said he's fine. They're both fine. He's with Skye but they're not coming back just yet.'

'What?' Shirley screeched. 'Why not? Are they being forced to stay?'

'Right, that's it!' Peter burst into the lounge. 'Time to call the police!'

'No, Peter,' Fiona snapped. 'Martin has assured me both he and Skye are fine. He said the police aren't needed.'

'Apparently, someone kidnapped him and kept him

prisoner in a cupboard and you think the police don't need to know?' Peter yelled. 'I want these people held accountable, so of course the police are bloody well needed! Being as Martin's no longer in the clutches of those lunatics, we won't be jeopardising his safety. That was your reasoning before, was it not? Well, it doesn't apply now.'

'Martin is *adamant* the police are not to be involved. He... erm, he said... said it was a misunderstanding?'

'A misunderstanding?'

'He said it was a misunderstanding and he wants to sort things out with Skye before he returns. Then they will be back,' Fiona mumbled.

'Skye's coming back,' Shirley repeated over and over to herself. 'She's coming back, thank God.'

'Thank God, my foot!' Peter snarled. 'If you think Martin is having anything to do with your daughter or *you* after this, then you're very much mistaken!'

'Peter!' Fiona scolded. 'Don't say things like th…'

'I like how it's conveniently escaped your brain that the stuff about Martin being in a cupboard was just like I said! Rubbish!' Peter paced the room, his usual anger returning. 'This was made-up nonsense from the start! What was said about the car was true. You wait until he gets back! He'll receive the end of my boot for this. Martin will be grounded for a very long time for dreaming up this stunt, no doubt with help from your daughter!' He glared at Shirley. 'Well, no more!'

Fiona and Shirley exchanged glances, both knowing this was not nonsense. Neither was it made-up, but if it made Peter feel better to think that, then it was easier to let him continue. Fiona knew she'd have to trust Martin's word on what he said and wait for him to return home when he was ready.

Then she'd find out what was going on, but Martin and Skye were both safe and that was the only thing that mattered. For now, she had to be patient.

• • • •

ZANE WAS GLAD that Skye had gone to her room for some space. He needed time away from her to process what she'd said. For her to admit that she'd manipulated and lied because of jealousy was disappointing, but it gnawed at his heart for her being so unhappy in her life to feel so resentful of him and his previous lack of presence.

But now he could put that right. Now Skye had admitted everything, despite the trouble it had caused, they could start again.

He squeezed Erin's hand, grateful as always that she was at his side. He needed her more than ever now. But as much as he wanted to concentrate on his daughter, there was the bombshell that Marco was out to deal with.

His brother was depleted when it came to power and muscle to pull on, but it was only a matter of time before he would rise from the ashes. And where he would do it…

He must be ready.

But there was another issue bothering Zane and that was what he endeavoured to uncover now. Erin being so adamant that Hazel wouldn't have signed that document supplying enough evidence to work in Marco's defence backed up what he, himself wanted to prove. He couldn't stomach the thought that Hazel could have done it either. None of them could. Not willingly, anyway so he needed more information – more clarity on it.

So, he'd asked. and now he should receive an answer.

Making sure Martin was out of earshot making the agreed call to his mother, Erin was the one to speak first. 'I still stand that Hazel wouldn't have signed that statement. She was terrified of Marco. She hated him!'

Zane nodded a signal for quiet as the line connected. 'Hey, yeah, it's me. You have? Okay - go on...' Frowning, he listened carefully to what his contact from the force, Dave Richards, relayed. Shaking with rage, it took all of his power not to launch the phone against the wall. 'You're sure? Yeah, okay... Thanks.'

Ending the call, Zane raised his eyes to meet those of Leo and Erin staring at him in anticipation. 'It was definitely the statement which got the charges dropped,' he muttered, the confirmation hard to comprehend. 'And it *was* signed by Hazel. The signature has been confirmed to be hers.'

'It could have been a good forgery?' Erin blathered.

Zane shook his head. 'It's not. Dave said it's kosher.'

'Then she must have been forced!' Erin continued scraping around for explanations. 'We already thought that could be feasible. Sandler went to the Starbright, forced Hazel to sign, killed her and then took that fucking document to th…'

'Except the statement was dated two days prior to that,' Zane muttered.

'Anyone can write a date on a piece of paper, Zane. It doesn't mean that sh…'

'The statement was sent to the police the day it was signed…' Zane's voice trailed off.

'Fuck!' Leo hissed. The unspoken assumption that they'd all clung to was that the alleged statement would be dated the day Hazel was *murdered*, making it clear she'd either been forced to sign or that the signature was forged, but this was now dead in the water.

And everyone knew what that meant.

Zane slumped into a chair - the news knocking the remaining wind out of his sails. He'd trusted Hazel; believed she'd put her devious past behind her.

Suddenly, another uncomfortable thought entered Zane's head: Hazel had been the one to initially suggest Erin could be mentally unstable as a result of trauma. Was befriending Erin, then getting her out of the picture and gaining his trust a ploy to open the doors for Marco? Had this been Hazel's plan all along?

Zane's hands began to tremble as adrenalin slammed through his veins. He didn't know what hurt more: that Hazel had set him up after giving her a new life, brought her into his family and trusted her with his daughter or that she'd been working for Marco all this time. Or was it merely that he'd fallen for it?

First Skye lying and now discovering Hazel had been too?

Was he losing his ability to see the wood for the trees? Had he turned into some kind of fucking mug?

As everyone sat in stunned silence, busy fighting their disbelief, Erin saw the expression on Zane's face. This had floored him. It had floored them all. It wasn't possible for Hazel to have done it. She couldn't have.

'I don't believe she did it,' Erin muttered, her voice loud in the still silence.

'Nor do I,' Leo said grimly. 'But it looks like she has...'

As much as Erin didn't believe that - didn't *want* to believe it, she couldn't deny that it seemed that way.

'Er... is it all right for me to come in?' Martin appeared thought the crack of the door. 'I've finished speaking to my mother.'

'What's been said?' Erin asked, grateful for the opportunity to slide off the subject of Hazel's betrayal hanging in the room.

Martin stepped into the sitting room and eyed the grave faces surrounding him. 'Is everything okay?'

'Everything's fine,' Erin lied. 'Your mother? Did you say what we agreed?'

Martin nodded. 'Yes, I made it clear that things are fine and that everything was a misunderstanding.'

'She believed you?'

'I don't know, but she won't involve the police. She promised.'

'And your father?' Erin pushed. 'What about him?'

'From what I saw of Mrs Bolt, I think Mr Bolt will do exactly as his wife says,' Leo said, recalling the woman's bottle.

'I also told her to let Shirley know that Skye is safe too.' Martin looked around. 'I hope that was the correct thing to do?'

'Yes, I guess so.' Erin glanced at Zane sitting in the chair locked in his own thoughts.

'Then if it's okay with you, could I go upstairs and speak to Skye?' Martin asked. 'I'd like to sort things out with her.

Regardless of what she's said and implied about me, I do love her and want to fix things between us if I can.'

Coming to life, Zane jerked his head in the direction of upstairs giving Martin the nod to do as he wished.

It was difficult to think of anything other than Hazel's betrayal after everything he'd done for her. Was that no one he could trust?

Perhaps the time he'd spent inside had depleted his ability to weigh people up because he seemed unable to do a decent job of it any longer. Maybe he'd finally lost his mojo and should throw the towel in to let Marco swan back into the city and take the control he so desperately craved.

He and Erin could buy a place in the country. He had enough money to buy whatever he liked. They could have a couple of kids and start again with a simpler life - one which didn't involve other people.

It was then that he clocked Erin and Leo - the concern for him etched over their faces as plain as day. What the hell was he thinking? Giving in? Handing his brother the key to restart his campaign to run riot over everything? Giving him the go ahead to ruin the city he loved, despite the troubles it brought?

Never.

He had Erin. He had Leo. They were both still by his side. Skye had turned a corner too. Admitting her shortfalls and the reasons behind them couldn't have been easy, yet she'd done it.

And yes, he still had to get to the bottom of what had happened with Shirley to make her hate him so, but while there was a breath left in his body and he had people around him who genuinely cared, his self-pity trip was superfluous.

Erin, Leo and Tiger had risked their all for him. He may have let Tiger down and lost his respect, friendship and presence because of the way he'd dealt with the incident with Skye, but one day the man might come round. And he would do everything he could to make that happen.

Either way, whilst he still Erin, Leo and his daughter looking to him to be the man he knew he still was, then he'd do anything required to keep his way of running things and looking after the city out of his brother's twisted hands.

And that started *now*.

Expelling a loud sigh, Zane spoke for the first time in what seemed like hours. 'Okay, so here's what we're going to do. The most immediate concern is Marco being out and Damon Sandler. Out of the two, it's Sandler that we go for first because my brother will do what he usually does before he gets started on anything useful. His first port of call will be to get off his head, book hookers and have an expensive blowout in the opulent surroundings of my penthouse.'

He paused to light a cigarette and blew the smoke slowly towards the ceiling. 'He'll be centring himself and scheming how to bring about my downfall, but doing nothing else so Sandler's the one we need to concentrate on initially. He's the immediate danger for Erin and Skye. I need him dispatched.'

Leo got to his feet. 'I'll get on to that. I know where he lives now so I'll go and do what's needed.'

Zane nodded. 'Once I hear that it's done, I'll update any men I haven't been able to reach on the phone.'

STRUTTING INTO THE PENTHOUSE, Marco went straight to the huge glass-fronted drinks cabinet and extracted a bottle of whisky, glad to see it had not been emptied during his absence.

Pouring himself a doubly large measure, he threw it down his throat like it was water and smacked his lips together in satisfaction.

By Christ, he needed that!

Moving to the floor-to-ceiling window offering a panoramic view of the Thames, he used the natural light to scan his trousers for Damon Sandler's blood splattering his clothes.

Pleased to see nothing, he smiled. That stupid fuck would be getting patched up in hospital by now – that's if he'd managed to get an ambulance.

His grin widened, hoping Sandler's predicament had been discovered otherwise it would spoil the fun of finishing the man off at a later date. He wanted that two-faced cunt sweating with fear, stressing as to exactly when his final moments would arrive. Because it would come.

But all in good time...

Turning away from the window, Marco eyed the open plan

lounge, knowing some of his men had remained guard here whilst he was unfairly detained. That was until the bunch of useless turds made the ill-informed decision to leg it, showing their true colours.

He sneered, his face twisting. He didn't need them anyway. They could be replaced easily enough and now he was out, people would queue up to get back in his good books. But the ones he'd been charitable enough to allow to work for him initially had better keep their heads down and well away. No one liked wankers with more faces than Big Ben.

Spotting a collection of empty beer cans on the floor at the side of one of his leather sofas his eyes narrowed. The cheeky bastards hadn't even the decency to clear up after themselves before running off to what they perceived a better outlook.

And was that a *cobweb*?

Everyone knew how much he hated dirt and mess.

This had best still be in here as well.

Striding over to a low wooden table, Marco yanked open the drawer, his temper calming on seeing the carved box inside. Pulling it out, he removed the large bag of finest Colombian and cut himself a line. Greedily snorting it, he dragged his hand under his nose and sniffed hard, relishing the burn.

That's better, he thought, lounging back in the leather armchair.

He knew Zane wouldn't have the balls to take the penthouse back. His brother was a fucking joke and recent events only underlined that.

Things were going well and foundations were nicely in place for him to crack on. There was just one more thing to ensure remained untouched.

Getting out of the chair, Marco walked up the stairs of the split-level penthouse and continued along the galleried landing. Entering the bedroom, he took a quick detour to pull down the Egyptian cotton duvet on the super king bed and inspected the base sheet.

The thought of any fucker taking it upon themselves to use

his bed in his absence filled him with horror. He wasn't lying on anyone's but his *own* bodily secretions. Thankfully, he didn't have to. It was all clean.

Good.

Now onto *this*...

Sliding open the smooth runner door of the immense walk-in wardrobe, Marco flicked on the light and stepped inside.

He pushed aside a row of handmade Savile Row suits and moved to the wall behind, flipping down two invisible catches at the top and bottom of a panel completely concealed within the silver and white textured wallpaper.

Cracking job this and unknown to a soul aside from him.

The man who had meticulously fashioned the built-in safe under Marco's express instructions the moment he'd commanded Zane's penthouse as his own had done a wonderful job. By dispatching the fucker the minute the job was completed, not only had Marco not parted with any brass for this feat of workmanship, but it would never be spoken of either.

Genius.

Pulling off the covering to reveal the silver metal of a safe, Marco had no problem remembering the code. He may have a sketchy memory over some things that his brain classed as superfluous but this wasn't one of them.

He tugged open the heavy door, his heart picking up a steady thrum of excitement to spot the bundles of cash within, secured together in chunks of set amounts.

He could see it a glance it was all there. This was his nest egg that he'd filched over the course of time for a rainy day. But this *was* a rainy day and therefore he'd be using it.

It was now just a case of getting things back on track and in motion.

And that started in earnest tomorrow.

• • • •

'LET'S HOPE SANDLER is in when you get there!' Erin said

hopefully.

'I don't think even he's that stupid to go out and show his face at the moment,' Leo said, shrugging his jacket on. 'Unless he's gone to the penthouse.'

'Is that because you think Marco's gone straight there?' Erin asked.

Zane's eyes narrowed. 'Where else would he go? My brother's such an arsehole he'll have walked back into his life like nothing's changed. Except that it has...'

Erin masked the smile flickering on her lips, relieved that Zane was back in the saddle. She'd thought for a minute that the update about Hazel had derailed him, but he was keeping it at bay.

From her side, the thought that Hazel had betrayed them all made her skin crawl with a thousand insects, but she wouldn't believe it - not until she knew for certain. And it would take a *lot* more than a date on a piece of paper to prove that the woman who was so vehemently against having anything more to do with Marco had set them up all along.

'How do you want me to play it if Sandler isn't at his flat?' Leo opened the front door, van keys in his hand.

'In that case, we'll have to regroup.' Zane chewed his lip. 'Give me a call either way and...' With the ringing of his mobile, he pulled it from his pocket, a tiny part of him hoping it was Dave Richards ringing back to tell him that he'd got it wrong about the statement date - like he'd got it wrong about Marco being charged... 'Yeah? Oh!'

Erin hovered in the hallway, hoping the call wasn't more unexpected and debilitating news.

'How did you know where to... Oh, right. Thanks, I really appreciate it, mate,' Zane continued. 'Look, can we... Yes, of course. Yeah, thanks, I'd like that.'

Hanging up, Zane turned away but Erin saw him swipe the beginnings of a tear from the corner of his eye. Concern mounting, she moved forward to touch his arm. 'Zane?'

'That was Tiger.' The slight crack in Zane's voice was

detectable despite him attempting to conceal it.

'Tiger?' Leo paused halfway out of the door. 'Is he all right? Fuck! Nothing's happened to him, has it? What did he say?'

'He's fine,' Zane said quickly. 'He said he may be pissed off with me, but felt the urge to check out Sandler's place on his way out of London regardless.'

'He what?' Leo gasped. 'How did Tiger know where Sandler lived?'

'No idea, but listen to this! He pulled up outside to see paramedics loading Sandler into the back of an ambulance.' A smile crossed Zane's face. 'He's not dead. Not yet anyway, judging by the noise Tiger said was coming out of Sandler's gob, but he's not in a good way.'

'Looks like someone got there before me,' Leo said with a tinge of disappointment. 'Does this mean Tiger's not leaving?'

'No, he is,' Zane said. 'Just for a while, but then we'll talk.' Humbled that Tiger had acted on his behalf despite the issue between them, Zane now knew things would be all right. Perhaps not today or tomorrow, but soon. And that alone lifted a weight from his shoulders.

'Let's sit on doing anything else for tonight. Nothing else can manifest now until the morning.' Zane clapped Leo on the shoulder. 'Go home and get some shut eye. We'll regroup first thing and work out how to deal with Marco.'

Nodding, Leo walked down the path towards his van leaving Zane and Erin standing in the doorway.

Wrapping her arms around Zane's waist, Erin glanced up the stairs. 'Being as Martin is sorting things out with Skye, why don't we take the opportunity to have an early night ourselves? Let's forget about everything else until tomorrow. We deserve a break.'

'I won't argue with that,' Zane grinned, sweeping Erin off her feet and ran up the stairs with her hoisted over his shoulder.

FORTY EIGHT

BUTTERING THE TOAST, Erin put Zane's plate down in front of him and leaned over to kiss his neck.

Despite the recent uncertainties, she'd been right to suggest they switch off for the night. Making love like they hadn't a care in the world had worked wonders for her state of mind as well as her body. And hopefully it had done the same for Zane. It was what they both needed - time away from the grief and stress.

Zane was more relaxed this morning, but how long that would last was dubious. It was no secret they'd only been granted a temporary respite and now things had to return to normal.

Unfortunately..

Buttering a piece of toast for herself, Erin sat down opposite. 'So, what now?'

Zane looked at Erin, the burden of the outstanding issues pressing down with a vengeance. 'Planning is now the key,' he said. 'Short of Sandler, we know Marco's has no men. From what Tiger said, Sandler's not in a good way and it will take Marco some time to rebuild.'

'You really believe Marco's gone to the penthouse?' Erin

queried. 'Are you *sure*?'

'He hasn't got anywhere else, so yes,' Zane muttered. 'He'll hole himself up in there until he's clawed together more men. He can do shag all on his own. I have an *army* compared to him, so time is on our side. We just have to make sure we leave no openings for him to hit one of us.' And Erin and Skye would be the first targets - those to cause the most pain.

Erin knew she was a prime target – there was no need for Zane to voice it. 'What about Shirley? How will you deal with her?'

'I'm not sure but it's something else I've got to sort out,' Zane sighed. 'But how do you feel about Skye? I appreciate you've taken the brunt of her issues.'

Erin paused. *How did she feel about Skye?* Skye's admission last night should have been a relief - a turning point to start again, but there was still something nagging. 'She's certainly troubled,' she said tactfully. 'I just hope she can move past her resentment.' *If that's what it truly was...* 'But if you're asking me whether I'll hold what she did and how she made me out to be against her, then the answer is no, I won't.' Reaching across, she took Zane's hand. 'She's your daughter, Zane. Your flesh and blood. I want her to be part of the family.'

Zane smiled, his face transforming. 'You really are a wonderful woman and I love you so much, even if sometimes it seems otherwise.' Bringing Erin's hand to his lips, he kissed her fingers. 'You centre me when no one else can.'

'It will be all right, you know.' Erin squeezed Zane's hand. 'Tiger will come back. You'll get to the bottom of what happened with Hazel and…'

'I have to accept Hazel betrayed me.' Zane's face darkened. 'I don't like it but there's no other explanation.' Dropping Erin's hand, he stood up. 'There's also no point in getting hung up about it. I screwed up where reading here was concerned.'

'I don't think you did,' Erin said. 'There must be another reason that expla…'

'I'm wasting no more time on it,' Zane said brusquely. 'I'm

going upstairs to see how Skye is this morning.'

'No need,' Skye said, entering the kitchen. 'Morning Erin. I wanted to ask you both something.'

Zane raised an eyebrow. 'Okay... What is it?'

'Do you mind if I go out for a while?'

'Go out?' Zane frowned. 'Why do you want to go out?'

Momentarily shocked by Skye's pleasant demeanour, Erin frowned. 'I'm not sure we can risk you leaving the house at the moment. Where's Martin?'

Skye plonked herself down at the table. 'He's upstairs. That's why I want to go out. I need to think and clear my head. Even after what I did, Martin wants to give things another go between us - *properly*.'

Zane studied his daughter. 'And what do *you* want to do?'

'I think I want that too.' Skye smiled shyly. 'Not that I deserve it, but I can put things right now. With everybody. But I need to think.'

'Okay you go out for a bit then but one of us will come with you.' Zane went to pick up his jacket.

'I want to be on my own,' Skye said. 'I just need a walk - somewhere away from the house.'

Zane paused. He understood that. He was exactly the same and fared better on his own when he needed to get his head straight. 'All right, but don't be long.'

Erin stared at Zane in surprise as Skye left the room. 'Is it a good idea, what with...'

'Marco won't be on the prowl yet, even if he's planning on being opportunistic.' Zane chucked his leather back on the chair. 'Besides, it's far too early for him to be up. I guarantee he'll be on a coke downer and have the mother of all hangovers.'

'Yes, but...'

'I want to give Skye the chance to sort things out with Martin,' Zane explained. 'I was wrong about him. He's a good kid. I know they're young, but for the bloke to risk his neck like he did to protect my daughter means I'm in his corner and I'm eager to make up for my judgement on him. Blokes like that don't come along very often.'

'You came along for me,' Erin smiled. 'I got lucky.'

'No.' Bending down, Zane kissed Erin softly on the lips. '*I* was the one who got lucky.'

• • • •

WITH THE BUZZING of the intercom, Marco moved quickly into the penthouse hallway. He glanced at his watch. Bang on time, just like he'd expected.

It was good being back where he belonged.

The concierge on reception wouldn't have impeded his visitor. The man knew better. Besides, he'd already informed the front desk he was expecting a visitor.

And he was looking forward to it.

This was the very reason why he'd gone steady on the powder and whisky last night. It would have been easy to have a blowout - God knew he was due one, but he had to be on top form today. It was more important than anything.

Opening the door, he grinned at the beautiful young woman on his doorstep and stepped aside to grant her free passage.

It was only after he shut the door behind him did he pull her into his arms. 'Well, I'm out!' he grinned, kissing her on the cheek. 'You've done well.'

'Hello, Dad.' Skye looked around, impressed. 'Nice place you've got here.'

'Isn't it just!' Marco gestured for his daughter to go through to the lounge area. 'And between us, there's a lot more yet to come.'

EPILOGUE

SITTING DOWN IN THE ARMCHAIR, Marco handed Skye a tumbler of whisky. 'You got out of the house without any grief?

'Yeah, I made-up some bullshit about clearing my head.' Skye sipped her drink, her nose wrinkling at the taste of the spirit.

'Fucking mugs! Still, it's good for us!' Marco tapped the side of his nose. 'What they don't know, we need to ensure stays that way!'

Sky laughed. 'Rest assured that's all in hand. Hey, did you offload that Sandler dickhead?'

'Partly, but I'm saving the final scene for later.' Marco's grin reflected his pleasure at spending *real* time with his daughter, rather than the couple of rushed meetings they'd managed. Since being locked up unexpectedly there had been only the one to confirm that she'd already posted the signed statement ensuring his release.

He knew Skye was just like him the moment he'd clapped eyes on her when she'd first got in contact weeks ago. It was a surprise to discover he had a daughter, but a good one. The best thing of all was that it gave him the perfect opportunity to fuck

Zane up good and proper.

His dear brother was far too stupid to work out that he wasn't the only one to have made Shirley Wilson's legs shake. Neither was Zane intelligent enough to work out why the silly tart disappeared from Battersea in the first place. But it had all worked out invariably well in Marco's favour - his daughter was stunningly beautiful. She'd not only inherited the Morelli good looks, but she was blessed with Marco's way of thinking too. That was a gene not offered to any but the elite and special. And Skye had that in bundles.

Marco then put on his stern look. 'I'm not sure whether I should be annoyed at you for offloading my wife and taking that pleasure away from me, or whether I'm impressed...'

Skye raised her eyebrows. 'Oh, come off it! It was the perfect solution. She was a simpering bitch! Palling up with Erin fucking Langley the way she did was a recipe for disaster! Between them they would have set me up.' Her eyes narrowed. 'Besides, what better way was there when Martin turned up out of the blue after being nabbed by Sandler but to fit those pair up for the murder? Anyway, it was cathartic shoving money down Hazel's throat. She was a grasping bitch, therefore she received a fitting end. It also gave me the perfect opportunity to steal her paperwork. And that obviously worked because you're out and that cow of a wife of yours is no longer. The bonus being is that Zane thinks it's Sandler.'

'Yeah.' Marco's face twisted in a grimace. 'It was hard pretending to Sandler that I wanted him onside when all along I knew he was out to steal my empire. But you're right, the paperwork you forged worked well. *Everything* has worked out well.'

'Hmm, Hazel was remiss for leaving signed paperwork in her desk. It was *begging* for someone to steal it. As much as I hate to admit it, Sandler didn't do a bad job preparing the statement, so it wasn't difficult for me to copy Hazel's signature on the bottom.'

'Tell me the latest on Zane and Erin. They're still

welcoming you with open arms?' Marco lined himself up another line of cocaine on the coffee table and snorted it loudly.

'Of course. I played a blinder with some shit about resenting Zane's absence from my life.' Skye looked pensive. 'There were a few close calls when Erin almost blew my cover and then Zane went to see my mum, but the rest was easy. Anyway, Zane loves having a daughter.'

Marco laughed. 'Shame he hasn't really got one then, isn't it!' He brushed aside his worry about Zane going to see Shirley. There was no need to stress. Shirley wouldn't say anything. She hated them all too much to discuss anything.

'It was a shame Sandler failed to kill the Langley whore though. It would have been gratifying hearing exactly how much *that* screwed Zane up,' Marco continued. 'Having to pretend I didn't know she was still alive was hard.'

'Ah, but like you said, Sandler's the fall guy – the one they think is behind everything!' Skye laughed. 'It's a perfect scenario. Plus, I'm sure you'll hear of Zane's distress over Erin's death soon,' she winked. Finishing her whisky, she placed the empty glass on the table. 'I didn't completely succeed in getting shot of Tiger though, which is a pain in the arse. I heard this morning that he'll be back at some point. That Leo twat is still hanging about like a bad smell too.'

Marco patted Skye's hand. 'Don't beat yourself up. You've done brilliantly!'

Skye glowed from the praise. 'What happens now then? How long before I can move in here with you?'

'Woah! Slow down!' Marco cried. 'There's plenty more work to be done before that can happen. You'll be my ears and eyes for some time to come.'

'But why should I have to stay in that hovel in Dalston with *them* when you're living *here*?' Skye waved her arm around the immense space. 'It's not fair!'

'Life ain't fair, darlin', but you need to be in situ at their place and in their business, with *them*.' Marco frowned. 'I want Zane to love you so much that his heart stops forever the day he finds out you're not his.'

'But he already loves me,' Skye pouted.

'I know my brother and he'll love you more every day. When he's on his knees because the rest of his life has disappeared back to where it belongs...' Marco slapped his broad chest, '...back with me, then I'll hit him with the truth about *you*. You'll get your payout in the end, sweetheart, believe me and I promise you, my most beautiful daughter, that you won't be disappointed.'

NEXT IN THIS SERIES

SCARRED #4
THE HARD TRUTH

COMING SOON...

MORE FROM THIS AUTHOR

ALLEGIANCE SERIES:

TAKEOVER | FALLOUT | VENDETTA | PAYBACK | JUDGEMENT

Daddy's girl Samantha Reynold hadn't bargained on unexpectedly needing to step into her father's shoes and take over the family casino business.

Pampered and spoiled, Sam knows nothing about the rules of this glamorous but deadly new world. She has a lot to learn and even more to prove. But she won't let her family down, especially when it looks like they could lose everything to their biggest rivals – the Stoker family.

Eldest son Sebastian hasn't got time to pander to pretty girl Samantha as she plays at being boss. Rumours are swirling around the streets of Birmingham that have the power to rip the Stoker family apart and destroy everything they've built.

MORE FROM THIS AUTHOR

RETRIBUTION SERIES:

AN OLD SCORE | FINDERS KEEPERS | THE FINAL TAKE

Three families... One prize...

Teagan Fraser had no idea what she was getting herself into when she took on an assignment as a live-in carer for Dulcie Adams – a retired dancer from a Soho club. Dulcie has waited forty years for her lover, Michael Pointer, to return, but she's been living in hope for a time that never came and left looking after something important, which Jonah Powell and his firm want back.

In addition to the notorious Powell firm, there are others wanting to claim what they believe is rightfully theirs and they'll do anything to get it back. If only Dulcie wasn't around it would be a lot easier, but she's difficult to shift...

A lot can happen in a short space of time and Teagan might wish she'd never become involved.

More From This Author

HUNTED SERIES:

THE STATUS DEBT | THE FAMILY LEGACY | THE TARGET OF LIES

Lillian Morgan would do anything to regain the status she lost by marrying beneath her and to cover the sordid details of her husband's death. This includes blackmail and the hand of marriage of her own daughter.

Tori thought her life couldn't get much worse, but someone is not being honest and secrets have the power to rip everyone to shreds.

Especially when life is built on lies.

** This series contains written depictions of graphic violence, sex and strong language. It also contains some themes that may be uncomfortable for certain readers. **

MORE FROM THIS AUTHOR

DOWNFALL SERIES:

UNTIL THE END OF TIME | ESCAPING THE PAST | VENGEFUL PAYBACK

Dive into Seth and Jane's train wreck of a life, where drugs, alcohol and obsessional love means this downright dangerous pair will do *anything* to ensure nothing gets in their way.

They do bad things. *Very* bad things and their promise to love each until the end of time turns into a war against each other.

A war neither of them can win.

** This series contains written depictions of graphic violence, sex and strong language. It also contains some themes that may be uncomfortable for certain readers. **

ABOUT THE AUTHOR

Over the years Edie has worked all over the UK as well as in several other countries and has met a lot of interesting people - several of whom have supplied ideas for some of the characters in her books! She has now settled back in central England with her partner and children, where she is pursuing her writing.

Edie writes gritty gangland and urban fiction for Boldwood Books and Athame Press.

Edie's series so far include her latest – the *Scarred* series; the *Allegiance* series, the *Retribution* series, *Hunted* series and *Downfall* series.

When she isn't writing, Edie enjoys reading and is a self-confessed book hoarder. She also enjoys crochet and music as well as loving anything quirky or unusual.

Visit www.ediebaylis.co.uk for the latest news, information about new releases, giveaways and to subscribe to her mailing list.

gangland | crime | urban

THRILLER AUTHOR

ACKNOWLEDGEMENTS

Firstly, special thanks goes to the ladies and gents (you know who you are) - who were brave enough to allow their names to be adopted by some of the characters in this story after winning a competition on Facebook. (I must point out that these characters are in no way anything to do with, or connected to, their namesakes in real life!) Just want to get that out there!

Also, many thanks to the people that kindly read my drafts of *Trusting Blood*. I appreciate your time and feedback.

As always, thanks to all of the supportive friends and readers who give me the incentive to keep on writing. And, of course, love and thanks to my family.

Thank you for reading *Trusting Blood*. I hope you enjoyed reading it as much as I did writing it!

If so, would you please consider leaving a review on Amazon and/or Goodreads. Reviews from readers are SOOOO helpful and especially important to us authors and without you we would have nobody to write for!

Thank you once again and hope you enjoy the rest of my books.

Edie xx

Printed in Great Britain
by Amazon